THE ANTHOLOGY OF LOVE AND ROMANCE

THE ANTHOLOGY
OF
Love and Romance

Edited by
KATE ALEXANDER

TIGER BOOKS INTERNATIONAL
LONDON

A copy of the British Library Cataloguing in Publication
Data for this title is available from the British Library.

This edition published in 1994 by
Tiger Books International PLC, Twickenham

ISBN 1-85501-505-6

Typeset in 10.5/13pt Bembo by
Hewer Text Composition Services, Edinburgh
Printed in Finland by Werner Söderström Oy

10 9 8 7 6 5 4 3 2 1

Contents

Acknowledgements

Acknowledgements are accorded to the following for the rights to reprint the stories in this anthology:

'Temporary Set Back' © Jilly Cooper. Reprinted by kind permission of Desmond Elliott (Agent)

'Full Moon' © Georgette Heyer 1960. Originally published by Wm Heinemann Ltd in the collection *Pistols For Two*. Reprinted by kind permission of Heron Enterprises Ltd.

'Cheap Excursion' © Estate of Noel Coward 1939. Reprinted by kind permission of Michael Imison Playwrights Ltd.

'Wonderful Copenhagen' © Marie Joseph. Reprinted by kind permission of Mary Irvine (Literary Agent).

'The Stone Boy' © Rosamunde Pilcher. Reprinted by kind permission of Felicity Bryan Associates.

Temporary Set-back

JILLY COOPER

JILLY COOPER was born in Hornchurch, Essex in 1937 and grew up in Yorkshire. Before starting to write her bestselling novels she was a journalist and short story writer. 'Temporary Set-Back' is one of her early stories, written in the 1960s, but already it is a typical Jilly Cooper story – amusing, irreverent and sexy.

MY first job was with a small publishers, Mildew and Rambridge. And how I hated it – nothing but washing up and running errands and cutting off people on the switchboard. I stayed there only because my typing school had gone on about holding down a first job for at least a year and, far more important, because I was nuts about Mr Rambridge. We all were: Miss Winn, his secretary, fairly drooled over him, and even fat Miss Truslove, who worked for Mr Mildew, was very free with the Devon Violets if she had to go to see him.

I don't know what made him so lovely. He was at least thirty – and he always looked tired out: like a weary lion, with his beautiful ravaged face, hair and great powerful body, that always seemed too big for his clothes as he sat reading manuscripts all day with his long legs up on his desk. I saw him only occasionally but he gave me a marvellous smile every time I took him his coffee, and I made sure that he and nobody else got the top of the milk. Recently his marriage had cracked up and, hope surging, Miss Winn had a home perm and Miss Truslove took to plucking out her beard with tweezers every morning.

The only other man in the firm besides Mr Rambridge and old Mr Mildew was Mr Curtis in Sales. Both Miss Winn and Miss Truslove disapproved of him and were pleased he was leaving at the end of the month. I was rather sad. He was lecherous but I liked him. He had a nice gipsy face and was a snappy dresser. But let's face it, he wasn't really in the same class as Mr Rambridge; I never gave Mr Curtis the top of the milk in his coffee.

It was a hot July and Miss Winn suddenly took a week's holiday. Mr Rambridge never gave her many letters, and I hoped she might let me do his work while she was away.

But she was quite determined to get a temporary in.

'Don't let her touch the filing,' she told me. 'Just see she does his letters and keeps his desk tidy. I told the agency to send us a really sensible older woman.'

At eleven o'clock on Monday the 'sensible older woman' rolled up. She was about nineteen, and she wore a tight sweater and short skirt. She had long hair, small eyes and a pug dog in her arms.

'I'm Stephanie Bathurst,' she said. 'Have I come to the right place?'

'You're late,' snapped Miss Truslove.

'Sorry, I overslept.'

'Is that your dog?' asked Miss Truslove. 'We can't have dogs here.'

At that moment Mr Rambridge wandered out of his office looking distraught.

'Could you ask Miss Winn to come in?' he said.

'She's on holiday,' said Miss Truslove.

'Oh God, I forgot.'

'This is your temporary,' added Miss Truslove with a sniff. 'She's brought her dog, but I told her we can't have dogs here.'

'He's very good,' said Stephanie, smiling dazzlingly at Mr Rambridge. 'He pines if he's left at home.'

'I don't see why he shouldn't stay,' said Mr Rambridge. 'Will you come in when you're ready?'

It took Stephanie at least half an hour to get ready. She looked ravishing. Her small eyes had become huge and thickly lashed, and she had put marvellous hollows in her cheeks. Mr Curtis in Sales, who'd just arrived, gave a long whistle.

'I say, I say, I say,' he said. 'Things *are* looking up.'

'Mr Rambridge is waiting,' snapped Miss Truslove. 'Will you go in at once.'

I was left to look after the pug, who was called Pomeroy. He was nice, but a perfect nuisance, whining and yapping and casting covetous eyes at Miss Truslove's knitting.

Stephanie was in with Mr Rambridge for hours. She came out yawning and I asked her if I could get her some sandwiches for lunch.

'No, thank you,' she said. 'I'm meeting someone, but I'll walk down the road with you if you like.'

She was just back from six weeks in the South of France, she told me.

'I'm so broke it isn't true, that's why I'm doing this awful temporary work. I can't type or do shorthand so I just smile all the time and show a lot of leg – it seems to work. Tell me – what gives with Rupert?'

'Rupert?'

'Rupert Rambridge – he's quite a dish! Married, I suppose?'

'Yes, very happily,' I lied.

'Pity! I really fancy him, and the other one – with the dark hair – he's not bad either.'

She got back from lunch at about half-past three and went into Mr Rambridge for more dictation. She then disappeared to do her face.

'Goodness, it's five o'clock,' she said, looking at her watch as she came out of the loo. 'Long past my going-home time. I can charge up to the agency for an extra half hour. Goodnight everyone,' and scooping up Pomeroy, she whisked out of the office before a spluttering Miss Truslove could say anything.

On Tuesday she arrived late, took two hours for lunch,

spent ages in Mr Rambridge's office taking dictation, and didn't type a word of it back. She was amazed he made no advances.

'He's still in love with his wife,' I told her crossly.

'They all say that,' sighed Stephanie, 'but it never makes any difference.'

On Wednesday afternoon Miss Truslove could bear it no longer and, as soon as Stephanie left the office, she waddled into Mr Rambridge.

'Three hours for lunch,' I heard, 'and not a single letter typed.'

'Never mind,' said Mr Rambridge mildly, 'I shall be away in Brighton most of tomorrow, so she can catch up then.'

But on the morning of the fourth day, Stephanie came in wearing a string vest over a body stocking and immediately disappeared to do her face.

'This is it,' Miss Truslove said and, marching into Mr Mildew's office, she slammed the door behind her.

'She spends all day in the toilet,' I heard Miss Truslove shouting, 'and today she's wearing a dress that makes her look quite nude.'

'I beg your pardon?' said Mr Mildew.

'Quite nude,' repeated Miss Truslove, warming to her subject. 'She's a bad influence on our little Jenny, it's only her first job, and they can pick up bad habits so easily at that age.'

'Can Jenny cope with Rupert's letters for the rest of the week?'

'I don't see why not, there are only two more days now.'

I couldn't believe my luck: I skipped round the office, hugging myself. At last – a chance to have a crack at Mr Rambridge. Perhaps I could nip up to Oxford Street in the lunch hour and buy a new dress.

Stephanie's face was quite expressionless when she came out of Mr Mildew's office.

'Goodbye,' she said to me. 'Thanks for looking after Pomeroy. Give my love to Rupert.'

Over my dead body, I thought. I was never so glad to see the back of anyone. Not that I disliked her, but it disturbed me to have her sitting hour after hour looking sexy in Mr Rambridge's office. I forgave her all, however, when I found she had written '*Dorothy Truslove has had more men than I've had hot dinners*' in lipstick on the wall of the loo.

The weather grew hotter. Miss Truslove's ankles swelled and swelled, and I wilted as I typed Mr Rambridge's letters over and over again until they were perfect. Mr Curtis badgered me to have a drink with him, and his gipsy face darkened when, as always, I turned down his offer.

By the time Mr Rambridge got back to the office after his day in Brighton everyone else had gone. Having driven an open car to the coast and back, his gleaming beauty was almost overwhelming, and I stammered as I explained the ousting of Stephanie.

'You shouldn't have waited,' he said, putting his beautiful black-ink signature at the bottom of each letter. 'These are splendid, you must have worked like a slave. How about a drink?'

He opened a cupboard and from it took a bottle of whisky and two glasses. Then he changed his mind. 'On second thoughts, let's go to a pub, it's too hot in here.'

I was too shy to ask if I could do my face so I only had time to comb my hair and empty a half bottle of scent over myself.

We sat in a lovely pub garden, surrounded by great wafts of Charlie. I was quite speechless with happiness, but Mr Rambridge seemed perfectly happy to do most of the talking anyway. I just listened.

'I hope you're enjoying the job,' he said.

'Oh yes, it gets better and better as I get more experienced.'

I was not used to drinking, and under the sun of his interest and a second drink I expanded like a flower. I told him all about myself and exactly why Stephanie had been thrown out and what she had written on the wall about Miss Truslove. Mr Rambridge loved that.

'She certainly was an odd girl,' he said. 'I used to be at school with some Pankhursts. I wonder if they were any relation?'

'Hardly,' I said. The drink was making me giggly. 'Her name was Bathurst.'

'Oh, Bathurst! I suppose she lives in extreme sordidity with hordes of girls, all draping their underwear over the bath.'

'No,' I said, 'she's staying in Kensington with her brother and his wife.'

Mr Rambridge looked at his watch. 'Heavens, I must go. Look, I'll drop you off at the nearest tube.'

I reeled home in a haze of drunken euphoria. I was so glad Mum and Dad had gone out to the pictures.

All night I was kept awake by delicious fantasies of becoming the second Mrs Rambridge: young, tender and understanding as I soothed away the hurt of his first marriage.

It was a beautiful morning next day, and I arrived at the office very early. I pinched twelve of Dad's prize roses, all velvety and dew-drenched, to put in Mr Rambridge's office. Then I decided that was going it a bit, so I picked out three with greenfly on them for Mr Mildew's desk. I spent hours in the loo doing my face, and when I came out Miss Truslove was answering the telephone.

'These summer colds are so treacherous,' she was saying, really laying it on. 'Now keep warm. I'll tell Mr Mildew you won't be in till Monday.' To me she said crossly, 'You should never leave the switchboard unattended. That was Mr Rambridge, he's caught a terrible chill and won't be in.'

I kicked myself for not being there to answer the telephone. Mr Rambridge knew I was always on the switchboard at that time and must have rung up especially to talk to me. Perhaps he even wanted me to go round and look after him. Now I'd have to exist for three long days until I saw him again. I imagined him lying in his great empty bed as sick with disappointment as I was.

That morning, Mr Mildew had one of his sporadic bursts

of efficiency and discovered two manuscripts were missing. Eventually I tracked down *British West Hampstead, A Geographical Survey* among the telephone books, but we couldn't find *Stubby, The Story of A Royal Corgi* anywhere.

'Perhaps Mr Rambridge has got it,' I said hopefully.

'Good idea,' said Mr Mildew. 'Ring him up and ask him.'

I was so excited, I could hardly pick up the telephone. If Mr Rambridge had the manuscript I could collect it. I could take him grapes and cook him a light lunch – me, who can't even boil an egg.

'Chinese laundry,' said a voice at the end of the telephone.

'Sorry, wrong number,' I said, and dialled again. I was completely thrown by a woman answering. 'Can I speak to Mr Rambridge?' I said. 'Wrong number,' said the voice and slammed down the phone.

I dialled carefully this time. The telephone rang for ages.

'Hello,' snapped the female voice; a dog was yapping hysterically in the background. 'Shut up, Pomeroy,' said the voice. 'It's all right, darling, go back to bed. Who did you say? Mr Rambridge? Sorry, you've got the wrong number,' and once again the phone was slammed down.

It took a few seconds to sink in – lovely, lovely Mr Rambridge and horrible Stephanie, or lovely, lovely Stephanie and horrible Mr Rambridge. But how had they got together? Then I remembered how last night at the pub I'd told him her surname, and that she was staying with her brother. Despite his lazy manner, he must have moved like lightning. I couldn't cry out loud, but I felt the tears pouring down my cheeks.

At that moment, Mr Curtis came in and said, 'Hello gorgeous,' then with real concern, 'Hey, what's the matter?'

I cried all over my desk, but bit by bit I managed to tell him the whole story.

He shrugged his shoulders. 'I could see it coming a mile off,' he said. 'There's a bird not famed for the strength of her knicker elastic I said to myself. She was sitting on his desk on Tuesday when I went in – skirt hitched up showing half a mile of thigh.'

'But Mr Rambridge isn't like that,' I sobbed.

'You've got him wrong, duckie. He's a really smooth operator.'

'I don't believe it, he was miserable when his wife left him.'

'And do you know why she left him? Because he was chasing every available skirt in London. She never knew where he was. Why do you think he always looks so clapped out in the mornings?'

'He never made a pass at anyone in the office.'

'He doesn't believe in shitting on his own doorstep. Anyway, can you imagine him having a go at Truslove or Winn?'

'Stephanie is terribly pretty,' I said.

'Sure, she's well packaged. You're much prettier – you just need to take your skirts up a few inches, get your hair cut properly, and stop letting old Mother Truslove dictate what you wear.'

I digested that for a minute. 'D'you think Mr Rambridge would fancy me then?'

'Course he would, if you're silly enough to want him.'

I stood up when Mr Curtis said that and looked at him. He was staring out of the window. I took my hand mirror out of my desk and had a quick look at my face: bloodshot piggy eyes and all my mascara running.

'You're a right mess,' said Mr Curtis, and took me in his arms and kissed me. That's the funny thing about men. You really don't know whether you fancy them until they touch you.

As suddenly as he had grabbed me, he let go. 'Sorry, I got carried away,' he said, taking a pair of dark glasses out of his pocket. 'Put these on and I'll buy you lunch.'

'I've got to get Miss Truslove some sandwiches.'

'To hell with Miss Truslove, she can live on her hump.'

'Thank you for being so kind,' I said.

'Purely ulterior motives,' he said.

*   *   *

That weekend I pottered down to the shops to get my hair cut and buy a new dress. I avoided thinking about the office or Mr Rambridge.

When I arrived on Monday, Miss Winn was having hysterics over the state of her in-tray. The friend she had expected to join her on holiday had not turned up and she was pouring out her heart to Miss Truslove, who had lost her tweezers and was surreptitiously trying to pluck her beard out with a bulldog clip.

'You've cut your hair,' Miss Truslove said to me. 'It's much neater. New dress, too, a bit short for the office. Taking a leaf out of that temporary's book,' and she started to tell Miss Winn about Stephanie.

Mr Rambridge came in at about ten. He looked exhausted. I was sitting by the switchboard.

'How's your cold?' I asked.

'Much better, thanks awfully. I stayed in bed all weekend, and managed to sweat it out.'

I bet you did, I thought sourly. He was looking at me with interest.

'I like your hair,' he said, 'and the dress. I did enjoy our drink, we must do it again soon.'

As I smiled at him very sweetly, I noticed that his hair was thinning, and where once I thought his great hairy body had seemed too big for his clothes I realised now that he just wore his clothes too tight.

While I was making coffee, I heard Mr Curtis come in. I poured the top of the milk into a cup and, picking it up, started for the door.

'I'll take Mr Rambridge's,' Miss Winn said, jumping up.

'This is for Mr Curtis,' I said shortly.

'But it's got cream in. You know Mr Rambridge always likes the cream.'

'Funny, so does Mr Curtis,' I said.

The Grey Frock

ANTHONY HOPE

ANTHONY HOPE (1863–1933). This was the pseudonym of Sir Anthony Hope Hawkins, knighted for his services in the Ministry of Information during the First World War. He gave the English language a new word when he invented the country of Ruritania for his novel The Prisoner of Zenda. *Here he writes of a young girl who fails in a test of love – or is it her fiancé who fails?*

THE rights and wrongs of the matter are perhaps a little obscure, and it is possible to take his side as well as hers. Or perhaps there is really no question of sides at all – no need to condemn anybody; only another instance of the difficulty people have in understanding one another's point of view. But here, with a few lines added by way of introduction, are the facts as related in her obviously candid and sincere narrative.

Miss Winifred Petheram's father had an income from landed estate of about five thousand a year, and spent, say, six or thereabouts; his manor house was old and beautiful, the gardens delightful, the stables handsome and handsomely maintained, the housekeeping liberal, hospitable, almost lavish. Mr Petheram had three sons and four daughters; but the sons were still young, and not the cause of any great expense. Mrs Petheram was a quiet body, the two girls in the schoolroom were no serious matter; in fact, apart from the horses, Mildred and Winifred were, in a pecuniary point of view, the most serious burden on the family purse. For both were pretty girls, gay and fond of society, given to paying

frequent visits in town and country, and in consequence
needing many frocks and a considerable supply of downright
hard cash. But everybody was very comfortable; only it was
understood that at a period generally referred to as 'some day'
there would be very little for anybody except the eldest son.
'Some day,' meant, of course, when Mr Petheram reluctantly
died, and thereby brought his family into less favourable
worldly circumstances.

From this brief summary of the family's position the duty
of Mildred and Winifred (and, in due course of time, of the
two girls in the schoolroom also) stands forth salient and
unmistakable. Mildred performed it promptly at the age of
nineteen years. He was the second son of a baronet, and his
elder brother was sickly and unmarried; but, like a wise young
man, he took no chances, went on the Stock Exchange, and
became exceedingly well-to-do in an exceedingly brief space
of time – something, in fact, 'came off' in South Africa, and
when that happens ordinary limits of time and probability
are suspended. So with Mildred all was very well; and it
was odds that one of the boys would be provided for by
his brother-in-law. Winifred had just as good chances –
nay, better; for her sensitive face and wondering eyes had
an attraction that Mildred's self-possessed good looks could
not exert. But Winifred shilly-shallied (it was her father's
confidential after-dinner word) till she was twenty-one, then
refused Sir Barton Amesbury (in itself a step of doubtful
sanity, as was generally observed), and engaged herself to
Harold Jackson, who made two hundred a year and had no
prospects except the doubtful one of maintaining his income
at that level – unless, that is, he turned out a genius, when
it was even betting whether a mansion or the workhouse
awaited him; for that depends on the variety of genius.
Having taken this amazing course, Winifred was resolute
and radiantly happy; her relatives, after the necessary amount
of argument, shrugged their shoulders – the very inadequate
ultima ratio to which a softening civilisation seems to have
reduced relatives in such cases.

'I can manage two hundred a year for her while I live,' said Mr Petheram, wiping his brow and then dusting his boots; he was just back from his ride. 'After that –'

'The insurance, my dear?' Mrs Petheram suggested. But her husband shook his head; that little discrepancy above noted, between five and six thousand a year, had before this caused the insurance to be a very badly broken reed.

Harold Jackson – for in him the explanation of Winifred's action must be sought – was tall, good-looking, ready of speech, and decidedly agreeable. There was no aggressiveness about him, and his quiet manners repelled any suspicion of bumptiousness. But it cannot be denied that to him Winifred's action did not seem extraordinary; he himself accounted for this by saying that she, like himself, was an Idealist, the boys by saying that he was 'stuck-up,' Mr Petheram by a fretful exclamation that in all worldly matters he was as blind as a new-born puppy. Whatever the truth of these respective theories, he was as convinced that Winifred had chosen for her own happiness as that she had given him his. And in this she most fully agreed. Of course, then, all the shrugging of shoulders in the universe could not affect the radiant contentment of the lovers, nor could it avert the swift passage of months which soon brought the wedding-day in sight, and made preparations for it urgent and indispensable.

Married couples, even though they have only a precarious four hundred a year, must live somewhere – no idealism is independent of a roof; on the contrary, it centres round the home, so Harold said, and the word 'home' seemed already sacred to Winifred as her glance answered his. It was the happiest day of her life when she put on her dainty new costume of delicate grey, took her parasol and gloves, matched to a shade with her gown, and mounted into the smart dog-cart which Jennie, the new chestnut mare, was to draw to the station. A letter had come from Harold to say that, after long search, he had found a house which would suit them, and was only just a trifle more expensive than the maximum sum they had decided to give for rent. Winifred knew that the delicate grey became her well, and that Harold would think her looking very pretty; and she was going to see her home and his. Her face was bright as she kissed her father and jumped down from the dog-cart; but he sighed when she had left him, and his brow was wrinkled as he drove Jennie back. He felt himself growing rather old; 'some day' did not seem quite as remote as it used, and pretty Winnie – well, there was no use in crying over it now. Wilful girls must have their way; and it was not his fault that confounded agitators had played the deuce with the landed interest. The matter passed from his thoughts as he began to notice how satisfactorily Jennie moved.

Winifred's lover met her in London, and found her eyes still bright from the reveries of her journey. Today was a gala day – they drove off in a hansom to a smart restaurant in Piccadilly, joking about their extravagance. Everything was perfect to Winifred, except (a small exception, surely!) that Harold failed to praise, seemed almost not to notice, the grey costume; it must have been that he looked at her face only!

'It's not a large house, you know,' he said at lunch, smiling at her over a glass of Graves.

'Well, I sha'n't be wanting to get away from you,' she answered, smiling. 'Not very far, Harold!'

'Are your people still abusing me?'

He put the question with a laugh.

'They never abused you, only me.' Then came the irrepressible question: 'Do you like my new frock? I put it on on purpose – for the house, you know.'

'Our home!' he murmured, rather sentimentally, it must be confessed. The question about the frock he did not answer; he was thinking of the home. Winifred was momentarily grateful to a stout lady at the next table, who put up her glass, looked at the frock, and with a nod of approval called her companion's attention to it. This was while Harold paid the bill.

Then they took another cab, and headed north – through

Berkeley Square, where Winifred would have liked, but did not expect, to stop, and so up to Oxford Street. Here they bore considerably to the east, then plunged north again and drove through one or two long streets. Harold, who had made the journey before, paid no heed to the route, but talked freely of delightful hours which they were to enjoy together, of books to read and thoughts to think, and of an intimate sympathy which, near as they were already to one another, the home and the home life alone could enable them fully to realise. Winifred listened; but far down in her mind now was another question, hardly easier to stifle than that about the frock. 'Where are we going to?' would have been its naked form; but she yielded no more to her impulse than to look about her and mark and wonder. At last they turned by a sharp twist from a long narrow street into a short narrower street, where a waggon by the curbstone forced the cab to a walk, and shrill boys were playing an unintelligible noisy game.

'What queer places we pass through!' she cried with a laugh, as she laid her hand on his arm and turned her face to his.

'Pass through! We're at home,' he answered, returning her laugh. 'At home, Winnie!' He pointed at a house on the right-hand side, and, immediately after, the cab stopped. Winifred got out, holding her skirt back from contact with the wheel. Harold, in his eagerness to ring the door bell, had forgotten to render her this service. She stood on the pavement for a moment looking about her. One of the boys cried: 'Crikey, there's a swell!' and she liked the boy for it. Then she turned to the house.

'It wants a lick of paint,' said Harold cheerfully, as he rang the bell again.

'It certainly does,' she admitted, looking up at the dirty walls.

An old woman opened the door; she might be said, by way of metaphor, to need the same process as the walls; a very narrow passage was disclosed behind her.

'Welcome!' said Harold, giving Winifred his hand and then

presenting her to the old woman. 'This is my future wife,' he explained. 'We've come to look at the house. But we won't bother you, Mrs Blidgett, we'd rather run over it by ourselves. We shall enjoy that, sha'n't we, Winnie?'

Winnie's answer was a little scream and a hasty clutch at her gown; a pail of dirty water, standing in the passage, had threatened ruin; she recoiled violently from this peril against the opposite wall and drew away again, silently exhibiting a long trail of dark dust on her new grey frock. Harold laughed as he led the way into a small square room that opened from the passage.

'That's the parlour,' said the old woman, wiping her arms with her apron. 'You can find your way upstairs; nothing's locked.' And with this remark she withdrew by a steep staircase leading underground.

'She's the caretaker,' Harold explained.

'She doesn't seem to have taken much care,' observed Winifred, still indignant about her gown and holding it round her as closely as drapery clings to an antique statue.

Miss Petheram's account of the house, its actual dimensions, accommodation, and characteristics, has always been very vague, and since she refused information as to its number in the street, verification of these details has remained impossible. Perhaps it was a reasonably capacious, although doubtless not extensive, dwelling; perhaps, again, it was a confined and well-nigh stifling den. She remembered two things – first, its all-pervading dirt; secondly, the remarkable quality which (as she alleged) distinguished its atmosphere. She thought there were seven 'enclosures,' this term being arrived at (after discussion) as a compromise between 'rooms' and 'pens'; and she knew that the windows of each of these enclosures were commanded by the windows of several other apparently similar and very neighbouring enclosures. Beyond this she could give no account of her first half-hour in the house; her exact recollection began when she was left alone in the enclosure on the first floor, which Harold asserted to be the drawing-room, Harold himself having gone downstairs to seek the old woman and elicit from her some information as to what were and what were not tenant's fixtures in the said enclosure. 'You can look about you,' he remarked cheerfully, as he left her, 'and make up your mind where you're going to have your favourite seat. Then you shall tell me, and I shall have the picture of you sitting there in my mind.' He pointed to a wooden chair, the only one then in the room. 'Experiment with that chair,' he added, laughing. 'I won't be long, darling.'

Mechanically, without considering things which she obviously ought to have considered, Winifred sank into the designated seat, laid her parasol on a small table, and leant her elbows on the same piece of furniture as she held her face between her gloved hands. The atmosphere again asserted its peculiar quality; she rose for a moment and opened the window; fresh air was gained at the expense of spoilt gloves, and was weighted with the drawbacks of a baby's cries and an inquisitive woman's stare from over the way. Shutting the window again, she returned to her chair – the symbol of what was to be her favourite seat in days to come, her chosen corner in the house which had been the subject of so many talks and so many dreams. There were a great many flies in the room; the noise of adjacent humanity in street and houses was miscellaneous and penetrating; the air was very close. And this house was rather more expensive than their calculations had allowed. They had immensely enjoyed making those calculations down there in the country, under the old yew hedge and in sight of the flower beds beneath the library window. She remembered the day they did it. There was a cricket match in the meadow. Mildred and her husband brought the drag over, and Sir Barton came in his tandem. It was almost too hot in the sun, but simply delightful in the shade. She and Harold had had great fun over mapping out their four hundred a year and proving how much might be done with it – at least compared with anything they could want when once they had the great thing that they wanted.

The vision vanished; she was back in the dirty little room

again; she caught up her parasol; a streak across the dust marked where it had lain on the table; she sprang up and twisted her frock round, craning her neck back; ah, that she had reconnoitred that chair! She looked at her gloves; then with a cry of horror she dived for her handkerchief, put it to her lips, and scrubbed her cheeks; the handkerchief came away soiled, dingy, almost black. This last outrage overcame her; the parasol dropped on the floor, she rested her arms on the table and laid her face on them, and she burst into sobs, just as she used to in childhood when her brothers crumpled a clean frock or somebody spoke to her roughly. And between her sobs she cried, almost loudly, very bitterly: 'Oh, it's too mean and dirty and horrid!'

Harold had stolen softly upstairs, meaning to surprise the girl he loved, perhaps to let a snatched kiss be her first knowledge of his return. He flushed red, and his lips set sternly; he walked across the room to her with a heavy tread. She looked up, saw him, and knew that her exclamation had been overheard.

'What in the world is the matter?' he asked in a tone of cold surprise.

It was very absurd – she couldn't stop crying; and from amid her weeping nothing more reasonable, nothing more adequate, nothing less trivial would come than confused murmurs of 'My frock, Harold!' 'My parasol!' 'Oh, my face, my gloves!' He smiled contemptuously. 'Don't you see?' she exclaimed, exhibiting the gloves and parasol.

'See what? Are you crying because the room's dirty?' He paused and then added, 'I'm sorry you think it mean and horrid. Very sorry, Winifred.'

Offence was deep and bitter in his voice; he looked at her with a sort of disgust; she stopped sobbing and regarded him with a gaze in which fright and expectation seemed mingled, as though there were a great peril, and just one thing that might narrowly avert it. But his eyes were very hard. She dried her tears, and then forlornly scrubbed her cheeks again. He watched her with hostile curiosity, appearing to think her a very strange spectacle. Presently he spoke. 'I thought you loved me. Oh, I daresay you thought so too till I came into competition with your new frock. I beg pardon – I must add your gloves and your parasol. As for the house, it's no doubt mean and horrid; we were going to be poor, you see.' He laughed scornfully, as he added, 'You might even have had to do a little dusting yourself now and then! Horrible!'

'I just sat there and looked at him.' That was Winifred's own account of her behaviour. It is not very explicit and leaves room for much conjecture as to what her look said or tried to say. But whatever the message was he did not read it. He was engrossed in his own indignation, readier to hurt than to understand, full of his own wrong, of the mistake he had made, of her extraordinary want of love, of courage, of the high soul. Very likely all this was a natural enough state of mind for him to be in. Justice admits his provocation; the triviality of her spoken excuses gave his anger only too fine an opportunity. He easily persuaded himself that here was a revelation of the real woman, a flash of light that showed her true nature, showing, too, the folly of his delusion about her. Against all this her look and what it asked for had very little chance, and she could find no words that did not aggravate her offence.

'This is really rather a ludicrous scene,' he went on. 'Is there any use in prolonging it?' He waited for her to speak, but she was still tongue-tied. 'The caretaker needn't be distressed by seeing the awful effects of her omission to dust the room; but, if you're composed enough, we might as well go.' He looked round the room. 'You'll be glad to be out of this,' he ended.

'I know what you must think of me,' she burst out; 'but – but you don't understand – you don't see –'

'No doubt I'm stupid, but I confess I don't. At least there's only one thing I see.' He bowed and waved his hand towards the door. 'Shall we go?' he asked.

She led the way downstairs, her skirt again held close and raised clear of her ankles; her care for it was not lost on

Harold as he followed her, for she heard him laugh again
with an obtrusive bitterness that made his mirth a taunt. The
old caretaker waited for them in the passage.

'When'll you be coming, sir?' she asked.

'I don't know. It's not certain we shall come,' said he. 'The
lady is not much taken with the house.'

'Ah, well!' sighed the old woman resignedly.

For an account of their drive back to the station materials
are, again, sadly wanting. 'He hardly said a word, and I
did nothing but try to get my face clean and my gloves
presentable,' was Winifred's history of their journey. But
she remembered – or chose to relate – a little more of what
passed while they waited for the train on the platform at
Euston. He left her for a few minutes on pretext of smoking
a cigarette, and she saw him walking up and down, apparently
in thought. Then he came back and sat down beside her. His
manner was grave now; to judge by his recorded words,
perhaps it was even a little pompous; but when may young
men be pompous, if not at such crises as these?

'It's no use pretending that nothing has happened, Winifred,'
he said. 'That would be the hollowest pretence, not worthy,
I think, of either of us. Perhaps we had better take time to
consider our course and – er – our relations to one another.'

'You don't want to marry me now?' she asked simply.

'I want to do what is best for our happiness,' he replied.
'We cannot forget what has happened to-day.'

'I know you would never forget it,' she said.

He did not contradict her; he looked first at his watch, then
along the platform for the approach of her train. To admit
that he might forget it was impossible to him; in such a case
forgetfulness would be a negation of his principles and a slur
on his perception. It would also be such a triumph over his
vanity and his pride as it did not lie in him to achieve, such a
forgiveness as his faults and virtues combined to put beyond
the power of his nature. She looked at him; and 'I smiled,' she
said, not seeming herself to know why she had smiled, but
conscious that, in the midst of her woe, some subtly amusing

thought about him had come into her mind. She had never been amused at him before; so she, too, was getting some glimmer of a revelation out of the day's experience – not the awful blaze of light that had flashed on Harold's eyes, but a dim ray, just enough to give cause to that puzzled smile for which she could not explicitly account.

So they parted, and for persons who have followed the affair at all closely it is hardly necessary to add that they never came together again. This issue was obvious, and Winifred seems to have made up her mind to it that very same evening, for she called her mother into her room (as the good lady passed on the way to bed) and looked up from the task of brushing the grey frock which she had spread out on the sofa.

'I don't think I shall marry Mr Jackson now, mother,' she said.

Mrs Petheram looked at her daughter and at her daughter's gown.

'You'd better tell me more about it to-morrow. You look tired to-night, dear,' she replied.

But Winifred never told her any more – in the first place, because the family was too delighted with the fact to care one straw about how it had come to pass, and, in the second place, on the more important ground that the thing was really too small, too trivial, and too absurd to bear telling – at least to the family. To me, for some reason or other, Winifred did tell it, or some of it – enough, anyhow, to enable me, with the help of a few touches of imagination, to conjecture how it occurred.

'Don't you think it was very absurd?' she asked at the end of her story. We were sitting by the yew hedge, near the library windows, looking across the flower beds to the meadow; it was a beautiful day, and the old place was charming. 'Because,' she added, 'I did love him, you know; and it seems a small thing to separate about, doesn't it?'

'If he had behaved differently—' I began.

'I don't see how he could be expected to,' she murmured.

'You expected him to,' I said firmly. She turned to me with an appearance of interest, as though I might be able to interpret to her something that had been causing her puzzle. 'Or you wouldn't have looked at him as you say you did – or smiled at him, as you admit you did. But you were wrong to expect him to, because he's not that kind of man.'

'What kind of man?'

'The kind of man to catch you in his arms, smother you in kisses (allow me the old phrase), tell you that he understood all you felt, knew all you were giving up, realised the great thing you were doing for him.'

Winifred was listening. I went on with my imaginary scene of romantic fervour.

'That when he contrasted that mean little place with the beauties you were accustomed to, with the beauties which were right and proper for you, when he saw your daintiness soiled by that dust, that gown whose hem he would willingly –'

'He needn't say quite as much as that,' interrupted Winifred, smiling a little.

'Well, or words to that effect,' said I. 'That when he did all this and saw all this, you know, he loved you more, and knew that you loved him more than he had dared to dream, with a deeper love, a love that gave up for him all that you loved next best and second only to him; that after seeing your tears he would never doubt again that you would face all trials and all troubles with him at your side – Don't you think, if he'd said something of that kind, accompanying his words with the appropriate actions—' I paused.

'Well?' asked Winifred.

'Don't you think you might have been living in that horrid little house now, instead of being about to contract an alliance with Sir Barton Amesbury?'

'How do you know I shall do that?' she cried.

'It needs,' I observed modestly, 'little skill to discern the approach of the inevitable.' I looked at her thoughtful face and at her eyes; they had their old look of wondering in them. 'Don't you think that if he'd treated the situation in that way—?' I asked.

'Perhaps,' she said softly. 'But he wouldn't think of all that. He was such an Idealist.'

I really do not know why she applied that term to him at that moment, except that he used to apply it to himself at many moments. But since it seemed to her to explain his conduct, there is no need to quarrel with the epithet.

'And I hope,' said I, 'that the grey frock wasn't irretrievably ruined?'

'I've never worn it again,' she murmured.

So I suppose it was ruined – unless she has some other reason. But she would be right to treat it differently from other frocks; it must mean a good deal to her, although it failed to mean anything except its own pretty self to Mr Jackson.

Miggles

FRANCIS BRET HARTE

FRANCIS BRET HARTE (1836–1902). This American writer went to California at the age of 18 and worked as a prospector, a teacher, a Wells Fargo expressman and a journalist, later using his experience in short stories. His 'Miggles' is certainly no lady, but her devotion to a helpless man is a true love story.

W E were eight, including the driver. We had not spoken during the passage of the last six miles, since the jolting of the heavy vehicle over the roughening road had spoiled the Judge's last poetical quotation. The tall man beside the Judge was asleep, his arm passed through the swaying strap and his head resting upon it – altogether a limp, helpless-looking object, as if he had hanged himself and been cut down too late. The French lady on the back seat was asleep, too, yet in a half-conscious propriety of attitude, shown even in the disposition of the handkerchief which she held to her forehead, and which partially veiled her face. The lady from Virginia City, travelling with her husband, had long since lost all individuality in a wild confusion of ribbons, veils, furs, and shawls. There was no sound but the rattling of wheels and the dash of rain upon the roof. Suddenly the stage stopped, and we became dimly aware of voices. The driver was evidently in the midst of an exciting colloquy with some one in the road – a colloquy of which such fragments as 'bridge gone,' 'twenty feet of water,' 'can't pass,' were occasionally distinguishable above the storm. Then came a lull, and a mysterious voice from the road shouted the parting adjuration –

'Try Miggles's.'

We caught a glimpse of our leaders as the vehicle slowly turned, of a horseman vanishing through the rain, and we were evidently on our way to Miggles's.

Who and where was Miggles? The Judge, our authority, did not remember the name, and he knew the country thoroughly. The Washoe traveller thought Miggles must keep a hotel. We only knew that we were stopped by high water in front and rear, and that Miggles was our rock of refuge. A ten minutes' splashing through a tangled by-road, scarcely wide enough for the stage, and we drew up before a barred and boarded gate in a wide stone wall or fence about eight feet high. Evidently Miggles's, and evidently Miggles did not keep a hotel.

The driver got down and tried the gate. It was securely locked.

'Miggles! O Miggles!'

No answer.

'Migg-ells! You Miggles!' continued the driver, with rising wrath.

'Migglesy!' joined in the expressman, persuasively. 'O Miggy! Mig!'

But no reply came from the apparently insensate Miggles. The Judge, who had finally got the window down, put his head out and propounded a series of questions, which if answered categorically would have undoubtedly elucidated the whole mystery, but which the driver evaded by replying that 'if we didn't want to sit in the coach all night, we had better rise up and sing out for Miggles.'

So we rose up and called on Miggles in chorus; then separately. And when we had finished, a Hibernian fellow-passenger from the roof called for 'Maygells!' whereat we all laughed. While we were laughing, the driver cried 'Shoo!'

We listened. To our infinite amazement the chorus of 'Miggles' was repeated from the other side of the wall, even to the final and supplemental 'Maygells.'

'Extraordinary echo,' said the Judge.

'Extraordinary d – d skunk!' roared the driver, contemptuously. 'Come out of that, Miggles, and show yourself! Be a man, Miggles! Don't hide in the dark; I wouldn't if I were you, Miggles,' continued Yuba Bill, now dancing about in an excess of fury.

'Miggles!' continued the voice, 'O Miggles!'

'My good man! Mr Myghail!' said the Judge, softening the asperities of the name as much as possible. 'Consider the inhospitality of refusing shelter from the inclemency of the weather to helpless females. Really, my dear sir – ' But a succession of 'Miggles,' ending in a burst of laughter, drowned his voice.

Yuba Bill hesitated no longer. Taking a heavy stone from the road, he battered down the gate, and with the expressman entered the enclosure. We followed. Nobody was to be seen. In the gathering darkness all that we could distinguish was that we were in a garden – from the rose-bushes that scattered over us a minute spray from their dripping leaves – and before a long, rambling wooden building.

'Do you know this Miggles?' asked the Judge of Yuba Bill.

'No, nor don't want to,' said Bill, shortly, who felt the Pioneer Stage Company insulted in his person by the contumacious Miggles.

'But, my dear sir,' expostulated the Judge, as he thought of the barred gate.

'Lookee here,' said Yuba Bill, with fine irony, 'hadn't you better go back and sit in the coach till yer introduced? I'm going in,' and he pushed open the door of the building.

A long room lighted only by the embers of a fire that was dying on the large hearth at its further extremity. The walls curiously papered, and the flickering firelight bringing out its grotesque pattern; somebody sitting in a large armchair by the fireplace. All this we saw as we crowded together into the room, after the driver and expressman.

'Hello, be you Miggles?' said Yuba Bill to the solitary occupant.

The figure neither spoke nor stirred. Yuba Bill walked wrathfully toward it, and turned the eye of his coach-lantern upon its face. It was a man's face, prematurely old and wrinkled, with very large eyes, in which there was that expression of perfectly gratuitous solemnity which I had sometimes seen in an owl's. The large eyes wandered from Bill's face to the lantern, and finally fixed their gaze on that luminous object, without further recognition.

Bill restrained himself with an effort.

'Miggles! Be you deaf? You ain't dumb anyhow, you know'; and Yuba Bill shook the insensate figure by the shoulder.

To our great dismay, as Bill removed his hand, the venerable stranger apparently collapsed – sinking into half his size and an undistinguishable heap of clothing.

'Well, dern my skin,' said Bill, looking appealingly at us, and hopelessly retiring from the contest.

The Judge now stepped forward, and we lifted the mysterious invertebrate back into his original position. Bill was dismissed with the lantern to reconnoitre outside, for it was evident that from the helplessness of this solitary man there must be attendants near at hand, and we all drew around the fire. The Judge, who had regained his authority, and had never lost his conversational amiability – standing before us with his back to the hearth – charged us, as an imaginary jury, as follows:

'It is evident that either our distinguished friend here has reached that condition described by Shakespeare as 'the sere and yellow leaf,' or has suffered some premature abatement of his mental and physical faculties. Whether he is really the Miggles –'

Here he was interrupted by 'Miggles! O Miggles! Migglesy! Mig!' and, in fact, the whole chorus of Miggles in very much the same key as it had once before been delivered unto us.

We gazed at each other for a moment in some alarm. The Judge, in particular, vacated his position quickly, as the voice seemed to come directly over his shoulder. The cause, however, was soon discovered in a large magpie who was perched upon a shelf over the fireplace, and who immediately relapsed into a sepulchral silence, which contrasted singularly with his previous volubility. It was, undoubtedly, his voice which we had heard in the road, and our friend in the chair was not responsible for the discourtesy. Yuba Bill, who re-entered the room after an unsuccessful search, was loath to accept the explanation, and still eyed the helpless sitter with suspicion. He had found a shed in which he had put up his horses, but he came back dripping and sceptical. 'Thar ain't nobody but him within ten mile of the shanty, and that 'ar d – d old skeesicks knows it.'

But the faith of the majority proved to be securely based. Bill had scarcely ceased growling before we heard a quick step upon the porch, the trailing of a wet skirt, the door was flung open, and with a flash of white teeth, a sparkle of dark eyes, and an utter absence of ceremony or diffidence, a young woman entered, shut the door, and, panting, leaned back against it.

'Oh, if you please, I'm Miggles!'

And this was Miggles! this bright-eyed, full-throated young woman, whose wet gown of coarse blue stuff could not hide the beauty of the feminine curves to which it clung; from the chestnut crown of whose head, topped by a man's oil-skin sou'wester, to the little feet and ankles, hidden somewhere in the recesses of her boy's brogans, all was grace – this was Miggles, laughing at us, too, in the most airy, frank, off-hand manner imaginable.

'You see, boys,' said she, quite out of breath, and holding one little hand against her side, quite unheeding the speechless discomfiture of our party, or the complete demoralization of Yuba Bill, whose features had relaxed into an expression of gratuitous and imbecile cheerfulness – 'you see, boys, I was mor'n two miles away when you passed down the road. I thought you might pull up here, and so I ran the whole way, knowing nobody was home but Jim – and – and – I'm out of breath – and – that lets me out.'

And here Miggles caught her dripping oil-skin hat from her head, with a mischievous swirl that scattered a shower of rain-drops over us; attempted to put back her hair; dropped two hair-pins in the attempt; laughed and sat down beside Yuba Bill, with her hands crossed lightly on her lap.

The Judge recovered himself first, and essayed an extravagant compliment.

'I'll trouble you for that thar har-pin,' said Miggles, gravely. Half a dozen hands were eagerly stretched forward; the missing hair-pin was restored to its fair owner; and Miggles, crossing the room, looked keenly in the face of the invalid. The solemn eyes looked back at hers with an expression we had never seen before. Life and intelligence seemed to struggle back into the rugged face. Miggles laughed again – it was a singularly eloquent laugh – and turned her black eyes and white teeth once more towards us.

'This afflicted person is – ' hesitated the Judge.

'Jim,' said Miggles.

'Your father?'

'No.'

'Brother?'

'No.'

'Husband?'

Miggles darted a quick, half-defiant glance at the two lady passengers who I had noticed did not participate in the general masculine admiration of Miggles, and said, gravely, 'No, it's Jim.'

There was an awkward pause. The lady passengers moved closer to each other; the Washoe husband looked abstractedly at the fire; and the tall man apparently turned his eyes inward for self-support at this emergency. But Miggles's laugh, which was very infectious, broke the silence. 'Come,' she said briskly, 'you must be hungry. Who'll bear a hand to help me get tea?'

She had no lack of volunteers. In a few moments Yuba Bill was engaged like Caliban in bearing logs for this Miranda; the expressman was grinding coffee on the verandah; to myself the arduous duty of slicing bacon was assigned; and the Judge lent each man his good-humoured and voluble counsel. And when Miggles, assisted by the Judge and our Hibernian 'deck passenger,' set the table with all the available crockery, we had become quite joyous, in spite of the rain that beat against windows, the wind that whirled down the chimney, the two ladies who whispered together in the corner, or the magpie who uttered a satirical and croaking commentary on their conversation from his perch above. In the now bright, blazing fire we could see that the walls were papered with illustrated journals, arranged with feminine taste and discrimination. The furniture was extemporized, and adapted from candleboxes and packing-cases; and covered with gay calico, or the skin of some animal. The arm-chair of the helpless Jim was an ingenious variation of a flour-barrel. There was neatness, and even a taste for the picturesque, to be seen in the few details of the long low room.

The meal was a culinary success. But more, it was a social triumph – chiefly, I think, owing to the rare tact of Miggles in guiding the conversation, asking all the questions herself, yet bearing throughout a frankness that rejected the idea of any concealment on her own part, so that we talked of ourselves, of our prospects, of the journey, of the weather, of each other – of everything but our host and hostess. It must be confessed that Miggles's conversation was never elegant, rarely grammatical, and that at times she employed expletives, the use of which had generally been yielded to our sex. But they were delivered with such a lighting up of teeth and eyes, and were usually followed by a laugh – a laugh peculiar to Miggles – so frank and honest that it seemed to clear the moral atmosphere.

Once, during the meal, we heard a noise like the rubbing of a heavy body against the outer walls of the house. This was shortly followed by a scratching and sniffling at the door. 'That's Joaquin,' said Miggles, in reply to our questioning glances, 'would you like to see him?' Before we could answer she had opened the door, and disclosed a half-grown grizzly, who instantly raised himself on his haunches, with his forepaws hanging down in the popular attitude of mendicancy, and looked admiringly at Miggles, with a very singular resemblance in his manner to Yuba Bill. 'That's my watch-dog,' said Miggles, in explanation. 'Oh, he don't bite,' she added, as the two lady passengers fluttered into a corner. 'Does he, old Toppy?' (the latter remark being addressed directly to the sagacious Joaquin). 'I tell you what, boys,' continued Miggles, after she had fed and closed the door on *Ursa Minor*, 'you were in big luck that Joaquin wasn't hanging round when you dropped in to-night.' 'Where was he?' asked the Judge. 'With me,' said Miggles. 'Lord love you; he trots round with me nights like as if he was a man.'

We were silent for a few moments, and listened to the wind. Perhaps we all had the same picture before us – of Miggles walking through the rainy woods, with her savage guardian at her side. The Judge, I remember, said something about Una and her lion, but Miggles received it as she did other compliments, with quiet gravity. Whether she was altogether unconscious of the admiration she excited – she could hardly have been oblivious of Yuba Bill's adoration – I know not; but her very frankness suggested a perfect sexual equality that was cruelly humiliating to the younger members of our party.

The incident of the bear did not add anything in Miggles's favour to the opinions of those of her own sex who were present. In fact, the repast over, a chillness radiated from the two lady passengers that no pine-boughs brought in by Yuba Bill and cast as a sacrifice upon the hearth could wholly overcome. Miggles felt it; and, suddenly declaring that it was time to 'turn in,' offered to show the ladies to their bed in an adjoining room. 'You, boys, will have to camp out here by the fire as well as you can,' she added, 'for thar ain't but the one room.'

Our sex – by which, my dear sir, I allude of course to the stronger portion of humanity – has been generally relieved from the imputation of curiosity, or a fondness for gossip. Yet I am constrained to say, that hardly had the door closed on

Miggles than we crowded together, whispering, snickering, smiling, and exchanging suspicions, surmises, and a thousand speculations in regard to our pretty hostess and her singular companion. I fear that we even hustled that imbecile paralytic, who sat like a voiceless Memnon in our midst, gazing with the serene indifference of the Past in his passionless eyes upon our wordy counsels. In the midst of an exciting discussion, the door opened again, and Miggles re-entered.

But not, apparently, the same Miggles who a few hours before had flashed upon us. Her eyes were downcast, and as she hesitated for a moment on the threshold, with a blanket on her arm, she seemed to have left behind her the frank fearlessness which had charmed us a moment before. Coming into the room, she drew a low stool beside the paralytic's chair, sat down, drew the blanket over her shoulders, and saying, 'If it's all the same to you, boys, as we're rather crowded, I'll stop here to-night,' took the invalid's withered hand in her own, and turned her eyes upon the dying fire. An instinctive feeling that this was only premonitory to more confidential relations, and perhaps some shame at our previous curiosity, kept us silent. The rain still beat upon the roof, wandering gusts of wind stirred the embers into momentary brightness, until, in a lull of the elements, Miggles suddenly lifted up her head, and, throwing her hair over her shoulder, turned her face upon the group and asked,

'Is there any of you that knows me?'

There was no reply.

'Think again! I lived at Marysville in '53. Everybody knew me there, and everybody had the right to know me. I kept the Polka Saloon until I came to live with Jim. That's six years ago. Perhaps I've changed some.'

The absence of recognition may have disconcerted her. She turned her head to the fire again, and it was some seconds before she again spoke, and then more rapidly,

'Well, you see, I thought some of you must have known me. There's no great harm done, anyway. What I was going to say was this: Jim here' – she took his hand in both of hers as she spoke – 'used to know me, if you didn't, and spent a heap of money upon me. I reckon he spent all he had. And one day – it's six years ago this winter – Jim came into my back room, sat down on my sofy, like as you see him in that chair, and never moved again without help. He was struck all of a heap, and never seemed to know what ailed him. The doctors came and said as how it was caused all along of his way of life – for Jim was mighty free and wild like – and that he would never get better, and couldn't last long anyway. They advised me to send him to Frisco to the hospital, for he was no good to any one and would be a baby all his life. Perhaps it was something in Jim's eye, perhaps it was that I never had a baby, but I said "No." I was rich then, for I was popular with everybody – gentlemen like yourself, sir, came to see me – and I sold out my business and bought this yer place, because it was sort of out of the way of travel, you see, and I brought my baby here.'

With a woman's intuitive tact and poetry, she had, as she spoke, slowly shifted her position so as to bring the mute figure of the ruined man between her and her audience, hiding in the shadow behind it, as if she offered it as a tacit apology for her actions. Silent and expressionless, it yet spoke for her; helpless, crushed, and smitten with the Divine thunderbolt, it still stretched an invisible arm around her.

Hidden in the darkness, but still holding his hand, she went on –

'It was a long time before I could get the hang of things about yer, for I was used to company and excitement. I couldn't get any women to help me, and a man I dursent trust; but what with the Indians here-about, who'd do odd jobs for me, and having everything sent from the North Fork, Jim and I managed to worry through. The Doctor would run up from Sacramento once in a while. He'd ask to see "Miggles's baby," as he called Jim, and when he'd go away, he'd say, "Miggles, you're a trump – God bless you!" and it didn't seem so lonely after that. But the last time he was here he said, as he opened the door to go, "Do you know, Miggles, your baby will grow up to be a man yet and an honour to his mother; but not here, Miggles, not here!" And I thought he went away sad – and – and' – and here Miggles's voice and head were somehow both lost completely in the shadow.

'The folks about here are very kind,' said Miggles, after a pause, coming a little into the light again. 'The men from the Fork used to hang around here, until they found they wasn't wanted, and the women are kind – and don't call. I was pretty lonely until I picked up Joaquin in the woods yonder one day, when he wasn't so high, and taught him to beg for his dinner; and then thar's Polly – that's the magpie – she knows no end of tricks, and makes it quite sociable of evenings with her talk, and so I don't feel like as I was the only living being about the ranch. And Jim here,' said Miggles, with her old laugh again, and coming out quite into the firelight, 'Jim – why, boys, you would admire to see how much he knows for a man like him. Sometimes I bring him flowers, and he looks at 'em just as natural as if he knew 'em; and times, when we're sitting alone, I read him those things on the wall. Why Lord!' said Miggles, with her frank laugh, 'I've read him that whole side of the house this winter. There never was such a man for reading as Jim.'

'Why,' asked the Judge, 'do you not marry this man to whom you have devoted your youthful life?'

'Well, you see,' said Miggles, 'it would be playing it rather low down on Jim, to take advantage of his being so helpless. And then, too, if we were man and wife, now, we'd both know that I was *bound* to do what I do now of my own accord.'

'But you are young yet and attractive –'

'It's getting late,' said Miggles, gravely, 'and you'd better all turn in. Good night, boys'; and, throwing the blanket over her head, Miggles laid herself down beside Jim's chair, her head pillowed on the low stool that held his feet, and spoke no more. The fire slowly faded from the hearth; we each sought our blankets in silence; and presently there was no sound in the long room but the pattering of the rain upon the roof, and the heavy breathing of the sleepers.

It was nearly morning when I awoke from a troubled dream. The storm had passed, the stars were shining, and through the shutterless window the full moon, lifting itself over the solemn pines without, looked into the room. It touched the lonely figure in the chair with an infinite compassion, and seemed to baptize with a shining flood the lowly head of the woman whose hair, as in the sweet old story, bathed the feet of him she loved. It even lent a kindly poetry to the rugged outline of Yuba Bill, half reclining on his elbow between them and his passengers, with savagely patient eyes keeping watch and ward. And then I fell asleep and only woke at broad day, with Yuba Bill standing over me, and 'All aboard' ringing in my ears.

Coffee was waiting for us on the table, but Miggles was gone. We wandered about the house and lingered long after the horses were harnessed, but she did not return. It was evident that she wished to avoid a formal leave-taking, and had so left us to depart as we had come. After we had helped the ladies into the coach, we returned to the house and solemnly shook hands with the paralytic Jim, as solemnly settling him back into position after each hand-shake. Then we looked for the last time around the long low room, at the stool where Miggles had sat, and slowly took our seats in the waiting coach. The whip cracked, and we were off!

But as we reached the high road, Bill's dexterous hand laid the six horses back on their haunches, and the stage stopped with a jerk. For there, on a little eminence beside the road, stood Miggles, her hair flying, her eyes sparkling, her white handkerchief waving, and her white teeth flashing a last 'good-bye.' We waved our hats in return. And then Yuba Bill, as if fearful of further fascination, madly lashed his horses forward, and we sank back in our seats. We exchanged not a word until we reached the North Fork and the stage drew up at the Independence House. Then, the Judge leading, we walked into the bar-room and took our places gravely at the bar.

'Are your glasses charged, gentlemen?' said the Judge, solemnly taking off his white hat.

They were.

'Well, then, here's to *Miggles*, GOD BLESS HER!'

Perhaps He had. Who knows?

The Stone Boy

ROSAMUNDE PILCHER

ROSAMUNDE PILCHER is as well known for her delightful short stories as for her bestselling novels, such as the universally popular The Shell Seekers. *'The Stone Boy' is typical of the stories she wrote for women's magazines in the 1980s.*

LIZ had never been to this particular Mediterranean island before, and yet the velvet blue darkness of night she remembered from other holidays, the constant chirp of cicadas, the warm smells of pine and juniper, blown through the open windows of the car on a wind that spoke of the sea.

Even arrival at her cousin and Harry's villa was something of a mystery. Harry parked the car some distance from the dark shape of the house. A string of lights illuminated a path, descending by means of small flights of steps. Denise led the way, and Liz followed, carrying her flight bag, and Harry brought up the rear, with her suitcase.

In front of the house ran a terrace, crowded with terracotta jars spilling a rainbow of flowers. Denise switched on a light, and everything was all at once floodlit, like a stage-set.

From the terrace a door led into the house. This was not a modern villa but an island 'quinta' which Denise and Harry had bought and reconstructed some years ago. The night was warm, but the thick-walled interior felt cool, with red-tiled floors and white walls.

Denise said, 'Now, would you like something to eat?'

'No, thanks. I'm not hungry. Just tired.'

'Bed, then.' Denise led the way up a narrow staircase. 'You're sleeping here . . .'

Liz followed her through a door into a small room of charming simplicity. Dark beams barred the white-washed ceiling. A goatskin rug, a few hooks for clothes, an old carved chest with a mirror hung over it.

'It's not very smart, I'm afraid, but it's not meant to be a very smart house. The bathroom's down the passage, and if you want, there's a mosquito net . . . just tuck it under the mattress. I'd advise you to use it, the mosquitos are bad here.' She gave Liz a kiss. 'Sleep well. We'll talk tomorrow.'

The door closed behind her. Left alone, Liz kicked off her shoes, felt the grateful coolness of polished tiles on the soles of her tired feet. She went to the little window, undid the shutters and folded them back. Harry had turned off the terrace lights, and she leaned her arms on the deep sill and took deep breaths of scented velvet-dark air. Instantly a mosquito introduced itself, whining around the room like a miniature jet. She went to the bed and unknotted the mosquito net which dropped, in filmy folds, to the floor, then she opened her suitcase and began to upack.

It was ten o'clock before Liz woke, and found the sun already high in the sky. She emerged, with some difficulty, from the mosquito net and went to the window. In the bright, hot light of morning, all was revealed, and it was even better than she had dared to anticipate.

Below was the terrace; to one side a small swimming-pool. Steps led down into the garden, shaded here and there with gnarled olive trees. Thick stone walls embraced this plot, and beyond these an almond orchard sloped to a narrow country road. Across the road stood another small house, and then the sea; not the open sea, but a wide inlet of blue water thrusting inland through groves of umbrella pines. The air smelt of lemons and warm resin. Liz turned from the window, found a bikini, brushed her long fair hair, wrapped herself in a towel robe, and went, barefoot, downstairs. There was no sign of

Harry, but she found Denise in the little kitchen, dressed in her swimsuit and a large cotton apron.

'Good morning.'

Denise turned from the sink. 'There you are! How did you sleep?'

'Like a log.'

'Fancy a cup of coffee?'

'Please.'

'Me too. Let's take it down to the pool.'

So breakfast was a juicy orange and a cup of black coffee, consumed in the little shaded pavilion, roofed with split cane, which served as a changing-room for the swimming-pool.

There were a number of brightly coloured chairs set around, and tubs of scarlet geraniums, and at the end of the pool stood a charming stone statue of a boy, his head turned, playing a little pipe.

'Where did you get the statue, Denise?'

'I found it in an antique shop in the village. I think he's meant to be a sort of Cupid. The swimming-pool was a bit dull until he arrived.'

'It's a heavenly house. Do you own the almond orchard, too?'

'Yes, and the other little house across the road. We call it the Casita. It was all part of the property, so we took a deep breath and bought the lot. We did up the Casita, put in a bathroom, and we let it out to holiday people. It helps pay a few of the expenses.'

'Have you got anyone living there now?'

'Yes. A rather nice man. He arrived a couple of days ago. I went down to introduce myself and make sure he'd got everything he wanted, and he seemed very content. In fact –' Denise's voice became elaborately casual – 'we've asked our great friends, the Hathaways, to come for dinner tonight. I wanted you to meet them. They live out here permanently, and he's a sculptor. Anyway, I asked our lodger to come as well. I thought it might be more amusing for you.'

'I hope you aren't matchmaking again.'

Denise said, 'Of *course* not,' but her cheeks were rosy and Liz knew that already her cousin had started to scheme. She was fifteen years older than Liz, an elegant forty-four, and in some ways more like an aunt than a cousin. Liz had been a small bridesmaid when Denise and Harry were married, and this seemed to give Denise a proprietory interest in Liz's love life. She was constantly producing suitable men, and being constantly disappointed by Liz's disinterest in them. She was even more disappointed by Liz's determination to carve a career for herself.

Starting as a junior typist with a glossy magazine, she had slowly climbed the ladder until now, at twenty-nine, she was one of the editors of the Fashion and Beauty sector. As her job had grown in responsibility, so had her salary, and she had made her way from a room in another person's house, to a basement flat, and finally, with the help of a small legacy when her grandmother died, to her own small red brick terrace house in Fulham. She had a car as well. She had her independence. She needed nothing more.

Nothing more. Sometimes, when she was tired or depressed, or another birthday loomed in the not-too-distant future, she had to tell herself this, firmly, aloud, as though she were speaking to another person. '*I have it all. I need nothing more.*'

'It's just,' Denise persisted, 'that I don't like to think of you never marrying. It would be so lonely.'

'I like being alone. I'm with other people all day.'

'But being with someone you love isn't being with other people. It's like being with the other half of yourself.'

'Not everyone's as lucky as you.' She tried diverting the conversation. 'Where is Harry, by the way?'

'He's gone to the garage to pick up a tyre. He'll be back for lunch. And anyway –' Liz realised that Denise was not to be diverted – 'you have to think about your old age.'

'I'm not thirty yet. I don't want to think about old age.'

'You're so gorgeous . . . yes, you are. You always have

been. I can't believe you've reached twenty-nine, and you've never once been in love.'

Liz lay back in her chair; observed, through dark glasses, the length of the pool, shifting and rippling as the breeze touched the surface of the water. At its end the stone boy stood, silhouetted against the sky.

She said at last, 'I was once, but it's over.'

'Oh, Liz. Why?'

'I suppose because I wasn't prepared for total commitment. And if you give your heart to a man, you have to trust him not to break it. I couldn't bear to become jealous and suspicious.'

'Why should you?'

'Because of his job. He was a photographer – always off on glamorous locations with a harem of gorgeous models.'

'Were you going to get married?'

'We talked about it.'

'Was he in love with you?'

'Oh, Denise, I don't know. I suppose so.'

'And you?'

In love. She remembered the excitement of those days. The sudden ecstasy of an unexpected telephone call. The brilliance and beauty of the most mundane objects. Laughter over nothing, shared across small candlelit tables; walking together on sunlit pavements; smelling lilac on a city street; driving in his car down to the country, with the sun roof open to the sky and a whole weekend ahead, and the sensation that there was nobody in the world but the two of them.

Denise was waiting for an answer. Liz smiled ruefully. 'Again . . . I suppose so. But it's over now.'

'Did you finish it, or did he?'

'I did. He went away for three weeks, and I was torn to pieces with every sort of shameful emotion. I hated every moment of it because I hated myself. I never knew I could be like that. Not just missing him, but imagining every sort of intrigue. You can't live with that sort of distrust.'

'When did this happen?' Denise asked.

'A couple of years ago. He went off to work in America.'

'Do you write?'

'No, he wrote me a letter, but I didn't reply. He's probably married by now, to some golden-skinned, wind-surfing American girl. And blissfully happy. Don't let's talk about him any more.' She pulled off her dark glasses and sat up. 'I'm too hot to lie here for another moment. Let's swim.'

She was at her mirror, coiling her long fair hair up into a chignon, when she heard the Hathaways arrive. From the terrace below, voices floated upwards, as Harry greeted his guests.

She turned from the mirror, and took from the bed an airy, lawn caftan and slipped it over her head. She fastened the tiny button at the neck, fixed her earrings, sprayed some scent, and then picked up her small jewelled evening bag and went down the stairs.

As she appeared on the terrace, Denise saw her and said her name, and the men got to their feet and she was introduced.

'This is my cousin Liz. Ken Hathaway, Liz, and Helen. Come and sit down, darling. I thought perhaps you'd gone to sleep and I was going to come and wake you.'

'I did sleep, but only for an hour.'

'You're looking marvellous,' said Helen Hathaway. 'Not burnt at all. Just brown. First days in this heat sometimes knock visitors out.'

'I'm much too careful for that.' Liz smiled.

'How long are you here for? Two weeks. Then Denise and Harry must bring you over to see us. We live here all the time, in a tiny house in the main street of the village. There's a yard at the back and a donkey shed that Ken's turned into a studio.'

Denise came to join them. 'Now, we're only waiting for our final guest. He's our lodger from the Casita, Helen.'

'All on his own?'

'Yes. A very self-contained person. Interesting, I thought. I hope he doesn't forget to come.'

'He hasn't forgotten,' said Liz. While they spoke, she had glimpsed the pale blur of a man's white shirt approaching the house by way of the almond orchard and the pool. As he passed the stone boy, and moved into the diffused light from the terrace, his figure took shape, a slightly built man, dark-headed, moving easily, wearing a white shirt, open-necked, and a pair of blue slacks. For an instant he disappeared behind the retaining wall, and then, almost at once, appeared again, climbing the steps which led up on to the terrace. Now, he stood in full light. 'He's here,' she finished.

Denise sprang to her feet. 'Oh, I am glad. I was afraid you'd forgotten.'

'Of course not.'

'How nice to have you with us, John.' Denise began the round of introductions. 'And this is my cousin Liz Searley, who's staying with us,' she ended.

His hand closed around her own. This surprised her, because she had no clear recollection of having put it out to greet him. She looked down, as though in need of confirmation, and saw their hands locked together.

He said, 'How nice to meet you.'

They ate dinner indoors, sitting around the scrubbed, candlelit table. For the occasion, Denise's maid Antonia had come in to cook one of her famous paellas, and there was rough, home-made bread, and huge wooden bowls of salads, and bottles of the local wine. After the paella, Antonia produced dishes of fresh fruit, goat's cheese, and tiny bowls of crystallised grapes.

All through dinner conversation bubbled, but Liz said little, content to listen.

At the end of the meal Harry smiled. 'Let's take coffee out on to the terrace.'

Liz found herself sitting next to John, this dark young man, not handsome, not tall, but compelling in an inexplicable way, and possessed of the most charming voice. At dinner he had told them little of himself. Ken had accused him of having a wife and brood of children but he assured them that there was no wife and family that he knew of, and one's own company could sometimes be the best.

'How long are you here for?' she asked him now, stirring her coffee and not looking into his face.

'Only a week.'

'You must be a busy man. Where do you work?'

'I'm working in Paris just now.'

'What do you do all day here?'

'Swim. Sit around. Paint.'

'*Paint?*'

He smiled. 'Not walls. Pictures. I started painting about a year ago. It's wonderful therapy.'

For some reason, Liz could think of nothing to say.

The Hathaways decided that it was time they left. Helen gave Denise a kiss. 'A perfect evening. When will you bring Liz to us . . . and John as well, if he'd like to come? We long to show you our little house.'

A date was fixed for the following evening.

'We'll give you a drink,' said Ken, 'and take you out for dinner at our local. They serve the best fresh fish in the world there.'

John set down his empty coffee cup and said that he, too, must take himself off. 'We'll be in touch,' Denise told him. 'We'll give you a lift to the Hathaways tomorrow.'

'That's very kind.'

Smiling, appreciative, he went from them the way he had come, down the steps, and along the edge of the swimming-pool. As he disappeared into the velvet darkness beyond the stone boy and was lost to them in the groves of almonds, Denise turned and began to stack the coffee cups.

'A nice man,' she said.

'Yes, and a heavenly evening. Thank you so much.'

Denise straightened, her eyes met Liz's own. 'I said, a nice man,' she repeated.

'Of course. Delightful.'

Cocks crowing and the discordant clamour of goat bells

awakened her. Early. So early after a late night. Liz reached for her watch, and saw that it was only a quarter-past seven. 'I should go back to sleep,' she told herself, and was instantly wide awake, knowing that she must be up and about, out of doors in the pearly cool of a new day.

Five minutes later, she was standing beside the swimming-pool, undoing the sash of her white towel robe. She poised and dived, shattering the surface of the water like broken glass. She swam a length and then another, back to the shallow end. She stood, shaking water from her face, smoothing back her wet hair with her hands. A voice said, 'Good morning.'

He seemed to have appeared out of nowhere, to stand by the stone boy and observe her. He wore a pair of swimming shorts and his bare feet were thrust into shabby leather sandals.

When he stood beside her in the water, she saw the neat strength of his body, the hard muscles beneath his tan, the very blueness of his eyes, spiked with wet black lashes.

'That was a good party last night.'

'Yes.'

'Are the others up yet?'

'I don't think so.'

'Come with me, and I'll give you breakfast. Fresh melon and boiled eggs. The sun's on my terrace, and everything's smothered in bougainvillaea.' When she hesitated, he went on, coaxing, practically bribing her to come with him. 'Black coffee, as much as you can drink. Fresh bread and orange blossom honey. No woman could want more than that.'

'You don't need to get carried away. You're only asking me to breakfast.'

'Then you'll come.'

She swam away from him. 'Yes, I'll come.'

A little later, when they had finished swimming, she followed him down the narrow stony track which wound beneath the almond trees. They crossed the road, then went through a gate and into the tiny garden of the Casita. The bougainvillaea was indeed a sight, covering the terrace; and

clambering up on to the red-tiled roof of the single-storied
house.

'Come and see inside.'

The door was open, but hung with a brightly coloured
bead curtain. He lifted this, stood aside, and she went in ahead
of him.

He said, 'I'll make coffee,' and went to fill the kettle.

The simple room was starkly shipshape, and she saw that
he had already made his bed. There was a small table by this,
with a lamp and a pile of paperbacks, and a photograph in a
leather frame. A photograph of a girl with long fair hair and
dark eyes, a girl laughing, her expression one of amusement
and affection. A happy girl. Herself.

She felt, quite suddenly, shaken and shocked. She knew that he
wasn't married, because he had told them so last night, but she
had never expected that he would still keep her photograph,
take it wherever he went, keep it by his bed. The beat of her
heart was all at once so strong that she was certain he must be
able to hear it.

Trembling, her knees weak, she went across the room,
meaning perhaps to take the photograph from the table, but
her legs suddenly felt wobbly and she ended up sitting on the
edge of the bed.

It was John who finally broke the laden silence.

He said, 'It goes everywhere with me. Has done ever since
you said goodbye and refused to see me again. I wanted you
to see it. I wanted you to know.'

'I thought you'd be married by now.'

'On the rebound from you?'

'No. I hoped, in love.'

'I thought the same about you. Did you never find what
you were looking for?'

'I think I stopped looking for it. How long did you stay in
America?'

'About eighteen months. Then I got this contract with a
French magazine. That's why I'm living in Paris.'

'You're happy? I wanted you to be happy.'

'Pity you weren't prepared to take the responsibility yourself.'

'That's not fair.'

'Why didn't you answer my letter?'

'I nearly did. I started to write, but I couldn't think of the
right words, so I tore it up and threw it away. It wasn't any
good. I knew too much about you.'

'I don't think you knew anything about me.'

'And I hated that something in myself which wouldn't let
you go. I seemed to want all of you for myself. Possessiveness
smothers. I didn't want to smother you, John.'

'The truth is, you didn't trust me.'

'No.' It was a horrible thing to have to say.

'What didn't you trust?' He abandoned the cooker and
crossed the room to sit beside her. 'Did you think every
time I left you I would start some new relationship? Or did
you think I mightn't come back?'

'I suppose I . . .' She felt as though she were digging for the
truth. 'I couldn't imagine any woman not – wanting you. The
way I wanted you.'

He shook his head. 'Luckily for all of us, we don't stimulate
the same reactions in every new person we meet. Otherwise
the world would be in a sorry mess.' He smiled. 'Oh, Liz,'
he told her, 'we'd have made a great team.'

'I'd have made you miserable.'

'I'd rather be miserable with you than miserable without
you.'

Ridiculously, her eyes filled with tears. Two years ago she
had turned her back on him, but he was still the most attractive
man she had ever known. Nothing had changed.

'How – how did you know I'd be here?' she managed at
last. 'It couldn't have been a coincidence. That only happens
in books!'

He smiled his gentle, caressing smile. 'Remember those
friends of your cousin's you introduced me to at a party in

London? Well, I contacted them and they gave me Denise's address here. I wrote. I didn't expect her to reply, but she did. She told me you were coming to stay and would I like to rent the Casita. She was surprisingly sympathetic.'

Denise would be! Suddenly Liz remembered her cousin's emphasis on 'a nice man' last night, the look in her eyes. She had known all along . . .

'I never stopped loving you,' he was saying.

A whistling sound came from the direction of the cooker. They both ignored it. She said, 'I can see clearly now. And, like you, I think I'd rather be miserable with you than miserable without you.'

'We won't be miserable. We'll be blissful. It would be foolish to pass up this second chance. What do you say, Liz? Shall we grab it, with both hands?'

'Like it was happening for the first time. No commitments. No promises.'

'An open-ended agreement.'

Solemnly they shook hands on it. She said, 'Do you know something?'

'Yes.' He put a hand on either side of her head, drew her face towards his, and began to kiss her. 'The kettle's boiling.'

The sun was high in the sky before they made their way back to the big house. They made their way, without haste, up the path through the orchard. Here it was shady, light filtering through the leaves of the trees, but the swimming-pool basked in full sunlight. By the statue of the stone boy, they paused.

'Denise said she thought he was a sort of Cupid. A little god of love.'

'More likely Pan, except he's missed out on the cloven hooves.' John patted the little figure. 'Whoever he is, he's brought us luck.'

Denise appeared on the terrace above them. 'There you are!' she called down to them. 'Everything all right, then?'

They left the stone boy, and went on up the steps to tell her.

Without Benefit of Clergy

RUDYARD KIPLING

RUDYARD KIPLING (1865–1936) was born in India. His father at that time was Professor of Architectural Sculpture in Bombay. By the age of 17 Kipling was assistant editor of the Civil and Military Gazette in Lahore, followed by two years with The Pioneer at Allahabad. This is when he wrote many of his Indian stories, from personal knowledge and intense sympathy with the people amongst whom he lived.

> *Before my Spring I garnered Autumn's gain,*
> *Out of her time my field was white with grain,*
> *The year gave up her secrets to my woe.*
> *Forced and deflowered each sick season lay,*
> *In mystery of increase and decay;*
> *I saw the sunset ere men saw the day,*
> *Who am too wise in that I should not know.*
>
> BITTER WATERS

I

BUT if it be a girl?'

'Lord of my life, it cannot be. I have prayed for so many nights, and sent gifts to Sheikh Badl's shrine so often, that I know God will give us a son – a man-child that shall grow into a man. Think of this and be glad. My mother shall be his mother till I can take him again, and the mullah of the Pattan mosque shall cast his nativity – God send he be born in an auspicious hour! – and then, and then thou wilt never weary of me, thy slave.'

'Since when hast thou been a slave, my queen?'

'Since the beginning – till this mercy came to me. How could I be sure of thy love when I knew that I had been bought with silver?'

'Nay, that was the dowry. I paid it to thy mother.'

'And she has buried it, and sits upon it all day long like a hen. What talk is yours of dower! I was bought as though I had been a Lucknow dancing-girl instead of a child.'

'Art thou sorry for the sale?'

'I have sorrowed; but today I am glad. Thou wilt never cease to love me now? – answer, my king.'

'Never – never. No.'

'Not even though the *mem-log* – the white women of thine own blood – love thee? And remember, I have watched them driving in the evening; they are very fair.'

'I have seen fire-balloons by the hundred. I have seen the moon, and – then I saw no more fire-balloons.'

Ameera clapped her hands and laughed. 'Very good talk,' she said. Then with an assumption of great stateliness, 'It is enough. Thou hast my permission to depart – if thou wilt.'

The man did not move. He was sitting on a low red-lacquered couch in a room furnished only with a blue-and-white floor-cloth, some rugs, and a very complete collection of native cushions. At his feet sat a woman of sixteen, and she was all but all the world in his eyes. By every rule and law she should have been otherwise, for he was an Englishman, and she a Mussulman's daughter bought two years before from her mother, who, being left without money, would have sold Ameera shrieking to the Prince of Darkness if the price had been sufficient.

It was a contract entered into with a light heart; but even before the girl had reached her bloom she came to fill the greater portion of John Holden's life. For her, and the withered hag her mother, he had taken a little house overlooking the great red-walled city, and found – when the marigolds had sprung up by the well in the courtyard, and Ameera had established herself according to her own ideas of comfort, and her mother had ceased grumbling at the inadequacy of the cooking-places, the distance from the daily market, and at matters of house-keeping in general – that the house was to him his home. Anyone could enter his bachelor's bungalow by day or night, and the life that he led there was an unlovely one. In the house in the city his feet only could pass beyond the outer courtyard to the women's rooms; and when the big wooden gate was bolted behind him he was king in his own territory, with Ameera for queen. And there was going to be added to this kingdom a third person whose arrival Holden felt inclined to resent. It interfered with his perfect happiness. It disarranged the orderly peace of the house that was his own. But Ameera was wild with delight at the thought of it, and her mother not less so. The love of a man, and particularly a white man, was at the best an inconstant affair, but it might, both women argued, be held fast by a baby's hands. 'And then,' Ameera would always say, 'then he will never care for the white *mem-log*. I hate them all – I hate them all.'

'He will go back to his own people in time,' said the mother; 'but by the blessing of God that time is yet afar off.'

Holden sat silent on the couch thinking of the future, and his thoughts were not pleasant. The drawbacks of a double life are manifold. The Government, with singular care, had ordered him out of the station for a fortnight on special duty in the place of a man who was watching by the bedside of a sick wife. The verbal notification of the transfer had been edged by a cheerful remark that Holden ought to think himself lucky in being a bachelor and a free man. He came to break the news to Ameera.

'It is not good,' she said slowly, 'but it is not all bad.

There is my mother here, and no harm will come to me
– unless indeed I die of pure joy. Go thou to thy work and
think no troublesome thoughts. When the days are done I
believe . . . nay, I am sure. And – and then I shall lay *him*
in thy arms, and thou wilt love me for ever. The train goes
tonight, at midnight, is it not? Go now, and do not let thy
heart be heavy by cause of me. But thou wilt not delay in
returning? Thou wilt not stay on the road to talk to the bold
white *mem-log*? Come back to me swiftly, my life.'

As he left the courtyard to reach his horse that was
tethered to the gate-post, Holden spoke to the white-haired
old watchman who guarded the house, and bade him under
certain contingencies dispatch the filled-up telegraph-form
that Holden gave him. It was all that could be done, and
with the sensations of a man who has attended his own
funeral Holden went away by the night mail to his exile.
Every hour of the day he dreaded the arrival of the telegram,
and every hour of the night he pictured to himself the death
of Ameera. In consequence his work for the State was not of
first-rate quality, nor was his temper towards his colleagues
of the most amiable. The fortnight ended without a sign
from his home, and, torn to pieces by his anxieties, Holden
returned to be swallowed up for two precious hours by a
dinner at the Club, wherein he heard, as a man hears in a
swoon, voices telling him how execrably he had performed
the other man's duties, and how he had endeared himself
to all his associates. Then he fled on horseback through the
night with his heart in his mouth. There was no answer at
first to his blows on the gate, and he had just wheeled his
horse round to kick it in when Pir Khan appeared with a
lantern and held his stirrup.

'Has aught occurred?' said Holden.

'The news does not come from my mouth, Protector of
the Poor, but –' He held out his shaking hand as befitted the
bearer of good news who is entitled to a reward.

Holden hurried through the courtyard. A light burned in
the upper room. His horse neighed in the gateway, and he

heard a shrill little wail that sent all the blood into the apple of his throat. It was a new voice, but it did not prove that Ameera was alive.

'Who is there?' he called up the narrow brick staircase.

There was a cry of delight from Ameera, and then the voice of the mother, tremulous with old age and pride: 'We be two women and – the – man – thy – son.'

On the threshold of the room Holden stepped on a naked dagger, that was laid there to avert ill-luck, and it broke at the hilt under his impatient heel.

'God is great!' cooed Ameera in the half-light. 'Thou hast taken his misfortunes on thy head.'

'Ay, but how is it with thee, life of my life? Old woman, how is it with her?'

'She has forgotten her sufferings for joy that the child is born. There is no harm; but speak softly,' said the mother.

'It only needed thy presence to make me all well,' said Ameera. 'My king, thou hast been very long away. What gifts hast thou for me? Ah, ah! It is I that bring gifts this time. Look, my life, look. Was there ever such a babe? Nay, I am too weak even to clear my arm from him.'

'Rest then, and do not talk. I am here, *bachari* [little woman].'

'Well said, for there is a bond and a heel-rope [*peecharee*] between us now that nothing can break. Look – canst thou see in this light? He is without spot or blemish. Never was such a man-child. *Ya illah!* he shall be a pundit – no, a trooper of the Queen. And, my life, dost thou love me as well as ever, though I am faint and sick and worn? Answer truly.'

'Yea. I love as I have loved, with all my soul. Lie still, pearl, and rest.'

'Then do not go. Sit by my side here – so. Mother, the lord of this house needs a cushion. Bring it.' There was an almost imperceptible movement on the part of the new life that lay in the hollow of Ameera's arm. 'Aho!' she said, her voice breaking with love. 'The babe is a champion from his birth. He is kicking me in the side with mighty kicks. Was there ever such a babe! And he is ours to us – thine and mine. Put thy hand on his head, but carefully, for he is very young, and men are unskilled in such matters.'

Very cautiously Holden touched with the tips of his fingers the downy head.

'He is of the Faith,' said Ameera; 'for lying here in the nightwatches I whispered the call to prayer and the profession of faith into his ears. And it is most marvellous that he was born upon a Friday, as I was born. Be careful of him, my life; but he can almost grip with his hands.'

Holden found one helpless little hand that closed feebly on his finger. And the clutch ran through his body till it settled about his heart. Till then his sole thought had been for Ameera. He began to realize that there was someone else in the world, but he could not feel that it was a veritable son with a soul. He sat down to think, and Ameera dozed lightly.

'Get hence, Sahib,' said her mother under her breath. 'It is not good that she should find you here on waking. She must be still.'

'I go,' said Holden submissively. 'Here be rupees. See that my *baba* gets fat and finds all that he needs.'

The chink of the silver roused Ameera. 'I am his mother, and no hireling,' she said weakly. 'Shall I look to him more or less for the sake of money? Mother, give it back. I have borne my lord a son.'

The deep sleep of weakness came upon her almost before the sentence was completed. Holden went down to the courtyard very softly with his heart at ease. Pir Khan, the old watchman, was chuckling with delight. 'This house is now complete,' he said, and without further comment thrust into Holden's hands the hilt of a sabre worn many years ago when he, Pir Khan, served the Queen in the Police. The bleat of a tethered goat came from the well-kerb.

'There be two,' said Pir Khan, 'two goats of the best. I bought them, and they cost much money; and since there is no birth-party assembled their flesh will be all mine. Strike craftily, Sahib! 'Tis an ill-balanced sabre at the best. Wait till they raise their heads from cropping the marigolds.'

'And why?' said Holden, bewildered.

'For the birth-sacrifice. What else? Otherwise the child being unguarded from fate may die. The Protector of the Poor knows the fitting words to be said.'

Holden had learned them once with little thought that he would ever speak them in earnest. The touch of the cold sabre-hilt in his palm turned suddenly to the clinging grip of the child upstairs – the child that was his own son – and a dread of loss filled him.

'Strike!' said Pir Khan. 'Never life came into the world but life was paid for it. See, the goats have raised their heads. Now! With a drawing cut!'

Hardly knowing what he did, Holden cut twice as he muttered the Mohammedan prayer that runs: 'Almighty! In place of this my son I offer life for life, blood for blood, head for head, bone for bone, hair for hair, skin for skin.' The waiting horse snorted and bounded in his pickets at the smell of the raw blood that spirted over Holden's riding-boots.

'Well smitten!' said Pir Khan, wiping the sabre. 'A swordsman was lost in thee. Go with a light heart, Heaven-born. I am thy servant, and the servant of thy son. May the Presence live a thousand years and . . . the flesh of the goats is all mine?' Pir Khan drew back richer by a month's pay. Holden swung himself into the saddle and rode off through the low-hanging wood-smoke of the evening. He was full of riotous exultation, alternating with a vast vague tenderness directed towards no particular object, that made him choke as he bent over the neck of his uneasy horse. 'I never felt like this in my life,' he thought. 'I'll go to the Club and pull myself together.'

A game of pool was beginning, and the room was full of men. Holden entered, eager to get to the light and the company of his fellows, singing at the top of his voice:

'*In Baltimore a-walking, a lady I did meet!*'

'Did you?' said the Club Secretary from his corner. 'Did she happen to tell you that your boots were wringing wet? Great goodness, man, it's blood!'

'Bosh!' said Holden, picking his cue from the rack. 'May I cut in? It's dew. I've been riding through high crops. My faith! my boots are in a mess though!

> '*And if it be a girl she shall wear a wedding-ring,*
> *And if it be a boy he shall fight for his King,*
> *With his dirk, and his cap, and his little jacket blue,*
> *He shall walk the quarter-deck –*'

'Yellow on blue – green next player,' said the marker monotonously.

'*He shall walk the quarter-deck* – Am I green, marker? *He shall walk the quarter-deck* – eh! that's a bad shot – *as his daddy used to do!*'

'I don't see that you have anything to crow about,' said a zealous junior Civilian acidly. 'The Government is not exactly pleased with your work when you relieved Sanders.'

'Does that mean a wigging from headquarters?' said Holden with an abstracted smile. 'I think I can stand it.'

The talk beat up round the ever-fresh subject of each man's work, and steadied Holden till it was time to go to his dark empty bungalow, where his butler received him as one who knew all his affairs. Holden remained awake for the greater part of the night, and his dreams were pleasant ones.

II

'How old is he now?'

'*Ya illah!* What a man's question! He is all but six weeks old; and on this night I go up to the house-top with thee, my life, to count the stars. For that is auspicious. And he was born on a Friday under the sign of the Sun, and it has been told to me that he will outlive us both and get wealth. Can we wish for aught better, beloved?'

'There is nothing better. Let us go up to the roof, and thou shalt count the stars – but a few only, for the sky is heavy with cloud.'

'The winter rains are late, and maybe they come out of season. Come, before all the stars are hid. I have put on my richest jewels.'

'Thou hast forgotten the best of all.'

'*Ai!* Ours. He comes also. He has never yet seen the skies.'

Ameera climbed the narrow staircase that led to the flat roof. The child, placid and unwinking, lay in the hollow of her right arm, gorgeous in silver-fringed muslin with a small skull-cap on his head. Ameera wore all that she valued most. The diamond nose-stud that takes the place of the Western patch in drawing attention to the curve of the nostril, the gold ornament in the centre of the forehead studded with tallow-drop emeralds and flawed rubies, the heavy circlet of beaten gold that was fastened round her neck by the softness of the pure metal, and the chinking curb-patterned silver anklets hanging low over the rosy ankle-bone. She was dressed in jade-green muslin as befitted a daughter of the Faith, and from shoulder to elbow and elbow to wrist ran bracelets of silver tied with floss silk, frail glass bangles slipped over the wrist in proof of the slenderness of the hand, and certain heavy gold bracelets that had no part in her country's ornaments, but, since they were Holden's gift and fastened with a cunning European snap, delighted her immensely.

They sat down by the low white parapet of the roof, overlooking the city and its lights.

'They are happy down there,' said Ameera. 'But I do not think that they are as happy as we. Nor do I think the white *mem-log* are as happy. And thou?'

'I know they are not.'

'How dost thou know?'

'They give their children over to the nurses.'

'I have never seen that,' said Ameera with a sigh, 'nor do I wish to see. *Ahi!*' – she dropped her head on Holden's shoulder – 'I have counted forty stars, and I am tired. Look at the child, love of my life, he is counting too.'

The baby was staring with round eyes at the dark of the heavens. Ameera placed him in Holden's arms, and he lay there without a cry.

'What shall we call him among ourselves?' she said. 'Look! Art thou ever tired of looking? He carries thy very eyes. But the mouth –'

'Is thine, most dear. Who should know better than I?'

' 'Tis such a feeble mouth. Oh, so small! And yet it holds my heart between its lips. Give him to me now. He has been too long away.'

'Nay, let him lie; he has not yet begun to cry.'

'When he cries thou wilt give him back – eh? What a man of mankind thou art! If he cried he were only the dearer to me. But, my life, what little name shall we give him?'

The small body lay close to Holden's heart. It was utterly helpless and very soft. He scarcely dared to breathe for fear of crushing it. The caged green parrot that is regarded as a sort of guardian-spirit in most native households moved on its perch and fluttered a drowsy wing.

'There is the answer,' said Holden. 'Mian Mittu has spoken. He shall be The Parrot. When he is ready he will talk mightily and run about. Mian Mittu is The Parrot in thy – in the Mussulman tongue, is it not?'

'Why put me so far off?' said Ameera fretfully. 'Let it be like unto some English name – but not wholly. For he is mine.'

'Then call him Tota, for that is likest English.'

'Ay, Tota, and that is still The Parrot. Forgive me, my lord, for a minute ago, but in truth he is too little to wear all the weight of Mian Mittu for name. He shall be Tota – our Tota to us. Hearest thou, O small one? Littlest, thou art Tota.' She touched the child's cheek, and he waking wailed, and it was necessary to return him to his mother, who soothed him with the wonderful rhyme of *Aré koko, Jaré koko!* which says:

Oh, crow! Go, crow! Baby's sleeping sound,
And the wild plums grow in the jungle, only a penny a pound.
Only a penny a pound, baba, *only a penny a pound.*

Reassured many times as to the price of those plums, Tota cuddled himself down to sleep. The two sleek, white well-bullocks in the courtyard were steadily chewing the cud of their evening meal; old Pir Khan squatted at the head of Holden's horse, his Police sabre across his knees, pulling drowsily at a big water-pipe that croaked like a bull-frog in a pond. Ameera's mother sat spinning in the lower veranda, and the wooden gate was shut and barred. The music of a marriage-procession came to the roof above the gentle hum of the city, and a string of flying-foxes crossed the face of the low moon.

'I have prayed,' said Ameera after a long pause, 'I have prayed for two things. First, that I may die in thy stead if thy death is demanded, and in the second, that I may die in the place of the child. I have prayed to the Prophet and to Bibi Miriam [the Virgin Mary]. Thinkest thou either will hear?'

'From thy lips who would not hear the lightest word?'

'I asked for straight talk, and thou hast given me sweet talk. Will my prayers be heard?'

'How can I say? God is very good.'

'Of that I am not sure. Listen now. When I die, or the child dies, what is thy fate? Living, thou wilt return to the bold white *mem-log*, for kind calls to kind.'

'Not always.'

'With a woman, no; with a man it is otherwise. Thou wilt in this life, later on, go back to thine own folk. That I could almost endure, for I should be dead. But in thy very death thou wilt be taken away to a strange place and a Paradise that I do not know.'

'Will it be Paradise?'

'Surely, for who would harm thee? But we two – I and the child – shall be elsewhere, and we cannot come to thee, nor canst thou come to us. In the old days, before the child was born, I did not think of these things; but now I think of them always. It is very hard talk.'

'It will fall as it will fall. Tomorrow we do not know, but today and love we know well. Surely we are happy now.'

'So happy that it were well to make our happiness assured. And thy Bibi Miriam should listen to me: for she is also a woman. But then she would envy me! It is not seemly for men to worship a woman.'

Holden laughed aloud at Ameera's little spasm of jealousy.

'Is it not seemly? Why didst thou not turn me from worship of thee, then?'

'Thou a worshipper! And of me? My king, for all thy sweet words, well I know that I am thy servant and thy slave, and the dust under thy feet. And I would not have it otherwise. See!'

Before Holden could prevent her she stooped forward and touched his feet; recovering herself with a little laugh she hugged Tota closer to her bosom. Then, almost savagely:

'Is it true that the bold white *mem-log* live for three times the length of my life? Is it true that they make their marriages not before they are old women?'

'They marry as do others – when they are women.'

'That I know, but they wed when they are twenty-five. Is that true?'

'That is true.'

'*Ya illah!* At twenty-five! Who would of his own will take a wife even of eighteen? She is a woman – ageing every hour. Twenty-five! I shall be an old woman at that age, and — Those *mem-log* remain young for ever. How I hate them!'

'What have they to do with us?'

'I cannot tell. I know only that there may now be alive on this earth a woman ten years older than I who may come to thee and take thy love ten years after I am an old woman, grey-headed, and the nurse of Tota's son. That is unjust and evil. They should die too.'

'Now, for all thy years thou art a child, and shalt be picked up and carried down the staircase.'

'Tota! Have a care for Tota, my lord! Thou at least art as foolish as any babe!' Ameera tucked Tota out of harm's way in the hollow of her neck, and was carried downstairs laughing in Holden's arms, while Tota opened his eyes and smiled after the manner of the lesser angels.

He was a silent infant, and, almost before Holden could realize that he was in the world, developed into a small gold-coloured little god and unquestioned despot of the house overlooking the city. Those were months of absolute happiness to Holden and Ameera – happiness withdrawn from the world, shut in behind the wooden gate that Pir Khan guarded. By day Holden did his work with an immense pity for such as were not so fortunate as himself and a sympathy for small children that amazed and amused many mothers at the little station-gatherings. At nightfall he returned to Ameera – Ameera, full of the wondrous doings of Tota; how he had been seen to clap his hands together and move his fingers with intention and purpose – which was manifestly a miracle – how, later, he had of his own initiative crawled out of his low bedstead on to the floor and swayed on both feet for the space of three breaths.

'And they were long breaths, for my heart stood still with delight,' said Ameera.

Then Tota took the beasts into his councils – the well-bullocks, the little grey squirrels, the mongoose that lived in a hole near the well, and especially Mian Mittu, the parrot, whose tail he grievously pulled, and Mian Mittu screamed till Ameera and Holden arrived.

'Oh, villain! Child of strength! This to thy brother on the house-top! *Tobah, tobah!* Fie! Fie! But I know a charm to make him wise as Suleiman and Aflatoun [Solomon and Plato]. Now look,' said Ameera. She drew from an embroidered bag a handful of almonds. 'See! we count seven. In the name of God!'

She placed Mian Mittu, very angry and rumpled, on the top of his cage, and seating herself between the babe and the bird she cracked and peeled an almond less white than her teeth. 'This is a true charm, my life, and do not laugh. See! I give the parrot one-half and Tota the other.' Mian Mittu with careful beak took his share from between Ameera's lips, and she kissed the other half into the mouth of the child, who ate it slowly with wondering eyes. 'This I will do each day of seven, and without doubt he who is ours will be a bold speaker and wise. Eh, Tota, what wilt thou be when thou art a man and I am grey-headed?' Tota tucked his fat legs into adorable creases. He could crawl, but he was not going to waste the spring of his youth in idle speech. He wanted Mian Mittu's tail to tweak.

When he was advanced to the dignity of a silver belt – which, with a magic square engraved on silver and hung round his neck, made up the greater part of his clothing – he staggered on a perilous journey down the garden to Pir Khan, and proffered him all his jewels in exchange for one little ride on Holden's horse, having seen his mother's mother chaffering with pedlars in the veranda. Pir Khan wept and set the untried feet on his own grey head in sign of fealty, and brought the bold adventurer to his mother's arms, vowing that Tota would be a leader of men ere his beard was grown.

One hot evening, while he sat on the roof between his father and mother watching the never-ending warfare of the kites that the city boys flew, he demanded a kite of his own with Pir Khan to fly it, because he had a fear of dealing with anything larger than himself, and when Holden called him a 'spark,' he rose to his feet and answered slowly in defence of his new-found individuality, '*Hum 'park nahin hai. Hum admi hai.* [I am no spark, but a man.]'

The protest made Holden choke and devote himself very seriously to a consideration of Tota's future. He need hardly have taken the trouble. The delight of that life was too perfect to endure. Therefore it was taken away as many things are taken away in India – suddenly and without warning. The little lord of the house, as Pir Khan called him, grew sorrowful and complained of pains who had never known the meaning of pain. Ameera, wild with terror, watched him through the night, and in the dawning of the second day the life was shaken out of him by fever – the seasonal autumn fever. It seemed altogether impossible that he could die, and neither Ameera nor Holden at first believed the evidence of the little body on the bedstead. Then Ameera beat her head against the wall and would have flung herself down the well in the garden had Holden not restrained her by main force.

One mercy only was granted to Holden. He rode to his office in broad daylight and found waiting him an unusually heavy mail that demanded concentrated attention and hard work. He was not, however, alive to this kindness of the Gods.

III

The first shock of a bullet is no more than a brisk pinch. The wrecked body does not send in its protest to the soul till ten or fifteen seconds later. Holden realized his pain slowly, exactly as he had realized his happiness, and with the same imperious necessity for hiding all trace of it. In the beginning he only felt that there had been a loss, and that Ameera needed comforting, where she sat with her head on her knees shivering as Mian Mittu from the house-top called, *Tota! Tota! Tota!* Later all his world and the daily life of it rose up to hurt him. It was an outrage that any one of the children at the band-stand in the evening should be alive and clamorous, when his own child lay dead. It was more than mere pain when one of them touched him, and stories told by over-fond fathers of their children's latest performances cut him to the quick. He could not declare his pain. He had neither help, comfort, nor sympathy; and Ameera at the end of each weary day would lead him through the hell of self-questioning reproach which is reserved for those who have lost a child, and believe that with a little – just a little more care – it might have been saved.

'Perhaps,' Ameera would say, 'I did not take sufficient heed. Did I, or did I not? The sun on the roof that day when he played so long alone and I was – *ahi!* braiding my hair – it may be that the sun then bred the fever. If I had warned him from the sun he might have lived. But, oh, my life, say that I am guiltless! Thou knowest that I loved him as I love thee. Say that there is no blame on me, or I shall die – I shall die!'

'There is no blame – before God, none. It was written, and how could we do aught to save? What has been, has been. Let it go, beloved.'

'He was all my heart to me. How can I let the thought go when my arm tells me every night that he is not here? *Ahi! Ahi!* Oh, Tota, come back to me – come back again, and let us be all together as it was before!'

'Peace, peace! For thine own sake, and for mine also, if thou lovest me – rest.'

'By this I know thou dost not care; and how shouldst thou? The white men have hearts of stone and souls of iron. Oh, that I had married a man of mine own people – though he beat me – and had never eaten the bread of an alien!'

'Am I an alien – mother of my son?'

'What else – Sahib? . . . Oh, forgive me – forgive! The death has driven me mad. Thou art the life of my heart, and the light of my eyes, and the breath of my life, and – and I have put thee from me, though it was but for a moment. If thou goest away, to whom shall I look for help? Do not be angry. Indeed, it was the pain that spoke and not thy slave.'

'I know, I know. We be two who were three. The greater need therefore that we should be one.'

They were sitting on the roof as of custom. The night was

a warm one in early spring, and sheet-lightning was dancing on the horizon to a broken tune played by far-off thunder. Ameera settled herself in Holden's arms.

'The dry earth is lowing like a cow for the rain, and I – I am afraid. It was not like this when we counted the stars. But thou lovest me as much as before, though a bond is taken away? Answer!'

'I love more because a new bond has come out of the sorrow that we have eaten together, and that thou knowest.'

'Yea, I knew,' said Ameera in a very small whisper. 'But it is good to hear thee say so, my life, who art so strong to help. I will be a child no more, but a woman and an aid to thee. Listen! Give me my *sitar* and I will sing bravely.'

She took the light silver-studded *sitar* and began a song of the great hero Rajah Rasalu. The hand failed on the strings, the tune halted, checked, and at a low note turned off to the poor little nursery-rhyme about the wicked crow:

'*And the wild plums grow in the jungle, only a penny a pound.*
Only a penny a pound, baba – *only* . . .'

Then came the tears, and the piteous rebellion against fate till she slept, moaning a little in her sleep, with the right arm thrown clear of the body as though it protected something that was not there. It was after this night that life became a little easier for Holden. The ever-present pain of loss drove him into his work, and the work repaid him by filling up his mind for nine or ten hours a day. Ameera sat alone in the house and brooded, but grew happier when she understood that Holden was more at ease, according to the custom of women. They touched happiness again, but this time with caution.

'It was because we loved Tota that he died. The jealousy of God was upon us,' said Ameera. 'I have hung up a large black jar before our window to turn the evil eye from us, and we must make no protestations of delight, but go softly underneath the stars, lest God finds us out. Is that not good talk, worthless one?'

She had shifted the accent on the word that means 'beloved,' in proof of the sincerity of her purpose. But the kiss that followed the new christening was a thing that any deity might have envied. They went about henceforward saying, 'It is naught, it is naught;' and hoping that all the Powers heard.

The Powers were busy on other things. They had allowed thirty million people four years of plenty, wherein men fed well and the crops were certain, and the birth-rate rose year by year; the Districts reported a purely agricultural population varying from nine hundred to two thousand to the square mile of the over-burdened earth; and the Member for Lower Tooting, wandering about India in top-hat and frock-coat, talked largely of the benefits of British rule, and suggested as the one thing needful the establishment of a duly qualified electoral system and a general bestowal of the franchise. His long-suffering hosts smiled and made him welcome, and when he paused to admire, with pretty wicked words, the blossom of the blood-red *dhak*-tree that had flowered untimely for a sign of what was coming, they smiled more than ever.

It was the Deputy-Commissioner of Kot-Kumharsen, staying at the Club for a day, who lightly told a tale that made Holden's blood run cold as he overheard the end.

'He won't bother anyone any more. Never saw a man so astonished in my life. By Jove, I thought he meant to ask a question in the House about it. Fellow-passenger in his ship – dined next him – bowled over by cholera and died in eighteen hours. You needn't laugh, you fellows. The Member for Lower Tooting is awfully angry about it; but he's more scared. I think he's going to take his enlightened self out of India.'

'I'd give a good deal if he were knocked over. It might keep a few vestrymen of his kidney to their own parish. But what's this about cholera? It's full early for anything of that kind,' said the warden of an unprofitable salt-lick.

'Don't know,' said the Deputy Commissioner reflectively. 'We've got locusts with us. There's sporadic cholera all along the north – at least we're calling it sporadic for decency's sake. The spring crops are short in five districts, and nobody seems to know where the rains are. It's nearly March now. I don't want to scare anybody, but it seems to me that Nature's going to audit her accounts with a big red pencil this summer.'

'Just when I wanted to take leave, too!' said a voice across the room.

'There won't be much leave this year, but there ought to be a great deal of promotion. I've come in to persuade the Government to put my pet canal on the list of famine-relief works. It's an ill-wind that blows no good. I shall get that canal finished at last.'

'Is it the old programme then,' said Holden; 'famine, fever, and cholera?'

'Oh no. Only local scarcity and an unusual prevalence of seasonal sickness. You'll find it all in the reports if you live till next near. You're a lucky chap. *You* haven't got a wife to send out of harm's way. The hill-stations ought to be full of women this year.'

'I think you're inclined to exaggerate the talk in the bazars,' said a young Civilian in the Secretariat. 'Now I have observed –'

'I daresay you have,' said the Deputy-Commissioner, 'but you've a great deal more to observe, my son. In the meantime, I wish to observe to you –' and he drew him aside to discuss the construction of the canal that was so dear to his heart. Holden went to his bungalow and began to understand that he was not alone in the world, and also that he was afraid for the sake of another – which is the most soul-satisfying fear known to man.

Two months later, as the Deputy had foretold, Nature began to audit her accounts with a red pencil. On the heels of the spring reapings came a cry for bread, and the Government, which had decreed that no man should die of want, sent wheat. Then came the cholera from all four quarters of the compass. It struck a pilgrim-gathering of half a million at a sacred shrine. Many died at the feet of their god; the others broke and ran over the face of the land carrying the pestilence with them. It smote a walled city and killed two hundred a day. The people crowded the trains, hanging on to the footboards and squatting on the roofs of the carriages, and the cholera followed them, for at each station they dragged out the dead and the dying. They died by the roadside, and the horses of the Englishmen shied at the corpses in the grass. The Rains did not come, and the earth turned to iron lest man should escape death by hiding in her. The English sent their wives away to the Hills and went about their work, coming forward as they were bidden to fill the gaps in the fighting-line. Holden, sick with fear of losing his chiefest treasure on earth, had done his best to persuade Ameera to go away with her mother to the Himalayas.

'Why should I go?' said she, one evening on the roof.

'There is sickness, and people are dying, and all the white *mem-log* have gone.'

'All of them?'

'All – unless perhaps there remain some old scald-head who vexes her husband's heart by running risk of death.'

'Nay; who stays is my sister, and thou must not abuse her, for I will be a scald-head too. I am glad all the bold *mem-log* are gone.'

'Do I speak to a woman or a babe? Go to the Hills, and I will see to it that thou goest like a queen's daughter. Think, child. In a red-lacquered bullock-cart, veiled and curtained, with brass peacocks upon the pole and red cloth hangings. I will send two orderlies for guard and –'

'Peace! Thou art the babe in speaking thus. What use are those toys to me? *He* would have patted the bullocks and played with the housings. For his sake, perhaps – thou hast made me very English – I might have gone. Now, I will not. Let the *mem-log* run.'

'Their husbands are sending them, beloved.'

'Very good talk. Since when hast thou been my husband to tell me what to do? I have but borne thee a son. Thou art only all the desire of my soul to me. How shall I depart when I know that if evil befall thee by the breadth of so much as my littlest finger-nail – is that not small? – I should be aware of it though I were in Paradise. And here, this summer, thou mayest die – *ai, janee*, die! and in dying they might call to tend thee a white woman, and she would rob me in the last of thy love!'

'But love is not born in a moment or on a death-bed!'

'What dost thou know of love, stoneheart? She would take thy thanks at least and, by God and the Prophet and Bibi Miriam the mother of thy Prophet, that I will never endure. My lord and my love, let there be no more foolish talk of going away. Where thou art, I am. It is enough.' She put an arm round his neck and a hand on his mouth.

There are not many happinesses so complete as those that are snatched under the shadow of the sword. They sat together and laughed, calling each other openly by every pet name that could move the wrath of the Gods. The city below them was locked up in its own torments. Sulphur fires blazed in the streets; the conches in the Hindu temples screamed and bellowed, for the Gods were inattentive in those days. There was a service in the great Mohammedan shrine, and the call to prayer from the minarets was almost unceasing. They heard the wailing in the houses of the dead, and once the shriek of a mother who had lost a child and was calling for its return. In the grey dawn they saw the dead borne out through the city gates, each litter with its own little knot of mourners. Wherefore they kissed each other and shivered.

It was a red and heavy audit, for the land was very sick and needed a little breathing-space ere the torrent of cheap life should flood it anew. The children of immature fathers and undeveloped mothers made no resistance. They were cowed and sat still, waiting till the sword should be sheathed in November if it were so willed. They were gaps among the English, but the gaps were filled. The work of superintending famine-relief, cholera-sheds, medicine-distribution, and what little sanitation was possible, went forward because it was so ordered.

Holden had been told to keep himself in readiness to move to replace the next man who should fall. There were twelve hours in each day when he could not see Ameera, and she might die in three. He was considering what his pain would be if he could not see her for three months, or if she died out of his sight. He was absolutely certain that her death would be demanded – so certain, that when he looked up from the telegram and saw Pir Khan breathless in the doorway, he laughed aloud. 'And?' said he –

'When there is a cry in the night and the spirit flutters into the throat, who has a charm that will restore? Come swiftly, Heavenborn! It is the black cholera.'

Holden galloped to his home. The sky was heavy with clouds, for the long-deferred Rains were near and the heat was stifling. Ameera's mother met him in the courtyard, whimpering, 'She is dying. She is nursing herself into death. She is all but dead. What shall I do, Sahib?'

Ameera was lying in the room in which Tota had been born. She made no sign when Holden entered, because the human soul is a very lonely thing and, when it is getting ready to go away, hides itself in a misty borderland where the living may not follow. The black cholera does its work quietly and without explanation. Ameera was being thrust out of life as though the Angel of Death had himself put his hand upon her. The quick breathing seemed to show that she was either afraid or in pain, but neither eyes nor mouth gave any answer to Holden's kisses. There was nothing to be said or done. Holden could only wait and suffer. The first drops of the rain began to fall on the roof and he could hear shouts of joy in the parched city.

The soul came back a little and the lips moved. Holden

bent down to listen. 'Keep nothing of mine,' said Ameera. 'Take no hair from my head. *She* would make thee burn it later on. That flame I should feel. Lower! Stoop lower! Remember only that I was thine and bore thee a son. Though thou wed a white woman tomorrow, the pleasure of receiving in thine arms thy first son is taken from thee for ever. Remember me when thy son is born – the one that shall carry thy name before all men. His misfortunes be on my head. I bear witness – I bear witness' – the lips were forming the words on his ear – 'that there is no God but – thee, beloved!'

Then she died. Holden sat still, and all thought was taken from him – till he heard Ameera's mother lift the curtain.

'Is she dead, Sahib?'

'She is dead.'

'Then I will mourn, and afterwards take an inventory of the furniture in this house. For that will be mine. The Sahib does not mean to resume it? It is so little, so very little, Sahib, and I am an old woman. I would like to lie softly.'

'For the mercy of God be silent a while. Go out and mourn where I cannot hear.'

'Sahib, she will be buried in four hours.'

'I know the custom. I shall go ere she is taken away. That matter is in thy hands. Look to it that the bed on which – on which she lies –'

'Aha! That beautiful red-lacquered bed. I have long desired –'

'That the bed is left here untouched for my disposal. All else in the house is thine. Hire a cart, take everything, go hence, and before sunrise let there be nothing in this house but that which I have ordered thee to respect.'

'I am an old woman. I would stay at least for the days of mourning, and the Rains have just broken. Whither shall I go?'

'What is that to me? My order is that there is a going. The house-gear is worth a thousand rupees and my orderly shall bring thee a hundred rupees tonight.'

'That is very little. Think of the cart-hire.'

'It shall be nothing unless thou goest, and with speed. O woman, get hence and leave me with my dead!'

The mother shuffled down the staircase, and in her anxiety to take stock of the house-fittings forgot to mourn. Holden stayed by Ameera's side, and the rain roared on the roof. He could not think connectedly by reason of the noise, though he made many attempts to do so. Then four sheeted ghosts glided dripping into the room and stared at him through their veils. They were the washers of the dead. Holden left the room and went out to his horse. He had come in a dead, stifling calm through ankle-deep dust. He found the courtyard a rain-lashed pond alive with frogs; a torrent of yellow water ran under the gate, and a roaring wind drove the bolts of the rain like buckshot against the mud walls. Pir Khan was shivering in his little hut by the gate, and the horse was stamping uneasily in the water.

'I have been told the Sahib's order,' said Pir Khan. 'It is well. This house is now desolate. I go also, for my monkey-face would be a reminder of that which has been. Concerning the bed, I will bring that to thy house yonder in the morning; but remember, Sahib, it will be to thee a knife turning in a green wound. I go upon a pilgrimage, and I will take no money. I have grown fat in the protection of the Presence whose sorrow is my sorrow. For the last time I hold his stirrup.'

He touched Holden's foot with both hands and the horse sprang out into the road, where the creaking bamboos were whipping the sky and all the frogs were chuckling. Holden could not see for the rain in his face. He put his hands before his eyes and muttered:

'Oh, you brute! You utter brute!'

The news of his trouble was already in his bungalow. He read the knowledge in his butler's eyes when Ahmed Khan brought in food, and for the first and last time in his life laid a hand upon his master's shoulder, saying, 'Eat, Sahib, eat. Meat is good against sorrow. I also have known. Moreover the shadows come and go, Sahib; the shadows come and go. These be curried eggs.'

Holden could neither eat nor sleep. The heavens sent down eight inches of rain in that night and washed the earth clean. The waters tore down walls, broke roads, and scoured open the shallow graves on the Mohammedan burying-ground. All next day it rained, and Holden sat still in his house considering his sorrow. On the morning of the third day he received a telegram which said only, 'Ricketts, Myndonie. Dying. Holden relieve. Immediate.' Then he thought that before he departed he would look at the house wherein he had been master and lord. There was a break in the weather, and the rank earth steamed with vapour.

He found that the rains had torn down the mud pillars of the gateway, and the heavy wooden gate that had guarded his life hung lazily from one hinge. There was grass three inches high in the courtyard; Pir Khan's lodge was empty, and the sodden thatch sagged between the beams. A grey squirrel was in possession of the veranda as if the house had been untenanted for thirty years instead of three days. Ameera's mother had removed everything except some mildewed matting. The *tick-tick* of the little scorpions as they hurried across the floor was the only sound in the house. Ameera's room and the other one where Tota had lived were heavy with mildew; and the narrow staircase leading to the roof was streaked and stained with rain-borne mud. Holden saw all these things, and came out again to meet in the road Durga Dass, his landlord – portly, affable, clothed in white muslin, and driving a Cee-spring buggy. He was overlooking his property to see how the roofs stood the stress of the first rains.

'I have heard,' said he, 'you will not take this place any more, Sahib?'

'What are you going to do with it?'

'Perhaps I shall let it again.'

'Then I will keep it on while I am away.'

Durga Dass was silent for some time. 'You shall not take

it on, Sahib,' he said. 'When I was a young man I also –, but today I am a member of the Municipality. Ho! Ho! No. When the birds have gone what need to keep the nest? I will have it pulled down – the timber will sell for something always. It shall be pulled down, and the Municipality shall make a road across, as they desire, from the burning-ghat to the city wall, so that no man may say where the house stood.'

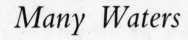

Many Waters

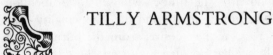

TILLY ARMSTRONG

TILLY ARMSTRONG was born in Sutton, Surrey. She began writing in 1976 and produced many short stories and serials for magazines before going on to write novels under two other pseudonyms. The lighthearted 'Many Waters' appeared in the Woman's Weekly *Fiction Series in 1979.*

I

THE trouble with me is, I get good ideas. My sister pointed out that our parents' Silver Wedding anniversary and Dad's fiftieth birthday fell not only in the same year, but in the same month, and asked me for suggestions for an unusual present to commemorate this double anniversary.

Quick as a flash, I came back with the idea of a family history. I ought to explain that, while our family has no claim to fame whatsoever and has always been noted chiefly for its decent obscurity, we do happen to have lived in one place for a long time. It was something Dad used to harp on when we were children and he was trying to get us to take an interest in our forebears.

'Candy, that's a wonderful idea!' Jacqueline said. 'If we could get together some pictures and a few anecdotes as well as a family tree, I could type it and I'm sure Bob would be able to arrange for it to be put into a nice binding. Do you think you can turn up some interesting information about the ancestors?'

'It might be possible,' I said doubtfully. As is my wont,

having spoken first I was now stopping to think. My sister, Jacqueline, is married and has a darling baby daughter; her husband, her house and her baby take up a great deal of her time. If it was going to be a question of doing any digging into our family background, I was the one who was going to use the spade.

'I don't know where to begin,' I said.

'Why don't you go and see someone at the Local History Museum?' she suggested helpfully. 'There was an article about it in the local paper a week or two ago, something to do with wanting to move it into that house the Council are thinking of pulling down.'

'Hopehill? I do hope they change their minds about that. I'd be really sorry to see Hopehill House disappear, although I realise it's a bit of a white elephant of a place.'

'Well, somebody was suggesting that it should be turned into a centre for local history and somebody else – I can't remember any of the details – said it would be a waste of money because no one would ever use it. If you feel really strongly about it you ought to go to the Museum and make some enquiries and then you can feel you are doing your bit, showing there is public demand.'

'Yes,' I agreed, but not very enthusiastically. I had a faint recollection of the so-called Local History Museum, housed in a couple of dark rooms in the Public Library and presided over by a nice, dim old man, who had taught my father at school before he retired. I doubted whether I was going to get much assistance from him.

My sister glanced at her watch. 'Help!' she said. 'I must fly! I turned the heating off before I came out and I want to get home and make sure the house is nice and warm before Bob comes in. Poor dear, I think he's starting a cold.'

I tried to suppress a grin, but didn't quite succeed. 'He's a grown man,' I pointed out. 'If he feels cold he's capable of turning up the heat for himself.'

'I like to look after him,' Jacqueline said defensively. 'You wait until you've got a husband, then you'll see what I mean.'

I didn't argue with her, but frankly I couldn't see myself pampering any man to that extent.

I work in our little town of Merryford, so I was able to drop into the Library in my lunch hour for a quick look at such facilities as the Local History Museum afforded. It seemed to have expanded since the last time I had visited it, which was in my school days. It had taken over an extra room, the lighting had been improved and the exhibits were set out in a far more orderly fashion and neatly labelled. What was more, there had been a change of curator and the new man had a minute office with his name on the door. *D. Denby*, it said. *Knock and enter.*

I knocked and entered and D. Denby hurriedly shovelled the cheese sandwich he had been eating into the drawer of his desk. He came as a considerable surprise to me. For one thing, he could only have been in his mid-twenties, about one-third the age of old Mr Morton. I didn't know historians came that young. On top of that, he was so *neat*! He wore a grey suit – a proper suit, with a striped shirt and tie – his hair was short and well-brushed, and he had very large, horn-rimmed glasses. He looked more like an aspiring young businessman than someone who worked in a museum. He waited patiently while I was taking this in, but when I didn't speak he said, 'Can I help you?'

'Yes,' I said, sitting down on the chair opposite his. 'I want to talk to you about a birthday present for my father.'

A faintly bewildered look came over his face and I realised that I had started at the wrong end as usual. 'I want to write him a family history,' I explained.

D. Denby began to look more interested. 'I might be able to help you,' he began cautiously. 'Was your father born here in Merryford?'

'Yes, and so was his father and, as far as I can gather, his father before him, and so on into the mists of antiquity.'

'What is your name?'

'Candida Marville.'

'One of the Marvilles of Waterford Street?' he asked, really sitting up and taking notice.

That was when I began to suspect that D. Denby really knew his stuff.

'My grandparents live in Waterford Street,' I replied. 'Dad hasn't lived there since he and Mum got married.'

'Interesting,' he said. 'I've come across your family name several times in the local records. It shouldn't be difficult to trace them, provided you are prepared to do a bit of work. The only thing is, I have to warn you that a lot of the records you may wish to examine are stored in boxes in the basement. How far back do you want to go?'

'How far can I go in three months?'

'Working on it every day?'

'For goodness' sake, no! Once a week for an hour or two was what I had in mind.'

I thought he looked disappointed, but it was better to make it clear at the outset that I was a mere dilettante and not a serious researcher.

'Look, all I want to do is to produce some sort of family tree, throw in a few spicy details about some of the ancestors, perhaps a picture or two if that's possible, put the whole thing together in book form and write "*Happy Birthday*" on the cover,' I explained.

'I'll get you started and then we'll see how you get on,' he said. 'But first of all, do you mind if I fill out an index card about your enquiry? I'm keeping a record of requests for information, trying to make a case for extending our facilities.'

I noticed that there was a large 'Save Hopehill' poster on his wall. 'Are you the chap who wants to move the Local History Museum to Hopehill?' I asked.

'I am indeed! It will be a crime to pull it down. Can I interest you in joining the campaign?'

'Possibly,' I said.

'I'll give you some literature about it,' he said. He got up and went over to his filing cabinet and I saw that he was tall and rather thin for his size.

'Do you always eat a sandwich at your desk for lunch?'
I asked.

'Usually. It's the time most people come in – as you
have done.'

He handed me a couple of leaflets, which I stuffed away in
my handbag. He was not exactly good-looking, but he had
some good points – nice grey eyes, rather obscured by those
horn-rimmed spectacles, which made it difficult to read their
expression. I watched his long-fingered, narrow hands riffling
through his card index and asked, 'Do you find it difficult to
get shoes to fit you?'

'Yes, I do. . .' He looked up and again I saw that baffled
expression on his face.

'I was just following a train of thought,' I explained.

He shook his head. 'If you are going to do genealogical
research you will have to curb this tendency to go off at a tan-
gent, otherwise you'll find yourself bogged down amongst the
second cousins instead of concentrating on the direct line.'

I was not too happy about the reference to genealogical research. It sounded rather more grand than the simple
enquiry I had had in mind. What was I letting myself in for?

He started to write on his card. 'Name?'

'I've already told you – Candida Marville.'

'Address?'

'18 Topaz Street.'

'Oh, yes, one of the "jewel" streets; built in the 1930s by a
local builder, called. . .' He looked up.

'Tom Marville,' I supplied. 'And yes, he was a relation.'

'Interesting.' He went back to his card. 'Age?'

I looked at him suspiciously. 'Why do you want to know
my age?'

'Most of the enquiries I get are from children wanting help
with school projects. I like to be able to distinguish between
them and the other enquiries.'

'Couldn't you just put "adult"?'

'I suppose I could, if you are reluctant to admit your age.'

'I'm not! All right, I'm twenty-one.'

'Occupation?'

I enjoyed answering that one. 'Garage attendant.'

He didn't turn a hair. 'Oh, yes, that will be Marville's Garage at the corner of the High Street? I quite often call there, but I've never seen you manning the pumps.'

'I'm more of a back-room girl,' I admitted. 'It's my uncle's business. I do the books and write the letters and make the tea. Actually, I'm studying to be an accountant.'

I thought I detected a twinkle behind the horn-rimmed spectacles. 'I didn't think you looked much like a motor mechanic.'

I was not amused. I am, in fact a very practical person, but there is something about being rather on the small size, with curly hair and a snub nose which makes all men believe you are helpless.

'Reason for enquiry – compiling family history. I think that's all we need bother with just now. Thank you for co-operating. Now, talk to me a little about what you have in mind.'

'One thing I thought of was that perhaps we could get hold of a picture or two of Merryford in the year when Dad was born, fifty years ago.'

He did a bit of mental arithmetic and said, 'That was one of the years when the Merrybrook overflowed. The local paper is sure to have published an account of it.'

I was impressed by this feat of memory and was about to tell him so, but we were interrupted by a boy who hesitated in the doorway when he saw that the office already contained a visitor. D. Denby got up again. 'Oh, Tom,' he said. 'I've found that book you wanted about nineteenth century natural history. I put it out for you – I'll just come and show you.'

Left on my own I had a good look round his tiny office. It was a bit cluttered, but in a tidy kind of way. Obviously D. Denby could put his hand on anything he needed at a moment's notice, even if he was forced by lack of space to keep some of his papers in piles instead of filing cabinets. I wondered what sort of enquiries he had been getting recently. I had had the impression that he had been pleased to see me come through the door, so perhaps business was not very brisk.

I drew the little card index box towards me and had a look at some of the cards. The enquiries had been surprisingly diverse, but I saw what he meant about the schoolchildren predominating. He had written a little comment on the bottom of some of the cards, usually about the progress they had made with the projects about which they had consulted him. I came to my own card. He had completed it just as he said, but at the bottom he had written, '*Not bad.*'

'Not bad'? The nerve of the man! In what way 'not bad'? Seizing a pencil I crossed it out and substituted, '*Charming and intelligent*'.

I just managed to slip it back into place and sit back on my chair looking innocent before he came back into the room. He plunged immediately into a lot of technical details about births, deaths and marriages and Parish Registers and things I had hardly known existed. I must say he managed to make it sound quite interesting, almost fun. I promised to dig out the basic information we needed before we could get started, and went away feeling that I had probably let myself in for more than I had intended, but that it might be worthwhile at that.

I was free on Saturday, so I called in on him again at lunchtime. As I had expected, D. Denby was working away at his desk. Not that it was an inviting day for going out; it was pouring with rain. I had ridden down the hill on my bicycle, wearing my yellow oilskin cape and big waterproof hat which tied under my chin.

'What are you having for lunch?' I asked as I entered his office.

'A cheese sandwich,' he said.

'I thought so. Is there somewhere I can hang up these wet things?'

He looked me over with a grin that sent one side of his mouth up and the other side down in an oddly attractive way. 'There's a hook behind the door. Where did you park your lifeboat?'

'It's rocking gently on the waves, chained to the Church railings.'

I dumped the basket I was carrying on his desk. 'Hot Cornish pasties straight out of the oven,' I said. 'Do you mind if I eat while I work?'

'I'd rather you didn't,' he said. 'Things do get spilt and, of course, we don't want to encourage mice by leaving crumbs.'

'I thought you'd probably say that, so I'll have it here. I brought enough for you, too. Two plates, two forks, a couple of apples, some shortbread and a flask of coffee, but before we start eating, what does the "D" stand for?'

He was quite quick on the up-take. 'Daniel,' he said.

'Daniel Denby. It sounds quite distinguished. Professor or Doctor, or anything?'

'Not yet. Doctor one day, I hope. I'm working on a thesis. I say, these pasties are good. Where did you get them?'

'I made them,' I said with dignity. 'And the shortbread, too.'

'Not only charming and intelligent, but a good cook, too!'

I remembered the card index but tried to look as though I didn't know what he was referring to. 'I've scraped together a lot of certificates and dates and things, and a few old family photographs, and I've decided how I'm going to put the thing together,' I said. 'It was your saying that the year of Dad's birth was the year the Merrybrook overflowed that gave me the idea. I'm going to take as many dates of events in the family as I can – marriages, births, deaths, special anniversaries, moving house – anything like that, and link them up with what was happening locally at the same time. I thought I could have the family news on the left hand page and the local history on the facing page. What do you think?'

'I think it sounds rather good, and it shouldn't be too difficult.'

'That's what I thought. It may not be quite the approach you would favour for your thesis, but it's within my capabilities. I'm not a – *scholar*, you know, and I haven't got time to learn Early English or Norman French.'

'Not in three months,' he agreed. 'And in any case, our local paper only goes back a hundred years. I think the newspaper files are your best bet, you know.'

'But I want to push it back a bit further than the grandparents,' I said. 'I'd like to tell Dad something he didn't know.'

'Do some of the easy bits this afternoon,' he suggested, through a mouthful of Cornish pasty. 'And I'll help you with the earlier history another day. I'm taking a party of visitors round Hopehill later this afternoon, trying to work up interest in opening it again.'

'Wouldn't it cost a fortune to make it usable?'

'Quite a lot of money,' he admitted ruefully. 'It could be raised, if I could only get people interested. I know the Council has other priorities, but it does seem such a shame that the one remaining house of any distinction should be reduced to rubble.'

'But it's not particularly old, is it?' I asked. To be perfectly honest, I was a bit puzzled about his preoccupation with Hopehill. It was just a big, slightly grim-looking house surrounded by prickly holly hedges, which had been occupied within my memory first by two eccentric old ladies and then, briefly, by a somewhat dubious nursing home, and was now standing empty.

'It was built in 1815 – Waterloo year. In fact, the house had a narrow escape from being called Waterloo House. It was built in and lived in by the Stallymore family right up until the last two descendants died within a few weeks of one another eight years ago.'

'Our family had some connection with the Stallymores,' I said. 'At least, so Dad has always said, but he was vague about what it was. One of my forebears probably dug the garden, or stoked the boiler, or something.'

'Doesn't that make you want to take a personal interest in saving it?'

'Do you mean you'd like me to come along and join your party this afternoon?'

'It might not be a bad idea,' he said. 'I could do with one or two to swell the numbers. On a day like this, I don't suppose many people will turn out.'

I put in a couple of hours work among his dusty archives in the basement and then he took me in his car to Hopehill. At least, he called it a car. Working where I do, I am something of a connoisseur of old cars and this one had to be seen to be believed.

'What do you use to keep it together?' I asked. 'String?'

'Paper clips. Come on, get in. At least it will get you up the hill in the dry, which is more than your bike will do.'

He managed to fix my bicycle to the roof rack, so that I could go straight home after our visit to Hopehill, which reminded me that I had not yet found out where he lived.

'I have a bedsitter in Mere Street,' he said, in response to my question.

'With a kitchen?'

'A sort of gas ring arrangement.'

I thought as much. I wondered when he had last had a square meal. I almost invited him back home with me for the evening, but that would have meant explaining him and I was trying to keep this family history project a secret. As it happened, I need not have worried because Daniel Denby got himself fixed up for that evening with no difficulty at all.

II

He was agreeably surprised when about twenty people turned up for his guided tour of Hopehill House. They were a fairly mixed bunch: a couple of schoolboys and three earnest girls from my old school, the curate of St Nicholas's Church, a sprinkling of middle-aged couples who remembered when Hopehill had still been inhabited, and a girl called Claire Burnside from the local Social Security Department.

Dan rather seemed to latch on to her, possibly because of her vehemently expressed determination to keep Hopehill standing at all costs. She was one of those brisk, capable young women who make me feel inadequate, very suitably dressed in a mannish beige raincoat with lots of buckles and buttons, tightly belted at the waist; the sort of thing that makes me look like a sack of flour tied up in the middle, but on her it looked smart and sexy, especially worn with shiny black boots and a dashing rain hat to match. She had a lot of black hair, which she wore tied back in a pony tail; a bit juvenile for a woman of her age, I thought.

She and Dan seemed to have a lot to talk about and I tried to look interested as she went on about the need for a crèche in the neighbourhood, and multi-purpose occupation, whatever that might mean. She was knowledgeable about the architecture, too. I got lost amongst the talk of cornices and architraves, confining myself to wandering around and looking instead of talking. I began to see what Dan had meant about it being a distinguished house. The rooms were beautifully proportioned and the fittings were very fine. My hand lingered on a satisfyingly round brass door knob on the drawing-room door, while my eyes admired the fireplace and the long sash windows.

'The chandelier in the dining-room is still intact,' Dan said. 'Come and have a look.'

It was a lovely thing. Even the fact that all the drops needed washing did not detract from its delicate beauty.

'It must be worth quite a lot of money,' Claire remarked. 'If it were taken down and sold it would produce a useful sum which could be used for something more essential.'

'It was specially made for this room,' Dan said. 'Imported from Italy. You are quite right, of course, but it would be a pity to take it away.'

'You have to balance sentiment against expediency,' she said, whatever that might mean. I left them to it again and went upstairs. The house smelt shut up and musty, but no damp seemed to have penetrated. It was in a deplorable state from a decorative point of view, but I began to see why Dan felt optimistic about being able to make use of it. It was in an astonishingly good state of preservation.

For some reason the bedrooms seemed even more unfurnished than the downstairs rooms, perhaps because downstairs there were things like the chandelier, and solid wooden fireplaces with overmantels, and shutters to the windows, whereas upstairs there was little to detract from the bareness of the walls and floors. There was something particularly pathetic about the faded patches of wall where pictures had once hung.

I found one room with bars on the windows. 'The nursery,' Dan said. He had come upstairs with Claire.

'How appalling,' she said. 'Just think of the effect those bars must have had on the psychological development of the children!'

'Well, at least they stopped them falling out of the window,' I pointed out. 'Dan, what's this room here, with all the shelves and drawers?'

'The linen store, I think.'

I drew open a drawer. In spite of its age and lack of use, it ran like silk. Was it my imagination or was there a faint, faint trace of something in the air which overcame the general mustiness for a moment?

'Not lavender,' I said, thinking aloud. 'More like violets.'

'Orris root,' said Dan. 'They used it to preserve the linen and keep it smelling sweet.'

He had given us a brief talk about the house when we first arrived, now he collected everyone together and explained how he thought it could be put to use for his Local History Museum combined with a community centre, including the crèche Claire set such store by. He answered a few questions, handed out some leaflets, and everyone began to drift towards the door.

One of the men who had had little to say previously suddenly found his tongue and kept Dan talking in the drawing-room. I went outside and walked round to the back of the house to take a look at the garden, but the everlasting rain drove me inside once more. It sounded as though the loquacious gentleman might be drawing to a close, but then I heard Claire's voice say, 'I've got those plans I was telling you about at home this weekend. Would you like to come round to my place and take a look at them?'

'Very much,' Dan said, with what I thought was somewhat overdone enthusiasm.

'I've got my car here, so you'd better follow me in yours.'

I was sorry about that. I would have liked to have seen her reaction to a drive in Dan's car. Obviously, he was in no need of my hospitality for the evening. It was a pity that it was necessary for me to wait around for him to offload my bicycle, but after that I would be off as fast as I could pedal for some nice hot tea and an evening in front of the television set.

I felt in my pocket and realised that my gloves were missing. Where had I last had them? I had been carrying them in my hand when I had been playing with the drawers of the linen cupboard.

I ran quickly up the stairs, through the green baize door which had once shut off the nursery and the servants' quarters from the more imposing rooms, up the second staircase and into the linen room. I found my gloves in exactly the spot I had expected. The light was growing dimmer and now I was alone in them the rooms looked gloomy and forlorn. I paused to sniff, but no trace of orris root lingered in the air with its evocative scent of a by-gone age. I ran down the stairs again.

When the green baize door refused to open I thought that it must have stuck. I rattled the handle and pushed, but nothing happened. Then I remembered that Dan had unlocked it to let us up the stairs. Thinking everyone had left, he must have come upstairs, almost immediately behind me, and locked it up again. What a crazy thing to happen! I wondered how long it would take him to realise that I was still inside. I called out, but my voice merely echoed up the staircase in a hollow way. The green baize door was all too effective. It had been designed to keep out noise and it was still performing its function to perfection.

I went back to the bedrooms and looked out of one of the windows. Below me I could see Dan unstrapping my bicycle from the car. He stopped one of the schoolgirls and spoke to her. She made a gesture towards the rear of the house. For the first time I began to feel a little uneasy. I tapped on the window, but no one in the little group down below took any notice. Dan propped my bicycle against the hedge and draped my yellow oilskin over the saddle to stop it getting wet, a thoughtful gesture I was in no mood to appreciate. Surely he was going to look up?

Again I rapped on the window, but just at that moment Claire started up her car. Dan looked round quickly, took a step towards the house, and then hesitated. I could follow his train of thought quite easily. Claire had invited him to follow her to her place of abode, but she had not, in my hearing at any rate, mentioned her address; quite possibly he did not know where she lived. I was, as far as he knew, meandering about the garden – getting dripping wet, but that did not seem to have occurred to him. I had my own means of transport; he could safely leave me to get myself home. He got into his car and drove away.

It looked as though I was going to have to rescue myself. It was a pity that Hopehill stood some way back from the road, but if I opened the window, leaned out and yelled, surely *someone* would hear me? Unfortunately, the fastenings to the large sash windows were out of my reach. Not for the first time I cursed my lack of inches. In order to open the window I needed something to stand on, and all the rooms were quite empty. I leaned against the wall and thought. Something to stand on. One of those smooth-running drawers from the linen closet, if I could manage to remove one of them. It was a happy thought.

I went and inspected the linen store. The drawers at the bottom were long and deep and obviously extremely heavy. I doubted whether I would be able to carry one of them once it was free of its support. The drawers above were smaller, but less easy for me to manoeuvre into a position where I could get one of them to come right out. I solved that by pulling out the lower drawers and using them as steps. I had a moment's qualm about the whole thing toppling over with me underneath, but the cupboard was built-in and seemed to be attached to the wall quite solidly.

The drawer I had chosen did not move as smoothly as the ones I had opened lower down, but I wriggled it about and eventually managed to get it to come out. Once I had detached it, I discovered the reason for its first lack of response to my attack. There was something wedged behind it which seemed to have slipped down from behind the range of cupboards above the drawers. I am, of course, the original of Kipling's elephant child when it comes to curiosity. So, as as soon as I had deposited my life-saving drawer on the floor, I climbed back up again to discover what the obstruction could be.

It was a book, a large, moderately thick book, in stiff red covers with marbled end-papers. I descended from my precarious perch and examined it. It was handwritten, but in the dim light of the linen store I could see no more than that. I carried it with me to the bedroom. No matter what it was – a child's exercise book, household accounts or, more likely, a laundry list – as long as the light lasted it would help to pass the time until I was rescued.

It would not be long before someone missed me – of course it wouldn't. My movements did tend to be a bit erratic, but I was usually very good about letting my parents know if I was going to be out unexpectedly. They would become uneasy when I failed to arrive home – wouldn't they? It was, of course, a pity that my visit to Hopehill had been unpremeditated. The only person who really knew where I was to be found was horrible Daniel Denby, living it up with equally horrible Claire.

I climbed on to my good, solid wooden drawer and struggled for several frustrated minutes with the catch on the window before I finally got it to open. I threw up the bottom of the sash window, leaned out and said, 'Help!' It sounded incredibly silly. I took a deep breath and tried yelling loudly, but I didn't feel that my voice was carrying far enough to be of much use. In any case, in that foul weather there were few people going by. Plenty of cars, but no pedestrians. I leaned even further out of the window. There were no creepers, no convenient drainpipes. Not that I would seriously have contemplated attempting to climb out; I didn't like the look of the drop to the gravel drive below. I called out again. No response.

I thought of the book I had discovered and took a quick look at it. It seemed to be some sort of diary, which might be quite interesting in other circumstances. At that particular time, I had another use for it. There were one or two blank pages and, although it seemed a pity, I tore one of them out, wrote on it in bright red lipstick, '*I am locked in Hopehill House*', made it into a paper aeroplane and launched it out of the window.

It was good, thick paper, but after soaring away quite successfully, my SOS caught the holly hedge and fell back into the garden. I felt discouraged, almost tearful. It was too ridiculous. There must be some way of getting out. Where were all my friends and my fond family? Had none of them missed me?

The shadows were beginning to close in on me. A nasty, cold, wet spring day, and I was beginning to feel hungry. After all, I had only had a snack lunch with Daniel Denby and how I wished now that I had not wasted my culinary efforts on him.

I was only shut up in my prison for about an hour, but it seemed like a very, very long time to me. The only thing that helped me pass the time was looking through the diary I had discovered, and even that became impossible as the light began to fade, until, even by sitting on the window-sill, I could not make out the fine, spidery writing, but by that time I had read enough to find it extremely interesting.

It seemed to have been written by the Stallymores' governess, which ought to have been a useful insight into the life of the family. I was looking forward to reading it properly in more comfortable circumstances, provided, of course, that I wasn't going to be left until my wasted skeleton came to light when the house was reopened.

From time to time I leaned out of the window and shouted my appeal for help. No one took any notice, until at last I saw a car's headlights stop near the front gate. Had Daniel Denby had qualms about me and come back? No, he had not. It was a policeman. In fact, it was two policemen. At first they seemed to be mainly interested in my bicycle which, with my bright yellow waterproof cape draped over it, had apparently attracted their attention from the road, but this time I was not letting my rescuers get away. I leaned out of the window and yelled with all my might. They looked up, shone a powerful torch up into the gathering darkness, then one of them said, 'Now then, what are you doing up there?'

I thought of several very good answers, but decided it would be better not to antagonise them. 'I'm locked in,' I replied with sweet reasonableness.

'And how did you get in there in the first place?'

Again I exercised restraint. 'I came with a party of visitors and was accidentally left behind.'

'Come downstairs and we'll try to get you out.'

'I can't come downstairs,' I said crossly. 'There's an internal door which is locked.'

'Who's got the keys, do you know?'

'A man called Daniel Denby, from the Local History Museum. He lives somewhere in Mere Street, but I don't know the exact address, and anyway I don't think he's at home this evening. They might have another set of keys at the Town Hall.'

They consulted together and then one of them walked round to the back of the house. The other one was speaking into his little radio. I stayed where I was and waited to be rescued, but the next moment my complacency about having two policemen to deliver me was shaken.

I could hear a most peculiar noise, a noise like footsteps, but curiously metallic footsteps, coming nearer and nearer, and then there was a rattling noise, like a door being violently shaken. I leaned out of the window once again. Policeman number one was out of sight round the back of the house; policeman number two was disappearing down the drive, presumably towards their car. Would either of them hear me if I screamed?

The strange noise began again, a weird metallic clattering, but this time it seemed to be disappearing. If one had been nervous, which of course one was not, one might have thought of ghosts. I sat on my window-sill and wished my policemen would come back. One of them did. Policeman number one reappeared from behind the house and called up to me. 'There's a fire escape round the far side. Can't you come down that?'

There was a fire escape round the far side. The idea had never occurred to me. Of course, there would have to be a fire escape, considering that the place had been used as a Nursing Home.

'I . . . I'll go and have a look,' I said with as much dignity as I could muster.

I closed the window before I left, it seemed the least I could do. I remembered to take the diary with me, too. Then I groped my way through the empty rooms and along a dark corridor to a door at the end which I had never so much as noticed. It had bolts at top and bottom, but it was not locked. The bolts were stiff, but I got them open, by which time the policeman had clattered back up the fire escape – clattered back with a strange metallic noise which made one think of armoured footsteps coming nearer.

I opened the door and stepped out, cringing with embarrassment. They were quite nice about it; to them I was just a silly girl who had got herself into a predicament and had not used her head. They watched indulgently while I struggled into my waterproof cape and waved goodbye as I cycled home.

The most frustrating thing of all was that I had to wait until Monday lunchtime before I could vent my spleen on Daniel Denby. I burst into his office without the formality of knocking.

'You beast, you fiend, you cold-blooded monster!' I said.

The elderly man behind the desk jumped to his feet in alarm. I glared at him. 'Where's D. Denby?' I asked.

'Er, Mr D-Denby had a message asking him to go round to Hopehill House and I said I would man the office for him until he returned. Apparently someone has been locked in.'

'What *again*?' I asked incredulously. I eyed the little man resentfully. He was looking nervous, as well he might, considering the way I had burst in on him. 'When Mr Denby comes back tell him Miss Marville is in the basement,' I said grandly. 'And I want to see him *immediately*!'

I swept out and took myself down to the basement to examine some of the enormous tomes Dan had recommended to me. When he eventually arrived he was looking harassed and something less than his usual tidy self.

'Sorry I wasn't here when you arrived,' he said. 'I had a rather worrying telephone call from the Town Hall. Someone going by Hopehill picked up this piece of paper and, as I still had the keys, they asked me to go round straight away to investigate.'

He felt in his pocket and pulled out a crumpled piece of paper. On it was written in bright red lipstick, '*I am locked in Hopehill House.*'

'The thing that worries me,' Dan went on, 'is that when I opened up the house and went all over it, I found that the fire escape was unbolted, so it looks as if someone really was locked up there. I can't understand it.'

I picked up the damp and crumpled piece of paper and looked at it with interest. The message was a little blurred, but quite easy to read. 'Fantastic,' I said. 'It just goes to show

that what the makers say about that lipstick is true. It really
does last.'

Dan looked at me with sudden suspicion, then he took
the lipstick message and held it against my face. It was,
as I knew, a perfect match for the lipstick I was wearing.

'Yes,' I said. 'Well, that's what I was going to tell you,
actually. It was me.' I thought about it. 'Or I, whichever is
correct.'

'Don't try to hide behind points of grammar,' Dan said. 'Do
you honestly mean that I had to go haring round to Hopehill
in my lunch hour to rescue someone who, as I thought, had
been sitting there since Saturday afternoon, when all the time
the culprit was waiting for me here?'

'Culprit! That's a fine word to use! Victim is more like
it! You drove away without a backward look and left me
stranded and now you are trying to blame me! Think what
a state I would have been in if I had had to wait until now to
be rescued!'

'I did think about it, all the way round to Hopehill,' Dan
said. 'I still can't understand how it happened.'

I told him. In great detail and with considerable bitterness.
He tried to look concerned, but by the time I had finished he
was grinning all over his silly face.

'You really are a complete nut case,' he said.

'As an apology I consider that inadequate.'

'Yes, I agree. I really am truly sorry. I thought you had gone
exploring round the back and I was anxious not to lose touch
with Claire, so I hurried off after her.'

'Without bothering about me – without even saying good-
bye! I hope she was worth it.'

'Yes, rather, very good value. I think Claire is going to be
an enormous help.'

'Oh, splendid,' I said, but he missed the sarcasm. I got up
off the bench where I had been perching. 'Well, I've said my
say, now I must go.'

'No lunch?' he asked.

'If you think I am feeding you after what you've done to me . . .'

'No, the other way round. I'll take you to lunch, to show you how truly sorry I am.'

'Where?' I asked suspiciously.

'Tellafords?'

I brightened up. Tellafords was by way of being our best restaurant. 'Done!' I said.

'You'll want to wash your hands after handling those dusty files. See you upstairs in my office in five minutes.'

When I got back upstairs the elderly man had gone, frightened away probably. While I was waiting for Dan I had a look at my index card, just to see whether he had added my cooking abilities to his notes about me. There was just one extra word on the card, '*Cuddly*'.

Cuddly! I thought about it. Was it a compliment or not? I was uneasily conscious that there was an inescapable suggestion of roundness about me. It was not that I was fat, by no means, but because of my shortness I do have to be particularly careful not to let my very reasonable measurements build up into something like plumpness. Cuddly! Perhaps I had better start dieting again – but not until after I had stung D. Denby for a very good lunch.

While we were eating I told him about the diary. Over the weekend I had read the volume I had taken away from Hopehill. As I had thought, it was written by the girl who had been engaged to look after the Stallymore children. She had obligingly written her name on the inside of the front cover, Eugenia Chorley; and, even better, had made a note of the little scraps of information she had gathered about the antecedents of the family and the house in which they lived.

'Benjamin Stallymore was the owner of Hopehill at the time Eugenia became governess,' I reported to Dan. 'The house had been built by his grandfather, whose name was Joseph, and Eugenia says he made his money as an India Merchant – what was that?'

'What we would call the import/export market,' Dan said. 'Go on, this is enthralling.'

'She was a bit snobbish about it, I thought. The next Stallymore was called Thomas. He died off in 1862 and Benjamin moved in with his wife and children and widowed mother. By the time Eugenia joined them in 1870 they had three children, two little girls of nine and eight, called Lucy and Belinda, and a boy of five called Edgar. She refers to them as "*the dear children*", but if you ask me they tried her patience at times.'

'What about her own family?'

'It's difficult to sort them out. She always says when she receives a letter from anyone, but of course she knew who they were so she only mentions their names, but not the relationship. I have gathered that her father was a clergyman because she refers to the Parish several times, and she certainly had a brother called Robert, who must have been younger than her, because she mentions his success in school examinations.'

'I can't wait to read it.'

'I'll pass it on to you,' I promised. 'But the really interesting thing is that I suspect there may be more volumes still in the house. You know the little cupboards right up by the ceiling in the linen room? I think they are up there.'

'We'll go and have a look straight after lunch,' Dan said.

'I have to go back to work,' I said regretfully. 'You'll let me know if you find anything else, won't you?'

'I'll ring you up,' he promised. 'Now, do you want anything from the sweets' trolley?'

I thought of my waistline and his wallet, and declined. I could see he was bursting to go off to Hopehill and look for the other diaries. It was almost worth making a fool of myself over getting locked in to give him so much pleasure.

He kept his word and telephoned me at the office that afternoon. 'Eight more volumes, one for every year right up to 1878,' he said, his voice cracking with excitement. 'What a find!'

'Who do they belong to?' I asked.

'That's a good question. To the Council, I suppose. They own the house, and I think that covers the contents. I'm afraid that even though you found them they are not likely to belong to you.'

'Of course not. I wasn't thinking of that. I was just wondering . . . Dan, if they all turned out to be as interesting to read as I found the first volume, do you think they might be publishable?'

'It's certainly a possibility. With a bit of editing and some research to establish who the people she mentions are.'

'And the profits, if any, could go towards the "Save Hopehill" fund.'

There was a brief pause. 'Now that really is an idea,' he said slowly. 'Look, we must meet and talk about it properly. I'm a bit tied up this week. Are you free Saturday evening?'

'No, I'm babysitting for my sister,' I said regretfully. It was a pity, but it was a long-standing promise and I could not let Jacqueline down.

'I suppose you wouldn't like some company?' he suggested, with a diffidence I found rather touching.

'Yes, of course, I'd be delighted. Bring the diaries with you and we'll compare notes on what we have read.'

It worked out quite well. Jacqueline and Bob had disappeared for their *tête-à-tête* dinner by the time Dan arrived, and baby Elizabeth had gone off to sleep like the angel she is. He was loaded with the eight additional volumes of Eugenia's diaries. I seized on them straight away. I had read to the end of 1870 and made a discovery and I was anxious to know what had happened next.

'She's fallen for her boss,' I announced. 'Tremendous drama! He kissed her under the mistletoe at Christmas and, although she fears he was a trifle inebriated and she doesn't intend to refine too much on it, she is obviously in a tremendous tizzy, not to mention searching her conscience like mad in case she encouraged him to think of her lightly.'

'Oh, that explains all the good resolutions about conducting herself with modesty and decorum that she made in January 1871,' Dan said.

'Obviously she must have decided to stay on as governess, since the diaries survived at Hopehill.'

We settled down in front of the fire, welcome in spite of the alleged arrival of spring. It was, of course, raining again.

'I hope your interest in Eugenia's diaries isn't distracting you from your family history?' Dan asked.

'No, I'm getting on famously with that, and I shall probably get some more information out of my grandmother tomorrow. She still lives in the old family house in Waterford Street and she's very good about remembering things that happened in the past.'

We began skimming through the diaries. As far as I could see, Eugenia's romance amounted to no more than that one solitary kiss arising out of the young master's too liberal enjoyment of the Christmas spirit, but when I came to the entry for the following Christmas I felt a pang of pity for the young girl, who must have been lonely in that great house with only the children for company, left out of most of the social occasions by her employers, too proud to mix with the servants.

'She says that there was no repetition of last year's unfortunate incident,' I said to Dan. 'It shows how it must have weighed on her mind. Just imagine remembering from one Christmas to the next that a man had kissed you under the mistletoe!'

'Imagine,' he said.

'In that day and age, I don't suppose any other man had ever kissed her.'

'No.' He gave me a curious, thoughtful look, which I pretended not to see. Then he got up to take another volume from the pile on the coffee table in front of us and sat down by my side on the sofa instead of in the armchair he had been occupying. I looked down demurely at the diary on my lap and waited for the next development.

The next development was that the baby started crying. I

went up to her, my long experience as a babysitter having taught me that it's better to pacify them immediately rather than to allow them to get into their stride. Elizabeth subsided as soon as she heard me come into the room.

I chided her gently. 'When you are grown up and I am still a maiden aunt, I shall tell you about how you spoilt all my chances with my boy friends,' I told her. Not that Dan was a boy friend exactly, more of a working colleague, but attractive and interesting and a bit out of the ordinary.

She was wet, so I changed her, patted her on the back, gave her a cuddle and put her down again. She let me get as far as the door when she started to yell in earnest. With a sigh, I went back and picked her up and took her downstairs. We went back to the living-room, Elizabeth blinking in the strong light like a mooncalf, although she is, in fact, a most intelligent baby.

'She shouldn't be hungry,' I said. 'And she is going to have to wait for a feed until Jacqueline gets home, but I'll give her a little drink in case she's thirsty. Would you mind holding her while I fetch it?'

Dan backed away into the corner of the sofa. 'I don't think I know how,' he said.

'For goodness sake, haven't you got any brothers or sisters?'

'No.'

'Suppose you had just finished writing your thesis and it was in loose sheets and you were going out in a high wind. How would you hold it?'

Instinctively his arms crossed over his chest as if he were hugging something to him.

'That's right. Now hold this precious bundle.'

I transferred Elizabeth to him and left the room before he could open his mouth to protest. When I returned he was leaning back with Elizabeth spread-eagled across his chest, her head turned against his shoulder, looking drowsy. 'She's stopped crying!' he said in a hoarse whisper.

'Splendid, you obviously have the right touch.' I leaned

over and offered Elizabeth the bottle of plain water. She sucked at it half-heartedly, but obviously it was not of any great interest to her. We sat quietly for a few minutes and her eyes closed.

'With any luck, she'll sleep now until Jacqueline gets home,' I said. 'Would you mind putting her down in her cot? If I take her from you she may wake up.'

He managed very well, but after I had tucked her up, he looked at her with a frown and said, 'She doesn't look very comfortable. Is it all right for her to lie flat like that?'

'You can't give pillows to small babies,' I said. 'They might smother themselves. You don't know much about it, do you?'

'Not a thing,' he admitted. He gave me that lop-sided grin which was beginning to do strange things to my insides. 'You are enlarging my experience.'

Bob and Jacqueline came home soon after that, early as I had known they would be, consumed with anxiety about their precious baby after an absence of nearly three hours. I saw Jacqueline looking thoughtful when I introduced her to Dan and followed the workings of her mind all too easily. My sister has been trying to get me married off ever since she achieved the state of bliss herself.

'The water in the Merrybrook is well up,' Bob remarked. 'We drove over the bridge and it was almost lapping the top. Does anyone happen to know when the next high tide is?'

'Wednesday night,' Dan said.

'It hasn't flooded for years and years,' Jacqueline said. 'And what has the tide to do with it? We aren't anywhere near the sea.'

'The Merrybrook flows into a tidal river,' Bob reminded her. 'If there's a particularly high tide, we sometimes get a sort of back-up effect.'

'Like the Severn bore,' Dan said.

'A bit like that, yes. That's always been the reason for any serious flooding in the past.'

Jacqueline looked round her pretty home, her fitted carpets, the furniture which was not yet paid for, the bright paint and newly-papered walls Bob had worked on so hard.

'It couldn't possibly affect us, could it?' she asked.

I saw Bob and Dan look at one another. 'I'm afraid it could,' Dan said. 'I'm a stranger in this town, but I have read a great deal about the effect of previous floods and there's no doubt that this part of Merryford has been under water in the past. The only comfort I can offer you is that you are better off here at the top of the road than you would be at the bottom.'

'There's a notice about it in the Town Hall,' Bob said. 'They're issuing sandbags to pile against outside doors, but having seen the Merrybrook tonight I think I'll take the carpets up before Wednesday, and move as much furniture upstairs as I can manage.'

'Could I help?' Dan asked with the diffidence I had noticed in him once or twice before.

Bob has three unmarried brothers, any one of whom could cheerfully carry a sofa upstairs with one hand, but with fierce concentration I willed him to accept Dan's offer. Fortunately, whether he got the message or not, my sister was on the right wavelength and, without giving him time to reply, she said, 'Thank you, Dan. We'd be very glad of your help. Could you come round tomorrow morning and stay to lunch?'

He accepted with alacrity and Jacqueline continued, carefully casual, 'What about you, Candy? Are you coming to help?'

I shook my head regretfully. 'It's my turn to cook lunch for Gran,' I said. I explained to Dan. 'Our grandmother – Dad's mother – is slightly handicapped after a stroke. She insists on living alone and she manages very well, but we have a rota in the family to see that she gets proper meals and this is my week to do the Sunday lunch.'

'That's nice,' Dan said. He smiled at me, a warm, intimate smile, and I felt that I had earned his approval, which made me feel just as pleased as he seemed to be. 'I must be going,' he said. 'Do you want a lift home?'

'No, I'm staying the night.'

'I'll see you out,' Bob said with unnecessary cordiality. I gave the door a dirty look as he closed it behind them.

'Well, well,' Jacqueline said. 'I thought there must be a new man in your life when I heard you were back on cottage cheese. You didn't tell me your helpful historian was a handsome young man.'

'I wouldn't call him handsome.'

'A nice face. Tell me all about it. Why hasn't the family spy system reported seeing you around with him before this?'

'Because he keeps himself shut up in the Library, and there's nothing to tell. We are just good friends, and thanks to your daughter and your husband that's all we are likely to be. I'm glad he's coming here tomorrow. For goodness sake, see that he gets a square meal. I'm sure he doesn't eat properly.'

For some reason this amused her, but she wouldn't explain and then her clamorous daughter claimed her attention and the matter was forgotten.

III

I went off to Gran's early the next morning. She liked her lunch punctually at one o'clock and she had very decided ideas on how a proper roast should be cooked. It was always rewarding to spend a day with her, and I enjoyed this one as usual, telling her all about the family history I was preparing, after swearing her to secrecy, and drawing on her for some interesting background information.

She produced some ancient photographs and was delighted to donate them to my book. Gran had been born in 1905 and she could remember Merryford when it was far smaller than it was now. She was still living in the house in Waterford Street and it occurred to me that she, too, might be affected if the Merrybrook flooded. She took the idea philosophically.

'It won't be the first time,' she said. 'The house has been flooded before now and survived. You'd better get your dad to come down and do a bit of furniture moving, unless he's too busy helping Bob and Jacqueline?'

'No, a friend of mine is helping them,' I said self-consciously.

'Oh?'

I groaned inwardly at the immediate spark of interest that woke in her.

'What's his name? Why haven't I heard about him before this?'

'He's just a friend,' I said patiently. 'He works in the Local History Museum.' I turned the conversation. 'Can you remember anything about your grandparents?'

'Of course I can. I haven't lost the use of my mind, you know. I was named after my grandfather. Robert his name was, and I was called Roberta after him. That was my mother's family, of course. I must admit I don't remember my other grandparents so well, because they lived in London and I rarely saw them, but my mother's father I can see as if it was yesterday. He was a fine-looking man and my grandmother was a pretty little woman, something after your type. Her parents kept the Golden Lion. I can just remember being taken in there, when I was very small and the bar was too high for me to see over. All I could see was a lot of dark wood, sawdust on the floor and a smell of beer inside, and straw and horses outside.'

'Fascinating. Of course, it's the male line I'm supposed to be pursuing, so I mustn't get too side-tracked by your family. What were granddad's family?'

'They were pork butchers, and very good ones. Had their own pig farm out Banley way. I can remember the smell of that, too! One of the brothers ran the farm and your great-grandfather ran the shop. They lived in this house, of course. It was a bit of a mystery to them when your granddad turned out to be more interested in engines than animals, but when he took his exams and became a proper engineer, they nearly burst with pride. My family lived half a dozen houses away up the street and your granddad and I went to school together.'

'Childhood sweethearts!' I sighed sentimentally.

'Oh, no! We didn't like one another. He improved as he grew up.'

It was on the tip of my tongue to tell her about the diaries, but for the moment I decided to keep their discovery to myself. Dan had particularly warned me that he did not want any premature publicity which might detract from the use he hoped to make of them to further his 'Save Hopehill' campaign.

It was not until the next day that it occurred to me that all Dan's precious archives were in the basement of the Library, and the Library was at the bottom of the hill, like Jacqueline's and Gran's house. I raced around there in my lunch hour. His office was piled high with cardboard boxes full of old books and newspapers, but Dan was not there. As I had expected, he was down in the basement. What I had not anticipated was that Claire was helping him.

'We've taken most of the really important stuff upstairs,' Dan said. 'Everything else will just have to go on the top shelves and take its chance.'

'But there's room for more upstairs, surely?'

'Possibly, but unfortunately there are regulations against overloading the upper floors and I think we've just about given them as much as they will stand.'

I had a flash of inspiration. 'What about Hopehill? Couldn't we move some of these heavy old books up there?'

Dan and Claire exchanged looks. 'We have other plans for Hopehill,' Claire said.

'Claire has arranged for the gas and electricity to be reconnected, and there are plans to use Hopehill to house people who may have to leave their homes in the event of a flood,' Dan explained.

'Oh, splendid,' I said with a pretence at enthusiasm. 'Pity about your books, of course.'

He grimaced in that rueful way he had and said, 'People first.'

It was a fine sentiment and I honoured him for it, but I

went away feeling a little lost and blank. There was nothing
for me to do. Everyone else was busy – everyone, that is,
who believed in the flood warnings. Most of the inhabitants
of Merryford ignored them. They had been caught by false
warnings before and few of them really believed that anything
was going to happen.

I was glad to know that Jacqueline and Bob were prepared, even to the extent of making reluctant plans to move
Jacqueline and the baby out to Bob's parents if it became really
necessary, while my father had moved all Gran's furniture to
the upper floor of her house and had then, in spite of her
protests, removed her completely to our house.

I went home and immersed myself in Eugenia's diaries. She
was a prim and proper miss, but I had a strange feeling of
sympathy with her. Behind her stilted words I detected a
lonely person, guiltily conscious of an attraction which she did
not entirely understand towards her employer, separated from
her family, for whom she clearly had a great affection, and
trying with no great success to educate three spoilt children.
I became quite excited when a new romance seemed to enter
her life.

She went on a holiday to her home and met her father's
new curate. She did not write up her diary while she was at
home, which was a pity. On her return to Hopehill her entries
were longer than usual, almost as if writing in the diary was
a comfort to her. She mentioned how satisfactory it was that
Papa should have a curate who was truly a gentleman and so
congenial to him as Arthur Pascoe.

A month passed and then she recorded that Mr Pascoe
had written to her – '*such a delightful letter, full of news of the
parish, just what one wants to hear*'. It was not a very frequent
correspondence, but she heard from him about every other
month and in the spring she recorded with some agitation
that he had called at Hopehill – '*being in the neighbourhood
unexpectedly he ventured to call and Mrs Stallymore most kindly
allowed me to receive him in the drawing-room for a full half hour,*

even though this took up the time she had intended to spend on afternoon calls.'

I read that again. Did it mean that Mrs Stallymore had been present at that rather touching meeting? Obviously it did. Poor Eugenia! What possible harm could there have been in allowing her to talk alone to a visitor from her home, and the curate at that? It must have been a frustrating interview, and yet I noticed a new warmth in her reference to him after that visit. Their correspondence flourished; he became '*Arthur*' instead of '*Mr Pascoe*', which seemed to imply no small degree of intimacy, even though nothing seemed to come of it. Why, I wondered? Lack of money, presumably.

Summer came and she was looking forward to another fortnight's holiday at home, and I was looking forward to some denouement to this slight romance, when she made her first reference to dear Papa having expressed anxiety about Arthur's health. I read on, sitting up in bed and hurrying through the pages. There was a fortnight's break in the story, presumably because, as before, she did not write in the diary while she was at home.

On her return to Hopehill once again the note of anxiety had intensified. He became '*dear Arthur*' and then, ominously, '*poor dear Arthur*'. By Christmas he was dead. I closed the diary for 1874, turned out the light and shed a few tears into my pillow for poor Eugenia. It was silly, but I felt so sorry for her, and I was feeling a bit low myself.

I took my gloom into the Library the next day. I hadn't intended bothering Dan, but his removals had upset the position of everything and I had to enlist his aid to find the file I wanted to see. My state of mind was not improved by finding Claire with him again.

'What's the matter?' he asked. 'You look miserable.'

'The curate died,' I explained.

He looked startled and then concerned. 'I'm sorry to hear that. Was he a close friend?'

'Not of mine. I mean Eugenia's curate. I think she might have married him if he had lived.'

'Oh, too bad! She doesn't have much luck, does she?'

'No. Born to be a maiden aunt, poor girl.'

I didn't add 'just like me', but it was what I was thinking.

'We haven't discovered what her fate was yet,' he pointed out. 'Take another couple of volumes and see if you can find anything in them to cheer yourself up.'

He took the four volumes I had not read out of the drawer of his desk. 'I'll take all four of them, I think,' I said. 'You don't mind?'

'They were your find, I feel you have first call on them.'

'What is all this?' Claire asked.

I thought that Dan hesitated, but then he answered her briefly, 'Candy discovered some diaries left behind in Hopehill by the Stallymores' governess. We are reading through them to see whether there is anything in them which might be of interest for publication.'

'How thrilling!' She reached out and took one of the red-covered books. 'May I read them?'

Again he hesitated. 'Not for the moment,' he said. 'But you shall certainly be one of the first to see them when we have decided what to do with them.'

It was rather nice of him to say 'we', I thought, because it was his decision really.

Claire's eyes were gleaming. 'There's a tremendous interest in the nineteenth century now,' she said. 'Some of the things which have been published recently must have made a fortune for their lucky owners. And, of course, the publicity would be wonderful for the "Save Hopehill" campaign. Have you thought of that?'

'Candy thought of it,' Dan said. 'I shall certainly make use of it if I can, but not just yet – not until I have had time to evaluate the diaries properly.'

'Oh, you are too cautious,' she said. 'Strike while the iron is hot is my motto.'

She sounded impatient, but Dan was quietly obstinate in

his determination not to let news of the diaries leak out prematurely and in the end she gave way, though not very graciously.

I took the four volumes I had not read and worked through them steadily that evening, partly because I had nothing better to do and partly because I felt restless and uneasy. The incessant rain and the constant talk of flooding was getting on my nerves. I shut my mind to the patter of raindrops on the window and applied myself to Eugenia and her problems.

The next anxiety was about her brother, Robert. He visited her in Merryford in 1875. She mentioned that he had come of age the previous month and she had kept his birthday present until she could give it to him in person. Infuriatingly, she did not say what the present was – that was the sort of unanswered question which made one long for the means of questioning her – but at least it fixed his age.

When she happened to say what a congenial companion he had become in spite of the six years' difference in their ages, I jumped with excitement because now I knew that she had been twenty-two when she came to Merrybrook and was twenty-seven in 1875. Twenty-seven! Poor Eugenia, I was afraid she was really and truly on the shelf.

Robert returned in the summer of 1876, to her great satisfaction, but it came as a surprise to her when he spent a further two weeks in Merryford in September. There followed a period of great agitation. Dear Robert had properly blotted his copybook. Eugenia could not believe that he would really do anything foolish, but it seemed that he had formed an attachment for the daughter of the people who kept the inn where he had been putting up in Merryford. He wanted her assistance in breaking the news to dear Papa, but how could she give him her support when she believed that the marriage he was contemplating would be his ruin?

'*I do not doubt that the Bromleys are very good people in their way,*' she wrote with what had obviously been a trembling hand, '*and Robert assures me that Miss Bromley has a most superior*

understanding, but nevertheless I cannot feel that it is fitting for a
Vicar's son to marry an innkeeper's daughter. Papa will be so grieved,
particularly since Robert appeared to have such a brilliant future in
front of him. He will be cutting himself off from all his friends by
this imprudent alliance. How can it prosper? I am torn by indecision.
Should I appeal to Miss Bromley to release him before it has gone too
far for him to draw back?'

This idea appeared to come to nothing. There was a
curiously touching episode in which Eugenia took her young
charges for a walk and deliberately went past the Golden Lion.
'A pretty inn, situated near the river bank. It seems well kept, and
there is a pleasant garden at the rear.'

I recognised the description, although the pleasant garden
had disappeared since I had known it. Eugenia stopped on
the bridge, ostensibly to look at the river, but really to have a
chance of observing this inn where her brother had so foolishly
lost his heart. There was a girl in the garden, throwing a ball
for a little dog. She wondered whether it was her future
sister-in-law, but lacked the courage to speak to her. Again,
one was left up in the air, for she never did say whether the
girl was Miss Bromley or not.

Robert married his innkeeper's daughter, and married her
in Merryford. After much heart-searching about whether she
should attend a ceremony which her father could not bring
himself to countenance, Eugenia went to the wedding and
recorded that Miss Bromley *'or Charlotte as I must now call her'*
was very pretty and seemed intelligent and well spoken *'and*
devoted to dear Robert, so that I think he must be happy if only he does
not regret the somewhat low connection with her family.' She also
recorded that Miss Bromley was very finely dressed, *'far better*
than I was myself and, indeed, I was sadly shabby in that company,
but no one appeared to notice and I think Mr and Mrs Bromley were
gratified that at least one of Robert's family was present.'

It was interesting to see how Eugenia's natural affections
had warred with her tendency to snobbishness, and I was glad
that in the end she had braved the wrath of her father and
the Stallymores' disapproval – *'Mrs Stallymore was astonished*

to learn that the report of Robert's intended marriage was true, since she had found him to be so truly a gentleman and Mr Stallymore had thought so highly of his talents. They both urged me to exert my influence to get him to break off the connection. I think that by saying nothing I gave them the impression that I would comply with their advice, but in truth I think Robert has gone too far now to draw back with any honour.'

It added a new dimension to Eugenia's diary. Robert settled in Merryford and she visited him and her new sister-in-law; not at the inn, she could never bring herself to enter that, but in their house in Waterford Street.

It was the reference to Waterford Street which pulled me up short. I sat back and thought about it. Robert had married the daughter of the people who had kept the Golden Lion. Gran had said that she remembered her own grandmother being the daughter of the people who kept that inn. I already knew that Gran's maiden name had been Pooley, so she wasn't descended from a son of Robert and Charlotte Chorley, but she said that she had been called Roberta after her grandfather. I could not resist it; blessing my father for bringing Gran to stay with us until the risk of flooding was over, I went and put my head round the door of the sitting-room where she was watching television.

'Gran, do you happen to remember your mother's maiden name?' I asked.

She dragged her eyes away from the screen with reluctance (Gran is a television addict) and said, 'Yes, of course I do.' She spoke with a hint of testiness that anyone should imagine she might have forgotten something. 'She was a Chorley. Maude Chorley, she was, until she married my father. I told you before that my grandad's name was Robert Chorley.'

She had not, in fact, told me that, but I was not going to argue. I gave her a hug and left the room before I betrayed my tremendous secret. I could have danced and sung, I was so excited. Robert Chorley was my – I shut my eyes and worked it out – my great-great-grandfather. His sister, Eugenia, was my great-great-aunt. It was the most extraordinary sensation, because I had been thinking of her as a girl, not much older than myself, whereas great-great-aunts were obviously terribly old women.

I went back and touched the diaries with reverential fingers. My great-great-aunt had handled these books. My great-great-aunt had written all those touching words. I was glad that she had had the courage to attend her brother's wedding and to think that she had become friends with the girl from the village inn who had become my great-great-grandmother. I longed to tell Dan about it, but he was not on the telephone and it was much too late to go in search of him. I would have to keep my news until I saw him again.

I read on, late into the night, until my eyes nearly dropped from their sockets. The friendship between Eugenia Chorley and her sister-in-law flourished and, to my delight, she was able to reconcile her father to the marriage to the extent of allowing Robert and Charlotte to visit him.

It was as well that Eugenia had the consolation of this friendship because the last volume of her diary was sombre. She was becoming uneasily conscious that the Stallymore girls would not require her services very much longer. The boy was away at school, the girls were growing up. Eugenia confided to her diary her anxiety at the thought of seeking another post after more than eight years in one household and when she was approaching the age of thirty.

Another thing which was causing concern was Mrs Stallymore's health. She appeared to be ailing for most of the year and, in October 1878, there was a blank period in the diary for which the only entry was, '*Much occupied in nursing Mrs Stallymore.*' She died at the beginning of November.

Again there was a blank space of a few days and then Eugenia wrote, '*My position in the house is difficult. Lucy is of an age to take charge, but she is prostrated with grief and can attempt nothing. The servants are bewildered and now that Mr Stallymore's sister has left us there is no one to give them instructions unless I take it upon myself to do so, which is not always well received. Little as I wish to trouble Mr Stallymore with these petty domestic disturbances, I think I must ask him to give me the necessary authority to take charge until Lucy is ready to assume her proper place. It is a thousand pities that Belinda is the younger, she is by far the more capable, but any attempt by her to assume her mother's mantle will be resented and it will be better for such resentment to fall on my shoulders than to be the cause of dissent between the sisters.'*

Two days later she recorded, *'I spoke to Mr Stallymore and he most readily agreed that I should for the time being become, as it were, housekeeper as well as governess. He spoke most affectingly of his loss, and I ventured to repeat some wise words from my father on the subject of bereavement. He listened carefully and seemed to find some comfort in what I said. He is a worldly man, but there is much to admire in him. His mind is open to the consolation of religion and he has not allowed himself to fall into the despair which afflicts poor Lucy.'*

Poor Lucy seemed to spend most of her time in the next week or two lying down on her bed, in floods of tears, or even hysterics. I was not surprised when Eugenia's patience finally gave way. *'I was forced to speak sharply to Lucy today. Deeply as I feel for her, her prolonged expressions of grief are excessive and cannot be allowed to continue. She is damaging her health. I called Dr Bunstead to her. He prescribed an iron tonic and, better still in my opinion, a brisk walk every day. She is to be out in the open air as much as the time of the year will permit.'*

There were consultations with Mr Stallymore, until at last Eugenia wrote. *'I have repeatedly urged on Mr Stallymore the benefit to be derived from a change of air, not only for the girls but for himself as well, but I did not expect that he would take them so far afield. They are to go to the South of France for the Christmas season and the whole of January. Lucy is quite revived by the news. Edgar, at his own request is to remain in England and will spend Christmas with his aunt and uncle in Bristol. For my part, I shall welcome the opportunity of passing the festive season amongst my own dear family. I have offered to return to Hopehill to supervise the opening of the house for the travellers homecoming. After that, I fear I shall have to seek another post. I must not repine, but I did not know until I undertook it how satisfying the ordering of a house can be. It will not be easy to return to nothing but the supervision of young children, particularly when I have recently had the advantage of contact with Mr Stallymore's more mature mind. My one consolation is that I have been of real use to him.'*

Perhaps it was my imagination, but I could not help suspecting that Eugenia still treasured a weakness for her employer, and her regret at parting from him, however staidly expressed, was real enough.

However, there was a change of plan. Her final entry, written in an almost illegible hand read, *'I cannot believe it, I cannot believe it. I am to go with them. Mr Stallymore spoke to me this evening after dinner and said that they had all become so dependent on what he was kind enough to call my great good sense that they cannot face the journey without me. I must try to compose myself sufficiently to write to dear Papa. He will be disappointed that I shall not be with him for Christmas but I think he must be glad for me. To travel to the South of France, perhaps even to Italy. No matter what may happen when I have to leave, at least I shall have had this, a memory to treasure to the end of my days.'*

I was glad for her, but how I wished that I could have had her journal of that holiday period. I lay awake for a long time, wondering whether it had come up to expectations. It was nice that the diary had ended on a happy note, but what had happened to her after that? Had she found another position? Had she been able to settle down again after her foreign travels? It was tantalising not to know.

I was bursting to tell Dan of my relationship to Eugenia. In fact, I could not wait. I rang him up at the Library from my office the next morning. He was interested, but not as enthusiastic as I had expected. When I had finished pouring it all out to him, he said, 'Candy, have you told anyone else about this?'

'Not a soul. It's most frustrating, because I'm dying to tell the family. The trouble is, once they get hold of it, it will be all over the town, which I know you don't want just yet.'

'No, I'd hoped to keep it quiet until I had at least read all eight volumes. The thing is, the news is out already. I have had a reporter from the local paper along to see me asking about the diaries and the story of how they were found and whether they are of any great importance.'

'Oh, what a nuisance!' I said disgustedly. 'But it doesn't really matter, does it?'

'Possibly not. Candy, you didn't let it out by accident, did you?' He sounded slightly embarrassed at asking, and I was certainly hurt that he felt it necessary to ask.

'No, of course I didn't.'

'Only he happened to mention that he was a cousin of yours.'

My heart sank. 'I can't help it, Dan,' I said. 'Merryford is littered with my cousins. But truly I haven't spoken to anyone about Eugenia and the diaries.'

'Oh, well, that's all right then,' he said, but I wished he had sounded more convinced. It quite took the edge off my pleasure in finding out about my great-great-aunt Eugenia.

I thought about it and then rang my cousin at the local newspaper. 'How did you find out about the diaries that I discovered at Hopehill?' I asked.

'Come, come, you can't expect me to reveal my sources,' he said, with a laugh.

'Don't play that game of pretending you are an ace reporter on a national daily with me,' I said. 'It's only a couple of years since I was tying up your cut knees and wiping your sniffly nose, you grubby brat. Was it Claire Burnside?'

'Yes,' he admitted. 'It sounded like a good story, and if you had any interest in promoting my career you would have given it to me yourself.'

'It will be a good story,' I said. 'Better than you think at the moment, but Dan doesn't want it to come out yet. Sit on it till I give you the word and I'll give you an exclusive interview.'

'Now who's playing at being a national celebrity? Is this on the level, Candy?'

'Strictly on the level,' I said. 'Can I tell Dan there will be nothing in this week's paper?'

'OK. My editor is an anti-Hopehill man anyway, so I don't suppose he'd be too keen on it. Who is this Dan Denby and what is he in your young life?'

'He's just a friend,' I said. I was getting tired of saying it.

IV

I grappled with my baser nature and managed not to ring Dan to tell him it was Claire who had broken the news about the diaries. I was surprised that he had not thought of it for himself, but it did not seem to have occurred to him. Perhaps because he thought so highly of her? Now there was a lowering thought. I was aggrieved that he should so readily have suspected me and made up my mind to keep out of his way for a day or two, but as it happened I met him by accident when we both went down to inspect the state of the river at lunchtime on Wednesday.

It was deep, deeper than I had ever seen it before, but I was cheered by the fact that the rain had stopped and the sun was actually shining. A feeble, watery kind of sunshine, but a vast improvement on the weather we had had lately. There is a small riverside park near the bridge where Eugenia had stood to observe her future sister-in-law and I took a stroll round it, delighted to see that the crocuses and daffodils had survived the recent deluge. When Dan spoke from behind me, he took me by surprise. He sounded breathless, as if he had been running.

'I saw you from the Library window,' he said. Had he come out specially in search of me? He did not say so, but it looked as if he had.

'The Merrybrook doesn't look too bad,' I said hopefully. 'If it rises no further than this, we shall be all right, shan't we?'

'We'll have to wait and see,' he said, in a noncommittal way that was not particularly reassuring.

I would have liked to have taken this opportunity to clear myself in his eyes over that newspaper article, but it was difficult to know how to do it without giving Claire away, and I was still reluctant to do that.

I ventured to say, 'I spoke to my cousin at the *Herald* office and he promised not to write up the story about the diaries until I gave the word. I held him at bay by promising further revelations – meaning the relationship with Eugenia, of course. She's his great-great-aunt, too. You won't mind him claiming a special interest when the time comes, will you?'

'Not a bit.' He was looking at me curiously. 'Did he tell you who gave him the story in the first place?'

I stared hard at a torn-off leaf swirling round in the dark water. 'It's not important, is it?' I asked uncomfortably. 'I know it wasn't me; that's all that interests me.'

'You know, you really are an extraordinarily nice person,' Dan said. I looked up quickly at his face and saw that he was smiling. 'It's all right, I've already worked it out for myself. It was Claire, of course. I rang her up and taxed her with it and she admitted it quite readily. She even seemed rather proud of herself. That's why I ran after you just now – to catch you and tell you. To apologise, if necessary, and to make sure you weren't annoyed with me.'

I sighed with relief. 'No apologies necessary, but I'm glad you know.'

'You weren't going to tell me, were you?'

'No.'

'Why not?'

'Difficult to say, except that you are rather friendly with Claire, aren't you? I thought it might hurt you if you knew she had spilled the beans after you'd particularly asked her not to.'

'I look on Claire as a useful ally and I admire her dedication and her organising ability. Apart from that, we haven't a lot in common. To tell you the truth, I'm a bit scared of her.'

'Me, too,' I admitted.

We stood on the wet gravel, steaming gently in the sun, and beamed at one another foolishly until at last he said, 'What are we doing about lunch today? I can't run to Tellafords twice in one month, but your news about great-great-aunt Eugenia calls for some sort of celebration.'

'Fish and chips, and we'll eat it here?' I suggested, flinging my diet to the winds. It was a happy thought. We sat on a park bench in a stone shelter festooned with creeping plants, and ate fish and chips with plastic forks and our fingers, and the sun shone and the birds sang. We talked about the diaries and what we were going to do with them; Dan told me about his home and the work he hoped to do in the future; I told him about my plans to qualify as an accountant. We discovered that we had similar views on politics, were poles apart on music (although I promised to let him try to convert me to Bach) and both preferred biographies to novels.

'Which is one reason why I find Eugenia so satisfying,' I said. 'She was a real person.' I glanced regretfully at my watch. 'I shall have to go. This has been nice. Such a relief to get out after all that wet weather.'

I gazed round me happily at the blossoming scene. Then I looked again. When we had sat down I had particularly noticed a clump of white crocuses with mauve veins on their petals, near the water's edge, and had thought how fresh and pretty they looked.

'Dan,' I said uneasily. 'Have you noticed the crocuses?'

'What crocuses?'

'That's the point. They've gone. I think they are under the water now. The river must still be rising.'

We both went to the edge of the river. I could see my crocuses, swaying gently, their petals flattened under the water.

I shivered. 'I don't think I like it very much,' I said. 'It's so stealthy, creeping up like that while we sat and talked.'

He took my hand and gave it a comforting squeeze, and then guided me away from the water's edge. We walked along slowly, without speaking, until we came to the entrance to the Library and stood there for a moment, hands loosely linked.

'I hate to go,' I said. 'I mean, because of the sunshine,' I added hastily.

'Of course. I agree, but I must go inside, I suppose.' He grinned in that lop-sided way that made me smile too. 'Amongst other things, I have a card index to keep up to date.'

'Sylph-like?' I asked, hoping that he might have noticed the new svelte Candida beginning to emerge from the old cuddly Candy.

He touched the tip of my nose with one of his long fingers. 'Adorable,' he said.

I floated up the High Street on a pink cloud, entered half a dozen transactions on the wrong side of the ledger, receipted a bill which had not yet been sent out and repeated an order for spare parts which had been delivered the day before. My uncle was disgusted with me. He rang up my mother and told her he thought I must be sickening for something, and she insisted on taking my temperature as soon as I got home, but even that did not cause my euphoria to evaporate. It took the flood warning to do that.

We had been too complacent about our preparedness for the flood which had been often threatened in the past and had never materialised. When at last the Merrybrook burst its banks, instead of merely over-flowing them by a few inches, we were as shocked as if the idea had never occurred to us. It was nothing like I had anticipated. I had seen the insidious encroachment of the stream and had felt uneasy about it, but this was nothing compared to the effect produced when the river quite literally turned round and flooded back on the town with a great rush of water and flung down our flimsy defences as contemptuously as a giant with a set of children's bricks.

I had foreseen the overflowing of the river, but no one had prepared me for the effect of sewers and drains backing up, with manhole covers and gratings tossed aside. We learned afterwards that, as Dan had predicted, Jacqueline and Bob's house was not too badly affected, with inches of water creeping in rather than feet, but one poor woman at the bottom of the hill described how she stood and watched in horror while her downstairs bathroom gushed water upwards like a fountain from every orifice.

We were roused from sleep by the pre-arranged warning, too startled at first to realise what it was. My mother, who belonged to the WRVS, had promised, if it really became necessary, to stand by to help with receiving the unfortunate people who were forced out of their homes. In the early hours of Thursday morning, I found myself pressed into service at Hopehill House.

It stood well up on the hill and I thought as we crunched up the drive that it had a welcoming air about it, with all the lights lit and the front door standing open. I thought Dan might have been there, since he had been a leading light in getting the house turned into a reception centre, but there was no sign of him. Claire was there, very efficient and, I thought, rather pleased with herself for her forethought. She set me to work, handing out blankets and cups of tea to the dazed, wet people who came streaming in, some of them still in their night clothes. We made them as comfortable as we could, but most of them had to make do with the floor for a bed since the supply of camp beds was limited. At least they were dry and safe and, once we had got organised, warm and fed as well.

I paused once by my mother and she said in a worried voice, 'I wish I knew what your father was up to. He went down into the town to see if he could do anything to help, but that was hours ago.'

'I expect he's helping to ferry people about,' I said vaguely, but with more sympathy for her anxiety that I would normally have felt, my opinion being that my father was well able to take care of himself. I had a worry of my own, which made me realise how Mum was feeling.

Irrational, but nagging at the back of my mind all the time

I dispensed bowls of soup and tried to soothe tired, fractious children, was the wish that I knew what Dan was doing. I told myself that I was an idiot, getting all worked up about a man to whom I had no real commitment, but it didn't stop me wanting to know that he was all right.

We were relieved at seven o'clock by a fresh team of helpers who came to cook breakfasts. I think they were a little staggered to see the numbers they were catering for, but they rallied and began to get down to it in the roomy kitchen.

'How fortunate that we have somewhere like this old house for an emergency like this,' someone commented.

'Yes, it will be a pity when it is pulled down,' I said, putting in a bit of propaganda for Dan's cause.

'Pulled down? That would be a shame. It's just the sort of place we need for our old people.'

'A Day Centre,' Claire's voice said behind us. 'That's one of the ideas I have in mind for Hopehill.'

Our eyes met and she gave me a conspiratorial smile. She was looking as brisk as she had five hours earlier. 'You must have heard that there was a campaign to save Hopehill?' she asked.

'I believe I did read something about it,' the other woman said vaguely. 'It didn't mean much to me at the time, but now I've seen inside the house I must say I'd be sorry to see it disappear.'

'It's just the sort of place where I'd like to have my wedding reception,' a young girl said dreamily. 'If it were smartened up a bit.'

'It's a crying shame to let that garden go to waste,' an older man said severely. 'Here am I crying out for an allotment, which I can't get, and there's all this ground not being used. I wouldn't mind keeping the flower beds tidy if they'd let me grow a few vegetables round the back.'

Claire looked at me again and this time she winked. 'I wish Dan was here,' she said in a low voice.

So did I wish Dan was there, though not for quite the same

reason. Where was he? Come to that, where was my father? And were Jacqueline and Bob and the baby all right? I began to walk home with Mum, both of us tired but not dissatisfied with our night's work.

'I expect we shall find your father at home in bed,' Mum said, but we both knew it was not likely. He would not have gone home without coming round to see us first. We opened the door hopefully, but no one was there, except Gran laboriously getting breakfast started.

'I thought you'd be in before long,' she said. 'Is George with you?'

'I haven't seen anything of him all night,' my mother said in a worried voice.

'I shouldn't fret about him,' Gran said. 'It's young Jacqueline and that little baby who are on my mind.'

'I'll go down into the town and see what the situation is and whether I can get any news,' I suggested.

'Have your breakfast first,' Mum said. 'And don't do anything foolhardy.'

'Don't worry,' I said flippantly. 'I won't go near the water.'

It was not raining, which made a nice change, but I put on my Wellington boots, since I foresaw a certain amount of paddling, and trudged down the hill. I hadn't got very far before the water was lapping at the edge of my boots. I looked at the scene in front of me with dismay. Not all the stories I had heard that night had quite prepared me for the lake which lay over what had once been the bottom of Merryford High Street.

A hand grasped my shoulder. 'Don't put your foot down a manhole, pint-size,' Dan's voice said. 'Or you'll be swept out to sea before we can haul you back.'

I turned so quickly that my face collided with his chest and I spoke with a voice muffled by the big woolly jersey he was wearing. 'I was worried about you.'

'I'm all right.' His arm crept round me and held me tight for a moment.

I freed myself and added, 'I really came down to see if I could find out what has happened to Dad.'

'He's probably out with one of the boats. We've organised a team of people to row up and down the streets to help with the evacuation.'

'Mum's fretting about him,' I explained. 'And about Jacqueline and the baby. I wish I could find out something to tell her. She needs a rest and she won't settle until she knows what has happened.'

'I could take you over to Bob and Jacqueline's place,' Dan offered. 'I've got one of those little boats from the children's play ground. Not very roomy, but quite useful in an emergency. Give me your hand. I meant what I said about falling down a manhole. It really is quite dangerous when you can't see where you are treading. Through the churchyard is the best way for us to go. I've got the boat tied up to the railings on the far side.'

'Where I chained my bicycle when I came to see you in the Library.'

'And made jokes about lifeboats – little did I know!'

He guided me very carefully through the churchyard, which was slightly raised above the level of the roadway and comparatively dry. 'Most of the Stallymores are buried just here,' he said in an absentminded voice, indicating some imposing monuments.

'No family vault?' I asked.

'No, apparently not. Individual headstones.' He glanced at the one we were passing. 'This urn and weeping angel belong to Thomas and his wife Adelaide – they'd be the parents of Eugenia's Mr Stallymore, I think. Joseph, the founder of the family fortune, has a much plainer monument.'

'And here's Benjamin,' I said with an interested look as we went past. 'Benjamin and his wife, Miranda, and . . .'

We both stopped dead in our tracks and stared. 'And his second wife, Eugenia,' Dan said in a stunned voice.

'She married him,' I said. 'Dan, she *married* him!'

'It looks like it,' he agreed.

'Oh, it *must* be the same Eugenia. Don't be so cautious! What a fantastic, wonderful end to the story, like a fairy tale come true. Oh, how I wish we'd got the next volume of her diary!'

'She probably never had the time, or the inclination, to write a diary again. I must admit it's tantalising not to have her own account of what happened, but it's tremendously satisfying to wrap up the end of her tale so neatly.'

We walked on, bubbling with excitement over our discovery. 'I could kick myself for not having looked at the monuments before,' Dan said. 'Or, at any rate, not having looked at them with a seeing eye, but everything has happened so fast.'

It was true. As I seated myself in the little boat (No. 22 and painted bright red), I reflected that Dan and I had only known each other a few weeks. I stole a look at his distinguished, bony profile. There was no doubt about it, he mattered tremendously, but was it perhaps a little too soon to imagine that he felt the same way about me, even if he did think I was adorable? I made a resolution to be a little more circumspect in my dealings with him in future. I really must stop flinging myself on his chest and telling him I was worried about him; it was too possessive, it took too much for granted.

In the meantime, I could at least admire the skill with which he guided our small craft across the fast-flowing river and into the entrance to the street where Bob and Jacqueline lived. He tethered it securely as soon as it ran aground and helped me out.

The water was almost up to my knees, but by the time we reached the house it was only inches deep. Bob was looking out of the window and saw us approach. He opened it and leaned out. 'If you are coming in, it will have to be through this,' he said. 'I'm not opening the doors at all, in the hope of keeping some of the water out.'

'Where are Jacqueline and Elizabeth?'

'Gone to my folks to stay. Jacqueline wasn't keen, but this

is no place for the baby. No gas, no electricity, no drinkable water and no toilet facilities. I'm leaving myself in a few minutes.' He gave Dan a friendly smile. 'That was good work we put in last weekend on the carpets and furniture. The damage is much less than I expected. Are you coming in?'

'Not much point,' I said. 'I'll go back and reassure Mum about her precious granddaughter. You haven't seen Dad, by any chance?'

'Yes, he stopped by earlier. He's still out with the boat as far as I know, unless he's gone home by this time.'

Dan and I walked back to our little boat. 'Well, that's very satisfactory,' I said. 'Now, if we can just catch a glimpse of Dad still alive and well, I can go home and get some sleep.'

'I'll row you up Mere Street,' Dan said. 'After that, whether we see your father or not, I think you ought to go home. You must be tired.'

'You too,' I said.

'Yes, I could do with a rest,' he agreed. 'How were things going at Hopehill? Will there be a corner for me? My digs are unusable.'

'You must come home with me,' I said. Over-possessive or not, I was certainly not going to let him camp out in Hopehill while we had a bed to spare in my own house. The words were hardly out of my mouth when we rounded the corner and I caught sight of a couple of boats in the water ahead of us; bigger, more practical boats than the little one we were using.

'That looks like Dad,' I said. 'Yes, it is.'

Dan glanced over his shoulder and began to steer us towards the two boats. One of them already had several people in it, and, as we watched, another elderly man was helped out of his living-room window, on to the window-sill, and from there the water was so high that it was only a step into the boat. I could see my father quite clearly now, in the second boat. He was looking upwards, apparently trying to coax some woman on the first floor to come downstairs and climb out of the window as the man had done. We bobbed nearer. Unbelievably, the woman was climbing out on to the window-sill of the bedroom window. I heard my father shout, 'Don't jump, don't jump! You might land on the railings!'

For one moment I could not think what he was talking about and then I remembered that these were houses with a basement area, fenced in by iron railings. It was a sickening thought that the woman might jump out of the window and land on those iron spikes. He stood up, balancing carefully, in an effort to make her hear and understand him, but she seemed to be oblivious to her peril, too panic-stricken perhaps to be rational. With an awkward, plunging movement, she sprang forward. Everyone seemed to be shouting at once, but it was too late to stop her. She actually landed in the boat, sprawling on her hands and knees on the far side of it. It rocked violently, my father, still on his feet, pitched forward, hit his head with a sickening crunch against the side of the house, and disappeared beneath the water.

Dan took two seconds to pull off his Wellington boots. 'He's gone down in the basement area,' he said. 'And he was wearing waders.'

I knew what he meant. Once those waist-high boots, fastening like dungarees, which Dad wore for his fishing expeditions, filled up with water, he had very little chance of coming up to the surface again, particularly if he was unconscious.

In the boat from which he had fallen, all was confusion, though fortunately it had not overturned. The woman who had caused all the trouble appeared to be having hysterics. The second boat was too full of people to be of much help. Dan slipped over the side of our little boat and swam strongly towards the house. He paused within feet of it and I wondered why he had stopped, then I realised he had reached the railings. He levered himself over them, glanced once over his shoulder towards me, and then dived beneath the water.

I sat where I was, frozen with horror, with nothing but an eddy in the water to show that anything was going on beneath the surface. I changed places, took the oars and made for the railings. It seemed an age, it was an age, before Dan surfaced, but when he did he had one arm round the neck of my unconscious father. He clutched at the invisible railings with the other hand; coughed, spluttered and shook the water from his head.

'We'll never get him out with these waders on,' he gasped. 'It's as much as I can do to support him. Tie the boat to the railings and then do you think you can keep his head above water while I go down and try to take them off?'

I nodded. I felt beneath the water for the iron railings and tied the little boat up with wet, cold fingers. Dan raised my father's arms and pushed them for support through the railings, while I knelt in the middle of the boat for balance and held his head above the water. His eyes were closed and a thin trickle of dark blood was oozing down over his forehead. In spite of the support of the railings he was a dragging weight on my arms as I knelt there. I hated seeing Dan disappear once more beneath that thick brown water, and once again it seemed like a lifetime before he reappeared. 'The fastenings are stiff,' he gasped. 'I've undone one side. Now for the next lot.'

Once more he went down and this time he seemed to be gone even longer, but just before his head reappeared I felt a lightening of the weight on my arms. Almost as if my father rose up in the water. Dan was gasping and choking, but he managed to speak. 'We must float him over the top of these railings,' he said. 'We don't want him catching on the points.'

It was not easy to manoeuvre Dad's inert weight, but between us we managed it. With Dan still in the water, and me in the boat, we got him into it over the end.

'Can you row?' Dan asked. 'Good girl! Make for the churchyard.'

He bent over my father in the confined space of the boat, doing his best to work on him to get rid of the water he had swallowed. I did not ask if he was going to be all right; I refused to admit to any other possibility. The other boats outstripped us, and by the time we reached a dry patch of ground there were plenty of hands to assist us, which was just as well because I discovered I was quite incapable of standing up.

I sat where I was, and Dan sat where he was. It was only the sight of Dad beginning to stir that roused me. I struggled to my feet and went to him. He seemed dazed and uncertain of his whereabouts, but I told him reassuringly that he was all right, which was vaguely comforting even if it was not quite true.

'That stupid woman,' he muttered.

'She's come to no harm,' I said. 'You've hit your head and swallowed a lot of nasty water, so you are going off to hospital for a little while.'

'Your mother . . .'

'Sound asleep in bed,' I lied. 'We've been up all night, remember. She'll be *furious* when she hears what you've been up to.'

That made him laugh weakly and then my cousin from the local newspaper came pushing through the group of people surrounding us.

'I say, is it really true?' he asked eagerly. 'Uncle George in the water, heroic rescue by daughter's boy friend, and all that?'

'No!' Dan said.

'Yes,' I said. 'Dad was – um, dislodged, by a woman *he* was rescuing, and you can say that Daniel Denby, curator of the Local History Museum and prominent campaigner to save Hopehill – which has played such a useful rôle in the present emergency – dived repeatedly below the water to free him and save him from drowning.'

'You traitor!' Dan hissed, but at that moment the ambulance arrived and I was too taken up with seeing Dad safely installed to pay any attention to his dismay at being turned into a hero.

'I think I ought to go to the hospital,' I said to Dan. I looked at him. His clothes were plastered to his body, his hair hung in wet rats' tails about his face. I tried to say 'thank you' but there didn't seem to be adequate words. Instead, I scowled at him and said, 'Don't stand about in those damp socks, you'll catch your death of cold.'

A smile lit his face. 'That's my girl,' he said fondly. 'If I wasn't so wet, I'd kiss you.'

'Always some excuse,' I said gloomily.

'Don't worry, I'll get round to it,' he said. 'And when I do, I'll promise you something.'

'What?'

'You'll remember it from one Christmas to the next.'

I beamed at him. 'Go and see my mother. She'll give you some dry clothes.'

'Is it all right if I tell her about us?'

'There isn't anything to tell,' I said. 'Is there?'

'Only that I'm head over heels in love with her daughter and one of these fine days I'm going to marry her. So start praying for sunshine, Candy, my little love.'

Exasperating man, he walked away laughing, leaving me in a state of total confusion, but as I rode off in the ambulance, holding Dad's hand, I was happily planning this year's entry for the family history. It was going to be quite a year: Dad's fiftieth birthday, the Silver Wedding, great-great-aunt Eugenia and her diaries, saving Hopehill, the great flood, the heroic rescue. And my wedding.

Cheap Excursion

NOEL COWARD

NOEL COWARD (1899–1973). Playwright, actor, lyricist and composer, he also wrote many short stories. This one uses his knowledge of the stage to deal with the love of a famous actress for a man who is not only younger, but well below her in the theatrical hierarchy. Today she would probably marry her young lover, but in the 1930s she feared the ridicule of her friends and the gossip which would smear the affair 'with dirty fingers'.

JIMMY said, 'Good night, Miss Reed,' as she passed him in the passage. He did it ordinarily, no overtones or undertones, not the slightest indication of any secret knowledge between them, not even a glint in his eye, nothing beyond the correct subservience of an assistant stage-manager to a star. She answered him vaguely, that well-known gracious smile, and went on to the stage door, her heart pounding violently as though someone had sprung at her out of the dark.

In the car, she sat very still with her hands folded in her lap, vainly hoping that this very stillness, this stern outward quietness might help to empty her mind. Presently she gave up and watched herself carefully taking a cigarette out of her case and lighting it. 'I am Diana Reed. *The* Diana Reed, lighting a cigarette. I am Diana Reed driving home in my expensive car to my expensive flat – I am tired after my performance and as I have a matinee to-morrow it is sane and sensible for me to go straight home to bed after the show. I am having supper with Jimmy to-morrow night and probably Friday night, too – there are hundreds of other nights and there is no reason whatsoever for me to feel lonely and agonised and without peace. I am Diana Reed – I am celebrated, successful, sought after – my play is a hit – my notices were excellent – except the *Sunday Times*. I am Diana Reed, famous, nearing forty and desperate. I am in love, not perhaps really in love like I was with Tony, nor even Pierre Chabron, but that was different, because it lasted such a little time and was foreign and mixed up with being abroad and everything, but I am in love all right and it's different again, it's always different and always difficult, and I wish to God I could be happy with it and give up to it, but there's too much to remember and too much to be careful of and too many people wanting to find out about it and gossip and smear it with their dirty fingers.'

She let down the window and flicked her cigarette on to the pavement. It fell at the feet of a man in a mackintosh and a bowler hat, he looked up quickly and she drew herself back guiltily into the corner of the car. When she let herself into her flat and switched on the lights in the sitting-room its smug tidy emptiness seemed to jeer at her. It was a charming room. The furniture was good, plain and luxuriously simple in line. There was the small 'Utrillo' that Tony had given her so many years ago – it had been in her flat in Cavendish Street for ages, and she had even taken it on tour with her. That sharp sunny little street with the pinkish-white walls and neat row of plane trees making shadows across the road. The only other picture in the room was a Marie Laurencin of a woman in a sort of turban. It was quite small and framed in glass. That she had bought herself a couple of years ago when she was in Paris with Barbara and Nicky. Nicky said it looked like a very pale peach with currants in it.

She pitched her hat on to the sofa where it lay looking apologetic, almost cringing, and went over and opened the window. Outside it was very quiet, only dark roof tops and an occasional light here and there, but there was a glow in the sky over Oxford Street, and she could hear the noise of traffic far away muffled by the houses and squares in between. Just round the corner in George Street she heard a taxi stop, the slam of its door and the sharp ping as the driver shut off the meter. It might so easily be Jimmy, knowing that she was coming home alone, knowing how happy it would make her if he just came along for ten minutes to say good night. The taxi with a grind of its gears started up and drove away, she could hear it for quite a while until there was silence again. It might still be Jimmy, he wouldn't be so extravagant as to keep a taxi waiting – he might at this very moment be coming up in the lift. In a few seconds she would hear the lift doors opening and then the front-door bell. She listened, holding her breath. He might, of course, come up the stairs in order not to be seen by the lift man. Jimmy was nothing if not cautious. She waited, holding on to the window-sill tight to prevent herself from going to the front door. There was no sound, and presently her tension relaxed and, after rather a disdainful glance at herself in the glass over the mantelpiece, she went and opened the front door anyhow. The landing was deserted. When she came back into the room again she discovered, to her great irritation, that she was trembling.

She sat on a chair by the door, bolt upright, like somebody in a dentist's waiting-room. It wouldn't have surprised her if a bright, professionally smiling nurse had suddenly appeared and announced that Doctor Martin was ready for her. Again she folded her hands in her lap. Someone had once told her that if you sat still as death with your hands relaxed, all the vitality ran out of the ends of your fingers and your nerves stopped being strained and tied up in knots. The frigidaire in the kitchen suddenly gave a little click and started whirring. She stared at various things in the room, as though by concentrating, identifying herself with them she could become part of them and not feel so alone. The pickled wood Steinway with a pile of highly-coloured American tunes on it; the low table in front of the fire with last week's *Sketch* and *Bystander*, and the week before last's *New Yorker*, symmetrically arranged with this morning's *Daily Telegraph* folded neatly on top; the Chinese horse on the mantelpiece, very aloof and graceful with its front hoof raised as though it were just about to stamp on something small and insignificant. Nicky had said it was 'Ming' and Eileen had sworn it was 'Sung' because she had once been to China on a cruise and became superior at the mention of anything remotely oriental.

There had been quite a scene about it culminating in Martha saying loudly that she'd settle for it being 'Gong' or 'Pong' if only everybody would bloody well shut up arguing and give her a drink.

Diana remembered how Jimmy had laughed, he was sitting on the floor next to Barbara. She looked at the empty space in front of the fireplace and saw him clearly, laughing, with his head thrown back and the firelight shining on his hair. That was during rehearsals, before anything had happened, before the opening night in Manchester and the fatal supper party at the Midland, when he had come over from his party at the other end of the French restaurant to tell her about the rehearsal for cuts the next afternoon. She remembered asking him to sit down and have a glass of champagne, and how politely he had accepted with a rather quizzical smile, almost an air of resignation. Then the long discussion about Duse and Bernhardt, and Jonathan getting excited and banging the table, and Jimmy sitting exactly opposite her where she could watch him out of the corner of her eye, listening intently to the conversation and twiddling the stem of his wine-glass. They had all been dressed, of course. Jonathan and Mary had come up from London especially for the first night, also Violet and Dick and Maureen. Jimmy was wearing a grey flannel suit and a blue shirt and navy blue tie; occasionally the corners of his mouth twitched as though he were secretly amused, but didn't want to betray it. Then he had caught her looking at him, raised his eyebrows just for the fraction of a second and, with the most disarming friendliness, patted her hand. 'You gave a brilliant performance to-night,' he said. 'I felt very proud to be there.' That was the moment. That was the spark being struck. If she had had any sense she'd have run like a stag, but instead of running, instead of recognising danger, there she had sat idiotically smiling, warmed and attracted.

Not content with having had a successful first night and
having given a good performance, not satisfied with the
fact that her friends, her close intimate friends had trailed
all the way from London to enjoy her triumph with her,
she had had to reach out greedily for something more. Well,
God knows she'd got it all right. Here it was, all the fun of the
fair. The fruits of those few weeks of determined fascination.
She remembered, with a slight shudder, how very much at her
best she had been, how swiftly she had responded to her new
audience, this nice-looking, physically attractive young man
at least ten years younger than herself. How wittily she had
joined in the general conversation. She remembered Jonathan
laughing until he cried at the way she had described the dress
rehearsal of *Lady from the East*, when the Japanese bridge had
broken in the middle of her love scene. All the time, through
all the laughter, through all the easy intimate jokes, she had
had her eye on Jimmy, watching for his response, drawing
him into the circle, appraising him, noting his slim wrists, the
way he put his head on one side when he asked a question,
his eyes, his thick eyelashes, his wide, square shoulders. She
remembered saying 'good night' to him with the others as
they all went up in the lift together. Her suite was on the
second floor, so she got out first. He was up on the top
floor somewhere, sharing a room with Bob Harley, one
of the small part actors. She remembered, also, looking at
herself in the glass in her bathroom and wondering, while
she creamed her face, how attractive she was to him really, or
how much of it was star glamour and position. Even then, so
early in the business, she had begun to doubt. It was inevitable,
of course, that doubt, particularly with someone younger
than herself, more particularly still when that someone was
assistant stage-manager and general understudy. A few days
after that, she had boldly asked him to supper in her suite.
She remembered at the time being inwardly horrified at such
flagrant indiscretion; however, no one had found out or even
suspected. He accepted with alacrity, arrived a little late,
having had a bath and changed his suit, and that was that.

Suddenly, the telephone bell rang. Diana jumped, and with a sigh of indescribable relief, went into her bedroom to answer it. Nobody but Jimmy knew that she was coming home early – nobody else would dream of finding her in at this time of night. She sat on the edge of the bed just in order to let it ring once more, just to give herself time to control the foolish happiness in her voice. Then she lifted the receiver and said 'Hallo,' in exactly the right tone of politeness only slightly touched with irritation. She heard Martha's voice at the other end, and the suddenness of the disappointment robbed her of all feeling for a moment. She sat there rigid and cold with a dead heart. 'My God,' Martha was saying, 'you could knock me down with a crowbar, I couldn't be more surprised. I rang up Jonathan and Barbara and Nicky, and finally the Savoy Grill – this is only a forlorn hope – I never thought for a moment you'd be in.' Diana muttered something about being tired and having a matinee to-morrow, her voice sounded false and toneless. Martha went on. 'I don't want to be a bore, darling, but Helen and Jack have arrived from New York, and they're leaving on Saturday for Paris, and they've been trying all day to get seats for your show, and the nearest they could get was the fourteenth row, and I wondered if you could do anything about the house seats.' With a great effort Diana said: 'Of course, darling, I'll fix it with the box-office to-morrow.' 'You're an angel – here are Helen and Jack, they want to say Hullo".' There was a slight pause, then Helen's husky Southern voice: 'Darling –'

Diana put her feet up and lay back on the bed, this was going to be a long business. She was in command of herself again, she had been a fool to imagine it was Jimmy, anyhow; he never telephoned unless she asked him to, that was one of the most maddening aspects of his good behaviour. Good behaviour to Jimmy was almost a religion. Excepting when they were alone together, he never for an instant betrayed by the flicker of an eyelash that they were anything more than casual acquaintances. There was no servility in his manner, no pandering to her stardom. On the contrary the brief words he had occasion to speak to her in public were, if anything, a trifle brusque, perfectly polite, of course, but definitely without warmth. Helen's voice went on. She and Jack had had a terrible trip on the *Queen Mary*, and Jack had been sick as a dog for three whole days. Presently Jack came to the telephone and took up the conversation where Helen had left off. Diana lay still, giving a confident, assured performance, laughing gaily, dismissing her present success with just enough disarming professional modesty to be becoming. 'But, Jack dear, it's a marvellous part – nobody could go far wrong in a part like that. You wait until you see it – you'll see exactly what I mean. Not only that, but the cast's good too, Ronnie's superb. I think it's the best performance he's given since *The Lights Are Low*, and, of course, he's heaven to play with. He does a little bit of business with the breakfast-tray at the beginning of the third act that's absolutely magical. I won't tell you what it is, because it would spoil it for you, but just watch out for it – No dear, I can't have supper to-morrow night – I've a date with some drearies that I've already put off twice – no, really I couldn't again – how about lunch on Friday? You'd better come here and bring old Martha, too – all right – it's lovely to hear your voice again. The seats will be in your name in the box-office to-morrow night. Come back-stage afterwards, anyhow, even if you've hated it – good-bye!'

Diana put down the telephone and lit a cigarette, then she wrote on the pad by the bed: 'Reminder fix house seats, Jack and Helen.' Next to the writing-pad was a thermos jug of Ovaltine left for her by Dora. She looked at it irritably and then poured some out and sipped it.

Jimmy had probably gone straight home. He generally did. He wasn't a great one for going out, and didn't seem to have many friends except, of course, Elsie Lumley, who'd been in repertory with him, but that was all over now and she was safely married, or was she? Elsie Lumley, judging from what she knew of her, was the type that would be reluctant to let any old love die, married or not married. Elsie Lumley! Pretty, perhaps rather over-vivacious, certainly talented. She'd be a star in a year or two if she behaved herself. The picture of Elsie and Jimmy together was unbearable – even though it all happened years ago – it *had* happened and had gone on for quite a long while, too. Elsie lying in his arms, pulling his head down to her mouth, running her fingers through his hair — Diana put down the cup of Ovaltine with a bang that spilt a lot of it into the saucer. She felt sick, as though something were dragging her heart down into her stomach. If Jimmy had gone straight home he'd be in his flat now, in bed probably, reading. There really wasn't any valid reason in the world why she shouldn't ring him up. If he didn't answer, he was out, and there was nothing else to do about it. If he was in, even if he had dropped off to sleep, he wouldn't really mind her just ringing up to say 'Good night.'

She put out her hand to dial his number, then withdrew it again. It would be awful if someone else was there and answered the telephone, not that it was very likely, he only had a bed-sitting room, but still he might have asked Bob Harley or Walter Grayson home for a drink. If Walter Grayson heard her voice on the telephone it would be all over the theatre by to-morrow evening. He was one of those born theatrical gossips, amusing certainly, and quite a good actor, but definitely dangerous. She could, of course, disguise her voice. Just that twang of refined cockney that she had used in *The Short Year*. She put out her hand again, and again withdrew it. 'I'll have another cigarette and by the time I've smoked it, I shall decide whether to ring him up or not.' She hoisted herself up on the pillow and lit a cigarette, methodically and with pleasure. The ache had left her heart and she felt happier – unaccountably so, really; nothing had happened except the possibility of action, of lifting the receiver and dialling a number, of hearing his voice – rather sleepy, probably – saying: 'Hallo, who is it?' She puffed at her cigarette luxuriously watching the smoke curl up into the air. It was blue when it spiralled up from the end of the cigarette and grey when she blew it out of her mouth. It might, of course, irritate him being rung up, he might think she was being indiscreet or tiresome or even trying to check up on him: trying to find out whether he'd gone straight home, and whether he was alone or not.

How horrible if she rang up and he wasn't alone: if she heard his voice say, just as he was lifting the receiver: 'Don't move, darling, it's probably a wrong number,' something ordinary like that, so simple and so ordinary, implying everything, giving the whole game away. After all, he was young and good-looking, and they had neither of them vowed any vows of fidelity. It really wouldn't be so surprising if he indulged in a little fun on the side every now and then. Conducting a secret liaison with the star of the theatre in which you work, must be a bit of a strain from time to time. A little undemanding, light, casual love with somebody else might be a relief.

Diana crushed out her cigarette angrily, her hands were shaking and she felt sick again. She swung her legs off the bed and, sitting on the edge of it, dialled his number viciously, as though she had found him out already; caught him red-handed. She listened to the ringing tone, it rang in twos – brrr-brrr – brrr-brrr. The telephone was next to his bed, that she knew, because once when she had dropped him home he had asked her in to see his hovel. It was a bed-sitting-room on the ground floor in one of those small, old-fashioned streets that run down to the river from John Street, Adelphi . . . brr-brr – brr-brrr – she might have dialled the wrong number. She hung up and then re-dialled it, again the ringing tone, depressing and monotonous. He was out – he was out somewhere – but where could he possibly be? One more chance, she'd call the operator and ask her to give the number a special ring, just in case there had been a mistake.

The operator was most obliging, but after a few minutes her voice, detached and impersonal, announced that there was no reply from the number and that should she call again later? Diana said no, it didn't matter, she'd call in the morning. She replaced the receiver slowly, wearily, as though it were too heavy to hold any longer, then she buried her face in her hands.

Presently she got up again and began to walk up and down

the room. The bed, rumpled where she had lain on it, but turned down, with her nightdress laid out, ready to get into, tortured her with the thought of the hours she would lie awake in it. Even medinal, if she were stupid enough to take a couple of tablets before a matinée, wouldn't be any use to-night. That was what was so wonderful about being in love, it made you so happy! She laughed bitterly aloud and then caught herself laughing bitterly aloud and, just for a second, really laughed. Just a grain of humour left after all. She stopped in front of a long glass and addressed herself in a whisper, but with clear, precise enunciation as though she were trying to explain something to an idiot child. 'I don't care,' she said, 'I don't care if it's cheap or humiliating or unwise or undignified or mad, I'm going to do it, so there. I'm going to do it now, and if I have to wait all night in the street I shall see him, do you understand? I shall see him before I go to sleep, I don't mind if it's only for a moment, I shall see him. If the play closes to-morrow night. If I'm the scandal of London. If the stars fall out of the sky. If the world comes to an end! I shall see him before I go to sleep to-night. If he's alone or with somebody else. If he's drunk, sober or doped, I intend to see him. If he is in and his lights are out I shall bang on the window until I wake him and if, when I wake him, he's in bed with man, woman or child, I shall at least know. Beyond arguments and excuses I shall *know*. I don't care how foolish and neurotic I may appear to him. I don't care how high my position is, or how much I trail my pride in the dust. What's position anyway, and what's pride? To hell with them. I'm in love and I'm desperately unhappy. I know there's no reason to be unhappy, no cause for jealousy and that I should be ashamed of myself at my age, or at any age, for being so uncontrolled and for allowing this God-damned passion or obsession or whatever it is to conquer me, but there it is. It can't be helped. No more fighting – no more efforts to behave beautifully. I'm going to see him – I'm going now – and if he is unkind or angry and turns away from me I shall lie down in the gutter and howl.'

She picked up her hat from the sofa in the sitting-room,

turned out all the lights, glanced in her bag to see if she had
her keys all right and enough money for a taxi, and went
out on to the landing, shutting the door furtively behind her.
She debated for a moment whether to ring for the lift or slip
down the stairs, finally deciding on the latter as it would be
better on the whole if the lift man didn't see her. He lived in
the basement and there was little chance of him catching her
unless by bad luck she happened to coincide with any of the
other tenants coming in. She got out into the street unobserved and set off briskly in the direction of Orchard Street.
It was a fine night, fortunately, but there had been rain earlier
on and the roads were shining under the lights. She waited on
the corner of Orchard Street and Portman Square for a taxi
that came lolling towards her from the direction of Great
Cumberland Place. She told the driver to stop just opposite
the Little Theatre in John Street, Adelphi, and got in. The
cab smelt musty and someone had been smoking a pipe in
it. On the seat beside her, something white caught her eye;
she turned it over gingerly with her gloved hand, and discovered that it was a programme of her own play, with a large
photograph of herself on the cover. She looked at the photograph critically. The cab was rattling along Oxford Street
now, and the light was bright enough. The photograph had
been taken a year ago in a Molyneux sports dress and small
hat. It was a three-quarter length and she was sitting on the
edge of a sofa, her profile half turned away from the camera.
She looked young in it, although the poise of the head was
assured, perhaps a trifle too assured. She looked a little hard
too, she thought, a little ruthless. She wondered if she was,
really. If this journey she was making now, this unwise, neurotic excursion, merely boiled down to being an unregenerate
determination to get what she wanted, when she wanted it, at
no matter what price. She thought it over calmly, this business of being determined. After all, it was largely that, plus
undoubted talent and personality, that got her where she was
to-day. She wondered if she were popular in the theatre. She
knew the stage-hands liked her, of course, they were easy;

just remembering to say 'thank you,' when any of them held
open a door for her or 'good evening,' when she passed them
on the stage was enough – they were certainly easy because
their manners were good, and so were hers; but the rest of
the company – not Ronnie, naturally, he was in more or less
the same position as herself; the others, little Cynthia French,
for instance, the ingenue, did she hate her bitterly in secret?
Did she envy her and wish her to fail? Was all that wide-
eyed, faintly servile eagerness to please, merely masking an
implacable ambition, a sweet, strong, female loathing? She
thought not on the whole, Cynthia was far too timid a creature, unless, of course, she was a considerably finer actress
off the stage than she was on. Walter Grayson, she knew,
liked her all right. She'd known him for years, they'd been in
several plays together. Lottie Carnegie was certainly waspish
at moments, but only with that innate defensiveness of an
elderly actress who hadn't quite achieved what she originally set out to achieve. There were several of them about,
old-timers without any longer much hope left of becoming
stars, but with enough successful work behind them to assure
their getting good character parts. They all had their little
mannerisms and peculiarities and private fortresses of pride.
Lottie was all right really, in fact as far as she, Diana, was
concerned she was all sweetness and light, but, of course,
that might be because she hated Ronnie. Once, years ago
apparently, he had been instrumental in having her turned
down for a part for which he considered her unsuitable. The
others liked her well enough, she thought, at least she hoped
they did; it was horrid not to be liked; but she hadn't any
illusions as to what would happen if she made a false step.
This affair with Jimmy, for example. If that became known
in the theatre the whole of London would be buzzing with
it. She winced at the thought. That would be horrible. Once
more, by the light of a street lamp at the bottom of the
Haymarket, she looked at the photograph. She wondered if
she had looked like that to the man with the pipe to whom
the programme had belonged; whether he had taken his wife

with him or his mistress; whether they'd liked the play and cried dutifully in the last act, or been bored and disappointed and wished they'd gone to a musical comedy. How surprised they'd be if they knew that the next person to step into the taxi after they'd left it was Diana Reed, Diana Reed herself, the same woman they had so recently been applauding, as she bowed and smiled at them in that shimmering silver evening gown – that reminded her to tell Dora at the matinée to-morrow that the paillettes where her cloak fastened were getting tarnished and that she must either ring up the shop or see if Mrs Blake could deal with it in the wardrobe.

The taxi drew up with a jerk opposite to the Little Theatre. Diana got out and paid the driver. He said: 'Good night, Miss,' and drove away down the hill, leaving her on the edge of the kerb feeling rather dazed, almost forgetting what she was there for. The urgency that had propelled her out of her flat and into that taxi seemed to have evaporated somewhere between Oxford street and here. Perhaps it was the photograph on the programme, the reminder of herself as others saw her, as she should be, poised and well-dressed with head held high, not in contempt, nothing supercilious about it, but secure and dignified, above the arena. Those people who had taken that taxi, who had been to the play – how shocked they'd be if they could see her now, not just standing alone in a dark street, that wouldn't of course shock them particularly, merely surprise them; but if they could know, by some horrid clairvoyance, why she was here. If, just for an instant, they could see into her mind. Diana Reed, that smooth, gracious creature whose stage loves and joys and sorrows they had so often enjoyed, furtively loitering about in the middle of the night in the hope of spending a few minutes with a comparatively insignificant young man whom she liked going to bed with. Diana resolutely turned in the opposite direction from Jimmy's street and walked round by the side of the Tivoli into the Strand. Surely it was a little more than that? Surely she was being unnecessarily hard on herself. There was a sweetness about Jimmy, a quality, apart from his damned sex appeal. To begin with, he was well-bred, a gentleman. (What a weak, nauseating alibi, as though that could possibly matter one way or the other and yet, of course, it did.) His very gentleness, his strict code of behaviour. His fear, so much stronger even than hers, that anyone should discover their secret. Also he was intelligent, infinitely more knowledgeable and better read than she. All that surely made a difference, surely justified her behaviour a little bit? She walked along the Strand towards Fleet Street, as though she were hurrying to keep an important appointment. There were still a lot of people about and on the other side of the street two drunken men were happily staggering along with their arms round each other's necks, singing 'Ramona.' Suddenly to her horror she saw Violet Cassel and Donald Ross approaching her, they had obviously been supping at the Savoy and decided to walk a little before taking a cab. With an instinctive gesture she jammed her hat down over her eyes and darted into Heppell's, so quickly that she collided with a woman who was just coming out and nearly knocked her down. The woman said, 'Christ, a fugitive from a chain gang?' and waving aside Diana's apologies, went unsteadily into the street. Diana, faced with the enquiring stare of the man behind the counter and slightly unhinged by her encounter in the doorway, and the fact that Donald and Violet were at that moment passing the shop, racked her brains for something to buy. Her eyes lighted on a bottle of emerald green liquid labelled 'Ess Viotto for the hands'. 'I should like that,' she said, pointing to it. The man, without looking at her again, wrapped it up and handed it to her. She paid for it and went out of of the shop. Violet and Donald were crossing over further down. She walked slowly back the way she had come. An empty taxi cruising along close to the kerb passed her and almost stopped. She hailed it, gave the driver her address, got in and sank thankfully back on to the seat. 'A fugitive from a chain gang.' She smiled and closed her eyes for a moment. 'What an escape!' She felt utterly exhausted as if he had passed through a tremendous crisis, she was safe,

safe as houses, safe from herself and humiliation and indignity. No more of such foolishness. She wondered whether or not she had replaced the stopper in the thermos. She hoped she had, because the prospect of sitting up, snug in bed, with a mind at peace and a cup of Ovaltine seemed heavenly. She opened her eyes as the taxi was turning into Lower Regent Street and looked out of the window. A man in a camel-hair coat and a soft brown hat was waiting on the corner to cross the road. Jimmy! She leant forward hurriedly and tried to slide the glass window back in order to tell the driver to stop, but it wouldn't budge. She rapped on the glass violently. The driver looked round in surprise and drew into the kerb. She was out on the pavement in a second, fumbling in her bag. 'I've forgotten something,' she said breathlessly. 'Here' – she gave him a half a crown and turned and ran towards Jimmy. He had crossed over by now and was just turning into Cockspur Street. She had to wait a moment before crossing because two cars came by and then a bus. When she got round the corner she could still see him just passing the lower entrance to the Carlton. She put on a great spurt and caught up with him just as he was about to cross the Haymarket. He turned his head slightly just as she was about to clutch at his sleeve. He was a pleasant-looking young man with fair hair and a little moustache. Diana stopped dead in her tracks and watched him cross the road, a stream of traffic went by and he was lost to view. She stood there trying to get her breath and controlling an overpowering desire to burst into tears. She stamped her foot hard as though by so doing she could crush her agonising, bitter disappointment into the ground.

A passing policeman looked at her suspiciously, so she moved miserably across the road and walked on towards Trafalgar Square, past the windows of the shipping agencies filled with smooth models of ocean liners. She stopped at one of them for a moment and rested her forehead against the cold glass, staring at a white steamer with two yellow funnels; its decks meticulously scrubbed and its paintwork shining in the light from the street lamps. Then, pulling herself together, she set off firmly in the direction of the Adelphi. No use dithering about any more. She had, in leaving the flat in the first place, obeyed an irresistible, but perfectly understandable impulse to see Jimmy. Since then, she had hesitated and vacillated and tormented herself into a state bordering on hysteria. No more of that, it was stupid, worse than stupid, this nerve-racking conflict between reason and emotion was insane. Reason had done its best and failed. No reason in the world could now woo her into going back to that empty flat without seeing Jimmy. Fate had ranged itself against reason. If Fate hadn't dressed that idiotic young man with a moustache in Jimmy's camel-hair coat and Jimmy's hat, all would have been well. If Fate had arbitrarily decided, as it apparently had, that she was to make a fool herself, then make a fool of herself she would. Jimmy was probably fast asleep by now and would be furious at being awakened. She was, very possibly, by this lamentable, silly behaviour, about to wreck something precious, something which, in future years, she might have been able to look back upon with a certain wistful nostalgia. Now of course, after she had observed Jimmy's irritation and thinly-veiled disgust, after he had kissed her and comforted her and packed her off home in a taxi, she would have to face one fact clearly and bravely and that fact would be that a love affair, just another love affair, was ended. Not a violent break or a quarrel or anything like that, just a gentle, painful decline, something to be glossed over and forgotten. By the time she had reached the top of Jimmy's street there were tears in her eyes.

She walked along the pavement on tip-toe. His windows were dark, she peered into them over the area railings. His curtains were not drawn, his room was empty. She walked over the road to where there was a street lamp and looked at her wrist-watch. Ten past two. She stood there leaning against a railing, not far from the lamp, for several minutes. There were no lights in any of the houses except one on the corner. On the top floor, a little square of yellow blind with a shadow occasionally moving behind it. On her left, beyond

the end of the road which was a cul-de-sac, were the trees
of the gardens along the embankment; they rustled slightly
in the damp breeze. Now and then she heard the noise of
a train rumbling hollowly over Charing Cross bridge, and
occasionally the mournful hoot of a tug on the river. Where
on earth could he be at this hour of the morning? He hated
going out, or at least so he always said. He didn't drink
much either. He wouldn't be sitting up with a lot of cronies
just drinking. He was very responsible about his job too and
in addition to a matinée to-morrow there was an understudy
rehearsal at eleven – she knew that because she had happened
to notice it on the board. He couldn't have gone home to his
parents; they lived on the Isle of Wight. She sauntered slowly
up to the corner of John Street and looked up and down it.
No taxi in sight, nothing, only a cat stalking along by the
railings. She stooped down and said 'Puss, puss' to it but it
ignored her and disappeared down some steps. Suddenly a
taxi turned into the lower end of the street. Diana took to her
heels and ran. Supposing it were Jimmy coming home with
somebody – supposing he looked out and saw her standing
on the pavement, watching him. Panic seized her. On the
left, on the opposite side of the road from the house where
he lived, was a dark archway. She dived into it and pressed
herself flat against the wall. The taxi turned into the street
and drew up. She peeped round the corner and saw a fat
man and a woman in evening dress get out of it and let
themselves into one of the houses. When the taxi had backed
and driven away she emerged from the archway. 'I'll walk,'
she said to herself out loud. 'I'll walk up and down this street
twenty times and if he hasn't come by then I'll – I'll walk up
and down it another twenty times.' She started walking and
laughing at herself at the same time, quite genuine laughter;
she listened to it and it didn't sound in the least hysterical.
I'm feeling better, she thought, none of it matters nearly as
much as I think it does, I've been making mountains out of
molehills. I'm enjoying this really, it's an adventure. There's
something strange and exciting in being out alone in the city

at dead of night, I must do it more often. She laughed again at the picture of herself solemnly setting out two or three times a week on solitary nocturnal jaunts. After about the fifteenth time she had turned and retraced her steps she met Jimmy face to face at the corner. He stopped in amazement and said, 'My God – Diana – what on earth –'

She held out to him the parcel she'd been holding.

'I've brought you a present,' she said with a little giggle. 'It's Ess Viotto – for the hands!'

The Little Mermaid

HANS CHRISTIAN ANDERSEN

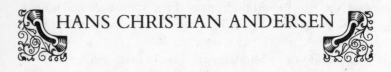

HANS CHRISTIAN ANDERSEN (1805–1875). This Danish writer is known the world over for his fairy stories. 'The Little Mermaid' is one of the most delightful and touching and is so famous that it is commemorated by a statue in the harbour in Copenhagen.

FAR out in the wide sea – where the water is blue as the loveliest cornflower, and clear as the purest crystal, where it is so deep that very, very many church-towers must be heaped one upon another, in order to reach from the lowest depth to the surface above – dwell the Mer-people.

Now you must not imagine that there is nothing but sand below the water: no, indeed, far from it! Trees and plants of wondrous beauty grow there, whose stems and leaves are so light, that they are waved to and fro by the slightest motion of the water, almost as if they were living beings. Fishes, great and small, glide in and out among the branches, just as birds fly about among our trees.

Where the water is deepest, stands the palace of the Mer-king. The walls of this palace are of coral, and the high, pointed windows are of amber; the roof, however, is composed of mussel-shells, which, as the billows pass over them, are continually opening and shutting. This looks exceedingly pretty, especially as each of these mussel-shells contains a number of bright, glittering pearls, one only of which would be the most costly ornament in the diadem of a king in the upper world.

The Mer-king who lived in this palace, had been for many

years a widower; his old mother managed the household affairs for him. She was, on the whole, a sensible sort of a lady, although extremely proud of her high birth and station, on which account she wore twelve oysters on her tail, whilst the other inhabitants of the sea, even those of distinction, were allowed only six. In every other respect she merited unlimited praise, especially for the affection she showed to the six little princesses, her grand-daughters. These were all very beautiful children; the youngest was, however, the most lovely; her skin was as soft and delicate as a roseleaf, her eyes were of as deep a blue as the sea, but like all other mermaids, she had no feet, her body ended in a tail like that of a fish.

The whole day long the children used to play in the spacious apartments of the palace, where beautiful flowers grew out of the walls on all sides around them. When the great amber windows were opened, fishes would swim into these apartments as swallows fly into our rooms; but the fishes were bolder than the swallows, they swam straight up to the little princesses, ate from their hands, and allowed themselves to be caressed.

In front of the palace there was a large garden, full of fiery red and dark blue trees, whose fruit glittered like gold, and whose flowers resembled a bright, burning sun. The sand that formed the soil of the garden was of a bright blue colour, something like flames of sulphur; and a strangely beautiful blue was spread over the whole, so that one might have fancied oneself raised very high in the air, with the sky at once above and below, certainly not at the bottom of the sea. When the waters were quite still, the sun might be seen looking like a purple flower, out of whose cup streamed forth the light of the world.

Each of the little princesses had her own plot in the garden, where she might plant and sow at her pleasure. One chose hers to be made in the shape of a whale, another preferred the figure of a mermaid, but the youngest had hers quite round like the sun, and planted in it only those flowers that were red, as the sun seemed to her. She was certainly a singular child, very quiet and thoughtful. Whilst her sisters were adorning themselves with all sorts of gay things that came out of a ship which had been wrecked, she asked for nothing but a beautiful white marble statue of a boy, which had been found in it. She put the statue in her garden, and planted a red weeping willow by its side. The tree grew up quickly, and let its long boughs fall upon the bright blue ground, where ever-moving shadows played in violet bues, as if boughs and root were embracing.

Nothing pleased the little princess more than to hear about the world of human beings living above the sea. She made her old grandmother tell her everything she knew about ships, towns, men, and land animals, and was particularly pleased when she heard that the flowers of the upper world had a pleasant fragrance (for the flowers of the sea are scentless), and that the woods were green, and the fishes fluttering among the branches of various gay colours, and that they could sing with a loud clear voice. The old lady meant birds, but she called them fishes, because her grand-children, having never seen a bird, would not otherwise have understood her.

'When you have attained your fifteenth year,' added she, 'you will be permitted to rise to the surface of the sea; you will then sit by moonlight in the clefts of the rocks, see the ships sail by, and learn to distinguish towns and men.'

The next year the eldest of the sisters reached this happy age, but the others – alas! the second sister was a year younger than the eldest, the third a year younger than the second, and so on; the youngest had still five whole years to wait till that joyful time should come when she also might rise to the surface of the water and see what was going on in the upper world; however, the eldest promised to tell the others of everything she might see, when the first day of her being of age arrived; for the grandmother gave them but little information, and there was so much that they wished to hear.

But none of all the sisters longed so ardently for the day

when she should be released from childish restraint as the youngest, she who had longest to wait, and was so quiet and thoughtful. Many a night she stood by the open windows, looking up through the clear blue water, whilst the fishes were leaping and playing around her. She could see the sun and the moon; their light was pale, but they appeared larger than they do to those who live in the upper world. If a shadow passed over them, she knew it must be either a whale or a ship sailing by full of human beings, who indeed little thought that, far beneath them, a little mermaiden was passionately stretching forth her white hands towards their ship's keel.

The day had now arrived when the eldest princess had attained her fifteenth year, and was therefore allowed to rise up to the surface of the sea.

When she returned she had a thousand things to relate. Her chief pleasure had been to sit upon a sandbank in the moonlight, looking at the large town which lay on the coast, where lights were beaming like stars, and where music was playing; she had heard the distant noise of men and carriages, she had seen the high church-towers, had listened to the ringing of the bells; and just because she could not go there she longed the more after all these things.

How attentively did her youngest sister listen to her words! And when she next stood at night time, by her open window, gazing upward through the blue waters, she thought so intensely of the great noisy city that she fancied she could hear the church-bells ringing.

Next year the second sister received permission to swim wherever she pleased. She rose to the surface of the sea, just when the sun was setting; and this sight so delighted her, that she declared it to be more beautiful than anything else she had seen above the waters.

'The whole sky seemed tinged with gold,' said she, 'and it is impossible for me to describe to you the beauty of the clouds. Now red, now violet, they glided over me; but still more swiftly flew over the water a flock of white swans, just where the sun was descending; I looked after them, but the sun disappeared, and the bright rosy light on the surface of the sea and on the edges of the clouds was gradually extinguished.'

It was now time for the third sister to visit the upper world. She was the boldest of the six, and ventured up a river. On its shores she saw green hills covered with woods and vine-yards, from among which arose houses and castles; she heard the birds singing, and the sun shone with so much power, that she was continually obliged to plunge below, in order to cool her burning face. In a little bay she met with a number of children, who were bathing and jumping about; she would have joined in their gambols, but the children fled back to land in great terror, and a little black animal barked at her in such a manner, that she herself was frightened at last, and swam back to the sea. She could not, however, forget the green woods, the verdant hills, and the pretty children, who, although they had no fins, were swimming about in the river so fearlessly.

The fourth sister was not so bold, she remained in the open sea, and said on her return home, she thought nothing could be more beautiful. She had seen ships sailing by, so far off that they looked like sea-gulls, she had watched the merry dolphins gambolling in the water, and the enormous whales, sending up into the air a thousand sparkling fountains.

The year after, the fifth sister attained her fifteenth year. Her birthday happened at a different season to that of her sisters; it was winter, the sea was of a green colour, and immense icebergs were floating on its surface. These, she said, looked like pearls; they were, however, much larger than the church-towers in the land of human beings. She sat down upon one of these pearls, and let the wind play with her long hair, but then all the ships hoisted their sails in terror, and escaped as quickly as possible. In the evening the sky was covered with sails; and whilst the great mountains of ice alternately sank and rose again, and beamed with a reddish glow, flashes of lightning burst forth from the clouds and the thunder rolled on, peal after peal. The sails of all the ships were instantly furled, and horror and affright reigned on board, but the princess sat still on the iceberg, looking unconcernedly at the blue zig-zag of the flashes.

The first time that either of these sisters rose out of the sea, she was quite enchanted at the sight of so many new and beautiful objects, but the novelty was soon over, and it was not long ere their own home appeared more attractive than the upper world, for there only did they find everything agreeable.

Many an evening would the five sisters rise hand in hand from the depths of the ocean. Their voices were far sweeter than any human voice, and when a storm was coming on, they would swim in front of the ships, and sing – oh! how sweetly did they sing! describing the happiness of those who lived at the bottom of the sea, and entreating the sailors not to be afraid, but to come down to them.

The mariners, however, did not understand their words; they fancied the song was only the whistling of the wind, and thus they lost the hidden glories of the sea; for if their ships were wrecked, all on board were drowned, and none but dead men ever entered the Mer-king's palace.

Whilst the sisters were swimming at evening time, the youngest would remain motionless and alone, in her father's palace, looking up after them. She would have wept, but mermaids cannot weep, and therefore, when they are troubled, suffer infinitely more than human beings do.

'Oh! if I were but fifteen!' sighed she, 'I know that I should love the upper world and its inhabitants so much.'

At last the time she had so longed for arrived.

'Well, now it is your turn,' said the grandmother, 'come here that I may adorn you like your sisters.' And she wound around her hair a wreath of white lilies, whose every petal was the half of a pearl, and then commanded eight large oysters to fasten themselves to the princess's tail, in token of her high rank.

'But that is so very uncomfortable!' said the little princess.

'One must not mind slight inconveniences when one wishes to look well,' said the old lady.

How willingly would the princess have given up all this splendour, and exchanged her heavy crown for the red flowers of her garden, which were so much more becoming to her. But she dared not do so. 'Farewell,' said she; and she rose from the sea, light as a flake of foam.

When, for the first time in her life, she appeared on the surface of the water, the sun had just sunk below the horizon, the clouds were beaming with bright golden and rosy hues, the evening star was shining in the pale western sky, the air was mild and refreshing, and the sea as smooth as a looking-glass. A large ship with three masts lay on the still waters; one sail only was unfurled, but not a breath was stirring, and the sailors were quietly seated on the cordage and ladders of the vessel. Music and song resounded from the deck, and after it grew dark hundreds of lamps all on a sudden burst forth into light, whilst innumerable flags were fluttering overhead. The little mermaid swam close up to the captain's cabin, and every now and then when the ship was raised by the motion of the water, she could look through the clear window panes. She saw within, many richly dressed men; the handsomest among them was a young prince with large black eyes. He could not certainly be more than sixteen years old, and it was in honour of his birthday that a grand festival was being celebrated. The crew were dancing on the deck, and when the young prince appeared among them, a hundred rockets were sent up into the air, turning night into day, and so terrifying the little mermaid, that for some minutes she plunged beneath the water. However, she soon raised her little head again, and then it seemed as if all the stars were falling down upon her. Such a fiery shower she had never seen before, never had she heard that men possessed such wonderful powers. Large suns revolved around her, bright fishes swam in the air, and everything was reflected perfectly on the clear surface of the sea. It was so light in the ship, that everything could be seen distinctly. Oh! how happy the young prince was! he shook hands with the sailors, laughed and jested with them, whilst sweet notes of music mingled with the silence of night.

It was now late, but the little mermaid could not tear herself away from the ship and the handsome young prince. She remained looking through the cabin window, rocked to and fro by the waves. There was a foaming and fermentation in the depths beneath, and the ship began to move on faster, the sails were spread, the waves rose high, thick clouds gathered over the sky, and the noise of distant thunder was heard. The sailors perceived that a storm was coming on, so they again furled the sails. The great vessel was tossed about on the tempestuous ocean like a light boat, and the waves rose to an immense height, towering over the ship, which alternately sank beneath and rose above them. To the little mermaid this seemed most delightful, but the ship's crew thought very differently. The vessel cracked, the stout masts bent under the violence of the billows, the waters rushed in. For a minute the ship tottered to and fro, then the main-mast broke, as if it had been a reed; the ship turned over, and was filled with water. The little mermaid now perceived that the crew was in danger, for she herself was forced to beware of the beams and splinters torn from the vessel, and floating about on the waves. But at the same time it became pitch dark so that she could not distinguish anything; presently, however, a dreadful flash of lightning disclosed to her the whole of the wreck. Her eyes sought the young prince – the same instant the ship sank to the bottom. At first she was delighted, thinking that the prince must now come to her abode, but she soon remembered that man cannot live in water, and that therefore if the prince ever entered her palace, it would be as a corpse.

'Die! no, he must not die!' She swam through the fragments with which the water was strewn regardless of the danger she was incurring, and at last found the prince all but exhausted, and with great difficulty keeping his head above water. He had already closed his eyes, and must inevitably have been drowned, had not the little mermaid come to his rescue. She seized hold of him and kept him above water, suffering the current to bear them on together.

Towards morning the storm was hushed; no trace, however, remained of the ship. The sun rose like fire out of the sea; his beams seemed to restore colour to the prince's cheeks, but his eyes were still closed. The mermaid kissed his high forehead and stroked his wet hair away from his face. He looked like the marble statue in her garden; she kissed him again and wished most fervently that he might recover.

She now saw the dry land with its mountains glittering with snow. A green wood extended along the coast, and at the entrance of the wood stood a chapel or convent, she could not be sure which. Citron and lemon trees grew in the garden adjoining it, an avenue of tall palm trees led up to the door. The sea here formed a little bay, in which the water was quite smooth but very deep, and under the cliffs there were dry firm sands. Hither swam the little mermaid with the seemingly dead prince; she laid him upon the warm sand, and took care to place his head high, and to turn his face to the sun.

The bells began to ring in the large white building which stood before her, and a number of young girls came out to walk in the garden. The mermaid went away from the shore, hid herself behind some stones, covered her head with foam, so that her little face could not be seen, and watched the prince with unremitting attention.

It was not long before one of the young girls approached. She seemed quite frightened at finding the prince in this state, apparently dead; soon, however, she recovered herself, and ran back to call her sisters. The little mermaid saw that the prince revived, and that all around smiled kindly and joyfully upon him – for her, however, he looked not, he knew not that it was she who had saved him, and when the prince was taken into the house, she felt so sad, that she immediately plunged beneath the water, and returned to her father's palace.

If she had been before quiet and thoughtful, she now grew still more so. Her sisters asked her what she had seen in the upper world, but she made no answer.

Many an evening she rose to the place where she had left the prince. She saw the snow on the mountains melt, the fruits in the garden ripen and gathered, but the prince she never saw, so she always returned sorrowfully to her subterranean abode. Her only pleasure was to sit in her little garden gazing on the beautiful statue so like the prince. She cared no longer for her flowers; they grew up in wild luxuriance, covered the steps, and entwined their long stems and tendrils among the boughs of the trees, so that her whole garden became a bower.

At last, being unable to conceal her sorrow any longer, she revealed the secret to one of her sisters, who told it to the other princesses, and they to some of their friends. Among them was a young mermaid who recollected the prince, having been an eye-witness herself to the festivities in the ship; she knew also in what country the prince lived, and the name of its king.

'Come, little sister!' said the princesses, and embracing her they rose together arm in arm, out of the water, just in front of the prince's palace.

This palace was built of bright yellow stones, a flight of white marble steps led from it down to the sea. A gilded cupola crowned the building, and white marble figures, which might almost have been taken for real men and women, were placed among the pillars surrounding it. Through the clear glass of the high windows one might look into magnificent apartments hung with silken curtains, the walls adorned with magnificent paintings. It was a real treat to the little royal mermaids to behold so splendid an abode; they gazed through the windows of one of the largest rooms, and in the centre saw a fountain playing, whose waters sprang up so high as to reach the glittering cupola above, through which the sunbeams fell dancing on the water, and brightening the pretty plants which grew around it.

The little mermaid now knew where her beloved prince dwelt, and henceforth she went there almost every evening. She often approached nearer the land than her sisters had ventured, and even swam up the narrow channel that flowed under the marble balcony. Here on a bright moonlight night, she would watch the young prince who believed himself alone.

Sometimes she saw him sailing on the water in a gaily-painted boat with many coloured flags waving above. She would then hide among the green reeds which grew on the banks, listening to his voice, and if any one in the boat noticed the rustling of her long silver veil, which was caught now and then by the light breeze, they only fancied it was a swan flapping his wings.

Many a night when the fishermen were casting their nets by the beacon's light, she heard them talking of the prince, and relating the noble actions he had performed. She was then so happy, thinking how she had saved his life when struggling with the waves, and remembering how his head had rested on her bosom, and how she had kissed him when he knew nothing of it, and could never even dream of such a thing.

Human beings became more and more dear to her every day; she wished that she were one of them. Their world seemed to her much larger than that of the mer-people; they could fly over the ocean in their ships, as well as climb to the summits of those high mountains that rose above the clouds; and their wooded domains extended much farther than a mermaid's eye could penetrate.

There were many things that she wished to hear explained, but her sisters could not give her any satisfactory answer; she was again obliged to have recourse to the old queen-mother, who knew a great deal about the upper world, which she used to call 'the country above the sea.'

'Do men when they are not drowned live for ever?' she asked one day. 'Do not they die as we do, who live at the bottom of the sea?'

'Yes,' was the grandmother's reply, 'they must die like us, and their life is much shorter than ours. We live to the age of three hundred years, but when we die, we become foam on the sea, and are not allowed even to share a grave among those that are dear to us. We have no immortal souls, we can never live again, and are like the grass which, when once cut down, is withered for ever. Human beings, on the contrary, have souls that continue to live, when their bodies become dust, and as we rise out of the water to admire the abode of man, they ascend to glorious unknown dwellings in the skies which we are not permitted to see.'

'Why have not *we* immortal souls?' asked the little mermaid. 'I would willingly give up my three hundred years to be a human being for only one day, thus to become entitled to that heavenly world above.'

'You must not think of that,' answered her grandmother, 'it is much better as it is; we live longer and are far happier than human beings.'

'So I must die, and be dashed like foam over the sea, never to rise again and hear the gentle murmur of the ocean, never again see the beautiful flowers and the bright sun! Tell me, dear grandmother, are there no means by which I may obtain an immortal soul?'

'No!' replied the old lady. 'It is true that if thou couldst so win the affections of a human being as to become dearer to him than either father or mother; if he loved thee with all his heart, and promised whilst the priest joined his hands with thine to be always faithful to thee; then his soul would flow into thine, and thou wouldst then become partaker of human bliss. But that can never be! for what in our eyes is the most beautiful part of our body, the tail, the inhabitants of the earth think hideous, they cannot bear it. To appear handsome to them, the body must have two clumsy props which they call legs.'

The little mermaid sighed and looked mournfully at the scaly part of her form, otherwise so fair and delicate.

'We are happy,' added the old lady, 'we shall jump and

swim about merrily for three hundred years; that is a long time, and afterwards we shall repose peacefully in death. This evening we have a court ball.'

The ball which the queen-mother spoke of was far more splendid than any that earth has ever seen. The walls of the saloon were of crystal, very thick, but yet very clear; hundreds of large mussel-shells were planted in rows along them; these shells were some of rose-colour, some green as grass, but all sending forth a bright light, which not only illuminated the whole apartment, but also shone through the glassy walls so as to light up the waters around for a great space, and making the scales of the numberless fishes, great and small, crimson and purple, silver and gold-coloured, appear more brilliant than ever.

Through the centre of the saloon flowed a bright, clear stream, on the surface of which danced mermen and mermaids to the melody of their own sweet voices, voices far sweeter than those of the dwellers upon earth. The little princess sang more harmoniously than any other, and they clapped their hands and applauded her. She was pleased at this, for she knew well that there was neither on earth or in the sea a more beautiful voice than hers. But her thoughts soon returned to the world above her; she could not forget the handsome prince; she could not control her sorrow at not having an immortal soul. She stole away from her father's palace, and whilst all was joy within, she sat alone lost in thought in her little neglected garden. On a sudden she heard the tones of horns resounding over the water far away in the distance, and she said to herself, 'Now he is going out to hunt, he whom I love more than my father and my mother, with whom my thoughts are constantly occupied, and to whom I would so willingly trust the happiness of my life! All! all, will I risk to win him – and an immortal soul! Whilst my sisters are still dancing in the palace, I will go to the enchantress whom I have hitherto feared so much, but who is, nevertheless, the only person who can advise and help me.'

So the little mermaid left the garden, and went to the foaming whirlpool beyond which dwelt the enchantress. She had never been this way before – neither flowers nor sea-grass bloomed along her path; she had to traverse an extent of bare grey sand till she reached the whirlpool, whose waters were eddying and whizzing like mill-wheels, tearing everything they could seize along with them into the abyss below. She was obliged to make her way through this horrible place, in order to arrive at the territory of the enchantress. Then she had to pass through a boiling, slimy bog, which the enchantress called her turf-moor: her house stood in a wood beyond this, and a strange abode it was. All the trees and bushes around were polypi, looking like hundred-headed serpents shooting up out of the ground; their branches were long slimy arms with finges of worms, every member, from the root to the uttermost tip, ceaselessly moving and extending on all sides. Whatever they seized they fastened upon so that it could not loosen itself from their grasp. The little mermaid stood still for a minute, looking at this horrible wood; her heart beat with fear, and she would certainly have returned without attaining her object, had she not remembered the prince – and immortality. The thought gave her new courage, she bound up her long waving hair, that the polypi might not catch hold of it, crossed her delicate arms over her bosom, and, swifter than a fish can glide through the water, she passed these unseemly trees, who stretched their eager arms after her in vain. She could not, however, help seeing that every polypus had something in his grasp, held as firmly by a thousand little arms as if enclosed by iron bands. The whitened skeletons of a number of human beings who had been drowned in the sea, and had sunk into the abyss, grinned horribly from the arms of these polypi; helms, chests, skeletons of land animals were also held in their embrace; among other things might be seen even a little mermaid whom they had seized and strangled! What a fearful sight for the unfortunate princess!

But she got safely through this wood of horrors, and then

arrived at a slimy place, where immense fat snails were crawling about, and in the midst of this place stood a house built of the bones of unfortunate people who had been shipwrecked. Here sat the witch caressing a toad in the same manner as some persons would a pet bird. The ugly fat snails she called her chickens, and she permitted them to crawl about her.

'I know well what you would ask of me,' said she to the little princess. 'Your wish is foolish enough, yet it shall be fulfilled, though its accomplishment is sure to bring misfortune on you, my fairest princess. You wish to get rid of your tail, and to have instead two stilts like those of human beings, in order that a young prince may fall in love with you, and that you may obtain an immortal soul. Is it not so?' Whilst the witch spoke these words, she laughed so violently that her pet toad and snails fell from her lap. 'You come just at the right time,' continued she; 'had you come after sunset, it would not have been in my power to have helped you before another year. I will prepare for you a drink with which you must swim to land, you must sit down upon the shore and swallow it, and then your tail will fall and shrink up to the things which men call legs. This transformation will, however, be very painful; you will feel as though a sharp knife passed through your body. All who look on you after you have been thus changed will say that you are the loveliest child of earth they have ever seen; you will retain your peculiar undulating movements, and no dancer will move so lightly, but every step you take will cause you pain all but unbearable; it will seem to you as though you were walking on the sharp edges of swords, and your blood will flow. Can you endure all this suffering? If so, I will grant your request.'

'Yes, I will,' answered the princess, with a faltering voice; for she remembered her dear prince, and the immortal soul which her suffering might win.

'Only consider,' said the witch, 'that you can never again become a mermaid, when once you have received a human form. You may never return to your sisters, and your father's palace; and unless you shall win the prince's love to such a degree, that he shall leave father and mother for you, that you shall be mixed up with all his thoughts and wishes, and unless the priest join your hands, so that you become man and wife, you will never obtain the immortality you seek. The morrow of the day on which he is united to another, will see your death; your heart will break with sorrow, and you will be changed to foam on the sea.'

'Still I will venture!' said the little mermaid, pale and trembling as a dying person.

'Besides all this, I must be paid, and it is no slight thing that I require for my trouble. Thou hast the sweetest voice of all the dwellers in the sea, and thou thinkest by its means to charm the prince; this voice, however, I demand as my recompense. The best thing thou possessest I require in exchange for my magic drink; for I shall be obliged to sacrifice my own blood, in order to give it the sharpness of a two-edged sword.'

'But if you take my voice from me,' said the princess, 'what have I left with which to charm the prince?'

'Thy graceful form,' replied the witch, 'thy modest gait, and speaking eyes. With such as these, it will be easy to infatuate a vain human heart. Well now! hast thou lost courage? Put out thy little tongue, that I may cut it off, and take it for myself, in return for my magic drink.'

'Be it so!' said the princess, and the witch took up her cauldron, in order to mix her potion. 'Cleanliness is a good thing,' remarked she, as she began to rub the cauldron with a handful of toads and snails. She then scratched her bosom, and let the black blood trickle down into the cauldron, every moment throwing in new ingredients, the smoke from the mixture assuming such horrible forms as were enough to fill beholders with terror, and a moaning and groaning proceeding from it, which might be compared to the weeping of crocodiles. The magic drink at length became clear and transparent as pure water; it was ready.

'Here it is!' said the witch to the princess, cutting out her tongue at the same moment. The poor little mermaid was now dumb: she could neither sing nor speak.

'If the polypi should attempt to seize you, as you pass through my little grove,' said the witch, 'you have only to sprinkle some of this magic drink over them, and their arms will burst into a thousand pieces.' But the princess had no need of this counsel, for the polypi drew hastily back, as soon as they perceived the bright phial, that glittered in her hand like a star; thus she passed safely through the formidable wood over the moor, and across the foaming mill-stream.

She now looked once again at her father's palace; the lamps in the saloon were extinguished, and all the family were asleep. She would not go in, for she could not speak if she did; she was about to leave her home for ever; her heart was ready to break with sorrow at the thought; she stole into the garden, plucked a flower from the bed of each of her sisters as a remembrance, kissed her hand again and again, and then rose through the dark blue waters to the world above.

The sun had not yet risen, when she arrived at the prince's dwelling, and ascended those well-known marble steps. The moon still shone in the sky when the little mermaid drank off the wonderful liquid contained in her phial, – she felt it run through her like a sharp knife, and she fell down in a swoon. When the sun rose, she awoke; and felt a burning pain in all her limbs, but – she saw standing close to her the object of her love, the handsome young prince, whose coal-black eyes were fixed inquiringly upon her. Full of shame she cast down her own, and perceived, instead of the long fish-tail she had hitherto borne, two slender legs; but she was quite naked, and tried in vain to cover herself with her long thick hair. The prince asked who she was, and how she had got there; and she, in reply, smiled and gazed upon him with her bright blue eyes, for alas! she could not speak. He then led her by the hand into the palace. She found that the witch had told her true; she felt as though she were walking on the edges of sharp swords, but she bore the pain willingly; on she passed, light as a zephyr, and all who saw her, wondered at her light undulating movements.

When she entered the palace, rich clothes of muslin and silk were brought to her; she was lovelier than all who dwelt there, but she could neither speak nor sing. Some female slaves, gaily dressed in silk and gold brocade, sung before the prince and his royal parents; and one of them distinguished herself by her clear sweet voice, which the prince applauded by clapping his hands. This made the little mermaid very sad, for she knew that she used to sing far better than the young slave. 'Alas!' thought she, 'if he did but know that, for his sake, I have given away my voice for ever.'

The slaves began to dance; our lovely little mermaiden then arose, stretched out her delicate white arms, and hovered gracefully about the room. Every motion displayed more and more the perfect symmetry and elegance of her figure; and the expression which beamed in her speaking eyes touched the hearts of the spectators far more than the song of the slaves.

All present were enchanted, but especially the young prince, who called her his dear little foundling. And she danced again and again, although every step cost her excessive pain. The prince then said she should always be with him; and accordingly a sleeping place was prepared for her on velvet cushions in the anteroom of his own apartment.

The prince caused a suit of male apparel to be made for her, in order that she might accompany him in his rides; so together they traversed the fragrant woods, where green boughs brushed against their shoulders, and the birds sang merrily among the fresh leaves. With him she climbed up steep mountains, and although her tender feet bled, so as to be remarked by the attendants, she only smiled, and followed her dear prince to the heights, whence they could see the clouds chasing each other beneath them, like a flock of birds migrating to other countries.

During the night, she would, when all in the palace were at rest, walk down the marble steps, in order to cool her feet in the deep waters; she would then think of those beloved ones, who dwelt in the lower world.

One night, as she was thus bathing her feet, her sisters swam together to the spot, arm in arm and singing, but alas! so mournfully! She beckoned to them, and they immediately recognized her, and told her how great was the mourning in her father's house for her loss. From this time the sisters visited her every night; and once they brought with them the old grandmother, who had not seen the upper world for a great many years; they likewise brought their father, the Mer-king, with his crown on his head; but these two old people did not venture near enough to land to be able to speak to her.

The little mermaiden became dearer and dearer to the prince every day; but he only looked upon her as a sweet, gentle child; and the thought of making her his wife never entered his head. And yet his wife she must be, ere she could receive an immortal soul; his wife she must be, or she would change into foam, and be driven restlessly over the billows of the sea!

'Dost thou not love me above all others?' her eyes seemed to ask, as he pressed her fondly in his arms, and kissed her lovely brow.

'Yes,' the prince would say, 'thou art dearer to me than any other, for no one is as good as thou art! Thou lovest me so much; and thou art so like a young maiden, whom I have seen but once, and may never see again. I was on board a ship, which was wrecked by a sudden tempest; the waves threw me on the shore, near a holy temple, where a number of young girls are occupied constantly with religious services. The youngest of them found me on the shore, and saved my life. I saw her only once, but her image is vividly impressed upon my memory, and her alone can I love. But she belongs to the holy temple; and thou who resemblest her so much hast been given to me for consolation; never will we be parted!'

'Alas! he does not know that it was I who saved his life,' thought the little mermaiden, sighing deeply; 'I bore him

over the wild waves, into the wooded bay, where the holy
temple stood; I sat behind the rocks, waiting till some one
should come. I saw the pretty maiden approach, whom he
loves more than me,' – and again she heaved a deep sigh,
for she could not weep – 'he said that the young girl belongs
to the holy temple; she never comes out into the world, so
they cannot meet each other again – and I am always with
him, see him daily; I will love him, and devote my whole
life to him.'

'So the prince is going to be married to the beautiful
daughter of the neighbouring king,' said the courtiers,
'that is why he is having that splendid ship fitted out. It is
announced that he wishes to travel, but in reality he goes to
see the princess; a numerous retinue will accompany him.' The
little mermaiden smiled at these and similar conjectures, for
she knew the prince's intentions better than any one else.

'I must go,' he said to her, 'I must see the beautiful princess; my parents require me to do so; but they will not compel me to marry her, and bring her home as my bride. And
it is quite impossible for me to love her, for she cannot be
so like the beautiful girl in the temple as thou art; and if I
were obliged to choose, I should prefer thee, my little silent
foundling, with the speaking eyes.' And he kissed her rosy
lips, played with her locks, and folded her in his arms, where-
upon arose in her heart a sweet vision of human happiness
and immortal bliss.

'Thou art not afraid of the sea, art thou, my sweet silent
child?' asked he tenderly as they stood together in the splendid ship, which was to take them to the country of the neighbouring king. And then he told her of the storms that sometimes agitate the waters; of the strange fishes that inhabit the
deep, and of the wonderful things seen by divers. But she
smiled at his words, for she knew better than any child of
earth what went on in the depths of the ocean.

At night time, when the moon shone brightly, and when
all on board were fast asleep, she sat in the ship's gallery,
looking down into the sea. It seemed to her, as she gazed

through the foamy track made by the ship's keel, that she saw her father's palace, and her grandmother's silver crown. She then saw her sisters rise out of the water, looking sorrowful and stretching out their hands towards her. She nodded to them, smiled, and would have explained that everything was going on quite according to her wishes; but just then the cabin boy approached, upon which the sisters plunged beneath the water so suddenly that the boy thought what he had seen on the waves was nothing but foam.

The next morning the ship entered the harbour of the king's splendid capital. Bells were rung, trumpets sounded, and soldiers marched in procession through the city, with waving banners, and glittering bayonets. Every day witnessed some new entertainments, balls and parties followed each other; the princess, however, was not yet in the town; she had been sent to a distant convent for education, and had there been taught the practice of all royal virtues. At last she arrived at the palace.

The little mermaid had been anxious to see this unparalleled princess; and she was now obliged to confess, that she had never before seen so beautiful a creature.

The skin of the princess was so white and delicate, that the veins might be seen through it, and her dark eyes sparkled beneath a pair of finely formed eye-brows.

'It is herself!' exclaimed the prince, when they met, 'it is she who saved my life, when I lay like a corpse on the seashore!' and he pressed his blushing bride to his beating heart.

'Oh, I am all too happy!' said he to his dumb foundling. 'What I never dared to hope for, has come to pass. Thou must rejoice in my happiness, for thou lovest me more than all others who surround me.' – And the little mermaid kissed his hand in silent sorrow; it seemed to her as if her heart was breaking already, although the morrow of his marriage day, which must inevitably see her death, had not yet dawned.

Again rung the church-bells, whilst heralds rode through the streets of the capital, to announce the approaching bridal. Odorous flames burned in silver candlesticks on all the altars;

the priests swung their golden censers; and bride and bride-groom joined hands, whilst the holy words that united them were spoken. The little mermaid, clad in silk and cloth of gold, stood behind the princess, and held the train of the bridal dress; but her ear heard nothing of the solemn music; her eye saw not the holy ceremony; she remembered her approaching end, she remembered that she had lost both this world and the next.

That very same evening, bride and bridegroom went on board the ship; cannons were fired, flags waved with the breeze, and in the centre of the deck stood a magnificent pavilion of purple and cloth of gold, fitted up with the richest and softest couches. Here the princely pair were to spend the night. A favourable wind swelled the sails, and the ship glided lightly over the blue waters.

As soon as it was dark, coloured lamps were hung out and dancing began on the deck. The little mermaid was thus involuntarily reminded of what she had seen the first time she rose to the upper world. The spectacle that now presented itself was equally splendid – and she was obliged to join in the dance, hovering lightly as a bird over the ship boards. All applauded her, for never had she danced with more enchant-ing grace. Her little feet suffered extremely, but she no longer felt the pain; the anguish her heart suffered was much greater. It was the last evening she might see him, for whose sake she had forsaken her home and all her family, had given away her beautiful voice, and suffered daily the most violent pain – all without his having the least suspicion of it. It was the last evening that she might breathe the same atmosphere in which he, the beloved one, lived; the last evening when she might behold the deep blue sea, and the starry heavens – an eternal night, in which she might neither think nor dream, awaited her. And all was joy in the ship; and she, her heart filled with thoughts of death and annihilation, smiled and danced with the others, till past midnight. Then the prince kissed his lovely bride, and arm in arm they entered the magnificent tent, prepared for their repose.

All was now still; the steersman alone stood at the ship's helm. The little mermaid leaned her white arms on the gallery, and looked towards the east, watching for the dawn; she well knew that the first sunbeam would witness her dissolution. She saw her sisters rise out of the sea; deadly pale were their features; and their long hair no more fluttered over their shoulders, it had all been cut off.

'We have given it to the witch,' said they, 'to induce her to help thee, so that thou mayest not die. She has given to us a penknife: here it is! before the sun rises, thou must plunge it into the prince's heart; and when his warm blood trickles down upon thy feet will they again be changed to a fish-tail; thou wilt once more became a mermaid, and wilt live thy full three hundred years, ere thou changest to foam on the sea. But hasten! either he or thou must die before sun-rise. Our aged mother mourns for thee so much, her grey hair has fallen off through sorrow, as ours fell before the scissors of the witch. Kill the prince, and come down to us! hasten! hasten! dost thou not see the red streaks on the eastern sky, announcing the near approach of the sun? A few minutes more and he rises, and then all will be over with thee.' At these words they sighed deeply and vanished.

The little mermaid drew aside the purple curtains of the pavilion, where lay the bride and bridegroom; bending over them, she kissed the prince's forehead, and then glancing at the sky, she saw that the dawning light became every moment brighter. The prince's lips unconsciously murmured the name of his bride – he was dreaming of her, and her only, whilst the fatal penknife trembled in the hand of the unhappy mermaid. All at once, she threw far out into the sea that instrument of death; the waves rose like blazing flames around, and the water where it fell seemed tinged with blood. With eyes fast becoming dim and fixed, she looked once more at her beloved prince; then plunged from the ship into the sea, and felt her body slowly but surely dissolving into foam.

Wonderful Copenhagen

MARIE JOSEPH

MARIE JOSEPH was born in Lancashire, a background she has used in her books. Her novel A Better World than This *won the Romantic Novel of the Year Award in 1987. In addition to being a prolific short story writer she has also written* One Step at a Time *which deals with her fight against rheumatoid arthritis.*

THERE I was, sitting all alone, listening to the band in Copenhagen's Tivoli Gardens, when quite suddenly I realised that I was free. The heartbreak of the past few months was over. I'd served my sentence of disillusionment, and I could start to live again. It was marvellous.

On that warm September evening, amidst the spangled image of countless coloured lanterns trimming the trees, I accepted the fact that Larry was going to marry someone else.

As the music soared into a Strauss waltz, I found that I was actually feeling glad for my ex-fiancé, actually wishing him well. When I flew back home with Gavin Lancing, my boss, at the end of our business trip to Denmark, I would start afresh.

Never again would I sit alone in my two-roomed flat in Balham, staring at the telephone, willing it to ring. Never again would I indulge myself in fantasies, where Larry discovered that his desertion of me had been a ghastly mistake. Where he rang my doorbell, and when I answered it, drew me into his arms, admitting that he must have been mad to think for one minute that we could live without each other, begging my forgiveness, my understanding.

It would be a long, long time before I fell in love again, a long time before any man could turn me into a willing slave, hanging on to his every word, dependent on his whims, his unpredictable moods, lifting me to the heights of happiness, or plunging me down into the depths of despair.

From the listening crowd standing behind the circle of chairs, an American woman called out a request for a 'toon'.

'I Left My Heart in San Francisco. C'n you play that?' she called, and her friends endorsed her request by clapping their hands noisily.

I turned away. For some perverse reason, I didn't want them to know that I was English. I was in no mood for exchanging pleasantries. I just wanted to sit quite still, savouring the new and heady feeling of absolute release.

Gavin Lancing, my boss, had gone to bed early in our hotel, the imposing building with its tall spire and dark blue blinds over-looking the square, nursing what he called a gyppy tummy. The outcome, as he'd readily admitted in his dry fashion, of the too-lavish hospitality of our Danish hosts and business contacts.

A married man in his early fifties, with two grown-up children and a house in the stockbroker belt of Surrey, my boss treated me with friendly deference, addressing me always as Miss Masters, regarding me merely as a taker of notes, a transcriber of shorthand, making it quite clear that if I had a life of my own away from my typewriter, it was certainly no concern of his.

Now the evening was gentle and warm, so warm that I slipped the shawl I was wearing from my shoulders, and lifted the weight of my hair from my neck.

The group of tourists applauded enthusiastically as the band went into a rather shaky, then increasingly confident rendering of I Left My Heart in San Francisco. The face of the American woman took on a wondering look, and I remembered that not all that long ago, any nostalgic tune would have brought the too-ready tears to my own eyes.

Across the enclosure, a man stared at me with frank admiration, waiting, I knew, for me to give him some sign that his attention wasn't unwelcome. I recalled the light-hearted teasing I'd had to put up with from the men in the office.

'Copenhagen, the city of vice,' they'd said. I knew that I was regarded as something of a prude, because at the great age of twenty-five, I still lived alone.

I should have been feeling lonely, I told myself, but I've always believed loneliness is merely a matter of not liking to be alone. And I was revelling in being alone, and never again would I allow myself to be so involved. In my relationship with Larry, I had been the one to do the loving – I could admit that now, and at last, my pride was restored.

The man caught my eye and smiled, and I got up and walked away, past the fairground, and the restaurants strung with fairy lights, back to the hotel, to sleep soundly as a child.

And the very next day I met Kurt Hansen, the sales representative of a firm dealing in glassware in Denmark.

Mr Lancing, more than a little pale and definitely hollow-eyed, insisted that he was well enough to take a taxi out to the factory on the outskirts of the city.

'As long as they don't offer us lunch, I can cope,' he said. 'It's the last day, anyway, and when we get back home, I have the weekend in which to recuperate. Megan knows what to give me when my tummy plays me up like this. She told me to bring a bottle of the stuff our local chemist makes up for me, but I forgot.'

Seeing in my mind's eye my boss's wife, short and square and motherly looking, in the tweed skirt and car coat she'd been wearing on the one occasion I'd met her, I murmured something non-committal.

'As long as they don't offer us lunch . . .' Mr Lancing

was saying again as we walked into the outer office, to be
met by a smiling Kurt Hansen, distinguished looking in a
lightweight tan suit, blue eyes twinkling beneath a thatch of
the yellowest hair I'd ever seen.

He was the Viking type all right, tall, lean and tanned, with
a myriad of fine lines radiating from those fantastically blue
eyes. Introductions were made, and in his thickly carpeted
room he listened intently to Mr Lancing's proposals, accepting some and rejecting others, then putting forward his own
ideas, going halfway to meet my boss but not an inch further.
Mr Lancing respected him.

Kurt Hansen was, like most of his fellow countrymen,
intensely patriotic. I discovered this when, over coffee, he
relaxed and talked to us about his country.

'For the rest of the day I am at your disposal,' he told us,
smiling. 'And now you must tell me what it is you would
like to see. I expect that already you have taken a boat trip
to see our Little Mermaid statue?'

Mr Lancing put down his untouched coffee and shook his
head. 'I'm afraid it's been mostly sheer grind. Miss Masters
knew that when she came along, and I – well, I'm not much
of a one for sight-seeing. I come abroad so often that one
European city is much like another to me.'

Kurt Hansen raised his eyebrows in mock dismay.

'But we must put that right at once. We will sail round the
harbour this afternoon, but first I will take you to lunch at
my favourite restaurant. Today we will sit in the sun on the
sidewalk. They serve the best open sandwich in Copenhagen
– smoked herring served with raw egg yolk and chopped
onions, and of course you cannot go home without having
one of our famous pastries.'

My boss actually closed his eyes, his face a suffering mask
of horror, and hoping I wasn't undermining his masculine
pride, I explained quickly about the gyppy tummy, and said
that under the circumstances I was sure Mr Lancing would
want to go straight back to our hotel.

Immediately, Kurt Hansen stood up, holding out his hand.

'But of course. You should have told me. I apologise for not realising sooner.'

Then, as I gathered the papers together and slipped them into my document case, he turned to me.

'I am willing to be your escort, Miss Masters, if that is permissible? It is monstrous that you should fly back tomorrow without having seen our Little Mermaid. It would be like visiting Paris without seeing the Eiffel Tower, or London without seeing your Buckingham Palace or the Tower.'

'It honestly doesn't matter,' I said. But Mr Lancing, obviously past caring what his secretary did with her time, and longing for nothing more than the sight of his hotel room with its comfortable bed, smiled weakly.

'Excellent idea, and very kind of you, old man. I'll be as right as rain tomorrow.'

'Rain is right?' Kurt Hansen said, and I smiled, but my boss was past seeing even the mildest of jokes, and allowed himself to be escorted outside to the large forecourt where our car waited.

'I'm not sure I ought to have let him go back alone. He does look awful,' I said as the car was driven away.

'Terrible,' the tall Dane said, his blue eyes twinkling. 'I think this afternoon we will take him a bottle of schnapps. We Danes think that will cure everything. What is it they say? A hair of the dog that bit?'

I was still worried. 'I feel responsible,' I said.

He looked solemn. 'To be too responsible is a terrible thing to be, Miss Masters, especially on a day like today. The sun does not always shine, even in Copenhagen, and may I call you by your first name? You must call me Kurt. To be too formal is also a terrible thing to be.'

'Fran, short for Frances,' I said. 'And the hair of the dog that bit would be the last thing Mr Lancing would appreciate. Once bitten twice shy, as we say.'

'You do? Your English idioms are a great puzzle to me.

You must teach me, but first we go and eat. Neither Paris nor Rome has anything like our outdoor restaurants. You will see by yourself.' He held the door for me.

'You were right,' I told him later, as we sat together at a small table underneath the spread of a green umbrella, watching the passers-by, and playing a game of trying to pick out the different languages.

'You knew Mr Lancing would have been annoyed with you if you hadn't been able to speak English,' I told him smiling, and he laughed.

'That I can believe. Danish is a very hard language to learn. Some of our words you could not say, but your sense of humour and ours are very much alike. You are not married at all, Fren?'

'Fran, and no, I'm not married at all. And you? Let me guess. You have a house way out in the suburbs, and a wife, and two small children, and at the weekends you drive to the beach, with a boat in tow, and swim and sail. All the businessmen I've met this week do just that.'

Kurt laughed again, and I thought how handsome he was, and how much I was enjoying myself, and how marvellous it was to sit and talk to a man with whom I felt no involvement, and whom, after I left tomorrow, I would never see again.

'To begin with,' he was saying, 'I hate fresh air, and I live all alone in a flat with my books and my records and I am the despair of my mother, because I have reached the age of twenty-eight without getting married even once. Sometimes when she looks at me, I see grandchildren in her eyes.'

'My mother is just the same,' I said, and almost started to tell this friendly stranger about Larry.

Coffee came, and we talked and talked, our sentences overlapping. I told him about the two-roomed flat in Balham, and the girl with whom I shared a bathroom. 'It's very convenient, because she believes that too much water is drying for the skin.'

He grinned. 'My next door neighbour plays the violin at

the Holmens Kirke, and he practises in the centre of the night.'

'Kirke? That's Scottish,' I told him, and as we walked towards his car, his hand comfortably underneath my elbow, Kurt expounded his theory about the closeness of his own language to the Gaelic.

I was fascinated. It seemed incredible that we had met only a few short hours ago. Usually I was reserved when meeting a man for the first time, but to have been shy in the face of such natural friendliness would have been an affectation, to say the least.

He pointed out places of interest as we drove along the road. Then by the quayside, he helped me down into the boat for our sail to Langelinie, where the statue of the Little Mermaid sat on her boulder in the harbour, dreaming of her prince.

'But she's tiny!' I said, and Kurt nodded.

'That is what everyone says. Not quite the Statue of Liberty, I admit, but beautiful all the same, don't you think? She represents the sea, and Copenhagen is a city of the sea.

'If you were staying for longer, I would take you to Odense, on our island of Funen, and show you the birthplace of our Hans Christian Andersen. It is commercialised, but there is his house and his bed, and the manuscripts of his stories. And his comb,' he added proudly. 'Now there would be a thing to tell your man when you go back to London. I have seen the comb of Hans Christian Andersen, you could say, and he would be tickled the pink.'

'I have no man to tickle pink,' I said.

'That is sad,' Kurt said, but he was smiling at me as the boat sailed out into the harbour, and the guide, a pretty girl, with long brown hair and long brown legs, spoke to us in fluent English, Spanish, French, and German.

When we got back to the landing-stage, I insisted that we went to the hotel to see how the invalid was faring.

'I feel mean,' I said, and Kurt said he didn't feel in the least mean, just rather happy, and we found Mr Lancing sitting out on his tiny iron-railed balcony, the papers on his knee.

'You are feeling better,' Kurt told him. 'That is good. So this evening I will take you to a special little restaurant down by the harbour. We will eat chatka crab, and Danish beef with fried egg, and then I will take you both to see our Royal Palaces. Then for ever you will remember Copenhagen and your visit.'

I saw the way Mr Lancing looked first at me, then at Kurt, and the way he winced at the mention of food and travelling.

'Not for me, old man, thanks all the same,' he said, taking off his horn-rimmed spectacles and rubbing his eyes. 'You take Miss Masters. I'm quite happy to have an early night. Mustn't ask for any trouble.'

'No, of course you must not,' Kurt said quickly. Too quickly, I thought. Then he held out his hand to Mr Lancing, bowing slightly from the waist.

'It has been a big pleasure to meet you, sir. I will be in touch with our man in London early next week, for sure.'

He turned to me. 'I will call for you at seven. Seven o'clock on the spot. Okay?'

'On the *dot*,' I said automatically, and when he'd gone I explained to Mr Lancing.

'His English is perfect in some ways, but he gets certain words wrong. I find him so funny, and he doesn't mind when I laugh at him. He doesn't seem to question the fact that I, for my part, don't speak a single word of Danish.'

'All foreigners with anything about them speak English,' said my boss, in a tone of voice that implied that this was rightly so, and I accused him of being insular-minded, and then held my breath, realising that perhaps for the first time, I was meeting him on common ground, treating him as just another man, instead of my superior officer.

'Maybe so,' he said drily. 'And now, if you can come down to earth for an hour or so, we'll go over this list of statistics. I want to have a clear picture to present to the management conference first thing on Monday morning.'

*　　*　　*

And so I took a small chair out on the balcony, and slipped back into my role as Miss Masters, private and personal secretary, a taker of notes, transcriber of shorthand outlines, sitting there in the late afternoon sun by my boss's side, my head bent over my pad, and my pencil skimming efficiently over the pages.

And all the time I was wondering what to wear that evening, and regretting that I hadn't packed my new dress, a sophisticated black with shoestring straps. I decided to wear my long black skirt with a cream silk shirt, and to pin my hair up on top, the way Larry had liked me to wear it.

Larry had never made me laugh the way Kurt Hansen made me laugh. Was that what had gone wrong with our relationship? Larry had always said I was too shy, too reserved, but Kurt thought I was warm and funny. He'd said so, except that he'd said hot and funny. Perhaps I could be natural with him because I wasn't involved. And being uninvolved was wonderful. As wonderful as Copenhagen itself.

'The relative contrast between our export drive and that of the Danish market, is so marginal as to be almost inadmissible . . .' I read back, as Mr Lancing continued to dictate, whilst down in the square, a group of tourists stared up at the sun-struck buildings, and clicked their cameras.

Kurt liked the way I'd done my hair, and said so as we sat at a corner table in the little restaurant by the harbour.

'Your face is a typical English face,' he said, and I said considering the fact that my mother was Scottish and my father Canadian, that was remarkable.

He recommended the pickled herring to start with, and he told me that our table was an actual deckplank from a ship which had lain on the bottom of the sea for over a hundred years.

I ran my hand over the polished timber. 'It's a pity Mr Lancing couldn't be with us,' I said and Kurt raised his glass, smiling at me warmly.

'You do not feel then, as I do, that he would have been a raspberry?'

'Gooseberry,' I said, laughing, 'and I can't decide whether you are clever enough to be getting your words mixed up on purpose.'

'I am clever, but of course,' Kurt nodded, 'and I admit I like to see you laugh. Your nose twitches itself like a rabbit's and your eye waters touchingly.'

'Oh, Kurt,' I said, 'that is the most flattering comment I've ever had made about me,' and once again I almost told him about Larry, who had hardly ever flattered me, and somehow managed most of the time to make me feel totally inadequate.

The waiter placed a dish of venison casserole before us, almost reverently, then walked away. 'I agree with your mother,' I said. 'It is time you were married. There must be a Danish girl somewhere whom you could make very, very happy.'

'I have looked,' Kurt assured me solemnly. 'I have spent many enjoyable years looking, but I have not been able to find a girl whose nose twitches at my jokes.'

'Perhaps they don't sound so funny in Danish,' I said, and he said I had a pointer, a very good pointer indeed.

And when coffee came, served with a plate of tiny macaroon cakes, he told me it was as if he had known me for every single one of his lives, and not for just one day.

'Me too,' I said ungrammatically, then sighed. 'Now you've got me doing it.'

It was only a short walk to the royal palace of Amalienborg and as we stood together in the courtyard, Kurt pointed out the small yellow house where Queen Alexandra had been born.

'It is natural that our kings and queens should choose to live by the harbour. Our royalty never sits on ceremony,' he said.

'Oh, Kurt . . .' I said, the wine I'd drunk making me light-headed, so that I leaned against him weakly. 'People *stand*, not sit on ceremony. I wonder what will you say next?'

Instantly his arm came round me, and there, in the shadow of the equestrian statue of Frederick the Fifth, Kurt tilted my chin, running his finger down my cheek lightly, before kissing me gently and thoroughly, so thoroughly that if I hadn't clung to him I'm sure I would have fallen down.

'I think I am falling in love with you, Fran,' he said softly. 'My mother would be very happy if she could see me now.'

I stared up at him, feeling my heartbeats quicken. This wasn't the way I had planned things.

'I must go back to the hotel,' I said. 'Right this minute, and you shouldn't have said that. I wish you hadn't said that.'

His face stiffened with hurt, but he dropped his arms, and started to walk back with me to the car, walking apart from me, only stretching out a hand to steady me when I stumbled on the rough cobbles.

And outside the hotel, I thanked him for a lovely evening, and when he said he couldn't leave me like that, that he would write, or telephone me, I said it would be better, honestly, if he didn't.

I would forget him, I told myself as I undressed for bed. I would forget the way he smiled, and the way he walked, proud and tall, and by this time the next week, our shared laughter would be just a pleasant memory.

It wasn't fair, I told myself childishly. Coming to Copenhagen had shown me how easy it was to forget one man; how uncomplicated life could be. I wasn't going to go back dreaming of another.

And early the next morning, it was Mr Lancing who tucked into his breakfast, causing me to shudder with distaste as he spread an iced Danish pastry thickly with creamy butter.

With his usual lack of interest, he asked no questions about my evening out with Kurt, but as our taxi drew away from the hotel, he said: 'Isn't that Kurt Hansen? Just rushing into the hotel?'

I was proud of the way I managed to keep my voice steady. 'It's the yellow hair, but then, a lot of Danes have yellow hair, haven't they?'

Then I turned round to sit stony-faced as the taxi gathered speed and turned off on the road to the airport.

As soon as we were airborne and Mr Lancing had unfastened his seat belt, he surprised me by saying: 'I met my wife during the war, Miss Masters. I married her just four weeks after we met. I was only twenty-three, and I didn't want to get involved. I hadn't even a future to build on. No one had in those days.

'But the day after we met, I telephoned her, and asked her to marry me, and I've never regretted it, not for one minute of the thirty years we've been together, and that *was* Kurt Hansen rushing into the hotel, wasn't it?'

When he had finished, he closed his eyes, folded his hands over his slight paunch, and appeared to go to sleep.

There was something about his sitting there beside me, in his clean white shirt, and his thinning hair sleeked back, that reminded me of my father, and to my dismay I felt the prick of tears behind my eyelids, threatening to emerge.

'Mr Lancing. Are you asleep?'

'Yes,' he said firmly. 'What is it, Miss Masters?'

He didn't open his eyes, and from his voice I could tell that our relationship was back onto its secretary-boss footing.

'Nothing,' I said, and I sat there, with the clouds whizzing by, or us whizzing by the clouds, telling myself what a wonderful life awaited me back in London.

I'd be free to go to parties, as I'd planned, to meet other men, to lead a life of total uninvolvement.

And it all sounded so dreary, I let a tear crawl down my cheek, and didn't bother to wipe it away.

Some day, when I was ready, I'd meet a man just as attractive as Kurt Hansen. Maybe he wouldn't have yellow hair, and maybe he wouldn't talk nonsense, but I'd love him. Oh, yes, I'd love him . . .

Another tear trickled down my cheek, mingling with the first one, to drip sadly off my chin.

'You could ring him at the office on Monday,' said Mr

Lancing, 'but if you'd like to pass my briefcase, I think I have his private number. There are times for running away, Miss Masters, and times, you'll find, for doing just the opposite. I have a point, my dear, haven't I?'

And as I passed the briefcase over, the plane flew out of the clouds into the sun, into heaven itself, or so it seemed to be.

'Yes, Mr Lancing,' I said. 'You have a point, a very good *pointer* indeed, as Kurt Hansen would say . . .'

A Love Affair
From *Cranford*

MRS GASKELL

MRS ELIZABETH GASKELL (1810–1865) was born in London, but after her marriage to a Unitarian minister her life was spent in the North of England. As well as Cranford, *from which this extract is taken, she wrote several powerful novels, including* Mary Barton, Ruth, North and South *and* Wives and Daughters.

AND *now* I come to the love affair.

It seems that Miss Pole had a cousin, once or twice removed, who had offered to Miss Matty long ago. Now this cousin lived four or five miles from Cranford on his own estate; but his property was not large enough to entitle him to rank higher than a yeoman; or rather, with something of the 'pride which apes humility,' he had refused to push himself on, as so many of his class had done, into the ranks of the squires. He would not allow himself to be called Thomas Holbrook, *Esq.*; he even sent back letters with this address, telling the postmistress at Cranford that his name was *Mr* Thomas Holbrook, yeoman. He rejected all domestic innovations; he would have the house door stand open in summer and shut in winter, without knocker or bell to summon a servant. The closed fist or the knob of the stick did this office for him if he found the door locked. He despised every refinement which had not its root deep down in humanity. If people were not ill, he saw no necessity for moderating his voice. He spoke the dialect of the country in perfection, and constantly used it in conversation; although Miss Pole (who gave me these particulars) added, that he read aloud more beautifully and with more feeling than any one she had ever heard, except the late rector.

'And how came Miss Matilda not to marry him?' asked I.

'Oh, I don't know. She was willing enough, I think; but you know cousin Thomas would not have been enough of a gentleman for the rector and Miss Jenkyns.'

'Well! but they were not to marry him,' said I, impatiently.

'No; but they did not like Miss Matty to marry below her rank. You know she was the rector's daughter, and somehow they are related to Sir Peter Arley: Miss Jenkyns thought a deal of that.'

'Poor Miss Matty!' said I.

'Nay, now, I don't know anything more than that he offered and was refused. Miss Matty might not like him – and Miss Jenkyns might never have said a word – it is only a guess of mine.'

'Has she never seen him since?' I inquired.

'No, I think not. You see Woodley, cousin Thomas's house, lies half-way between Cranford and Misselton; and I know he made Misselton his market-town very soon after he had offered to Miss Matty; and I don't think he has been into Cranford above once or twice since – once when I was walking with Miss Matty, in High Street, and suddenly she darted from me, and went up Shire Lane. A few minutes after I was startled by meeting cousin Thomas.'

'How old is he?' I asked, after a pause of castle-building.

'He must be about seventy, I think, my dear,' said Miss Pole, blowing up my castle, as if by gunpowder into small fragments.

Very soon after – at least during my long visit to Miss Matilda – I had the opportunity of seeing Mr Holbrook; seeing, too, his first encounter with his former love, after thirty or forty years' separation. I was helping to decide whether any of the new assortment of coloured silks which they had just received at the shop would do to match a grey and black mousseline-de-laine that wanted a new breadth, when a tall, thin, Don Quixote-looking old man came into the shop for some woollen gloves. I had never seen the person (who was rather striking) before, and I watched him rather attentively while Miss Matty listened to the shopman. The stranger wore a blue coat with brass buttons, drab breeches, and gaiters, and drummed with his fingers on the counter until he was attended to. When he answered the shop-boy's question, 'What can I have the pleasure of showing you to-day, sir?' I saw Miss Matilda start, and then suddenly sit down; and instantly I guessed who it was. She had made some inquiry which had to be carried round to the other shopman.

'Miss Jenkyns wants the black sarsenet two-and-twopence the yard,' and Mr Holbrook had caught the name, and was across the shop in two strides.

'Matty – Miss Matilda – Miss Jenkyns! God bless my soul! I should not have known you. How are you? how are you?' He kept shaking her hand in a way which proved the warmth of his friendship; but he repeated so often, as if to himself, 'I should not have known you!' that any sentimental romance which I might be inclined to build was quite done away with by his manner.

However, he kept talking to us all the time we were in the shop; and then waving the shopman with the unpurchased gloves on one side, with 'Another time, sir! another time!' he walked home with us. I am happy to say my client, Miss Matilda, also left the shop in an equally bewildered state, not having purchased either green or red silk. Mr Holbrook was evidently full with honest, loud-spoken joy at meeting his old love again; he touched on the changes that had taken place; he even spoke of Miss Jenkyns as 'Your poor sister! Well, well! we have all our faults,' and bade us good-bye with many a hope that he should soon see Miss Matty again. She went straight to her room, and never came back till our early tea-time, when I thought she looked as if she had been crying.

A few days after, a note came from Mr Holbrook, asking us – impartially asking both of us – in a formal, old-fashioned style, to spend a day at his house – a long June day – for it was June now. He named that he had also invited his cousin, Miss Pole; so that we might join in a fly, which could be put up at his house.

I expected Miss Matty to jump at this invitation; but, no! Miss Pole and I had the greatest difficulty in persuading her to go. She thought it was improper; and was even half annoyed when we utterly ignored the idea of any impropriety in her going with two other ladies to see her old lover. Then came a more serious difficulty. She did not think Deborah would have liked her to go. This took us half a day's good hard talking to get over; but, at the first sentence of relenting, I seized the opportunity, and wrote and despatched an acceptance in her name – fixing day and hour, that all might be decided and done with.

The next morning she asked me if I would go down to the shop with her; and there, after much hesitation, we chose out three caps to be sent home and tried on, that the most becoming might be selected to take with us on Thursday.

She was in a state of silent agitation all the way to Woodley. She had evidently never been there before; and, although she little dreamt I knew anything of her early story, I could perceive she was in a tremor at the thought of seeing the place which might have been her home, and round which it is probable that many of her innocent girlish imaginations had clustered. It was a long drive there, through paved jolting lanes. Miss Matilda sat bolt upright, and looked wistfully out of the windows as we drew near the end of our journey. The aspect of the country was quiet and pastoral. Woodley stood among fields; and there was an old-fashioned garden where roses and currant-bushes touched each other, and where the feathery asparagus formed a pretty background to the pinks and gilly-flowers; there was no drive up to the door. We got out at a little gate, and walked up a straight box-edged path.

'My cousin might make a drive, I think,' said Miss Pole, who was afraid of ear-ache, and had only her cap on.

'I think it is very pretty,' said Miss Matty, with a soft plaintiveness in her voice, and almost in a whisper, for just then Mr Holbrook appeared at the door, rubbing his hands in very effervescence of hospitality. He looked more like my idea of Don Quixote than ever, and yet the likeness was only external. His respectable housekeeper stood modestly at the door to bid us welcome; and, while she led the elder ladies upstairs to a bedroom, I begged to look about the garden. My request evidently pleased the old gentleman, who took me all round the place, and showed me his six-and-twenty cows, named after the different letters of the alphabet. As we went along, he surprised me occasionally by repeating apt and beautiful quotations from the poets, ranging easily from Shakespeare and George Herbert to those of our own day. He did this as naturally as if he were thinking aloud, and their true and beautiful words were the best expression he could find for what he was thinking or feeling. To be sure he called Byron 'my Lord Byrron,' and pronounced the name of Goethe strictly in accordance with the English sound of the letters – 'As Goethe says, "Ye ever-verdant palaces," ' etc. Altogether, I never met with a man, before or since, who had spent so long a life in a secluded and not impressive country, with ever-increasing delight in the daily and yearly change of season and beauty.

When he and I went in, we found that dinner was nearly ready in the kitchen – for so I suppose the room ought to be called, as there were oak dressers and cupboards all round, all over by the side of the fireplace, and only a small Turkey carpet in the middle of the flag-floor. The room might have been easily made into a handsome dark oak dining-parlour by removing the oven and a few other appurtenances of a kitchen, which were evidently never used, the real cooking-place being at some distance. The room in which we were expected to sit was a stiffly-furnished, ugly apartment; but that in which we did sit was what Mr Holbrook called the counting-house, when he paid his labourers their weekly wages at a great desk near the door. The rest of the pretty sitting-room – looking into the orchard, and all covered over with dancing tree-shadows – was filled with books. They lay on the ground, they covered the walls, they strewed the table. He was evidently half-ashamed and half-proud of his extravagance in this respect. They were of all kinds – poetry and wild weird tales prevailing. He evidently chose his books in accordance with his own tastes, not because such and such were classical or established favourites.

'Ah!' he said, 'we farmers ought not to have much time for reading; yet somehow one can't help it.'

'What a pretty room!' said Miss Matty, *sotto voce*.

'What a pleasant place!' said I, aloud, almost simultaneously.

'Nay! if you like it,' replied he; 'but can you sit on these great black leather three-cornered chairs? I like it better than the best parlour; but I thought ladies would take that for the smarter place.'

It was the smarter place, but, like most smart things, not at all pretty, or pleasant, or home-like; so, while we were at dinner, the servant-girl dusted and scrubbed the counting-house chairs, and we sat there all the rest of the day.

We had pudding before meat; and I thought Mr Holbrook was going to make some apology for his old-fashioned ways, for he began:

'I don't know whether you like new-fangled ways.'

'Oh, not at all!' said Miss Matty.

'No more do I,' said he. 'My housekeeper *will* have these in her new fashion; or else I tell her that, when I was a young man, we used to keep strictly to my father's rule, "No broth, no ball; no ball, no beef" and always began dinner with broth. Then we had suet puddings, boiled in the broth with the beef; and then the meat itself. If we did not sup our broth, we had no ball, which we liked a deal better; and the beef came last of all, and only those had it who had done justice to the broth and the ball. Now folks begin with sweet things, and turn their dinners topsy-turvy.'

When the ducks and green peas came, we looked at each other in dismay; we had only two-pronged, black-handled forks. It is true the steel was as bright as silver; but what were we to do? Miss Matty picked up her peas, one by one, on the point of the prongs, much as Aminé ate her grains of rice after her previous feast with the Ghoul. Miss Pole sighed over her delicate young peas as she left them on one side of her plate untasted, for they *would* drop between the prongs. I looked at my host: the peas were going wholesale into his capacious mouth, shovelled up by his large, round-ended knife. I saw, I imitated, I survived! My friends, in spite of my precedent, could not muster up courage enough to do an ungenteel thing; and, if Mr Holbrook had not been so heartily hungry, he would probably have seen that the good peas went away almost untouched.

After dinner, a clay pipe was brought in, and a spittoon; and, asking us to retire to another room, where he would soon join us, if we disliked tobacco-smoke, he presented his pipe to Miss Matty, and requested her to fill the bowl. This was a compliment to a lady in his youth; but it was rather inappropriate to propose it as an honour to Miss Matty, who had been trained by her sister to hold smoking of every kind in utter abhorrence. But if it was a shock to her refinement, it was also a gratification to her feelings to be thus selected; so she daintily stuffed the strong tobacco into the pipe, and then we withdrew.

'It is very pleasant dining with a bachelor,' said Miss Matty, softly, as we settled ourselves in the counting-house. 'I only hope it is not improper; so many pleasant things are!'

'What a number of books he has!' said Miss Pole, looking round the room. 'And how dusty they are!'

'I think it must be like one of the great Dr Johnson's rooms,' said Miss Matty. 'What a superior man your cousin must be!'

'Yes!' said Miss Pole, 'he's a great reader; but I am afraid he has got into very uncouth habits with living alone.'

'Oh! uncouth is too hard a word. I should call him eccentric; very clever people always are!' replied Miss Matty.

When Mr Holbrook returned, he proposed a walk in the fields; but the two elder ladies were afraid of damp, and dirt, and had only very unbecoming calashes to put on over their caps; so they declined, and I was again his companion in a turn which he said he was obliged to take to see after his men. He strode along, either wholly forgetting my existence, or soothed into silence by his pipe – and yet it was not silence exactly. He walked before me, with a stooping gait, his hands clasped behind him; and, as some tree or cloud, or glimpse of distant upland pastures, struck him, he quoted poetry to himself, saying it out loud in a grand, sonorous voice, with just the emphasis that true feeling and appreciation give. We came upon an old cedar-tree, which stood at one end of the house –

The cedar spreads his dark-green layers of shade.

'Capital term – "layers!" Wonderful man!' I did not know whether he was speaking to me or not; but I put in an assenting 'wonderful,' although I knew nothing about it, just because I was tired of being forgotten, and of being consequently silent.

He turned sharp round. 'Ay! you may say "wonderful." Why, when I saw the review of his poems in "Blackwood," I set off within an hour, and walked seven miles to Misselton (for the horses were not in the way) and ordered them. Now, what colour are ash-buds in March?'

Is the man going mad? thought I. He is very like Don Quixote.

'What colour are they, I say?' repeated he, vehemently.

'I am sure I don't know, sir,' said I, with the meekness of ignorance.

'I knew you didn't. No more did I – an old fool that I am!

– till this young man comes and tells me. Black as ash-buds in March. And I've lived all my life in the country; more shame for me not to know. Black: they are jet-black, madam.' And he went off again, swinging along to the music of some rhyme he had got hold of.

When we came back, nothing would serve him but he must read us the poems he had been speaking of; and Miss Pole encouraged him in his proposal, I thought, because she wished me to hear his beautiful reading, of which she had boasted; but she afterwards said it was because she had got to a difficult part of her crochet, and wanted to count her stitches without having to talk. Whatever he had proposed would have been right to Miss Matty; although she did fall sound asleep within five minutes after he had begun a long poem, called 'Locksley Hall,' and had a comfortable nap, unobserved, till he ended; when the cessation of his voice wakened her up, and she said, feeling that something was expected, and that Miss Pole was counting –

'What a pretty book!'

'Pretty, madam! it's beautiful! Pretty, indeed.'

'Oh yes! I meant beautiful!' said she, fluttered at his disapproval of her word. 'It is so like that beautiful poem of Dr Johnson's my sister used to read – I forget the name of it; what was it, my dear?' turning to me.

'Which do you mean, ma'am? What was it about?'

'I don't remember what it was about, and I've quite forgotten what the name of it was; but it was written by Dr Johnson, and was very beautiful, and very like what Mr Holbrook has just been reading.'

'I don't remember it,' said he, reflectively. 'But I don't know Dr Johnson's poems well. I must read them.'

As we were getting into the fly to return, I heard Mr Holbrook say he should call on the ladies soon, and inquire how they got home; and this evidently pleased and fluttered Miss Matty at the time he said it; but after we had lost sight of the old house among the trees her sentiments towards the master of it were gradually absorbed into a distressing wonder as to whether Martha had broken her word, and seized on the opportunity of her mistress's absence to have a 'follower.' Martha looked good, and steady, and composed enough, as she came to help us out; she was always careful of Miss Matty, and to-night she made use of this unlucky speech:

'Eh! dear ma'am, to think of your going out in an evening in such a thin shawl! It's no better than muslin. At your age, ma'am, you should be careful.'

'My age!' said Miss Matty, almost speaking crossly, for her, for she was usually gentle – 'My age! Why, how old do you think I am, that you talk about my age?'

'Well, ma'am, I should say you were not far short of sixty: but folks' looks is often against them – and I'm sure I meant no harm.'

'Martha, I'm not yet fifty-two!' said Miss Matty, with grave emphasis; for probably the remembrance of her youth had come very vividly before her this day, and she was annoyed at finding that golden time so far away in the past.

But she never spoke of any former and more intimate acquaintance with Mr Holbrook. She had probably met with so little sympathy in her early love, that she had shut it up close in her heart; and it was only by a sort of watching, which I could hardly avoid since Miss Pole's confidence, that I saw how faithful her poor heart had been in its sorrow and its silence.

She gave me some good reason for wearing her best cap every day, and sat near the window in spite of her rheumatism, in order to see, without being seen, down into the street.

He came. He put his open palms upon his knees, which were far apart, as he sat with his head bent down, whistling, after we had replied to his inquiries about our safe return. Suddenly, he jumped up:

'Well, madam! have you any commands for Paris? I am going there in a week or two.'

'To Paris!' we both exclaimed.

'Yes madam! I've never been there, and always had a wish to go; and I think if I don't go soon, I mayn't go at all; so as soon as the hay is got in I shall go, before harvest time.'

We were so much astonished that we had no commissions.

Just as he was going out of the room, he turned back, with his favourite exclamation:

'God bless my soul, madam! but I nearly forgot half my errand. Here are the poems for you you admired so much the other evening at my house.' He tugged away at a parcel in his coat-pocket. 'Good-bye, miss,' said he; 'good-bye, Matty! take care of yourself.' And he was gone. But he had given her a book, and he had called her Matty, just as he used to do thirty years ago.

'I wish he would not go to Paris,' said Miss Matilda, anxiously. 'I don't believe frogs will agree with him; he used to have to be very careful what he ate, which was curious in so strong-looking a young man.'

Soon after this I took my leave, giving many an injunction to Martha to look after her mistress, and to let me know if she thought that Miss Matilda was not so well; in which case I would volunteer a visit to my old friend, without noticing Martha's intelligence to her.

Accordingly I received a line or two from Martha every now and then; and, about November, I had a note to say her mistress was 'very low and sadly off her food,' and the account made me so uneasy that, although Martha did not decidedly summon me, I packed up my things and went.

I received a warm welcome, in spite of the little flurry produced by my impromptu visit, for I had only been able to give a day's notice. Miss Matilda looked miserably ill; and I prepared to comfort and cosset her.

I went down to have a private talk with Martha.

'How long has your mistress been so poorly?' I asked, as I stood by the kitchen fire.

'Well! I think it's better than a fortnight; it is, I know; it was one Tuesday, after Miss Pole had been, that she went into this moping way. I thought she was tired, and it would go off with a night's rest; but no! she has gone on and on ever since, till I thought it my duty to write to you, ma'am.'

'You did quite right, Martha. It is a comfort to think she has so faithful a servant about her. And I hope you find your place comfortable?'

'Well, ma'am, missus is very kind, and there's plenty to eat and drink, and no more work but what I can do easily – but —' Martha hesitated.

'But what, Martha?'

'Why, it seems so hard of missus not to let me have any followers; there's such lots of young fellows in the town; and many a one has as much as offered to keep company with me; and I may never be in such a likely place again, and it's like wasting an opportunity. Many a girl as I know would have 'em unbeknownst to missus; but I've given my word, and I'll stick to it; or else this is just the house for missus never to be the wiser if they did come: and it's such a capable kitchen – there's such good dark corners in it – I'd be bound to hide any one. I counted up last Sunday night – for I'll not deny I was crying because I had to shut the door in Jem Hearn's face, and he's a steady young man, fit for any girl; only I had given missus my word.' Martha was all but crying again; and I had little comfort to give her, for I knew, from old experience, of the horror with which both the Miss Jenkynses looked upon 'followers,' and in Miss Matty's present nervous state this dread was not likely to be lessened.

I went to see Miss Pole the next day, and took her completely by surprise, for she had not been to see Miss Matilda for two days.

'And now I must go back with you, my dear, for I promised to let her know how Thomas Holbrook went on; and, I'm sorry to say, his housekeeper has sent me word to-day that he hasn't long to live. Poor Thomas! that journey to Paris was quite too much for him. His housekeeper says he has hardly ever been round his fields since, but just sits with his hands on his knees in the counting-house, not reading or anything, but only saying what a wonderful city Paris was! Paris has much to answer for if it's killed my cousin Thomas, for a better man never lived.'

'Does Miss Matilda know of his illness?' asked I – a new light as to the cause of her indisposition dawning upon me.

'Dear! to be sure, yes! Has not she told you? I let her know a fortnight ago, or more, when first I heard of it. How odd she shouldn't have told you!'

Not at all, I thought; but I did not say anything. I felt almost guilty of having spied too curiously into that tender heart, and I was not going to speak of its secrets – hidden, Miss Matty believed, from all the world. I ushered Miss Pole into Miss Matilda's little drawing-room, and then left them alone. But I was not surprised when Martha came to my bedroom door, to ask me to go down to dinner alone, for that missus had one of her bad headaches. She came into the drawing-room at tea-time, but it was evidently an effort to her; and, as if to make up for some reproachful feeling against her late sister, Miss Jenkyns, which had been troubling her all the afternoon, and for which she now felt penitent, she kept telling me how good and how clever Deborah was in her youth; how she used to settle what gowns they were to wear at all the parties (faint, ghostly ideas of grim parties, far away in the distance, when Miss Matty and Miss Pole were young!); and how Deborah and her mother had started the benefit society for the poor, and taught girls cooking and plain sewing; and how Deborah had once danced with a lord; and how she used to visit at Sir Peter Arley's, and try to remodel the quiet rectory establishment on the plans of Arley Hall, where they kept thirty servants; and how she had nursed Miss Matty through a long, long illness, of which I had never heard before, but which I now dated in my own mind as following the dismissal of the suit of Mr Holbrook. So we talked softly and quietly of old times through the long November evening.

The next day Miss Pole brought us word that Mr Holbrook was dead. Miss Matty heard the news in silence; in fact, from the account of the previous day, it was only what we had to expect. Miss Pole kept calling upon us for some expression of regret, by asking if it was not sad that he was gone, and saying:

'To think of that pleasant day last June, when he seemed so well! And he might have lived this dozen years if he had not gone to that wicked Paris, where they are always having revolutions.'

She paused for some demonstration on our part. I saw Miss Matty could not speak, she was trembling so nervously; so I said what I really felt; and after a call of some duration – all the time of which I have no doubt Miss Pole thought Miss Matty received the news very calmly – our visitor took her leave.

Miss Matty made a strong effort to conceal her feelings – a concealment she practised even with me, for she has never alluded to Mr Holbrook again, although the book he gave her lies with her Bible on the little table by her bedside. She did not think I heard her when she asked the little milliner of Cranford to make her caps something like the Honourable Mrs Jamieson's, or that I noticed the reply –

'But she wears widows' caps, ma'am?'

'Oh? I only meant something in that style; not widows', of course, but rather like Mrs Jamieson's.'

This effort at concealment was the beginning of the tremulous motion of head and hands which I have seen ever since in Miss Matty.

The evening of the day on which we heard of Mr Holbrook's death, Miss Matilda was very silent and thoughtful; after prayers she called Martha back, and then she stood, uncertain what to say.

'Martha!' she said, at last, 'you are young' – and then she made so long a pause that Martha, to remind her of her half-finished sentence, dropped a curtsey, and said –

'Yes, please, ma'am; two-and-twenty last third of October, please, ma'am.'

'And perhaps, Martha, you may some time meet with a

young man you like, and who likes you. I did say you were not to have followers; but if you meet with such a young man, and tell me, and I find he is respectable, I have no objection to his coming to see you once a week. God forbid!' said she, in a low voice, 'that I should grieve any young hearts.' She spoke as if she were providing for some distant contingency, and was rather startled when Martha made her ready eager answer.

'Please, ma'am, there's Jem Hearn, and he's a joiner making three-and-sixpence a-day, and six foot one in his stocking-feet, please, ma'am; and if you'll ask about him to-morrow morning, every one will give him a character for steadiness; and he'll be glad enough to come to-morrow night, I'll be bound.'

Though Miss Matty was startled, she submitted to Fate and Love.

The Gift of the Magi

O. HENRY

O. HENRY (1862–1910) was born in North Carolina and began writing short stories while serving a prison sentence for alleged embezzlement. He is the master of the short story with the twist in the tail.

ONE dollar and eighty-seven cents. That was all. And sixty cents of it was in pennies. Pennies saved one and two at a time by bulldozing the grocer and the vegetable man and the butcher until one's cheek burned with the silent imputation of parsimony that such close dealing implied. Three times Della counted it. One dollar and eighty-seven cents. And the next day would be Christmas.

There was clearly nothing left to do but flop down on the shabby little couch and howl. So Della did it. Which instigates the moral reflection that life is made up of sobs, sniffles, and smiles, with sniffles predominating.

While the mistress of the home is gradually subsiding from the first stage to the second, take a look at the home. A furnished flat at $8 per week. It did not exactly beggar description, but it certainly had that word on the look-out for the mendicancy squad.

In the vestibule below was a letter-box into which no letter would go, and an electric button from which no mortal finger could coax a ring. Also appertaining thereunto was a card bearing the name 'Mr James Dillingham Young.'

The 'Dillingham' had been flung to the breeze during a former period of prosperity when its possessor was being paid $30 per week. Now, when the income was shrunk to $20, the letters of 'Dillingham' looked blurred, as though they were thinking seriously of contracting to a modest and unassuming D. But whenever Mr James Dillingham Young came home and reached his flat above he was called 'Jim' and greatly hugged by Mrs James Dillingham Young, already introduced to you as Della. Which is all very good.

Della finished her cry and attended to her cheeks with the powder rag. She stood by the window and looked out dully at a grey cat walking a grey fence in a grey backyard. Tomorrow would be Christmas Day, and she had only $1.87 with which to buy Jim a present. She had been saving every penny she could for months, with this result. Twenty dollars a week doesn't go far. Expenses had been greater than she had calculated. They always are. Only $1.87 to buy a present for Jim. Her Jim. Many a happy hour she had spent planning for something nice for him. Something fine and rare and sterling – something just a little bit near to being worthy of the honour of being owned by Jim.

There was a pier-glass between the windows of the room. Perhaps you have seen a pier-glass in an $8 flat. A very thin and very agile person may, by observing his reflection in a rapid sequence of longitudinal strips, obtain a fairly accurate conception of his looks. Della, being slender, had mastered the art.

Suddenly she whirled from the window and stood before the glass. Her eyes were shining brilliantly, but her face had lost its colour within twenty seconds. Rapidly she pulled down her hair and let it fall to its full length.

Now, there were two possessions of the James Dillingham Youngs in which they both took a mighty pride. One was Jim's gold watch that had been his father's and his grandfather's. The other was Della's hair. Had the Queen of Sheba lived in the flat across the airshaft, Della would have let her hair hang out the window some day to dry just to depreciate Her Majesty's jewels and gifts. Had King Solomon been the janitor, with all his treasures piled up in the basement, Jim would have pulled out his watch every time he passed, just to see him pluck at his beard from envy.

So now Della's beautiful hair fell about her, rippling and shining like a cascade of brown waters. It reached below her knee and made itself almost a garment for her. And then she did it up again nervously and quickly. Once she faltered for a minute and stood still while a tear or two splashed on the worn red carpet.

On went her old brown jacket; on went her old brown hat. With a whirl of skirts and with the brilliant sparkle still in her eyes, she fluttered out of the door and down the stairs to the street.

Where she stopped the sign read: 'Mme. Sofronie. Hair Goods of All Kinds.' One flight up Della ran, and collected herself, panting. Madame, large, too white, chilly, hardly looked the 'Sofronie.'

'Will you buy my hair?' asked Della.

'I buy hair,' said Madame. 'Take yer hat off and let's have a sight at the looks of it.'

Down rippled the brown cascade.

'Twenty dollars,' said Madame, lifting the mass with a practised hand.

'Give it to me quick,' said Della.

Oh, and the next two hours tripped by on rosy wings. Forget the hashed metaphor. She was ransacking the stores for Jim's present.

She found it at last. It surely had been made for Jim and no one else. There was no other like it in any of the stores, and she had turned all of them inside out. It was a platinum fob chain simple and chaste in design, properly proclaiming its value by substance alone and not by meretricious ornamentation – as all good things should do. It was even worthy of The Watch. As soon as she saw it she knew that it must be Jim's. It was like him. Quietness and value – the description applied to both. Twenty-one dollars they took from her for it, and she hurried home with the 87 cents. With that chain on his watch Jim might be properly anxious about the time in any company. Grand as the watch was, he sometimes looked at it on the sly on account of the old leather strap that he used in place of a chain.

When Della reached home her intoxication gave way a little to prudence and reason. She got out her curling irons and lighted the gas and went to work repairing the ravages made by generosity added to love. Which is always a tremendous task, dear friends – a mammoth task.

Within forty minutes her head was covered with tiny, close-lying curls that made her look wonderfully like a truant schoolboy. She looked at her reflection in the mirror long, carefully, and critically.

'If Jim doesn't kill me,' she said to herself, 'before he takes a second look at me, he'll say I look like a Coney Island chorus girl. But what could I do – oh! what could I do with a dollar and eighty-seven cents?'

At seven o'clock the coffee was made and the frying-pan was on the back of the stove, hot and ready to cook the chops.

Jim was never late. Della doubled the fob chain in her hand and sat on the corner of the table near the door that he always entered. Then she heard his step on the stair away down on the first flight, and she turned white for just a moment. She had a habit of saying little silent prayers about the simplest everyday things, and now she whispered: 'Please God, make him think I am still pretty.'

The door opened and Jim stepped in and closed it. He looked thin and very serious. Poor fellow, he was only twenty-two – and to be burdened with a family! He needed a new overcoat and he was without gloves.

Jim stepped inside the door, as immovable as a setter at the scent of quail. His eyes were fixed upon Della, and there was an expression in them that she could not read, and it terrified her. It was not anger, nor surprise, nor disapproval, nor horror, nor any of the sentiments that she had been prepared for. He simply stared at her fixedly with that peculiar expression on his face.

Della wriggled off the table and went for him.

'Jim, darling,' she cried, 'don't look at me that way. I had my hair cut off and sold it because I couldn't have lived through Christmas without giving you a present. It'll grow out again – you won't mind, will you? I just had to do it. My hair grows awfully fast. Say "Merry Christmas!" Jim, and let's be happy. You don't know what a nice – what a beautiful, nice gift I've got for you.'

'You've cut off your hair?' asked Jim, laboriously, as if he had not arrived at that patent fact yet even after the hardest mental labour.

'Cut it off and sold it,' said Della. 'Don't you like me just as well, anyhow? I'm me without my hair, ain't I?'

Jim looked about the room curiously.

'You say your hair is gone?' he said with an air almost of idiocy.

'You needn't look for it,' said Della. 'It's sold, I tell you – sold and gone, too. It's Christmas Eve, boy. Be good to me, for it went for you. Maybe the hairs of my head were numbered,' she went on with a sudden serious sweetness, 'but nobody could ever count my love for you. Shall I put the chops on, Jim?'

Out of his trance Jim seemed quickly to wake. He enfolded his Della. For ten seconds let us regard with discreet scrutiny some inconsequential object in the other direction. Eight dollars a week or a million a year – what is the difference? A mathematician or a wit would give you the wrong answer. The magi brought valuable gifts, but that was not among them. This dark assertion will be illuminated later on.

Jim drew a package from his overcoat pocket and drew it upon the table.

'Don't make any mistake, Dell,' he said, 'about me. I don't think there's anything in the way of a haircut or a shave or a shampoo that could make me like my girl any less. But if you'll unwrap that package you may see why you had me going awhile at first.'

White fingers and nimble tore at the string and paper. And

then an ecstatic scream of joy; and then, alas! a quick feminine change to hysterical tears and wails, necessitating the immediate employment of all the comforting powers of the lord of the flat.

For there lay The Combs – the set of combs, side and back, that Della had worshipped for long in a Broadway window. Beautiful combs, pure tortoise-shell, with jewelled rims – just the shade to wear in the beautiful vanished hair. They were expensive combs, she knew, and her heart had simply craved and yearned over them without the least hope of possession. And now they were hers, but the tresses that should have adorned the coveted adornments were gone.

But she hugged them to her bosom, and at length she was able to look up with dim eyes and a smile and say: 'My hair grows so fast, Jim!'

And then Della leaped up like a little singed cat and cried, 'Oh, oh!'

Jim had not yet seen his beautiful present. She held it out to him eagerly upon her open palm. The dull precious metal seemed to flash with a reflection of her bright and ardent spirit.

'Isn't it a dandy, Jim? I hunted all over town to find it. You'll have to look at the time a hundred times a day now. Give me your watch. I want to see how it looks on it.'

Instead of obeying, Jim tumbled down on the couch and put his hands under the back of his head and smiled.

'Dell,' said he, 'let's put our Christmas presents away and keep 'em awhile. They're too nice to use just at present. I sold the watch to get the money to buy your combs. And now suppose you put the chops on.'

The magi, as you know, were wise men – wonderfully wise men – who brought gifts to the Babe in the manger. They invented the art of giving Christmas presents. Being wise, their gifts were no doubt wise ones, possibly bearing the privilege of exchange in case of duplication. And here I have lamely related to you the uneventful chronicle of two foolish children in a flat who most unwisely sacrificed for each other the greatest treasures of their house. But in a last word to the wise of these days, let it be said that of all who give gifts these two were the wisest. Of all who give and receive gifts, such as they are wisest. Everywhere they are wisest. They are the magi.

Her Who Loves
You Best

From *Jane Eyre*

CHARLOTTE BRONTE

*CHARLOTTE BRONTE (1816–1855) grew up with her
sisters, Emily and Anne, and their brother, in Haworth,
Yorkshire. The three sisters all achieved literary fame and in*
Jane Eyre *Charlotte produced one of the great romantic classics
of English literature.*

THE manor-house of Ferndean was a building of considerable antiquity, moderate size, and no architectural pretensions, deep buried in a wood. I had heard of it before. Mr
Rochester often spoke of it, and sometimes went there. His
father had purchased the estate for the sake of the game cov-
erts. He would have let the house, but could find no tenant, in consequence of its ineligible and insalubrious site.
Ferndean then remained uninhabited and unfurnished with
the exception of some two or three rooms fitted up for the
accommodation of the squire when he went there in the season to shoot.

To this house I came just ere dark, on an evening marked
by the characteristics of sad sky, cold gale, and continued,
small, penetrating rain. The last mile I performed on foot,
having dismissed the chaise and driver with the double remu-
neration I had promised. Even when within a very short
distance of the manor-house, you could see nothing of it, so

thick and dark grew the timber of the gloomy wood about it. Iron gates between granite pillars showed me where to enter, and passing through them, I found myself at once in the twilight of close ranked trees. There was a grass-grown track descending the forest aisle between hoar and knotty shafts and under branched arches. I followed it, expecting soon to reach the dwelling, but it stretched on and on, it wound far and farther: no sign of habitation or grounds was visible.

I thought I had taken a wrong direction and lost my way. The darkness of natural as well as of sylvan dusk gathered over me. I looked round in search of another road. There was none: all was interwoven stem, columnar trunk, dense summer foliage – no opening anywhere.

I proceeded: at last my way opened, the trees thinned a little; presently I beheld a railing, then the house – scarce, by this dim light, distinguishable from the trees; so dank and green were its decaying walls. Entering a portal, fastened only by a latch, I stood amidst a space of enclosed ground, from which the wood swept away in a semicircle. There were no flowers, no garden-beds; only a broad gravel walk girdling a grass plot, and this set in the heavy frame of the forest. The house presented two pointed gables in its front; the windows were latticed and narrow, the front door was narrow too, one step led up to it. The whole looked, as the host of the Rochester Arms had said, 'quite a desolate spot.' It was as still as a church on a week-day: the pattering rain on the forest leaves was the only sound audible in its vicinage.

'Can there be life here?' I asked.

Yes, life of some kind there was; for I heard a movement – that narrow front door was unclosing, and some shape was about to issue from the grange.

It opened slowly: a figure came out into the twilight and stood on the step – a man without a hat. He stretched forth his hand as if to feel whether it rained. Dusk as it was, I had recognised him; it was my master, Edward Fairfax Rochester, and no other.

I stayed my step, almost my breath, and stood to watch him – to examine him, myself unseen, and alas! to him invisible. It was a sudden meeting, and one in which rapture was kept well in check by pain. I had no difficulty in restraining my voice from exclamation, my step from hasty advance.

His form was of the same strong and stalwart contour as ever: his port was still erect, his hair was still raven black: nor were his features altered or sunk: not in one year's space, by any sorrow, could his athletic strength be quelled or his vigorous prime blighted. But in his countenance I saw a change: that looked desperate and brooding – that reminded me of some wronged and fettered wild beast or bird, dangerous to approach in his sullen woe. The caged eagle, whose gold-ringed eyes cruelty has extinguished, might look as looked that sightless Samson.

And reader, do you think I feared him in his blind ferocity? – if you do, you little know me. A soft hope blent with my sorrow that soon I should dare to drop a kiss on that brow of rock, and on those lips so sternly sealed beneath it; but not yet. I would not accost him yet.

He descended the one step, and advanced slowly and gropingly towards the grass plot. Where was his daring stride now? Then he paused, as if he knew not which way to turn. He lifted his hand and opened his eyelids; gazed blank, and with a straining effort, on the sky, and toward the amphitheatre of trees: one saw that all to him was void darkness. He stretched his right hand (the left arm, the mutilated one, he kept hidden in his bosom); he seemed to wish by touch to gain an idea of what lay around him: he met but vacancy still; for the trees were some yards off where he stood. He relinquished the endeavour, folded his arms, and stood quiet and mute in the rain, now falling fast on his uncovered head. At this moment John approached him from some quarter.

'Will you take my arm, sir?' he said; 'there is a heavy shower coming on: had you not better go in?'

'Let me alone,' was the answer.

John withdrew, without having observed me. Mr Rochester

now tried to walk about: vainly – all was too uncertain. He groped his way back to the house, and, re-entering it, closed the door.

I now drew near and knocked: John's wife opened for me. 'Mary,' I said, 'how are you?'

She started as if she had seen a ghost: I calmed her. To her hurried, 'Is it really you, miss, come at this late hour to this lonely place?' I answered by taking her hand; and then I followed her into the kitchen, where John now sat by a good fire. I explained to them, in few words, that I had heard all which had happened since I left Thornfield, and that I was come to see Mr Rochester. I asked John to go down to the turnpike-house, where I had dismissed the chaise, and bring my trunk, which I had left there: and then, while I removed my bonnet and shawl, I questioned Mary as to whether I could be accommodated at the Manor House for the night; and finding that arrangements to that effect, though difficult, would not be impossible, I informed her I should stay. Just at this moment the parlour-bell rang.

'When you go in,' said I 'tell your master that a person wishes to speak to him, but do not give my name.'

'I don't think he will see you,' she answered, 'he refuses everybody.'

When she returned, I inquired what he had said.

'You are to send in your name and your business,' she replied. She then proceeded to fill a glass with water, and place it on a tray, together with candles.

'Is that what he rang for?' I asked.

'Yes: he always has candles brought in at dark, though he is blind.'

'Give the tray to me; I will carry it in.'

I took it from her hand: she pointed me out the parlour door. The tray shook as I held it; the water spilt from the glass; my heart struck my ribs loud and fast. Mary opened the door for me, and shut it behind me.

This parlour looked gloomy: a neglected handful of fire burnt low in the grate; and, leaning over it, with his head supported against the high, old-fashioned mantel-piece, appeared the blind tenant of the room. His old dog, Pilot, lay on one side, removed out of the way, and coiled up as if afraid of being inadvertently trodden upon. Pilot pricked up his ears when I came in: then he jumped up with a yelp and a whine, and bounded towards me: he almost knocked the tray from my hands. I set it on the table; then patted him, and said softly, 'Lie down!' Mr Rochester turned mechanically to *see* what the commotion was: but as he *saw* nothing, he returned and sighed.

'Give me the water, Mary,' he said.

I approached him with the now only half-filled glass; Pilot followed me, still excited.

'What is the matter?' he inquired.

'Down, Pilot!' I again said. He checked the water on its way to his lips, and seemed to listen: he drank, and put the glass down. 'This is you, Mary, is it not?'

'Mary is in the kitchen,' I answered.

He put out his hand with a quick gesture, but not seeing where I stood, he did not touch me. 'Who is this? Who is this?' he demanded, trying, as it seemed, to *see* with those sightless eyes – unavailing and distressing attempt! 'Answer me – speak again!' he ordered, imperiously and aloud.

'Will you have a little more water, sir? I spilt half of what was in the glass,' I said.

'*Who* is it? *What* is it? Who speaks?'

'Pilot knows me, and John and Mary know I am here. I came only this evening,' I answered.

'Great God! – what delusion has come over me? What sweet madness has seized me?'

'No delusion – no madness: your mind, sir, is too strong for delusion, your health too sound for frenzy.'

'And where is the speaker? Is it only a voice? Oh! I *cannot* see, but I must feel, or my heart will stop and my brain burst. Whatever, whoever you are, be perceptible to the touch, or I cannot live!'

He groped; I arrested his wandering hand, and prisoned it in both mine.

'Her very fingers!' he cried; 'her small, slight fingers! If so, there must be more of her.'

The muscular hand broke from my custody; my arm was seized, my shoulder, neck, waist – I was entwined and gathered to him.

'Is it Jane? *What* is it? This is her shape – this is her size –'

'And this her voice,' I added. 'She is all here: her heart, too. God bless you, sir! I am glad to be so near you again.'

'Jane Eyre! – Jane Eyre!' was all he said.

'My dear master,' I answered, 'I am Jane Eyre: I have found you out – I am come back to you.'

'In truth? – in the flesh? My living Jane?'

'You touch me, sir – you hold me, and fast enough: I am not cold like a corpse, nor vacant like air, am I?'

'My living darling! These are certainly her limbs, and these her features; but I cannot be so blest, after all my misery. It is a dream; such dreams as I have had at night when I have clasped her once more to my heart, as I do now; and kissed her, as thus – and felt that she loved me, and trusted that she would not leave me.'

'Which I never will, sir, from this day.'

'Never will, says the vision? But I always woke and found it an empty mockery; and I was desolate and abandoned – my life dark, lonely, hopeless – my soul athirst and forbidden to drink – my heart famished and never to be fed. Gentle, soft dream, nestling in my arms now, you will fly, too, as your sisters have fled before you: but kiss me before you go – embrace me, Jane.'

'There, sir – and there!'

I pressed my lips to his once brilliant and now rayless eyes – I swept his hair from his brow, and kissed that too. He suddenly seemed to arouse himself: the conviction of the reality of all this seized him.

'It is you – is it, Jane? You are come back to me, then?'

'I am.'

'And you do not lie dead in some ditch, under some stream? And you are not a pining outcast amongst strangers?'

'No, sir! I am an independent woman now.'

'Independent! What do you mean, Jane?'

'My uncle in Madeira is dead, and he left me five thousand pounds.'

'Ah! this is practical – this is real!' he cried: 'I should never dream that. Besides, there is that peculiar voice of hers, so animating and piquant, as well as soft: it cheers my withered heart; it puts life into it. What, Janet! Are you an independent woman? A rich woman?'

'Quite rich, sir. If you won't let me live with you, I can build a house of my own close up to your door, and you may come and sit in my parlour when you want company of an evening.'

'But as you are rich, Jane, you have now, no doubt, friends who will look after you, and not suffer you to devote yourself to a blind lameter like me?'

'I told you I am independent, sir, as well as rich: I am my own mistress.'

'And you will stay with me?'

'Certainly – unless you object. I will be your neighbour, your nurse, your housekeeper. I find you lonely: I will be your companion – to read to you, to walk with you, to sit with you, to wait on you, to be eyes and hands to you. Cease to look so melancholy, my dear master; you shall not be left desolate, so long as I live.'

He replied not: he seemed serious – abstracted; he sighed; he half-opened his lips as if to speak: he closed them again. I felt a little embarrassed. Perhaps I had too rashly overleaped conventionalities; and he, like St John, saw impropriety in my inconsiderateness. I had indeed made my proposal from the idea that he wished and would ask me to be his wife: an expectation, not the less certain because unexpressed, had buoyed me up, that he could claim me at once as his own. But no hint to that effect escaping him, and his countenance becoming more overcast, I suddenly remembered that I might have been all wrong, and was perhaps playing the fool unwittingly; and I began to gently withdraw myself from his arms – but he eagerly snatched me closer.

'No – no – Jane; you must not go. No – I have touched you, heard you, felt the comfort of your presence – the sweetness of your consolation: I cannot give up these joys. I have little left in myself – I must have you. The world may laugh – may call me absurd, selfish – but it does not signify. My very soul demands you; it will be satisfied, or it will take deadly vengeance on its frame.'

'Well, sir, I will stay with you: I have said so.'

'Yes; but you understand one thing by staying with me; and I understand another. You, perhaps, could make up your mind to be about my hand and chair – to wait on me as a kind little nurse (for you have an affectionate heart and a generous spirit, which prompt you to make sacrifices for those you pity), and that ought to suffice for me, no doubt. I suppose I should now entertain none but fatherly feelings for you: do you think so? Come, tell me.'

'I will think what you like, sir: I am content to be only your nurse, if you think it better.'

'But you cannot always be my nurse, Janet: you are young – you must marry some day.'

'I don't care about being married.'

'You should care, Janet: if I were what I once was, I would try to make you care – but – a sightless block!'

He relapsed again into gloom. I, on the contrary, became more cheerful, and took fresh courage: these last words gave me an insight as to where the difficulty lay; and as it was no difficulty with me, I felt quite relieved from my previous embarrassment. I resumed a livelier vein of conversation.

'It is time some one undertook to rehumanise you,' said I, parting his thick and long uncut locks; 'for I see you are being metamorphosed into a lion, or something of that sort. You have a *faux air* of Nebuchadnezzer in the fields about you, that is certain: your hair reminds me of eagles' feathers; whether your nails are grown like bird's claws or not, I have not yet noticed.'

'On this arm I have neither hand nor nails,' he said, drawing the mutilated limb from his breast, and showing it to me. 'It is a mere stump – a ghastly sight! Don't you think so, Jane?'

'It is a pity to see it; and a pity to see your eyes – and the scar of fire on your forehead: and the worst of it is, one is in danger of loving you too well for all this; and making too much of you.'

'I thought you would be revolted, Jane, when you saw my arm, and my cicatrised visage.'

'Did you? Don't tell me so – lest I should say something disparaging to your judgment. Now, let me leave you an instant to make a better fire, and have the hearth swept up. Can you tell when there is a good fire?'

'Yes; with the right eye I see a glow – a ruddy haze.'

'And you see the candles?'

'Very dimly – each is a luminous cloud.'

'Can you see me?'

'No, my fairy: but I am only too thankful to hear and feel you.'

'When do you take supper?'

'I never take supper.'

'But you shall have some to-night. I am hungry: so are you, I dare say, only you forget.'

Summoning Mary, I soon had the room in more cheerful order: I prepared him, likewise, a comfortable repast. My spirits were excited, and with pleasure and ease I talked to him during supper, and for a long time after. There was no harassing restraint, no repressing of glee and vivacity with him; for with him I was at perfect ease, because I knew I suited him; all I said or did seemed either to console or revive him. Delightful consciousness! It brought to life and light my whole nature: in his presence I thoroughly lived; and he lived in mine. Blind as he was, smiles played over his face, joy dawned on his forehead: his lineaments softened and warmed.

After supper, he began to ask me many questions, of where I had been, what I had been doing, how I had found him out; but I gave him only very partial replies: it was too late to enter into particulars that night. Besides, I wished to touch no deep-thrilling chord – to open no fresh well of emotion in his heart, my sole present aim was to cheer him. Cheered, as I have said, he was: and yet but by fits. If a moment's silence broke the conversation he would turn restless, touch me, then say, 'Jane.'

'You are altogether a human being, Jane? You are certain of that?'

'I conscientiously believe so, Mr Rochester.'

'Yet, how, on this dark and doleful evening could you so suddenly rise on my lone hearth? I stretched my hand to take a glass of water from a hireling, and it was given me by you: I asked a question, expecting John's wife to answer me, and your voice spoke at my ear.'

'Because I had come in, in Mary's stead, with the tray.'

'And the enchantment there is in the very hour I am now spending with you. Who can tell what a dark, dreary, hopeless life I have dragged on for months past? Doing nothing, expecting nothing; merging night in day; feeling but the sensation of cold when I let the fire go out, of hunger when I forgot to eat; and then a ceaseless sorrow, and, at times, a very delirium of desire to behold my Jane again. Yes: for her restoration I longed, far more than for that of my lost sight. How can it be that Jane is with me, and says she loves me? Will she not depart as suddenly as she came? To-morrow, I fear I shall find her no more.'

A commonplace, practical reply, out of the train of his own disturbed ideas, was, I was sure, the best and most reassuring for him in this frame of mind. I passed my finger over his eyebrows, and remarked that they were scorched, and that

I should apply something which would make them grow as broad and black as ever.

'Where is the use of doing me good in any way, beneficent spirit, when, at some fatal moment, you will again desert me – passing like a shadow, whither and how to me unknown, and for me remaining afterwards undiscoverable?'

'Have you a pocket-comb about you, sir?'

'What for, Jane?'

'Just to comb out this shaggy black mane. I find you rather alarming, when I examine you close at hand: you talk of my being a fairy, but I am sure you are more like a brownie.'

'Am I hideous, Jane?'

'Very, sir; you always were, you know.'

'Humph! The wickedness has not been taken out of you, wherever you have sojourned.'

'Yet I have been with good people; far better than you: a hundred times better people; possessed of ideas and views you never entertained in your life: quite more refined and exalted.'

'Who the deuce have you been with?'

'If you twist in that way you will make me pull the hair out of your head; and then I think you will cease to entertain doubts of my substantiality.'

'Who have you been with, Jane?'

'You shall not get it out of me to-night, sir; you must wait till to-morrow; to leave my tale half told, will, you know, be a sort of security that I shall appear at your breakfast-table to finish it. By the by, I must mind not to rise on your hearth with only a glass of water then: I must bring you an egg at least, to say nothing of fried ham.'

'You mocking changeling – fairy-born and human-bred! You make me feel as I have not felt these twelve months. If Saul could have had you for his David, the evil spirit would have been exorcised without the aid of the harp.'

'There, sir, you are redd up and made decent. Now I'll leave you: I have been travelling these last three days, and I believe I am tired. Good-night.'

'Just one word, Jane: were there only ladies in the house where you have been?'

I laughed and made my escape, still laughing as I ran upstairs. 'A good idea!' I thought with glee. 'I see I have the means of fretting him out of his melancholy for some time to come.'

Very early the next morning I heard him up and astir, wandering from one room to another. As soon as Mary came down I heard the question: 'Is Miss Eyre here?' Then: 'Which room did you put her into? Was it dry? Is she up? Go and ask if she wants anything; and when she will come down.'

I came down as soon as I thought there was a prospect of breakfast. Entering the room very softly, I had a view of him before he discovered my presence. It was mournful indeed, to witness the subjugation of that vigorous spirit to a corporeal infirmity. He sat in his chair – still, but not at rest: expectant evidently; the lines of now habitual sadness marking his strong features. His countenance reminded one of the lamp quenched, waiting to be re-lit; and alas! it was not himself that could now kindle the lustre of animated expression: he was dependent on another for that office! I had meant to be gay and careless, but the powerlessness of the strong man touched my heart to the quick: still I accosted him with what vivacity I could.

'It is a bright sunny morning, sir,' I said. 'The rain is over and gone, and there is a tender shining after it: you shall have a walk soon.'

I had wakened the glow: his features beamed.

'Oh, you are indeed there, my skylark! Come to me. You are not gone, not vanished? I heard one of your kind an hour ago, singing high over the wood; but its song had no music for me, any more than the rising sun had rays. All the melody on earth is concentrated in my Jane's tongue to my ear. I am glad it is not naturally a silent one; all the sunshine I can feel is in her presence.'

The water stood in my eyes to hear this avowal of his dependence; just as if a royal eagle, chained to a perch, should be forced to entreat a sparrow to become its purveyor. But I would not be lachrymose: I dashed off the salt drops, and busied myself with preparing breakfast.

Most of the morning was spent in the open air. I led him out of the wet and wild wood into some cheerful fields: I described to him how brilliantly green they were; how the flowers and hedges looked refreshed; how sparklingly blue was the sky. I sought a seat for him in a hidden and lovely spot, a dry stump of a tree; nor did I refuse to let him, when seated, place me on his knee. Why should I, when both he and I were happier near than apart? Pilot lay beside us: all was quiet. He broke out suddenly while clasping me in his arms –

'Cruel, cruel deserter! Oh, Jane, what did I feel when I discovered you had fled from Thornfield, and when I could nowhere find you: and, after examining your apartment, ascertained that you had taken no money, nor anything which could serve as an equivalent! A pearl necklace I had given you lay untouched in its little casket; your trunks were left corded and locked as they had been prepared for the bridal tour. What could my darling do, I asked, left destitute and penniless? And what did she do? Let me hear now.'

Thus urged, I began the narrative of my experience for the last year. I softened considerably what related to the three days of wandering and starvation, because to have told him all would have been to inflict unnecessary pain: the little I did say lacerated his faithful heart deeper than I wished.

I should not have left him thus, he said, without any means of making my way: I should have told him my intention. I should have confided in him: he would never have forced me to be his mistress. Violent as he had seemed in his despair, he, in truth, loved me far too well and too tenderly to constitute himself my tyrant: he would have given me half his fortune, without demanding so much as a kiss in return, rather than I should have flung myself friendless on the wide world. I had endured, he was certain, more than I had confessed to him.

'Well, whatever my sufferings had been, they were very

short,' I answered: and then I proceeded to tell him how I had been received at Moor House; how I had obtained the office of schoolmistress, etc. The accession of fortune, the discovery of my relations, followed in due order. Of course St John River's name came in frequently in the progress of the tale. When I had done, that name was immediately taken up.

'This St John, then is your cousin?'

'Yes.'

'You have spoken of him often: do you like him?'

'He was a very good man, sir; I could not help liking him.'

'A good man. Does that mean a respectable, well-conducted man of fifty? Or what does it mean?'

'St John was only twenty-nine, sir.'

' "*Jeune encore*," as the French say. Is he a person of low stature, phlegmatic, and plain? A person whose goodness consists rather in his guiltlessness of vice, than in his prowess in virtue?'

'He is untiringly active. Great and exalted deeds are what he lives to perform.'

'But his brain? That is probably rather soft? He means well: but you shrug your shoulders to hear him talk?'

'He talks little, sir: what he does say is ever to the point. His brain is first-rate, I should think not impressible, but vigorous.'

'Is he an able man, then?'

'Truly able.'

'A thoroughly educated man?'

'St John is an accomplished and profound scholar.'

'His manners, I think you said, are not to your taste? – priggish and parsonic?'

'I never mentioned his manners; but, unless I had a very bad taste, they must suit it; they are polished, calm, and gentleman-like.'

'His appearance – I forgot what description you gave of his appearance; – a sort of raw curate, half strangled with his white neckcloth, and stilted up on his thick-soled high-lows, eh?'

'St John dresses well. He is a handsome man: tall, fair, with blue eyes, and a Grecian profile.'

(*Aside*) 'Damn him!' – (*To me*) 'Did you like him, Jane?'

'Yes, Mr Rochester, I liked him: but you asked me that before.'

I perceived, of course, the drift of my interlocutor. Jealousy had got hold of him: she stung him; but the sting was salutary: it gave him respite from the gnawing fang of melancholy. I would not, therefore, immediately charm the snake.

'Perhaps you would rather not sit any longer on my knee, Miss Eyre?' was the next somewhat unexpected observation.

'Why not, Mr Rochester?'

'The picture you have just drawn is suggestive of a rather too overwhelming contrast. Your words have delineated very prettily a graceful Apollo: he is present to your imagination – tall, fair, blue-eyed, and with a Grecian profile. Your eyes dwell on a Vulcan – a real blacksmith, brown, broad-shouldered; and blind and lame into the bargain.'

'I never thought of it before; but you certainly are rather like Vulcan, sir.'

'Well, you can leave me, ma'am: but before you go' (and he retained me by a firmer grasp than ever), 'you will be pleased just to answer me a question or two.' He paused.

'What questions, Mr Rochester?'

Then followed this cross-examination.

'St John made you schoolmistress of Morton before he knew you were his cousin?'

'Yes.'

'You would often see him? He would visit the school sometimes?'

'Daily.'

'He would approve of your plans, Jane? I know they would be clever, for you are a talented creature!'

'He approved of them – yes.'

'He would discover many things in you he could not have expected to find? Some of your accomplishments are not ordinary.'

'I don't know about that.'

'You had a little cottage near the school, you say: did he ever come there to see you?'

'Now and then.'

'Of an evening?'

'Once or twice.'

A pause.

'How long did you reside with him and his sisters after the cousinship was discovered?'

'Five months.'

'Did Rivers spend much time with the ladies of his family?'

'Yes; the back parlour was both his study and ours: he sat near the window, and we by the table.'

'Did he study much?'

'A good deal.'

'What?'

'Hindustani.'

'And what did you do meantime?'

'I learnt German at first.'

'Did he teach you?'

'He did not understand German.'

'Did he teach you nothing?'

'A little Hindustani.'

'Rivers taught you Hindustani?'

'Yes, sir.'

'And his sisters also?'

'No.'

'Only you?'

'Only me.'

'Did you ask to learn?'

'No.'

'He wished to teach you?'

'Yes.'

A second pause.

'Why did he wish it? Of what use could Hindustani be to you?'

'He intended me to go with him to India.'

'Ah! here I reach the root of the matter. He wanted you to marry him?'

'He asked me to marry him.'

'That is a fiction – an impudent invention to vex me.'

'I beg your pardon, it is the literal truth: he asked me more than once, and was as stiff about urging his point as ever you could be.'

'Miss Eyre, I repeat it, you can leave me. How often am I to say the same thing? Why do you remain pertinaciously perched on my knee, when I have given you notice to quit?'

'Because I am comfortable there.'

'No, Jane, you are not comfortable there, because your heart is not with me: it is with this cousin – this St John. Oh, till this moment, I thought my little Jane was all mine! I had a belief she loved me even when she left me: that was an atom of sweet in much bitter. Long as we have been parted, hot tears as I have wept over our separation, I never thought that while I was mourning her, she was loving another! But it is useless grieving. Jane, leave me: go and marry Rivers.'

'Shake me off, then, sir – push me away, for I'll not leave you of my own accord.'

'Jane, I ever like your tone of voice: it still renews hope, it sounds so truthful. When I hear it, it carries me back a year. I forget that you have formed a new tie. But I am not a fool – go —'

'Where must I go, sir?'

'Your own way – with the husband you have chosen.'

'Who is that?'

'You know – this St John Rivers.'

'He is not my husband, nor ever will be. He does not love me: I do not love him. He loves (as he *can* love, and that is not as you love) a beautiful young lady called Rosamond. He wanted to marry me only because he thought I should make a suitable missionary's wife, which she would not have done. He is good and great, but severe; and, for me, cold as an iceberg. He is not like you, sir. I am not happy at his side, nor near him, nor with him. He has no indulgence for me – no fondness. He sees nothing attractive in me; not even youth – only a few useful mental points – Then I must leave you, sir, to go to him?'

I shuddered involuntarily, and clung instinctively closer to my blind but beloved master. He smiled.

'What, Jane! Is this true? Is such really the state of matters between you and Rivers?'

'Absolutely, sir! Oh, you need not be jealous! I wanted to tease you a little to make you less sad: I thought anger would be better than grief. But if you wish me to love you, could you but see how much I *do* love you, you would be proud and content. All my heart is yours, sir: it belongs to you; and with you it would remain, were fate to exile the rest of me from your presence for ever.'

Again, as he kissed me, painful thoughts darkened his aspect.

'My seared vision! My crippled strength!' he murmured regretfully.

I caressed, in order to soothe him. I knew of what he was thinking, and wanted to speak for him, but dared not. As he turned aside his face a minute, I saw a tear slide from under the sealed eyelid, and trickle down the manly cheek. My heart swelled.

'I am no better than the old lightning-struck chestnut-tree in Thornfield orchard,' he remarked ere long. 'And what right would that ruin have to bid a budding woodbine cover its decay with freshness?'

'You are no ruin, sir – no lightning-struck tree: you are green and vigorous. Plants will grow about your roots, whether you ask them or not, because they take delight in your bountiful shadow; and as they grow they will lean towards you, and wind round you, because your strength offers them so safe a prop.'

Again he smiled: I gave him comfort.

'You speak of friends, Jane?' he asked.

'Yes, of friends,' I answered rather hesitatingly: for I knew

I meant more than friends, but could not tell what other word to employ. He helped me.

'Ah! Jane. But I want a wife.'

'Do you, sir?'

'Yes: is it news to you?'

'Of course: you said nothing about it before.'

'Is it unwelcome news?'

'That depends on circumstances, sir – on your choice.'

'Which you shall make for me, Jane. I will abide by your decision.'

'Choose then, sir – *her who loves you best.*'

'I will at least choose – *her I love best.* Jane, will you marry me?'

'Yes, sir.'

'A poor blind man, whom you will have to lead about by the hand?'

'Yes, sir.'

'A crippled man, twenty years older than you, whom you will have to wait on?'

'Yes, sir.'

'Truly, Jane?'

'Most truly, sir.'

'Oh! my darling! God bless you and reward you!'

'Mr Rochester, if ever I did a good deed in my life – if ever I thought a good thought – if ever I prayed a sincere and blameless prayer – if ever I wished a righteous wish – I am rewarded now. To be your wife is, for me, to be as happy as I can be on earth.'

'Because you delight in sacrifice.'

'Sacrifice! What do I sacrifice? Famine for food, expectation for content. To be privileged to put my arms round what I value – to press my lips to what I love – to repose on what I trust: is that to make a sacrifice? If so, then certainly I delight in sacrifice.'

'And to bear with my infirmities, Jane: to overlook my deficiencies.'

'Which are none, sir, to me. I love you better now, when

I can really be useful to you, than I did in your state of proud independence, when you disdained every part but that of the giver and protector.'

'Hitherto I have hated to be helped – to be led: henceforth, I feel I shall hate it no more. I did not like to put my hand into a hireling's, but it is pleasant to feel it circled by Jane's little fingers. I preferred utter loneliness to the constant attendance of servants; but Jane's soft ministry will be a perpetual joy. Jane suits me: do I suit her?'

'To the finest fibre of my nature, sir.'

'The case being so, we have nothing in the world to wait for: we must be married instantly.'

He looked and spoke with eagerness: his old impetuosity was rising.

'We must become one flesh without any delay, Jane: there is but the licence to get – then we marry.'

'Mr Rochester, I have just discovered the sun is far declined from its meridian, and Pilot is actually gone home to his dinner. Let me look at your watch.'

'Fasten it into your girdle, Janet, and keep it henceforward: I have no use for it.'

'It is nearly four o'clock in the afternoon, sir. Don't you feel hungry?'

'The third day from this must be our wedding day, Jane. Never mind fine clothes and jewels, now: all that is not worth a fillip.'

'The sun has dried up all the raindrops, sir. The breeze is still: it is quite hot.'

'Do you know, Jane, I have your little pearl necklace at this moment fastened round my bronze scrag under my cravat? I have worn it since the day I lost my only treasure, as a memento of her.'

'We will go home through the wood: that will be the shadiest way.'

He pursued his own thoughts without heeding me.

'Jane! you think me, I dare say, an irreligious dog: but my heart swells with gratitude to the beneficent God of this earth just now. He sees not as man sees, but far clearer: judges not as man judges, but far more wisely. I did wrong: I would have sullied my innocent flower – breathed guilt on its purity: the Omnipotent snatched it from me. I, in my stiff-necked rebellion, almost cursed the dispensation: instead of bending to the decree, I defied it. Divine justice pursued its course; disasters came thick on me: I was forced to pass through the valley of the shadow of death. *His* chastisements are mighty; and one smote me which has humbled me for ever. You know I was proud of my strength: but what is it now, when I must give it over to foreign guidance, as a child does its weakness? Of late, Jane – only – only of late – I began to see and acknowledge the hand of God in my doom. I began to experience remorse, repentance, the wish for reconcilement to my Maker. I began sometimes to pray: very brief prayers they were, but very sincere.

'Some days since: nay, I can number them – four; it was last Monday night, a singular mood came over me; one in which grief replaced frenzy – sorrow, sullenness. I had long had the impression that since I could nowhere find you, you must be dead. Late that night – perhaps it might be between eleven and twelve o'clock – ere I retired to my dreary rest, I supplicated God, that, if it seemed good to Him, I might soon be taken from this life, and admitted to that world to come, where there was still hope of joining Jane.

'I was in my own room and sitting by the window, which was open: it soothed me to feel the balmy night-air; though I could see no stars, and only by a vague luminous haze knew the presence of the moon. I longed for thee, Janet! Oh, how I longed for thee both with soul and flesh! I asked of God, at once in anguish and humility, if I had not been long enough desolate, afflicted, tormented; and might not soon taste bliss and peace once more. That I merited all I endured, I acknowl- edged – that I could scarcely endure more, I pleaded; and the alpha and omega of my heart's wishes broke involuntarily from my lips in the words, – 'Jane! Jane! Jane!'

'Did you speak these words aloud?'

'I did, Jane. If any listener had heard me, he would have thought me mad, I pronounced them with such frantic energy.'

'And it was last Monday night, somewhere near midnight?'

'Yes; but the time is of no consequence: what followed is the strangest point. You will think me superstitious – some superstition I have in my blood, and always had: nevertheless, this is true – true at least it is that I heard what I now relate.

'As I exclaimed, "Jane! Jane! Jane!" a voice – I cannot tell whence the voice came, but I know whose voice it was – replied, "I am coming; wait for me;" and a moment after, went whispering on the wind the words, "Where are you?"

'I tell you, if I can, the idea, the picture these words opened to my mind: yet it is difficult to express what I want to express. Ferndean is buried, as you see, in a heavy wood, where sound falls dull, and dies unreverberating. "Where are you?" seemed spoken amongst mountains; for I heard a hill-sent echo repeat the words. Cooler and fresher at the moment the gale seemed to visit my brow: I could have deemed that in some wild, lone scene, I and Jane were meeting. In spirit, I believe, we must have met. You no doubt were, at that hour, in unconscious sleep, Jane: perhaps your soul wandered from its cell to comfort mine; for those were your accents as certain as I live, they were yours!'

Reader, it was on Monday night – near midnight – that I too had received the mysterious summons: those were the very words by which I replied to it. I listened to Mr Rochester's narrative, but made no disclosure in return. The coincidence struck me as too awful and inexplicable to be communicated or discussed. If I told anything, my tale would be such as must necessarily make a profound impression on the mind of my hearer: and that mind, yet from its sufferings too prone to gloom, needed not the deeper shade of the supernatural. I kept these things then, and pondered them in my heart.

'You cannot now wonder,' continued my master, 'that

when you rose upon me so unexpectedly last night, I had difficulty in believing you any other than a mere voice and vision, something that would melt to silence and annihilation, as the midnight whisper and mountain echo had melted before. Now, I thank God! I know it to be otherwise. Yes, I thank God!'

He put me off his knee, rose, and reverently lifting his hat from his brow, and bending his sightless eyes to the earth, he stood in mute devotion. Only the last words of the worship were audible –

'I thank my Maker, that, in the midst of judgment, He has remembered mercy. I humbly entreat my Redeemer to give me strength to lead henceforth a purer life than I have done hitherto!'

Then he stretched his hand out to be led. I took that dear hand, held it a moment to my lips, and then let it pass round my shoulder: being so much lower of stature than he, I served both for his prop and guide. We entered the wood, and wended homeward.

Something Childish But Very Natural

KATHERINE MANSFIELD

*KATHERINE MANSFIELD (1888–1923) was a New Zea-
lander. She died tragically young of tuberculosis. In her chosen genre
of the short story she is acknowledged as one of the finest writers of
her time.*

I

WHETHER he had forgotten what it felt like, or his head
had really grown bigger since the summer before, Henry
could not decide. But his straw hat hurt him: it pinched
his forehead and started a dull ache in the two bones just
over the temples. So he chose a corner seat in a third-class
'smoker,' took off his hat and put it in the rack with his large
black cardboard portfolio and his Aunt B.'s Christmas-present
gloves. The carriage smelt horribly of wet india-rubber and
soot. There were ten minutes to spare before the train went,
so Henry decided to go and have a look at the book-stall.
Sunlight darted through the glass roof of the station in long
beams of blue and gold; a little boy ran up and down carrying
a tray of primroses; there was something about the people –
about the women especially – something idle and yet eager.
The most thrilling day of the year, the first real day of Spring
had unclosed its warm delicious beauty even to London eyes.
It had put a spangle in every colour and a new tone in every
voice, and city folks walked as though they carried real live

bodies under their clothes with real live hearts pumping the stiff blood through.

Henry was a great fellow for books. He did not read many nor did he possess above half a dozen. He looked at all in the Charing Cross Road during lunch-time and at any odd time in London; the quantity with which he was on nodding terms was amazing. By his clean neat handling of them and by his nice choice of phrase when discussing them with one or another bookseller you would have thought that he had taken his pap with a tome propped before his nurse's bosom. But you would have been quite wrong. That was only Henry's way with everything he touched or said. That afternoon it was an anthology of English poetry, and he turned over the pages until a title struck his eye – *Something Childish But Very Natural!*

> Had I but two little wings,
> And were a little feathery bird,
> To you I'd fly, my dear,
> But thoughts like these are idle things,
> And I stay here.
>
> But in my sleep to you I fly,
> I'm always with you in my sleep,
> The world is all one's own,
> But then one wakes and where am I?
> All, all alone.
>
> Sleep stays not though a monarch bids,
> So I love to wake at break of day,
> For though my sleep be gone,
> Yet while 'tis dark one shuts one's lids,
> And so, dreams on.

He could not have done with the little poem. It was not the words so much as the whole air of it that charmed him! He might have written it lying in bed, very early in the morning, and watching the sun dance on the ceiling. 'It is *still*, like that,' thought Henry. 'I am sure he wrote it when he was half-awake some time, for it's got a smile of a dream on it.' He stared at the poem and then looked away and repeated it by heart, missed a word in the third verse and looked again and again, until he became conscious of shouting and shuffling and he looked up to see the train moving slowly.

'God's thunder!' Henry dashed forward. A man with a flag and a whistle had his hand on a door. He clutched Henry somehow . . . Henry was inside with the door slammed, in a carriage that wasn't a 'smoker,' that had not a trace of his straw hat or the black portfolio or his Aunt B.'s Christmas-present gloves. Instead, in the opposite corner, close against the wall, there sat a girl. Henry did not dare to look at her, but he felt certain she was staring at him. 'She must think I'm mad,' he thought, 'dashing into a train without even a hat, and in the evening, too.' He felt so funny. He didn't know how to sit or sprawl. He put his hands in his pockets and tried to appear quite indifferent and frown at a large photograph of Bolton Abbey. But feeling her eyes on him he gave her just the tiniest glance. Quick she looked away out of the window, and then Henry, careful of her slightest movement, went on looking. She sat pressed against the window, her cheek and shoulder half hidden by a long wave of marigold-coloured hair. One little hand in a grey cotton glove held a leather case on her lap with the initials E. M. on it. The other hand she had slipped through the window-strap, and Henry noticed a silver bangle on the wrist with a Swiss cow-bell and a silver shoe and a fish. She wore a green coat and a hat with a wreath round it. All this Henry saw while the title of the new poem persisted in his brain – *Something Childish But Very Natural*. 'I suppose she goes to some school in London,' thought Henry. 'She might be in an office. Oh no, she is too young. Besides, she'd have her hair up if she was. It isn't even down her back.' He could not keep his eyes off that beautiful waving hair. ' "My eyes are like two drunken bees . . .." Now, I wonder if I read that or made it up?'

That moment the girl turned round and, catching his glance,

she blushed. She bent her head to hide the red colour that flew in her cheeks, and Henry, terribly embarrassed, blushed too. 'I shall have to speak – have to – have to!' He started putting up his hand to raise the hat that wasn't there. He thought that funny; it gave him confidence.

'I'm – I'm most awfully sorry,' he said, smiling at the girl's hat. 'But I can't go on sitting in the same carriage with you and not explaining why I dashed in like that, without my hat even. I'm sure I gave you a fright, and just now I was staring at you – but that's only an awful fault of mine; I'm a terrible starer! If you'd like me to explain – how I got in here – not about the staring, of course,' – he gave a little laugh – 'I will.'

For a minute she said nothing, then in a low, shy voice – 'It doesn't matter.'

The train had flung behind the roofs and chimneys. They were swinging into the country, past little black woods and fading fields and pools of water shining under an apricot evening sky. Henry's heart began to thump and beat to the beat of the train. He couldn't leave it like that. She sat so quiet, hidden in her fallen hair. He felt that it was absolutely necessary that she should look up and understand him – understand him at least. He leant forward and clasped his hands round his knees.

'You see I'd just put all my things – a portfolio – into a third-class 'smoker' and was having a look at the bookstall,' he explained.

As he told the story she raised her head. He saw her grey eyes under the shadow of her hat and her eyebrows like two gold feathers. Her lips were faintly parted. Almost unconsciously he seemed to absorb the fact that she was wearing a bunch of primroses and that her throat was white – the shape of her face wonderfully delicate against all that burning hair. 'How beautiful she is! How simply beautiful she is!' sang Henry's heart, and swelled with the words, bigger and bigger and trembling like a marvellous bubble – so that he was afraid to breathe for fear of breaking it.

'I hope there was nothing valuable in the portfolio,' said she, very grave.

'Oh, only some silly drawings that I was taking back from the office,' answered Henry airily. 'And – I was rather glad to lose my hat. It had been hurting me all day.'

'Yes,' she said, 'it's left a mark,' and she nearly smiled.

Why on earth should those words have made Henry feel so free suddenly and so happy and so madly excited? What was happening between them? They said nothing, but to Henry their silence was alive and warm. It covered him from his head to his feet in a trembling wave. Her marvellous words, 'It's made a mark,' had in some mysterious fashion established a bond between them. They could not be utter strangers to each other if she spoke so simply and so naturally. And now she was really smiling. The smile danced in her eyes, crept over her cheeks to her lips and stayed there. He leant back. The words flew from him – 'Isn't life wonderful!'

At that moment the train dashed into a tunnel. He heard her voice raised against the noise. She leant forward.

'I don't think so. But then I've been a fatalist for a long time now' – a pause – 'months.'

They were shattering through the dark. 'Why?' called Henry.

'Oh . . .'

Then she shrugged, and smiled and shook her head, meaning she could not speak against the noise. He nodded and leant back. They came out of the tunnel into a sprinkle of lights and houses. He waited for her to explain. But she got up and buttoned her coat and put her hands to her hat, swaying a little. 'I get out here,' she said. That seemed quite impossible to Henry.

The train slowed down and the lights outside grew brighter. She moved towards his end of the carriage.

'Look here!' he stammered. 'Shan't I see you again?' He got up too, and leant against the rack with one hand. 'I *must* see you again.' The train was stopping.

She said breathlessly, 'I come down from London every evening.'

'You – you – you do – really?' His eagerness frightened her. He was quick to curb it. Shall we or shall we not shake hands? raced through his brain. One hand was on the door-handle, the other held the little bag. The train stopped. Without another word or glance she was gone.

II

Then came Saturday – a half-day at the office – and Sunday between. By Monday evening Henry was quite exhausted. He was at the station far too early, with a pack of silly thoughts at his heels as it were driving him up and down. 'She didn't say she came by this train!' 'And supposing I go up and she cuts me.' 'There may be somebody with her.' 'Why do you suppose she's ever thought of you again?' 'What are you going to say if you do see her?' He even prayed, 'Lord, if it be Thy will, let us meet.'

But nothing helped. White smoke floated against the roof of the station – dissolved and came again in swaying wreaths. Of a sudden, as he watched it, so delicate and so silent, moving with such mysterious grace above the crowd and the scuffle, he grew calm. He felt very tired – he only wanted to sit down and shut his eyes – she was not coming – a forlorn relief breathed in the words. And then he saw her quite near to him walking towards the train with the same little leather case in her hand. Henry waited. He knew, somehow, that she had seen him, but he did not move until she came close to him and said in her low, shy voice – 'Did you get them again?'

'Oh yes, thank you, I got them again,' and with a funny half-gesture he showed her the portfolio and the gloves. They walked side by side to the train and into an empty carriage. They sat down opposite to each other, smiling timidly but not speaking, while the train moved slowly, and slowly gathered speed and smoothness. Henry spoke first.

'It's so silly,' he said, 'not knowing your name.' She put

back a big piece of hair that had fallen on her shoulder, and
he saw how her hand in the grey glove was shaking. Then
he noticed that she was sitting very stiffly with her knees
pressed together – and he was, too – both of them trying
not to tremble so. She said, 'My name is Edna.'

'And mine is Henry.'

In the pause they took possession of each other's names and
turned them over and put them away, a shade less frightened
after that.

'I want to ask you something else now,' said Henry. He
looked at Edna, his head a little on one side. 'How old are
you?'

'Over sixteen,' she said, 'and you?'

'I'm nearly eighteen . . .'

'Isn't it hot?' she said suddenly, and pulled off her grey
gloves and put her hands to her cheeks and kept them there.
Their eyes were not frightened – they looked at each other
with a sort of desperate calmness. If only their bodies would
not tremble so stupidly! Still half hidden by her hair, Edna
said:

'Have you ever been in love before?'

'No, never! Have you?'

'Oh, never in all my life.' She shook her head. 'I never even
thought it possible.'

His next words came in a rush. 'Whatever have you been
doing since last Friday evening? Whatever did you do all
Saturday and all Sunday and to-day?'

But she did not answer – only shook her head and smiled
and said, 'No, you tell *me*.'

'I?' cried Henry – and then he found he couldn't tell her
either. He couldn't climb back to those mountains of days,
and he had to shake his head too.

'But it's been agony' he said, smiling brilliantly – 'agony.'
At that she took away her hands and started laughing, and
Henry joined her. They laughed until they were tired.

'It's so – so extraordinary,' she said. 'So suddenly, you
know, and I feel as if I'd known you for years.'

'So do I . . .' said Henry. 'I believe it must be the Spring. I believe I've swallowed a butterfly – and it's fanning its wings just here.' He put his hand on his heart.

'And the really extraordinary thing is,' said Edna, 'that I had made up my mind that I didn't care for – men at all. I mean all the girls at College –'

'Were you at College?'

She nodded. 'A training college, learning to be a secretary.' She sounded scornful.

'I'm in an office,' said Henry. 'An architect's office – such a funny little place up one hundred and thirty stairs. We ought to be building nests instead of houses, I always think.'

'Do you like it?'

'No, of course I don't. I don't want to do anything, do you?'

'No, I hate it . . . And,' she said, 'my mother is a Hungarian – I believe that makes me hate it even more.'

That seemed to Henry quite natural. 'It would,' he said.

'Mother and I are exactly alike. I haven't a thing in common with my father; he's just . . . a little man in the City – but mother has got wild blood in her and she's given it to me. She hates our life just as much as I do.' She paused and frowned. 'All the same, we don't get on a bit together – that's funny – isn't it? But I'm absolutely alone at home.'

Henry was listening – in a way he was listening, but there was something else he wanted to ask her. He said, very shyly, 'Would you – would you take off your hat?'

She looked startled. 'Take off my hat?'

'Yes – it's your hair. I'd give anything to see your hair properly.'

She protested. 'It isn't really . . .'

'Oh, it *is*,' cried Henry, and then, as she took off the hat and gave her head a little toss, 'Oh, Edna! it's the loveliest thing in the world.'

'Do you like it?' she said, smiling and very pleased. She pulled it round her shoulders like a cape of gold. 'People generally laugh at it. It's such an absurd colour.' But Henry would not believe that. She leaned her elbows on her knees and cupped her chin in her hands. 'That's how I often sit when I'm angry and than I feel it burning me up . . . Silly?'

'No, no, not a bit,' said Henry. 'I knew you did. It's your sort of weapon against all the dull horrid things.'

'However did you know that? Yes, that's just it. But however did you know?'

'Just knew,' smiled Henry. 'My God!' he cried, 'what fools people are! All the little pollies that you know and that I know. Just look at you and me. Here we are — that's all there is to be said. I know about you and you know about me — we've just found each other — quite simply — just by being natural. That's all life is — something childish and very natural. Isn't it?'

'Yes — yes,' she said eagerly. 'That's what I've always thought.'

'It's people that make things so — silly. As long as you can keep away from them you're safe and you're happy.'

'Oh, I've thought that for a long time.'

'Then you're just like me,' said Henry. The wonder of that was so great that he almost wanted to cry. Instead he said very solemnly: 'I believe we're the only two people alive who think as we do. In fact, I'm sure of it. Nobody understands me. I feel as though I were living in a world of strange beings — do you?'

'Always.'

'We'll be in that loathsome tunnel again in a minute,' said Henry. 'Edna! can I — just touch your hair?'

She drew back quickly. 'Oh no, please don't,' and as they were going into the dark she moved a little away from him.

III

'Edna! I've bought the tickets. The man at the concert hall didn't seem at all surprised that I had the money. Meet me outside the gallery doors at three, and wear that cream blouse and the corals — will you? I love you. I don't like sending

these letters to the shop. I always feel those people with
"Letters received" in their window keep a kettle in their back
parlour that would steam open an elephant's ear of an envelope. But it really doesn't matter, does it, darling? Can you
get away on Sunday? Pretend you are going to spend the day
with one of the girls from the office, and let's meet at some
little place and walk or find a field where we can watch the
daisies uncurling. I do love you, Edna. But Sundays without
you are simply impossible. Don't get run over before Saturday, and don't eat anything out of a tin or drink anything
from a public fountain. That's all, darling.'

My dearest, yes, I'll be there on Saturday – and I've
arranged about Sunday too. That is one great blessing.
I'm quite free at home. I have just come in from the
garden. It's such a lovely evening. Oh, Henry, I could
sit and cry, I love you so to-night. Silly – isn't it? I either
feel so happy I can hardly stop laughing or else so sad I
can hardly stop crying, and both for the same reason.
But we are so young to have found each other, aren't
we? I am sending you a violet. It is quite warm. I wish
you were here now, just for a minute even. Good-night,
darling.

                                        I am, Edna.

IV

'Safe,' said Edna, 'safe! And excellent places, aren't they,
Henry?'

She stood up to take off her coat and Henry made a movement to help her. 'No – no – it's off.' She tucked it under the
seat. She sat down beside him. 'Oh, Henry, what have you
got there? Flowers?'

'Only two tiny little roses.' He laid them in her lap.

'Did you get my letter all right?' asked Edna, unpinning
the paper.

'Yes,' he said, 'and the violet is growing beautifully. You should see my room. I planted a little piece of it in every corner and one on my pillow and one in the pocket of my pyjama jacket.'

She shook her hair at him. 'Henry, give me the programme.'

'Here it is – you can read it with me. I'll hold it for you.'

'No, let me have it.'

'Well, then, I'll read it for you.'

'No, you can have it after.'

'Edna,' he whispered.

'Oh, please don't,' she pleaded. 'Not here – the people.'

Why did he want to touch her so much and why did she mind? Whenever he was with her he wanted to hold her hand or take her arm when they walked together, or lean against her – not hard – just lean lightly so that his shoulder should touch her shoulder – and she wouldn't even have that. All the time that he was away from her he was hungry, he craved the nearness of her. There seemed to be comfort and warmth breathing from Edna that he needed to keep him calm. Yes, that was it. He couldn't get calm with her because she wouldn't let him touch her. But she loved him. He knew that. Why did she feel so curiously about it? Every time he tried to or even asked for her hand she shrank back and looked at him with pleading, frightened eyes as though he wanted to hurt her. They could say anything to each other. And there wasn't any question of their belonging to each other. And yet he couldn't touch her. Why, he couldn't even help her off with her coat. Her voice dropped into his thoughts.

'Henry!' He leaned to listen, setting his lips. 'I want to explain something to you. I will – I will – I promise – after the concert.'

'All right.' He was still hurt.

'You're not sad, are you?' she said.

He shook his head.

'Yes, you are, Henry.'

'No, really not.' He looked at the roses lying in her hands.

'Well, are you happy?'

'Yes. Here comes the orchestra.'

It was twilight when they came out of the hall. A blue net of light hung over the streets and houses, and pink clouds floated in a pale sky. As they walked away from the hall Henry felt they were very little and alone. For the first time since he had known Edna his heart was heavy.

'Henry!' She stopped suddenly and stared at him. 'Henry, I'm not coming to the station with you. Don't – don't wait for me. Please, please leave me.'

'My God!' cried Henry, and started, 'what's the matter – Edna – darling – Edna, what have I done?'

'Oh, nothing – go away,' and she turned and ran across the street into a square and leaned up against the square railings – and hid her face in her hands.

'Edna – Edna – my little love – you're crying. Edna, my baby girl!'

She leaned her arms along the railings and sobbed distractedly.

'Edna – stop – it's all my fault. I'm a fool – I'm a thundering idiot. I've spoiled your afternoon. I've tortured you with my idiotic mad bloody clumsiness. That's it. Isn't it, Edna? For God's sake.'

'Oh,' she sobbed, 'I do hate hurting you so. Every time you ask me to let – let you hold my hand or – or kiss me I could kill myself for not doing it – for not letting you. I don't know why I don't even.' She said wildly, 'It's not that I'm frightened of you – it's not that – it's only a feeling, Henry, that I can't understand myself even. Give me your handkerchief, darling.' He pulled it from his pocket. 'All through the concert I've been haunted by this, and every time we meet I know it's bound to come up. Somehow I feel if once we did that – you know – held each other's hands and kissed, it would be all changed – and I feel we wouldn't be free like we are – we'd be doing something secret. We wouldn't be children any more . . . silly, isn't it? I'd feel

awkward with you, Henry, and I'd feel shy, and I do so feel
that just because you and I are you and I, we don't need that
sort of thing.' She turned and looked at him, pressing her
hands to her cheeks in the way he knew so well, and behind
her as in a dream he saw the sky and half a white moon and
the trees of the square with their unbroken buds. He kept
twisting, twisting up in his hands the concert programme.
'Henry! You do understand me – don't you?'

'Yes, I think I do. But you're not going to be frightened
any more, are you?' He tried to smile. 'We'll forget, Edna.
I'll never mention it again. We'll bury the bogy in this square
– now – you and I – won't we?'

'But,' she said, searching his face – 'will it make you love
me less?'

'Oh no,' he said. 'Nothing could – nothing on earth could
do that.'

V

London became their playground. On Saturday afternoons
they explored. They found their own shops where they
bought cigarettes and sweets for Edna – and their own
tea-shop with their own table – their own streets – and
one night when Edna was supposed to be at a lecture at the
Polytechnic they found their own village. It was the name that
made them go there. 'There's white geese in that name,' said
Henry, telling it to Edna. 'And a river and little low houses
with old men sitting outside them – old sea captains with
wooden legs winding up their watches, and there are little
shops with lamps in the windows.'

It was too late for them to see the geese or the old men, but
the river was there and the houses and even the shops with
lamps. In one a woman sat working a sewing-machine on
the counter. They heard the whirring hum and they saw her
big shadow filling the shop. 'Too full for a single customer,'
said Henry. 'It is a perfect place.'

The houses were small and covered with creepers and ivy.

Some of them had worn wooden steps leading up to the doors. You had to go down a little flight of steps to enter some of the others; and just across the road – to be seen from every window – was the river, with a walk beside it and some high poplar trees.

'This is the place for us to live in,' said Henry. 'There's a house to let, too. I wonder if it would wait if we asked it. I'm sure it would.'

'Yes, I would like to live there,' said Edna. They crossed the road and she leaned against the trunk of a tree and looked up at the empty house with a dreamy smile.

'There is a little garden at the back, dear,' said Henry, 'a lawn with one tree on it and some daisy bushes round the wall. At night the stars shine in the tree like tiny candles. And inside there are two rooms downstairs and a big room with folding doors upstairs and above that an attic. And there are eight stairs to the kitchen – very dark, Edna. You are rather frightened of them, you know. "Henry, dear, would you mind bringing the lamp? I just want to make sure that Euphemia has raked out the fire before we go to bed." '

'Yes,' said Edna. 'Our bedroom is at the very top – that room with the two square windows. When it is quiet we can hear the river flowing and the sound of the poplar trees far, far away, rustling and flowing in our dreams, darling.'

'You're not cold – are you?' he said suddenly.

'No – no, only happy.'

'The room with the folding doors is yours.' Henry laughed. 'It's a mixture – it isn't a room at all. It's full of your toys and there's a big blue chair in it where you sit curled up in front of the fire with the flames in your curls – because though we're married you refuse to put your hair up and only tuck it inside your coat for the church service. And there's a rug on the floor for me to lie on, because I'm so lazy. Euphemia – that's our servant – only comes in the day. After she's gone we go down to the kitchen and sit on the table and eat an apple, or perhaps we make some tea, just for the sake of hearing the kettle sing. That's not joking. If you listen to a kettle right through it's like an early morning in Spring.'

'Yes, I know,' she said. 'All the different kinds of birds.'

A little cat came through the railings of the empty house and into the road. Edna called it and bent down and held out her hands – 'Kitty! Kitty!' The little cat ran to her and rubbed against her knees.

'If we're going for a walk just take the cat and put it inside the front door,' said Henry, still pretending. 'I've got the key.'

They walked across the road and Edna stood stroking the cat in her arms while Henry went up the steps and pretended to open the door.

He came down again quickly. 'Let's go away at once. It's going to turn into a dream.'

The night was dark and warm. They did not want to go home. 'What I feel so certain of is,' said Henry, 'that we ought to be living there now. We oughtn't to wait for things. What's age? You're as old as you'll ever be and so am I. You know,' he said, 'I have a feeling often and often that it's dangerous to wait for things – that if you wait for things they only go further and further away.'

'But, Henry, – money! You see we haven't any money.'

'Oh, well – perhaps if I disguised myself as an old man we could get a job as caretakers in some large house – that would be rather fun. I'd make up a terrific history of the house if anyone came to look over it, and you could dress up and be the ghost moaning and wringing your hands in the deserted picture gallery, to frighten them off. Don't you ever feel that money is more or less accidental – that if one really wants things it's either there or it doesn't matter?'

She did not answer that – she looked up at the sky and said, 'Oh dear, I don't want to go home.'

'Exactly – that's the whole trouble – and we oughtn't to go home. We ought to be going back to the house and find an odd saucer to give the cat the dregs of the milk-jug in. I'm not really laughing – I'm not even happy. I'm lonely for you, Edna – I would give anything to lie down and cry' . . . and he added limply, 'with my head in your lap and your darling cheek in my hair.'

'But, Henry,' she said, coming closer, 'you have faith, haven't you? I mean you are absolutely certain that we shall have a house like that and everything we want – aren't you?'

'Not enough – that's not enough. I want to be sitting on those very stairs and taking off these very boots this very minute. Don't you? Is faith enough for you?'

'If only we weren't so young . . .' she said miserably. 'And yet,' she sighed, 'I'm sure I don't feel very young – I feel twenty at least.'

VI

Henry lay on his back in the little wood. When he moved the dead leaves rustled beneath him, and above his head the new leaves quivered like fountains of green water steeped in sunlight. Somewhere out of sight Edna was gathering primroses. He had been so full of dreams that morning that he could not keep pace with her delight in the flowers. 'Yes, love, you go and come back for me. I'm too lazy.' She had thrown off her hat and knelt down beside him, and by and by her voice and her footsteps had grown fainter. Now the wood was silent except for the leaves, but he knew that she was not far away and he moved so that the tips of his fingers touched her pink jacket. Ever since waking he had felt so strangely that he was not really awake at all, but just dreaming. The time before Edna was a dream, and now he and she were dreaming together and somewhere in some dark place another dream waited for him. 'No, that can't be true because I can't ever imagine the world without us. I feel that we two together mean something that's got to be there just as naturally as trees or birds or clouds.' He tried to remember what it had felt like without Edna, but he could not get back to those days. They were hidden by her; Edna with the marigold hair and strange, dreamy smile filled him up to the brim. He breathed her; he ate and drank her. He walked about with a shining ring of Edna keeping the world away or touching whatever it lighted on with its own beauty. 'Long after you have stopped laughing,' he told her, 'I can hear your laugh running up and down my veins – and yet – are we a dream?' And suddenly he saw himself and Edna as two very small children walking through the streets, looking through windows, buying things and playing with them, talking to each other, smiling – he saw even their gestures and the way they stood, so often, quite still, face to face – and then he rolled over and pressed his face in the leaves – faint with longing. He wanted to kiss Edna, and to put his arms round her and press her to him and feel her cheek hot against his kiss, and kiss her until he'd no breath left and so stifle the dream.

'No, I can't go on being hungry like this,' said Henry, and jumped up and began to run in the direction she had gone. She had wandered a long way. Down in a green hollow he saw her kneeling, and when she saw him she waved and said – 'Oh, Henry – such beauties! I've never seen such beauties. Come and look.' By the time he had reached her he would have cut off his hand rather than spoil her happiness. How strange Edna was that day! All the time she talked to Henry her eyes laughed; they were sweet and mocking. Two little spots of colour like strawberries glowed on her cheeks and 'I wish I could feel tired,' she kept saying. 'I want to walk over the whole world until I die. Henry – come along. Walk faster – Henry! If I start flying suddenly, you'll promise to catch hold of my feet, won't you? Otherwise I'll never come down.' And 'Oh,' she cried, 'I am so happy. I'm so frightfully happy!' They came to a weird place, covered with heather. It was early afternoon and the sun streamed down upon the purple.

'Let's rest here a little,' said Edna, and she waded into the heather and lay down. 'Oh, Henry, it's so lovely. I can't see anything except the little bells and the sky.'

Henry knelt down by her and took some primroses out of her basket and made a long chain to go round her throat. 'I could almost fall asleep,' said Edna. She crept over to his knees and lay hidden in her hair just beside him. 'It's like being under the sea, isn't it, dearest, so sweet and so still?'

'Yes,' said Henry, in a strange, husky voice. 'Now I'll make you one of violets.' But Edna sat up. 'Let's go on,' she said.

They came back to the road and walked a long way. Edna said, 'No, I couldn't walk over the world – I'm tired now.' She trailed on the grass edge of the road. 'You and I are tired, Henry! How much further is it?'

'I don't know – not very far,' said Henry, peering into the distance. Then they walked in silence.

'Oh,' she said at last, 'it really is too far, Henry, I'm tired and I'm hungry. Carry my silly basket of primroses.' He took them without looking at her.

At last they came to a village and a cottage with a notice 'Teas Provided.'

'This is the place,' said Henry. 'I've often been here. You sit on the little bench and I'll go and order the tea.' She sat down on the bench, in the pretty garden all white and yellow with spring flowers. A woman came to the door and leaned against it watching them eat. Henry was very nice to her, but Edna did not say a word. 'You haven't been here for a long spell,' said the woman.

'No – the garden's looking wonderful.'

'Fair,' said she. 'Is the young lady your sister?' Henry nodded Yes, and took some jam.

'There's a likeness,' said the woman. She came down into the garden and picked a head of white jonquils and handed it to Edna. 'I suppose you don't happen to know anyone who wants a cottage,' said she. 'My sister's taken ill and she left me hers. I want to let it.'

'For a long time?' asked Henry politely.

'Oh,' said the woman vaguely, 'that depends.'

Said Henry, 'Well – I might know of somebody – could we go and look at it?'

'Yes, it's just a step down the road, the little one with the apple trees in front – I'll fetch you the key.'

While she was away Henry turned to Edna and said, 'Will you come?' She nodded.

They walked down the road and in through the gate and up the grassy path between the pink and white trees. It was a tiny place – two rooms downstairs and two rooms upstairs. Edna leaned out of the top window, and Henry stood at the doorway. 'Do you like it?' he asked.

'Yes,' she called, and then made a place for him at the window. 'Come and look. It's so sweet.'

He came and leant out of the window. Below them were the apple trees tossing in a faint wind that blew a long piece of Edna's hair across his eyes. They did not move. It was evening – the pale green sky was sprinkled with stars. 'Look!' she said – 'stars, Henry.'

'There will be a moon in two T's,' said Henry.

She did not seem to move and yet she was leaning against Henry's shoulder; he put his arm round her – 'Are all those trees down there – apple?' she asked in a shaky voice.

'No, darling,' said Henry. 'Some of them are full of angels and some of them are full of sugar almonds – but evening light is awfully deceptive.' She sighed. 'Henry – we mustn't stay here any longer.'

He let her go and she stood up in the dusky room and touched her hair. 'What has been the matter with you all day?' she said – and then did not wait for an answer but ran to him and put her arms round his neck, and pressed his head into the hollow of her shoulder. 'Oh,' she breathed, 'I do love you. Hold me, Henry.' He put his arms round her, and she leaned against him and looked into his eyes. 'Hasn't it been terrible, all to-day?' said Edna. 'I knew what was the matter and I've tried every way I could to tell you that I wanted you to kiss me – that I'd quite got over the feeling.'

'You're perfect, perfect, perfect,' said Henry.

*   *   *

VII

'The thing is,' said Henry, 'how am I going to wait until evening?' He took his watch out of his pocket, went into the cottage and popped it into a china jar on the mantel-piece. He'd looked at it seven times in one hour, and now he couldn't remember what time it was. Well, he'd look once again. Half-past four. Her train arrived at seven. He'd have to start for the station at half-past six. Two hours more to wait. He went through the cottage again – downstairs and upstairs. 'It looks lovely,' he said. He went into the garden and picked a round bunch of white pinks and put them in a vase on the little table by Edna's bed. 'I don't believe this,' thought Henry. 'I don't believe this for a minute. It's too much. She'll be here in two hours and we'll walk home, and then I'll take that white jug off the kitchen table and go across to Mrs Biddie's and get the milk, and then come back, and when I come back she'll have lighted the lamp in the kitchen and I'll look through the window and see her moving about in the pool of lamplight. And then we shall have supper, and after supper (Bags I washing up!) I shall put some wood on the fire and we'll sit on the hearth-rug and watch it burning. There won't be a sound except the wood and perhaps the wind will creep round the house once . . . And then we shall light our candles and she will go up first with her shadow on the wall beside her, and she will call out, Good-night, Henry – and I shall answer – Good-night, Edna. And then I shall dash upstairs and jump into bed and watch the tiny bar of light from her room brush my door, and the moment it disappears will shut my eyes and sleep until morning. Then we'll have all to-morrow and to-morrow and to-morrow night. Is she thinking all this, too? Edna, come quickly!

> Had I but two little wings,
> And were a little feathery bird,
> To you I'd fly, my dear –

'No, no dearest . . . Because the waiting is a sort of Heaven, too, darling. If you can understand that. Did you ever know a cottage could stand on tiptoe. This one is doing it now.'

He was downstairs and sat on the doorstep with his hands clasped round his knees. That night when they found the village – and Edna said, 'Haven't you faith, Henry?' 'I hadn't then. Now I have,' he said, 'I feel just like God.'

He leaned his head against the lintel. He could hardly keep his eyes open, not that he was sleepy, but . . . for some reason . . . and a long time passed.

Henry thought he saw a big white moth flying down the road. It perched on the gate. No, it wasn't a moth. It was a little girl in a pinafore. What a nice little girl, and he smiled in his sleep, and she smiled, too, and turned in her toes as she walked. 'But she can't be living here,' thought Henry. 'Because this is ours. Here she comes.'

When she was quite close to him she took her hand from under her pinafore and gave him a telegram and smiled and went away. There's a funny present! thought Henry, staring at it. 'Perhaps it's only a make-believe one, and it's got one of those snakes inside it that fly up at you.' He laughed gently in the dream and opened it very carefully. 'It's just a folded paper.' He took it out and spread it open.

The garden became full of shadows – they spun a web of darkness over the cottage and the trees and Henry and the telegram. But Henry did not move.

Jack

M. H. LAWSON

M. H. LAWSON is a Canadian, living in England with her husband and two sons. Her story, 'Jack', harks back to the part of Ontario in which she grew up and is one of many Mary Lawson has written for magazines in this country.

MY great-great-grandmother fixed a book-rest to her spinning wheel so that she could read while she was spinning, or so the story goes. And one Saturday evening she became so absorbed in her book that when she finally looked up she found that it was half-past midnight, and she had spun for half an hour on the Sabbath day. A grievous sin.

There was a picture of her in my parents' room while I was growing up. I used to stand in front of it, as a very small child, daring myself to meet her eye. She was small, tight-lipped, and straight, dressed in black with an impossibly white lace collar (scrubbed ruthlessly, no doubt, every single evening, and ironed mercilessly before dawn each day). She looked severe, disapproving, and entirely without humour. And well she might: she had fourteen children in thirteen years, and 500 acres of barren farmland. How she ever found time to spin, let alone read, I'll never know. My brother Jack looked a bit like her sometimes; he was far from grim, but he had the same straight mouth and steady grey eyes. If I fidgeted in church and got a sharp glance from my mother I would peer sideways up at Jack to see if he had noticed. And he always had, and looked severe, and then at the last possible moment, just as I was beginning to despair, he would wink.

We lived in a small farming community in northern Ontario, and you can't get a more serious-minded background than that. My father was the first member of the Morrison family to manage to leave the farm. He worked in a bank in the nearest town, and wore a suit to work, and owned a car and built a house out by the lake, away from the dust and the flies of the farmyard. But his ideals and principles were pretty much the same as great-great-grandmother Morrison's: the community we lived in wasn't given to rapid change. It was linked to the outside world by one dusty road and the railroad tracks. The trains didn't stop unless you flagged them down, and the road led only south, there being no reason for anyone to want to go further north. Apart from half a dozen farms, a general store, and a few new houses out by the lake, there was nothing there but the church and the school.

Jack was ten years older than I, tall and serious and clever. His great passion was the ponds, a mile or two away, across the railroad tracks. They were old gravel pits, abandoned years ago and filled by nature with all manner of marvellous wriggling creatures. When Jack first started taking me back to the ponds I was so small that he had to carry me on his shoulders – through the woods with their luxuriant growth of poison ivy, along the tracks, past the dusty box-cars, lined up to receive their loads of sugar beets, down the steep sandy path to the ponds themselves. There we would lie on our bellies while the sun beat down on our backs, gazing into the dark water, waiting to see what we would see.

There is no image of my childhood that I carry with me as clearly as that; a boy of perhaps 15 or 16, dark haired and lanky; beside him a little girl, fair hair in braids, thin brown legs burning yet more deeply in the sun. They are both lying perfectly still, chins resting on the backs of their hands. He is showing her things. Or rather, things are drifting out from under rocks and shadows and showing themselves, and he is telling her about them.

'Just move your finger, Peg. Just waggle it in the water. He'll come over. Can't resist.'

Cautiously, the little girl waggles her finger; cautiously a small snapping turtle slides over to inspect.

'See? They're very curious when they're young. When he gets older, though, he'll be suspicious and bad-tempered and mean.'

'Why?' (The old snapper she and Jack had trapped out on land once had looked sleepy rather than mean. He had a wrinkled, rubbery head, and she had wanted to pat it. Jack held out a finger-thick branch, and the snapper chopped it clean in two.)

'Their shells are small for the size of their bodies, see? So a lot of their skin is exposed. More than most turtles. Makes them nervous.'

The little girl nods, and the ends of her braids bob up and down in the water, making tiny ripples. She is completely absorbed.

Hundreds of hours, we must have spent that way over the years. I came to know the tadpoles of the leopard frogs, the fat grey tadpoles of the bullfrogs, the tiny black wriggling ones of toads. I knew the turtles and the catfish, the waterstriders and the newts, the whirlygigs spinning hysterically over the surface of the water. Hundreds of hours, while the seasons changed, and the pond life died and renewed itself many times, and I grew too big to ride on Jack's shoulders and instead picked my way through the woods behind him. I was unaware of these changes of course – they happened so gradually, and children have very little concept of time. Tomorrow is forever, and years pass in no time at all.

'He's a very fortunate young man,' my mother said. 'Not everybody gets an opportunity like that. Not everybody, by any means.' Her tone was brisk, matter-of-fact. Jack had won a scholarship to study biology at the University of Toronto. My parents were modest in their pride; they did not praise him, or drop casual comments to the neighbours. That would have been unseemly, and besides, there was no need. It had been announced, banner headlines, in the church newsletter. Everybody knew. I was eight, and Jack

eighteen. He was taller than my father now, and gravely
good-looking.
'Mum says you're going away.'
'I'm going to university, Peg.'
'How long for?'
He hesitates and smiles at her. 'A few years, I guess.'
'Don't you like it here any more?'
'Sure I do. And I'll come back lots.'
'How often? Every weekend?'
'Well, maybe not every weekend.'
*A long silence, while she tries to work something out. 'Mum says
Toronto is 300 miles away.'*
*He reaches out and tugs one of her braids. 'I'll come back often, Peg.
I promise. But I can learn a lot there. I've got to go.'*
'When?'
*'Not until the end of September. Three whole months. We'll have
the whole summer together.'*

But we did not have the whole summer together. The
scholarship covered tuition and lodging, but not food or the
cost of textbooks, so at the end of June when school finished,
Jack took a job working on Mr Pye's farm back near the
gravel pits. Mr Pye had 6 kids of his own, but by some cruel
stroke of fate they were all girls. He was known to be a hard
man, though honest, and terribly strict – I once heard my
mother say that Calvin Pye was too hard on his kids, and
would do better to ease up on them a bit – but Jack never
complained about him. He worked long hours, though, six
days a week, and by the time he got home in the evenings he
was too tired to do anything but flop on his bed and read.

School had finished for me too, and I spent the days sitting on the back step, drawing patterns in the dust with
my toes, or resentfully doing jobs for my mother. I waited
for Sundays, when Jack would be free. And at first he was,
and took me back to the ponds as before, but then, as the
summer wore on, he frequently seemed to vanish straight
after church on Sunday, and sometimes didn't get home until
dinner time.

'Where's Jack?'

'He said he was going out.' Mother gives me a reproving glance. *'He works hard. He needs a bit of time to himself.'*

'When will he be back? Will he take me to the ponds this evening?'

'Don't you go pestering him, young lady. He's taken you to those old ponds often enough, heaven knows.'

'But where's he gone?'

'I expect he's off with his friends, Peggy! Give him some peace, child! You'd think you owned him!'

Which was true.

Most bitter in my mind was the thought of how few hours I had left with Jack. And in a sorry parody of adult jealousies, I managed to spoil those few. Jack did take me back to the ponds once or twice, but neither of us enjoyed it. I was too busy being resentful; he seemed uneasy, unable to concentrate. I interrogated him about where he went, what he did, and he snapped at me, which he had never done before.

I was forbidden to go back to the ponds alone. They were deep, and a child had been drowned there once. Perhaps that is why I went – simply to break the rules. I do not think that I expected to find Jack there, though it may have been in my mind to look for him.

It was an extremely hot day, heavy and still. I walked tight-rope along the rails, feeling the heat of the steel through the soles of my shoes, and then slid down the path to the nearest pond. For a while I lay on my stomach and stared into the water, but everything that could move was in hiding from the sun. Even if you poked about you only got a brief flurry of activity and then stillness again. I sighed and stood up, slightly dizzy from the heat. If Jack had been here, he would have sought the shade on the other side of the bank between this pond and the next. At the foot of the bank I hesitated, thinking that I heard voices. Then I scrambled up the side, using the tufts of grass as hand-holds, and hauled myself onto the flat grassy top. There was no doubt now about the voices. I stood up and peered over the side.

Marie Pye was the eldest of Mr Pye's six daughters. She was Jack's age, soft and pretty and nervous-looking, with a halo of fine pale hair and wide startled eyes. She and Jack were lying in the shade of the overhanging bank, about 30 feet below and to the left of where I stood. Jack had taken off his shirt and spread it on the ground, and they were both lying on that. I remember thinking that it was awfully hot to be so close to someone else.

Marie was crying. From where I stood I could not see her face, but I could hear her, and Jack trying to comfort her. He kept saying he was sorry, that it would be all right. His voice was urgent, frightened even, and it occurred to me that he must have done something wrong. He had hit her, perhaps, and knocked her down. I was surprised by this, and then angry with Marie, for Jack was mild and even-tempered, and it would have taken quite something to make him hit anyone.

Then I noticed his shirt again, and realized that he would not have spread it out in order to knock her down on it. But still I was angry with her. Whatever he had done, she had driven him to it: I was sure of that. I am sure of it still.

At length he helped her up and tried to put his arms around her. She turned away. She was wearing a thin cotton print dress; it was creased and rumpled and had come almost completely undone. She began doing it up, sniffling and fumbling. Jack watched her, his hands clenched at his sides, his expression utterly wretched.

'I'm sorry,' he said again. 'I didn't mean it to happen. I really didn't.' She shook her head. I hated her. You could see how upset he was, and she would not accept it. She finished doing herself up, then straightened and smoothed her hair back and it was then that she saw me. She gave a cry of absolute terror, and Jack jerked back, and then saw me himself. For a minute all three of us were frozen. Then

Marie started crying hysterically. Her fear was so great that it communicated itself to me, and I turned and ran, slithered down the other side of the bank, around the edge of the pond, running as I had never run, my heart pounding with fear. I was halfway up the path to the railroad tracks when Jack caught me. 'Peggy! Peggy, stop!' He caught me around the waist and held me, kicking and struggling. 'Peggy, for goodness sake stop! What are you afraid of? I'm not cross with you. Stop!'

'I want to go home!'

'We will. In just a minute. We'll go home together. But we must go back to Marie first.'

'I'm not going back to her! She's horrible! Screaming like that – she's horrible!'

'She's just upset, Peg. You startled her. Come on now.'

She was standing where we had left her, arms wrapped around herself, shivering in the blazing heat. Jack brought me up to her, but he didn't know what to say. It was Marie who spoke.

'She'll tell.' She was white as white. A big healthy farm girl, white as a fish's belly, trembling, weeping, snivelling.

'No she won't. You won't tell, will you Peg?'

'Tell what?' I had recovered from my fright, felt outraged, scornful, and cruel.

'Oh Jack! She will! She'll tell!' More weeping. Jack turned first to her and then to me.

'Peg, you must promise. Promise me you won't tell you saw us here.'

I wouldn't look at him. I watched Marie, this dull girl whom Jack preferred to me, who could have no possible interest in the ponds, who accused Jack and refused to forgive him, who thought I was a sneak, a tattle-tale.

'I promise I won't tell on you,' I said at last, turning to Jack. But he was too smart for that.

'Or on Marie. You must promise not to tell that you saw her with anyone. Word of honour.' The silence grew. 'Word of honour, Peg. Promise on all the times I've brought you to these ponds. Promise on the life of every creature in these ponds.'

I had no choice then. Sullenly, mumbling, I gave my word. Marie looked a little less fearful. Jack put an arm around her and led her a few yards away. I watched them, jealousy making my lower lip quiver. He talked to her very quietly, for a long time. Finally she nodded, and walked off across the sand towards the path that led up to the farms.

Jack and I walked home together. Several times I looked up at him, hoping that he would smile, but he seemed unaware of my presence. In the coolness of the woods I drew up the courage to ask if he was mad at me.

'No. No, I'm not mad at you.' He gave me a smile of such misery that I was shamed out of my own self-pity.

'It's all right isn't it?' I said. 'Everything will be all right?'

Jack was different after that. Subdued. He continued working on the farm, but in the evenings and on Sundays he shut himself in his room. I can imagine now what he must have gone through, as one week followed another, waiting, and hoping, and no doubt praying too, for we had been brought up to believe in a merciful god.

In September, a couple of weeks before he was due to leave, he called me into his room. For a few minutes he just fiddled with his pencil, not looking at me. He was very white, and I began to get scared. Finally he looked up.

'I have to tell Mum and Dad something, Peg, and I wanted to tell you first.'

I nodded, too frightened now to speak.

'It's going to cause a lot of trouble – everyone's going to be upset and everything – and I want you to understand.'

Poor Jack. As if there was any hope that I would understand.

They were married in our little local church. I guess the shame of it nearly finished off Mum and Dad. They could

not find it in their hearts to forgive Mr and Mrs Pye for
bringing up such a slut of a daughter, and Mr and Mrs Pye
felt likewise, so the smiles at the wedding reception were false
as charity.

As for Jack and Marie; Mr Pye had said that Jack should
live with them, but my father would sooner have died than
have Jack go back to farming. When Jack tried to protest,
said that he didn't mind, my father told him to shut up in
such a tone as no one in the house had ever heard him use.
At great personal sacrifice, by borrowing from his family
and the bank and shaming Calvin Pye into contributing, he
managed to buy Jack and Marie a mean little house off the
Northern Side Road. Then, by doing some begging, he got
Jack a job at the bank. Any punishment would have seemed
a picnic by comparison.

And in due course, it was I who took up a scholarship and
went to Toronto to study biology.

All this was 18 years ago. Their son, Simon, was born at the
end of April, and a fortnight ago I was invited to his 18th
birthday party. I took a bit of time off work, and drove up
from Toronto the day before. The roads are paved most of
the way now; it is only for the last half hour that you feel you
are really going back in time.

Jack and Marie met me at the door. They live in a pleasant
chalet-style house now, down by the lake. Jack is manager
of the bank in town. I know that he has been offered bigger
jobs in bigger towns, but Marie will not leave her family.
Her parents are old, and Marie's debt to them has not yet
been paid off, nor ever will be. Our parents are both dead,
so Jack's years of penance are over.

Marie and I did not embrace: we smiled the polite smile of
acquaintances. Jack hugged me, and I returned his pressure
hard, making up for long absences. We are both shamefully
bad at writing letters. Simon stood in the doorway to the
livingroom, watching us with an interested smile. He is very

clever, like Jack – considerably more so than his three sisters, who were hovering and giggling in the kitchen.

'Hi Auntie,' he said. 'Do I get a kiss?'

He calls me Auntie to tease: there is less than nine years between us. In the fall he is coming to the university to study chemistry. I lecture there now. I don't suppose I'll see much of him, but I have threatened to keep an eye on him, and he has looked suitably horrified at the thought.

After dinner, an excellent, wholesome meal – Marie has been a "good wife" to Jack, and looks after him well – Jack said, 'Come outside, Peg. We want to show you something.'

'I'll just help Marie with the dishes first. That was a beautiful meal.'

'No no,' Marie got up from the table. 'You go and look before it gets dark. They've been dying to show you. It's your sort of thing.'

It was a pond. Jack and Simon had dug it themselves. They have half an acre of land beside the house, and they'd borrowed Calvin Pye's tractor and stuck a shovel on its nose and dug out a pond.

'What do you think?' said Jack. He and Simon were watching me excitedly.

'It's great! *Great!*'

I squatted down and gazed into the pond, so as not to have to look at Jack. All that future, all that dedication and love of learning, and all he had was a little pond beside his house, with tadpoles and turtles and the odd catfish. 'Snappers even,' I said admiringly. 'You must have been poaching.'

'Yes,' he said. 'The gravel pits.'

'If you wind him up, Auntie, he'll recite every god-forsaken creature in there from amoeba on up,' said Simon. 'So please don't. He's even more boring on the subject than you.'

I looked up. 'I know,' I said.

We stayed out there, prodding around in the mud until the cold drove us in. Jack and Simon began clearing the livingroom for tomorrow's party. I forced myself to go into the kitchen, where Marie was making about two dozen desserts. There was no sign of the girls.

'Can I help?'

'Oh . . . thanks. Could you . . .?' she looked around helplessly, trying to think of something I could safely be entrusted with. She considers me a liability in the kitchen, and she is right. 'What did you think of the pond?'

'Oh it's excellent!' Hearty and enthusiastic. I am hearty and enthusiastic with no one but Marie. 'They must have had great fun with it!'

She stood by the refrigerator, a jug of cream in her hands.

'Yes,' she said. 'They do have a good time together.' She turned and looked at me. She has changed very little over the years. If anything, her looks have improved. Her eyes are less fearful now.

'What do you think of Simon?' she asked. 'On the eve of his birthday – what do you think of him?'

It was such a strange question that I flushed, and stared. He was the same age as Jack had been the summer of their disastrous affair, and though I was sure that he was far too street-wise to make his father's mistakes, I wondered if she was worrying about him. 'I like him very much. He's a . . . fine boy. An extremely nice boy.' It sounded ridiculously old fashioned and patronising, but Marie nodded. Her face was flushed too, but she seemed grim rather than embarrassed. Fierce, almost. It was so unlike her that I was quite unnerved.

'How does Jack strike you?' she said. 'Does he seem well to you?'

'I think he's looking very well. Very well.'

'Happy, would you say?'

I was alarmed now. We do not ask such questions in our family. It is the ultimate in bad taste. 'He seems happy to me, Marie. Why? What's wrong?'

'Nothing.' She gave a brief smile. 'I just wondered if you could see it. Could see that he is well and happy, and has a fine son, who he loves and has a good time with, and three good daughters. I just wanted you to see it, for once, after all this time.'

In the silence we could hear Jack and Simon heaving furniture about. Something had become stuck in the doorway; Jack was cursing, Simon was hooting with laughter.

Marie smiled at me again. 'If you knew,' she said. 'If you only knew how much your opinion matters to him. And to me, of course, but mostly to him. He could live with your parents' disappointment, he could accept that. But yours has been so hard for him to bear.'

Great-great-grandmother Morrison, you have a lot to answer for. It is you, with your love of books, your determination to learn and understand, who set the standard against which I have somehow judged everyone around me, all of my life. If I were to look at your portrait now, would I see myself? Humourless and disapproving, at the age of twenty-six? In all these years of single-minded pursuit of knowledge, have I learned nothing at all?

Simon came in then, and saved us from ourselves – which is the great gift of the young – by sticking his fingers in the desserts and getting shouted at by both of us. The atmosphere was eased after that, and we were able to work together very well.

Toxin

OUIDA

OUIDA (1839–1908). Her real name was Marie Louise de la Remée and her writing name was taken from a childish version of 'Louise'. She was born in Bury St Edmunds, where her father taught French. Her best known novel is probably Under Two Flags, *about the Foreign Legion. In their day her novels were considered hot stuff, and kept out of the hands of impressionable young girls.*

I

'OH! my necklace!' cried a fair woman as she leaned over the side of her gondola.

A string of opals, linked and set in gold, had been loosened from her throat, and had slid down into the water of the lagoon, midway between the Lido and the city of Venice. But the gondola was moving swiftly under the impulsion of a rower fore and aft, and, though they stopped a few moments after at her cry, the spot where it had fallen was already passed and left behind. She was vexed and provoked. She had many jewels, but the opal necklace was an heirloom, and of fine and curious workmanship. The gondoliers did their best to find it, but in vain. They were in the deeper water of the sailing roads, which were marked out by the lines of poles, and the necklace, a slight thing, had been borne away by the current setting in from the open sea.

It was a pale afternoon in late summer; the heat was still great; the skies and the waters were of the same soft, dreamy, silvery hue, and the same transparency and ethereality were on the distant horizons of the hills, west and east. The only colour there was came from the ruddy painted sails of some fruit-laden market boats which were passing to leeward.

Neither of the men could swim; many Venetians cannot; but they got over the side, and waded up to their waists in the water, and with their oars struck and sounded the sandy bottom, whilst she encouraged them with praise and extravagant promise of reward. Their efforts were of no avail. The lagoon, which has been the grave of so many, kept the drowned opals.

'We will go back and send divers,' she said to her men who, wet to their waists, were well content to turn the head of the gondola back to the city.

They wore white clothes with red sashes and red ribbons round their straw hats; they were in her private service; they steered quickly home again over the calm water-way, and in and out the crowded craft, by the Schiavone, past the Customs House, and S. Giorgio, and the Salvatore, until they reached a palace on the Grand Canal, which was their mistress's residence, with poles painted red and white, with coronets on their tops, marking the landing-stairs in the old Venetian fashion.

'I have lost my opals in the water!' she cried to a friend who was on one of the balconies of the first floor.

'I am glad you have lost them,' replied her friend. 'They are stones of misfortune.'

'Nonsense! They were beautiful, and they were Ninetta Zaranegra's, poor Carlo's great-great-grandmother; they were one of her nuptial presents a hundred and twenty years ago. I must have the men dive and dredge till they are found. The water is so shallow. I cannot think how the collar can have vanished so completely in such a moment of time.'

She ascended her palace steps, and dismissed her gondoliers with a gesture, as she paused in the entrance hall to tell her major-domo of her loss, and consult him as to the best means to recover the necklace. The hall was painted in fresco, with beautiful Moorish windows, and a groined and gilded ceiling, and a wide staircase of white marble, uncarpeted. Opposite the entrance was a latticed door, through which was seen the bright green of acacias, cratægus and laurel growing in a garden.

On the morrow, when it was known through Venice that the rich and generous Countess Zaranegra had lost her jewels, all the best divers hurried to the place where the opals had dropped, and worked sedulously from daybreak to find it, sailors and fishermen and boatmen all joining in the search, in hope to merit the reward she promised. But no one of them succeeded. Their efforts were useless. The tenacious water would not yield up its prey. The opals were gone, like spindrift.

II

The winter came and went, wrapping Venice in its mists, driving the sea-birds into the inland canals, making the pigeons sit ruffled and sad on the parapets of the palaces, and leaving many a gondolier unemployed, to warm his hands over little fires of driftwood under the snow-sprinkled rafters and naked vine branches of his traghetto. The gondoliers of the Ca' Zaranegra were more fortunate; they could sit round the great bronze brazier in the hall of their lady's house, and the gondola was laid up high and dry to await the spring, and their wages were paid with regularity and liberality by the silent and austere major-domo who reigned in the forsaken palace, for their lady was away on warmer shores than the windbeaten, surge-drowned sea-walls of their city.

The winter was hard; snow lay long on the Istrian hills and on the Paduan pastures; there was ice on the rigging of the Greek brigs in the Giudecca, and the huge ocean steamers from the east looked like uncouth prehistoric beasts, black and gigantic, as they loomed through the fogs, moving slowly towards the docks under cautious pilotage. There were laughter and warmth in the theatres, and the sounds of music came from some of the palaces; but in the Calle, in the fishermen's quarters, on the islands, on board the poor rough sailing craft, and amongst the maritime population generally, there were great suffering and much want; and by the bar of Malomocco and off the coast of Chioggia there were wrecks, which strewed the waters with broken timbers and dashed drowning sailors like seaweed on to the wooden piles. Stout boats were broken like shells, and strong seafaring men were washed to and fro like driftwood. But the frail opal necklace of the Countess Zaranegra was safe in the midst of the strife; it had fallen into a hollow in a sunken pile, and lay there unharmed, whilst above it the stormy tides rose and fell, and the winds churned the cream of the surf. There it lay, all through the rough winter weather, whilst the silvery gulls died of hunger, and the sea swallows were hurled by the hurricane on to the lanterns of lighthouses and against the timbers of vessels.

It weathered many storms, this frail toy, made to lie on the warm breasts of women, whilst the storm kings drew down to their death the bread-winners for whom wife and children vainly prayed on shore, and the daring mariners for whom the deep had had no terrors.

In the hollow of the old oak pile the opals remained all winter long, lying like bird's eggs in a nest, whilst the restless waters washed and swirled above its sanctuary. The worn stump of the wood had kept its place for centuries, and many a corpse had drifted past it outward to the sea in days when the white marbles of St Mark's city had run red with blood. It had once been the base of a sea-shrine, of a Madonna of the waters, to whom the boatmen passing had invoked the Stella Maris Virgine, so dear to fishermen and sailors.

But the painted shrine had long disappeared, and only the piece of timber, down underneath the waters, rooted in the sand amongst the ribbon weed and mussels, had had power to resist the forces of tide and tempest.

All the winter long the old wood kept the opals safe and sound. When the cold passed, and the blasts from the

Dolomite glaciers softened, and the orchards of the fruit islands were in bud, the opals were still in their hollow, covered from the sea by the bend of the wood above them, so that, though often wet, they were never washed away.

But one day, when the peach and pear and plum trees had in turn burst into blossom on the isles, and the flocks of gulls who had survived the stress of famine and frost had returned to their feeding-places on the outer lagoons, a large iron ship, coming from the Black Sea, gave a rude shock, in passing, to the old oak pile; the top of it under the blow parted and fell asunder; the necklace was washed out of its hiding-place, and, carried in the heavy trough of the steamer's path, was floated nearer to the isles, farther from the city. It became entangled with some algæ, and, rocked on the weed as on a little raft, was borne to and fro by a strong wind rushing from the north-east, and so was driven round past San Cristoforo and Burano, and was finally carried ashore up the creeks into the long grasses and reeds beneath the Devil's Bridge at Torcello. The yellow water iris was then flowering, and two little reed warblers were nesting amongst the flags, as the opals were drifted up under some hemlock leaves and there rested.

'I think they are eggs, but they are all strung together,' said the warbler to his mate.

'They look more like the spawn of a fish,' said the little winged lady, with scorn.

A water rat came up and smelt at them, then went away disdainfully; they were not good to eat. For birds and beasts do not care for jewels: it is only humanity, which thinks itself superior to them, which sees any value in stones, and calls such toys precious.

III

The devil is credited with building many bridges on the earth; it is hard to know why he should have done so, since waters, however wide, cannot possibly have been an obstacle in his own path.

But Devil's Bridges there are, from the Hebrides to the Isles of Greece. The Devil's Bridge at Torcello has been so called from the height and breadth of its one arch, but there is nothing diabolic or infernal in its appearance; it is of old brick, made beautiful in its hues by age, and has many seeding grasses and weeds growing in its crevices. Its banks are rich in grass, in flags, in sea-lavender, and about it grow hazel trees and pear trees.

There is nowhere in the world any grass richer than that of Torcello, and forget-me-nots, honeysuckle and wild roses grow down to the water's edge and around the hoary stones of the deserted isle.

'What a God-forgotten place!' said a young man as he sprang from a boat on to the bank by the bridge.

'Torcello was the mother of Venice; the daughter has slain her,' replied an older man, as he laid down his oars in the boat and prepared to follow his companion.

His foot trod amongst the hemlock leaves and was entangled by them; he stooped, and his eyes, which were very keen, caught sight of the string of opals.

'A woman's necklace!' he said, as he drew it out from under the salt seaweed and the dewy dock leaves. It was discoloured, and had sand and mud on it, and bore little traces of its former beauty; but he recognised that it was a jewel of worth; he perceived, even dulled as they were, that the stones were opals.

'What have you there?' cried the younger man from above on the bank. 'The skull of an Archimandrite?'

The other threw the necklace up on to the grass.

'You would have been a fitter finder of a woman's collar than I am.'

'Opals! The stones of sorrow!' said the younger man, gravely, as he raised it and brushed off the sand. 'It has been beautiful,' he added. 'It will be so again. It is not really hurt, only a little bruised and tarnished.

The necklace interested him; he examined it minutely as the sun shone on the links of dimmed gold. It awakened in him an image of the woman who might have possessed and worn it.

'What will you do with it?' he said to his companion, who had mounted on to the bank after securing the boat.

'What does one always do with things found? Send them to the police, I believe.'

'Oh, you Goth!' said the younger. 'Let us spend our lives in discovering the owner.'

'You can spend yours so if you like, prince. Mine is already in bond to a severer mistress.'

'Lend me your glass,' said the younger man; the glass was of strong magnifying power. When it was handed to him he looked through it at some little marks on the back of the clasp of the opal collar. 'Zaranegra, 1770,' he read aloud. 'Zaranegra is a Venetian name.'

There was an inscription so minute, that to the unaided eye it was invisible; through the glass it was possible to read it. It was this –

NINA DELLA LUCEDIA
CONTESSA ZARANEGRA
Capo d'Anno
1770.

'Zaranegra!' repeated the younger man. 'That is a Venetian name. Lucedia is a name of the Marches of Ancona. There is a Ca' Zaranegra on the Grand Canal. It is next to the Loredàn. You admired its Moorish windows on the second storey this morning. Carlo Zaranegra died young; he left a widow who is only twenty now. She is a daughter of the Duke of Monfalcone, a family of the Trentino, but pure Italians in blood. Their place is in the mountains above Gorizia. It must be she who owns this necklace, an heirloom probably.'

'Take it to her,' said the finder of it, with indifference. 'I cede you my rights.'

The younger laughed.

'Ah! who knows what they may become?'

'Whatever they may become they are yours. I do not appreciate that kind of reward.'

'Really?' said the younger man. 'If so, I pity you!'

'Nay, I pity you,' said the elder.

The young man still stood with the opals in his hands; with a wisp of grass he had cleared the sand in a measure off them. The pearly softness and the roseate flame of the stones began to show here and there; two alone of their number were missing.

'Come,' said his companion, with impatience, 'put that broken rubbish in your pocket, and let us go and see the Cathedral and S. Fosca, for it will soon grow dark.'

They walked along the dyke of turf which traverses the isle, past the low fruit trees and the humble cabins of the few peasants who dwell there; the grass was long, and full of ox-eyed daisies and purple loosestrife and pink campion. They soon reached the green and quiet place where the sacred buildings of S. Maria and S. Fosca stand in the solitude of field and sea.

They entered first of all the old church of S. Fosca. The younger man went straight to the altar with uncovered head and knelt before it, a soft and serious look upon his face as his lips moved.

The elder cast a glance, contemptuous and derisive, on him, and turned to look at the five arcades, with their columns, so precious to those who understand the laws of architecture.

He was learned in many things, and architecture and archæology were the studies which were to him pastimes, in the rare hours of recreation which he allowed himself.

'Have you prayed to find the mistress of the opals?' he said to the younger man who, risen from his knees, approached him, a red light of the late afternoon slanting in from an upper window in the apse and falling on his bright hair and beautiful classic face.

The young man coloured.

'I prayed that the stones may bring us no evil,' he said, with ingenuous simplicity. 'Laugh as you will, a prayer

can never do harm, and you know opals are stones of
sorrow.'

'I know you are a credulous child – a superstitious peasant
– though you are twenty-four years old and have royal and
noble blood in your veins.'

'If you had not saved my life I would throw you into the
sea,' replied the other, half in jest half in anger. 'Leave my
faiths alone. Lead your own barren life as you choose, but do
not cut down flowers in the garden of others.'

'Life is truly a garden for you,' said the elder man, with a
touch of envy in the tone of his voice.

It was dusk in S. Fosca, for the day was far advanced and
the sun was setting without beyond the world of waters.

Two peasant women were saying their aves before low
burning lamps. The scent of the grass and the smell of the
sea came in through the open door. A cat walked noiselessly
across the altar. As the church was now, so it had been a
thousand years earlier.

'Does this place say nothing to you?' asked the younger
man.

'Nothing,' replied the other. 'What should it say?'

IV

When the young Sicilian prince, Lionello Adrianis, head of
an ancient Hispano-Italian family, had met with a hunting
accident, and the tusks of an old boar had brought him near
to death, an English surgeon, by name Frederic Damer, who
was then in Palermo, did for him what none of the Italian
surgeons dared to do, and, so far as the phrase can ever be
correct of human action, saved his life. A year had passed
since then; the splendid vitality of the Sicilian had returned
to all its natural vigour; he was only twenty-four years of
age, and naturally strong as a young oak in the woods of
Etna. But he had a mother who loved him, and was anxious;
she begged the Englishman to remain awhile near him; the
Sicilian laughed but submitted; he and Damer had travelled

together in Egypt and India during several months, and were now about in another month to part company; the Sicilian to return to his own people, the Englishman to occupy a chair of physiology in a town of northern Europe.

Their lives had been briefly united by accident and would have parted in peace: a collar of opals was by chance washed up amongst the flags and burdocks of Torcella, and the shape of their fate was altered.

With such trifles do the gods play when they stake the lives of men on the game.

Damer was the son of a country physician, but his father had been poor, the family numerous, and he, a third son, had been sent out into the world with only his education as his capital. He practised surgery to live; he practised physiology to reach through it that power and celebrity for which his nature craved and his mental capacity fitted him. But at every step his narrow means galled and fretted him, and he had been a demonstrator, an assistant, a professor in schools, when his vast ability and relentless will fitted him for the position of a Helmholtz or a Virchow in that new priesthood which has arisen to claim the rule of mankind, and sacrifices to itself all sentient races.

In Adrianis he saw all the powers of youth and of wealth concentrated in one who merely used them for a careless enjoyment and a thoughtless good nature, which seemed, to himself, as senseless as the dance in the sun of an amorous negro.

Adrianis and the whole of his family had shown him the utmost gratitude, liberality and consideration, and the young prince bore from him good-humouredly sarcasms and satires which he would not have supported from an emperor; but Damer in his turn felt for the Sicilian and his people nothing but the contempt of the great intellect for the uncultured mind, the irritation of the wise man who sees a child gaily making a kite to divert itself out of the parchments of a treatise in an unknown tongue which, studied, might have yielded up to the student the secret of perished creeds and of lost nations.

There is no pride so arrogant, no supremacy so unbending, as those of the intellect. It may stand, like Belisarius, a beggar at the gate; but, like Belisarius, it deems itself the superior of all the crowds who drop their alms to it, and while it stretches out its hand to them, its lips curse them.

V

They went, without visiting the basilica, back to Venice in the twilight which deepened into night as they drew near the city; the moon was high and the air still. They dined in the spacious rooms set aside in the hotel for the young prince. When the dinner was over, Adrianis rose.

'Will you come?' he asked.

'Where?' asked Damer.

'To the Ca' Zaranegra,' he replied, with a boyish laugh.

'Not I,' replied Damer.

'A rivederci, then,' said Adrianis.

But he lingered a moment.

'It will not be fair to you,' he said, 'for me to take the credit of having found this necklace.'

'Whatever honour there may be in the salvage I cede it, I tell you, willingly.'

'Of course I shall tell her that it was you.'

'There is no need to do so; I am not a squire of dames. She will prefer a Sicilian prince to a plain man of science. However, you must find the lady first. The true owner lies under some mossgrown slab in some chapel crypt, no doubt.'

'Why will you speak of death? I hate it.'

'Hate it as you may, it will overtake you. Alexander hated it, but still! When we shall have found the secret of life we may perhaps find the antidote to death. But that time is not yet.'

He looked at his companion as he spoke, and thought what he did not speak, –

'Yes, strong as you are, and young as you are, and fortunate as you are, you too will die like the pauper, and the cripple, and the beggar!'

The reflection gratified him; for of the youth, of the beauty, of the fortune, he was envious, and with all his scorn of higher intellect he despised the childlike, happy, amorous temperament, and the uncultured mind which went with them.

'If I had only his wealth,' he thought often. 'Or if he only had my knowledge!'

'When we shall have penetrated the secret of life we shall perhaps be able to defy death,' repeated Adrianis. 'What use would that be? You would soon have the world so full that there would be no standing room; and what would you do with the choking multitudes?'

'I never knew you so logical,' said the elder man, con- temptuously. 'But have no fear. We are far enough off the discovery; when it is made, it will remain in the hands of the wise. The immortality of fools will never be contemplated by science.'

'The wise will not refuse to sell the secret to the wealthy fools,' thought his companion, but he forbore to say so. He was generous of temper, and knew that his companion had both wisdom and poverty.

A few seconds later the splash of the canal water beneath the balcony told the other that the gondola was moving.

'What a child!' thought Damer, with impatient contempt; he turned up the light of his reading-lamp, opened a number of the French *Journal de Physiologie*, and began to read, not heeding the beauty of the moonlit marbles of the Salvatore in front of him, or listening to the song from Mignon which a sweet-voiced lad was singing in a boat below. He read on thus in solitude for three hours; the great tapestried and gilded room behind him, the gliding water below; the beautiful church in front of his balcony, the laughter, the music, the swish of oars, the thrill of lutes and guitars, all the evening movement on the canal as the crowds went to and from the Piazza, not disturbing him from his studies, of which every now and then he made a note in pencil in a pocket-book.

It was twelve o'clock when, into the empty, brilliantly-lighted room, Adrianis entered and came across it to where Damer sat on the balcony.

'I have found her!' he said, with joyous triumph. The moonlight shone on his dark, starry eyes, his laughing mouth, his tall figure, full of grace and strength like the form of the Greek Hermes in the Vatican.

Damer laid aside his papers with impatience.

'And she has welcomed you, apparently? It is midnight, and you look victorious.'

Adrianis made a gesture of vexed protestation.

'Pray do not suspect such things. I sent in my card and begged her major-domo to say that I had found her necklace. She sent word for me to go upstairs that she might thank me. Of course, my name was known to her. She had a duenna with her. It was all solemn and correct. She was enchanted to find her necklace. It was an heirloom which Zaranegra gave her. He was killed in a duel, as I told you, two years ago. She is very beautiful, and looks twenty years old, even less. I was very honest; I told her that an Englishman, who was travelling with me, had enjoyed the honour of finding the opals; and she wishes to see you to-morrow. I promised to take you *in prima sera*; you surely ought to be grateful.'

Damer shrugged his shoulders and looked regretfully at his papers and pencils.

'Women only disturb one,' he said ungraciously.

Adrianis laughed.

'It is that disturbance which perfumes our life and shakes the rose leaves over it. But I remember, to attract you a woman must be lying, dead or alive, on an operating-table.'

'Alive by preference,' said Damer. 'The dead are little use to us; their nervous system is still, like a stopped clock.'

'A creature must suffer to interest you?'

'Certainly.'

Adrianis shuddered slightly.

'Why did you save me?'

Damer smiled.

'My dear prince, it is my duty to save when I can. I should have preferred to let you alone, and study your natural powers of resistance in conflict with the destruction which was menacing them. But I could not follow my preferences. I was called in to assist your natural powers by affording them artificial resistance; and I was bound to do so.'

Adrianis made a grimace which signified disappointment and distaste.

'If my mother knew you looked at it in that way she would not adore you, my friend, as she does.'

'The princess exaggerates,' said Damer, putting out his lamp. 'Mothers always do; I do not think I ever said anything to lead her to deceive herself with regard to me. She knows what my interests and my pursuits are.'

'But,' said Adrianis, wistfully, 'surely there are many men of science, many surgeons, whose desire is to console, to amend, who care for the poor human material on which they work?'

'There are some,' replied Damer; 'but they are not in the front ranks of their profession, nor will science ever owe much to them.'

The young man was silent; he felt in his moral nature as he had sometimes felt in his physical, when a chill icy wind had risen and passed through the sunshine of a balmy day. He shook off the impression with the mutability of a happy temper.

'Eh via!' he cried. 'You make me feel cold in the marrow of my bones. Good-night. I am tired, and I go to dream of the lady of the opals. Like you, I prefer living women to dead ones, but I do not wish them to suffer. I wish them to enjoy – for my sake and their own!'

Damer, left alone, relit his lamp, took up his papers and books, went into the room, for the night was fresh, and remained reading and writing until daybreak.

VI

Veronica Zaranegra was charmed to find her necklace; she was still more charmed to find an adventure through it.

This beautiful youth with his starry eyes, soft with admiration, who had brought her back the opals, looked like a knight out of fairyland. She was young; she was weary of the seclusion of her widowhood; she was kept in close constraint by those who had authority over her; she was ready to re-enter life in its enjoyments, its amusements, its affections, its desires. The tragic end of her husband had impressed and saddened her, but she had recovered from its shock. The marriage had been arranged by their respective families, and the hearts of neither had been consulted. Zaranegra, however, had become much in love with her, and had left her all which it was in his power to leave, and that had been much.

She was like a picture of Caterina Cornaro as she stood on the balcony of her house; her golden hair was enclosed in a pearl-sown net, she had some crimson carnations at her throat, and her cloak of red satin lined with sables lay on her shoulders and fell to her feet like the robes of a Dogaressa.

The balcony was filled with spiræa, whose white blossoms were like snow about her in the starlight and lamplight as the gondola which brought the Sicilian prince and his companion to her palace paused below at the water-stairs.

'How clever it was of you to see my opals under the grass and the sand!' she said, a few moments later, as Adrianis presented Damer in the long, dim room hung with tapestries and rich in bronzes, marbles, pictures and mosaics.

She threw her cloak on a couch as she spoke; she was dressed in black, but the gauze sleeves of the gown showed her fair arms, and the bodice was slightly open on her bosom; her face was bright like a rose above the deep shadow of the gown; her hair had been a little ruffled by the wind of the evening as she had stood on the balcony.

'Madame,' said Damer, as he bowed to her with a strange and unwelcome sense of embarrassment, 'Prince Adrianis should not have told you that I had such good fortune. I am no fit squire of dames: he is.'

'But how came you to see them, all dull and muddy as they were?'

'Sight is a matter of training; I use my eyes. Most people do not use theirs.'

She looked at him curiously and laughed. The answer seemed to her very droll.

'Everybody sees except the blind,' she said, somewhat puzzled.

'And the purblind,' added Damer.

She did not catch his meaning. She turned from him a little impatiently and addressed Adrianis.

She spoke of music. Adrianis was accomplished in that art; there was a mandoline lying on the grand piano; he took it up and sang to it a Sicilian love song; she took it from him and sang Venetian barcarolle and stornelli; then they sang together, and their clear, youthful voices blent melodiously. People passing on the canal stopped their gondolas under the balcony to listen; some Venetian professional musicians in a boat below applauded. Damer sat in the shadow, and listened, and looked at them. Music said little or nothing to him; he had scarcely any comprehension of it; but something in the sound of those blended voices touched a chord in his nature; made him feel vaguely sad, restlessly desirous, foolishly irritated. The light fell on the handsome head of the youth, on the carnations at the lady's throat, on the rings on their hands, which touched as they took the mandoline one from the other; behind them were the open casement, the balcony with its white flowers, the lighted frontage of a palace on the opposite side of the canal.

As they ceased to sing the people below on the water applauded again, and cried, 'Brava! brava! Bis, bis!'

Adrianis laughed and rose, and, going out on to the balcony, threw some money to the boat-load of ambulant musicians who had left off their playing and singing to listen.

'Those artistes below are very kind to us amateurs,' said Adrianis, with a little branch of spiræa in his hand, which he proceeded to fasten in his buttonhole as he came back into the light of the room.

'You are more than an amateur.'

'Oh, all Sicilians sing. The syrens teach us.'

'Prince Adrianis is a poet,' said Damer, with a harsh tone in his voice.

'Who never wrote a verse,' said Adrianis, as he handed a cup of coffee to his hostess.

'Shut the windows,' said the Countess Zaranegra to her servants, who brought in coffee and wine, lemonade and syrups.

Through the closed windows the sound of a chorus sung by the strolling singers below came faintly and muffled into the room; the lamplight shone on the white spray of the spiræa in his coat, which looked like a crystal of snow.

'If I had found the opals I should have been inspired by them,' he added. 'As it is, I am dumb and unhappy.'

Veronica Zaranegra smiled.

'If you are dumb, so was Orpheus.'

'And if you are unhappy, so was Prince Fortunatus,' added Damer. 'You are only sad out of wantonness, because the gods have given you too many gifts.'

'Or because he has stolen a piece of spiræa.'

'I may keep my theft?' asked Adrianis.

'Yes. For you brought back the opals, though you did not find them.'

Soon after they both took their leave of her and went down to the waiting gondola. The boat-load of musicians had drifted upwards towards Rialto, the colours of their paper lanthorns glowing through the dark. There was no moon. They did not speak to each other in the few minutes which carried them to their hotel. When they reached it, they parted with a brief Good-night. Neither asked the other what his impressions of the lady, and of the evening, had been.

The night was dark. Mists obscured the stars. The lights

at the Dogana and of the lamps along the Schiavone were shining brightly, and many other lights gleamed here and there, where they shone in gondolas, or boats, or at the mastheads of vessels anchored in the dock of S. Mark. The hour was still early; eleven o'clock and the canal was not yet deserted. There was the liquid sound of parting water as people went to and fro on its surface. At such an hour Venice is still what it was in the days of Paul Veronese, or of Virginia di Leyva.

Adrianis sat by the sea-wall of the hotel garden and looked absently down the dark expanse studded with lights like diamonds, and thought exclusively of the woman he had quitted. He saw her golden hair shining in the lamplight, the red of the knot of carnations at her throat, the slender, jewelled hand on the mandoline, the smiling, rose-like mouth; he heard the clear, fresh, unstrained voice rising and falling with his own, whilst her eyes smiled and her eyes met his.

'Stones of sorrow! stones of sorrow!' he thought. 'No, no. They shall be jewels of joy to me, to her. Love is born of a glance, of a note, of a murmur. It is the wonder flower of life. It blossoms full-grown in an instant. It needs neither time nor reflection.'

His heart beat gladly in him; his nerves were thrilled and throbbing; his welcome of a new and profound emotion was without fear.

In such a mood the merest trifle has eloquence. He was sorry when he looked down on the spray of spiræa in his coat, and saw that all the little starry flowers of it had fallen off, and vanished, as though it had indeed been snow which had melted at a breath of sirocco.

VII

Two weeks passed, and brought the month of May. On the many island banks long sprays of dog-rose and honeysuckle hung down over the water, and the narrow canals which ran through them were tunnels of blossom and verdure; on the sunny shallows thousands of white-winged gulls were fishing and bathing all the day long; and in the churches azaleas and lilies and arums were grouped round the altars under the dark-winged angels of Tintoretto and the golden-haired cherubim of Tiepolo.

The nights were still cold, but the days were warm, were at noontide even hot; and Veronica Zaranegra passed almost all her time on the water. There was a little orchard island, which belonged to the family, out beyond Mazzorbo; in the previous century a small summer-house or pavilion, with a red-tiled dome like a beehive, had been erected on it and was still there; a pretty toy still, though its frescoed walls were faded and its marble landing-steps eaten away by the incessant washing of the sea; it was embowered in peach and plum and pear trees, and looked westward. Here she came often for breakfast, or for afternoon tea, or the evening merenda of fruit, sweetmeats and wine, and here she was often accompanied by a gay party of Venetians of her own years and by the two strangers who had given her back her opals. The weather was rainless and radiant; the gondolas glided like swallows over the lagoons; she was rich, childlike, fond of pleasure; she tried to bring back the life of the eighteenth century, and amused herself with reviving its customs, its costumes, its comedies, as they had been before the storms of revolution and the smoke of war had rolled over the Alps, and Arcole and Marengo had silenced the laughter of Italy.

'I wish I had lived when this collar was new,' she said, when her jewellers returned to her the opals restored to their pristine brilliancy. 'Life in Venice was one long festa then; I have read of it. It was all masque, and serenade, and courtship, and magnificence. People were not philosophical about life then; they lived. Nina Zaranegra was a beautiful woman. They have her portrait in the Belle Arte. She holds a rose to her lips and laughs. She was killed by her husband for an amour. She had these opals on her throat when he drove the stiletto through it. At least so Carlo used to tell me. But perhaps it was not true.'

'Do not wear them,' said Adrianis, to whom she was speaking. 'Do not wear them if they are bloodstained. You know they are stones of sorrow.'

She laughed.

'You Sicilians are superstitious. We Northerners are not. I like to wear them for that very reason of their tragedy.'

She took up the necklace and clasped it round her throat; some tendrils of her hair caught in the clasp; she gave an involuntary little cry of pain. Adrianis hastened to release her hair from the clasp. His hand trembled; their eyes met, and said much to each other. Damer, who was near, drew nearer.

'I have seen the portrait in the Belle Arte,' he said. 'The Countess Nina symbolises silence with her rose, but she has the face of a woman who would not keep even her own secrets. Indeed, a charming woman is always "*bavarde comme les pies*," as the French say.'

'You despise women,' said Veronica Zaranegra, with vexation.

'Oh, no. But I should not give them my confidence any more than I should give a delicate scientific instrument to a child.'

'Not even to a woman whom you loved?'

'Still less to a woman whom I loved.'

'You are a mysterious sage,' she said, a little impatiently. 'You regard us as if we were children indeed, incapable of any comprehension.'

Damer did not dispute the accusation.

'Did I hear you say,' he asked, 'that the lovely original of that portrait was murdered by her husband?'

'Yes, and he would not even allow her Christian burial, but had her body carried out on to the Orfano Canal, and thrown into the water, with a great stone tied to her feet.'

'He was primitive,' said Damer. 'Those are rough, rude ways of vengeance.'

'What would you have done?'

'I hardly know; but I should not have so stupidly wasted

such a beautiful organism. Besides, the end was too swift to be any great punishment.'

She was silent, looking at him with that mixture of curiosity, interest and vague apprehension which he always aroused in her. She was not very intelligent, but she had quick susceptibilities; there was that in him which alarmed them and yet fascinated them.

'He awes me,' she said later in the day to Adrianis. 'So often one cannot follow his meaning, but one always feels his reserve of power.'

It was a grave speech for a light-hearted lover of pleasure. Adrianis heard it with vexation, but he was loyal to the man who, as he considered, had saved his life.

'He is a person of great intellect,' he answered; 'we are pigmies beside him. But –'

'But what?'

'He used his brains to cure my body. So I must not dispute the virtue of his use of them. Yet sometimes I fancy that he has no heart. I think all the forces in him have only nourished his mind, which is immense. But his heart, perhaps, has withered away, getting no nourishment. He would say I talk nonsense; but I think you will understand what I mean.'

'I think I understand,' said Veronica, thoughtfully.

She had thought very little in her careless young life; she had begun to think more since these two men had come into it.

'Adrianis merits better treatment than you give him,' said her duenna to her that day. 'How long will you keep him in suspense? You ought to remember "what hell it is in waiting to abide." '

'A hell?' said Veronica, with the colour in her face. 'You mean a paradise!'

'A fool's paradise, I fear,' replied the elder woman. 'And what does that other man do here? He told me he was due at some university in Germany.'

'How can I tell why either of them stays?' said Veronica, disingenuously as her conscience told her. 'Venice allures many people, especially in her spring season.'

'So does a woman in her spring,' said the elder lady, drily, with an impatient gesture.

'You are angry with me,' said Veronica, mournfully.

'No, my dear. It is as useless to be angry with you as to be angry with a young cat because in its gambols it breaks a vase of which it knows nothing of the preciousness.'

Veronica Zaranegra did not resent or reply. She knew the vase was precious; she did not mean to break it; but she wanted to be free awhile longer. Mutual love was sweet, but it was not freedom. And what she felt ashamed of was a certain reluctance which moved her to allow Damer to see or know that she loved a man of so little intellectual force as Adrianis, a man who had nothing but his physical beauty and his gay, glad temper and kind heart.

'Do you want nothing more than these?' the gaze of Damer seemed in her imagination to say to her.

She was angered with herself for thinking of him or of his opinion; he was not of her world or of her station; he was a professional man, a worker, a teacher; natural pride of lineage and habit made her regard him as in no way privileged to be considered by her. And yet she could not help being influenced by that disdain of the mental powers of others which he had never uttered, but which he continually showed. Indecision is the greatest bane of women; obstinacy costs them much, but indecision costs them more. The will of Veronica flickered like a candle in the wind, veered hither and thither like a fallen leaf in a gust of wind and rain.

Adrianis was delightful to her; his beauty, his gaiety and his homage were all sympathetic to her. She knew that he loved her, but she prevented him telling her so; she liked her lately-acquired liberty; she did not want a declaration which would force her to decide in one way or another what to do with her future. And she was affected, without being aware of it, by the scarcely disguised contempt which his companion had for him. It was seldom outspoken, but it was visible in every word of Damer, in every glance.

'He is beautiful, yes,' he said once to her. 'So is an animal.'

'Do you not like animals?'

'I do not like or dislike them. The geologist does not like or dislike the stones he breaks up, the metallurgist does not like or dislike the ore he fuses.'

She did not venture to ask him what he meant; she had a vague conception of his meaning, and it gave her a chill as such replies gave to Adrianis: a chill such as the north wind, when it comes down from the first snows on the Dolomite peaks, gives to the honeysuckle flowers hanging over the sea-walls. She was not clever or much educated, but she had seen a good deal of the world, and she had heard men talk of science, of its pretensions and its methods, its self-worship and its tyrannies. She had put her rosy fingers in her ears and run away when they had so spoken, but some things she had heard and now remembered.

'You are what they call a physiologist?' she said once, suddenly.

'I am,' replied Damer.

She looked at him under her long silky lashes as a child looks at what it fears in the dusk of a fading day. He attracted her and repelled her, as when she had herself been a little child she had been at once charmed and frightened by the great ghostly figures on the tapestries, and the white and grey busts of gods and sages on the grand staircase of her father's house in the Trentino. She would have liked to ask him many things – things of mystery and of horror – but she was afraid. After all, how much better were the sea, the sunshine, the dog-rose, the barcarolle, the laughter, the lute!

She turned to Adrianis, who at that moment came along the sands of the beach, his hands filled with spoils from the blossoming hedges; turned to him as when, a little child on the staircase in the dusk, she had run to reach the shelter of a warmed and lighted room. He was of her own country, her own age, her own temperament; he carried about him a sense of gladness, an atmosphere of youth; he was of her own rank; he was as rich as she, and richer. There was no leaven of self-seeking in the love he bore her; the passion she had roused in him was pure of any alloy; it was the love of the poets and the singers. If she accepted it, her path, from youth to age, would be like one of those flowering meadows of his own Sicily, which fill the cloudless day with perfume.

She knew that; her foot was ready to tread the narcissus-filled grass, but by an unaccountable indecision and caprice she would not let him invite her thither. She continually evaded or eluded the final words which would have united them or parted them.

Again and again, when that moment of decision could not have been postponed, the sombre shadow of Damer had appeared, as in the moment when the clasp of the necklace had been entangled in the little curls at the back of her throat.

It might be chance, it might be premeditation; but he was always there in those moments when the heart of Adrianis leapt to his eyes and lips and called to hers.

VIII

In the evening she was usually at home. She did not as yet go to balls or theatres; the aristocratic society of Venice flocked to her rooms, and what was best in the foreign element. In the evenings neither Adrianis nor Damer saw her alone; but in the daytime, on the island or in the water excursions, sometimes one or the other was beside her for a few minutes with no listener near.

Adrianis eagerly sought such occasions; Damer never seemed to seek them. He was often in her palace and on her island, but appeared to be so chiefly because he went where Adrianis went. No one could have told that he took pleasure in doing so.

But Adrianis, somewhat surprised at his lingering so long, thought to himself, 'He was to be in Gottenberg by the 10th of May, and it is now the 23d.'

'Have you given up your appointment?' he asked once, directly.

Damer merely answered, 'No.' He did not offer any explanation; but he continued to stay on in Venice, though he had removed from the fine apartments occupied by his friend to a house on the Fondamenti Nuovi, where he had hired two chambers.

Adrianis, who was very generous, and had always a grateful and uneasy sense of unrepaid obligation, vainly urged him to remain at his hotel. But Damer, somewhat rudely, refused.

'I cannot pursue any studies there,' he replied.

The house he had chosen was obscure and uninviting, standing amidst the clang of coppersmiths' hammers and the stench of iron foundries, in what was once the most patrician and beautiful garden quarter of Venice, but which is now befouled, blackened, filled with smoke and clamour and vileness, where once the rose-terraces and the clematis-covered pergole ran down to the lagoon, and the marble stairs were white as snow under silken awnings.

'What do you do there?' Veronica Zaranegra wished to ask him; but she never did so; she felt vaguely afraid, as a woman of the Middle Ages would have feared to ask a magician what he did with his alembics and his spheres.

Although the eyes of lovers are proverbially washed by the collyrium of jealousy, those of Adrianis were blind to the passion which Damer, like himself, had conceived. The reserve and power of self-restraint in Damer were extreme, and served to screen his secret from the not very discerning mind of his companion. Moreover, the pride of race, which was born and bred in Adrianis, rendered it impossible for him to suspect that he possessed a rival in one who was, however mentally superior, so far socially inferior to himself and to the woman he loved.

That a man who was going to receive a stipend as a teacher in a German university could lift his eyes to Veronica Zaranegra, would have seemed wholly impossible to one who had been reared in patrician and conservative tenets. He never noticed the fires which slumbered in the cold, wide-opened eyes of his friend and monitor. He never observed how frequently Damer watched him and her when they were together, listened from afar to their conversation, and invariably interrupted them at any moment when their words verged on more tender or familiar themes. He was himself tenderly, passionately, romantically enamoured; his temper was full of a romance to which he could not often give adequate expression; his love for her had the timidity of all sincere and nascent passion; he was pained and chafed by the manner in which she avoided his definite declaration of it, but he did not for a moment trace it to its right cause, the magnetic influence which the Englishman had upon her, the hesitation which was given her by vague hypnotic suggestion. If any looker-on had warned him, he would have laughed and said that the days of magic were past.

He himself only counted time by the hours which brought him into her presence on the water, on the island, or in the evening receptions in the palace. He made water festivals and pleasure cruises to please her; he had sent for his own sailing yacht from Palermo. The long, light days of late spring and earliest summer passed in a series of ingenious amusements of which the sole scope was to obtain a smile from her. Often she did smile, the radiance of youth and of a woman's willingness to be worshipped shining on her fair countenance as the sun shone on the sea. Sometimes also the smile ceased suddenly when, from a distance, her eyes encountered those of Damer.

All that was most delightful in life offered itself to her in the homage of Adrianis: his mother's welcome, his southern clime, his great love, his infinite tenderness and sweetness of temper, his great physical beauty. She longed to accept these great gifts; she longed to feel his arms folded about her and his cheek against hers; and yet she hesitated, she delayed, she avoided, because in the eyes of another man, whom she disliked and feared, she read mockery, disdain and superiority. She could not have said what it was that she felt any more than the young spaniel could tell what moves it as it looks up into human eyes, and reads authority in them, and crouches, trembling.

Why did he stay here? she asked herself, this cold, still, irresponsive man, who had nothing in him which was not alien to the youthful and pleasure-loving society in which he found himself, and who was by his own admission already overdue at the university to which he had been appointed.

'Are you not losing time?' she said once to him; 'we are so frivolous, so ignorant, so unlike you.'

'I never lose time,' replied Damer. 'An amœba in a pool on the sand is companion enough for me.'

Seeing that she had no idea of what he meant, he added, –

'A man of science is like an artist; his art is everywhere, wherever natural forms exist.'

'Or like a sportsman,' said Adrianis, who was listening; 'his sport is everywhere, wherever there are living things to kill.'

'Put it so if you please,' said Damer. But he was annoyed; he disliked being answered intelligently and sarcastically by one whom he considered a fool. Whatever Adrianis said irritated him, though it was almost perpetually courteous and simple, as was the nature of the speaker.

Damer read the young man's heart like an open book, and he knew that it was wholly filled with the image of Veronica. He had never liked Adrianis; he had no liking for youth or for physical beauty, or for kindliness and sweetness and simplicity of character. Such qualities were not in tune with him; they were no more to him than the soft, thick fur of the cat in his laboratory, which he stripped off her body that he might lay bare her spinal cord; the pretty, warm skin was nothing to science – no more than was the pain of the bared nerves.

He had saved the life of Adrianis because it had interested and recompensed him to do so; he had travelled with him for a year because it suited him financially to do so; but he had never liked him, he had never been touched by any one of the many generous and delicate acts of the young man, nor by the trust which the mother of Adrianis continually expressed in her letters to himself. Where jealousy sits on the threshold of the soul, goodness and kindness and faith knock in vain for admittance. Envy is hatred in embryo; and only waits in the womb of time for birth.

IX

One day Veronica asked him to go and see an old servant of the Zaranegra household who was very ill and in hospital; they had begged him not to go to the hospital, but he had wished to do so, and had been allowed to fulfil his wish. Damer went to visit him. He found the man at death's door with cancer of the food and air passages.

'If he be not operated on he will die in a week,' said the Englishman.

None of the hospital surgeons dared perform such an operation.

'I will operate if you consent,' said Damer.

The surgeons acquiesced.

'Will Biancon recover?' asked Veronica, when he returned and told her on what they had decided.

'In his present state he cannot live a week,' replied Damer, evasively.

'Does he wish for the operation?'

'He can be no judge. He cannot know his own condition. He cannot take his own prognosis.'

'But it will be frightful suffering.'

'He will be under anæsthetics.'

'But will he recover?'

'Madame, I am not the master of Fate.'

'But what is probable?'

'What is certain is that the man will die if left as he is.'

He performed the operation next day. The man ceased to breathe as it was ended; the shock to the nervous system had killed him.

When she heard that he was dead she burst into tears.

'Oh! why, oh! why,' she said passionately to Damer, later

in the day, 'why, if you knew he must die, did you torture him in his last moments?'

'I gave him a chance,' he replied indifferently. 'Anyhow, he would never have survived the operation more than a few weeks.'

'Why did you torture him with it then?' said Veronica, indignantly.

'It was a rare, and almost unique, opportunity. I have solved by it a doubt which has never been solved before, and never could have been without a human subject.'

She shrank from him in horror.

'You are a wicked man!' she said faintly. 'Oh, how I wish, how I wish I had never asked you to see my poor Biancon! He might have lived!'

'He would most certainly have died,' said Damer, unmoved. 'The life of a man at sixty is not an especially valuable thing, and I believe he did nothing all his life except polish your palace floors with bees-wax or oil; I forget which it is they use in Venice.'

She looked at him with a mixture of horror and fear.

'But you have killed him! – and you can jest.'

'I did not kill him. His disease killed him,' replied Damer, with calm indifference. 'And his end has been a source of knowledge. I should wish my own end to be as fruitful.'

She shuddered, and motioned to him to leave her.

'Go away, go away, you have no heart, and no conscience.'

Damer smiled slightly.

'I have a scientific conscience; it is as good as a moral one, and does better work.'

'Why did you bring that man to Venice?' she said to Adrianis some hours later. 'He has killed my poor Biancon, and he cares nothing.'

'Why do you receive him?' said Adrianis, feeling the reproach unjust. 'Cease to receive him. That is very simple. If you banish him, he is proud, he will not persist.'

'He would not perhaps persist; but he would be revenged,'

she thought, but she did not say so. Though her life was short, she had learned in it that men are like detonators which you cannot throw against each other without explosion.

Adrianis began to desire the exile of his companion, though his loyalty withheld him from trying to obtain it by any unfair means or unjust attack. He was mortified and disquieted. Why had he not had patience, and waited to carry the opals to the Ca' Zaranegra until the Englishman had been safe on the sea on his way to Trieste? He began to perceive that Damer had an influence on the Countess Veronica which was contrary to his own, and adverse to his interests. He did not attach importance to it, because he saw that it was purely intellectual; but he would have preferred that it had not existed. So would she.

It was such an influence as the confessor obtains over the devotee; against which husband, lover, children, all natural ties, struggle altogether in vain.

It is not love; it is alien to love, but it is frequently stronger than love, and casts down the winged god maimed and helpless.

'Pierres de malheur! Pierres de malheur!' she said, as she looked at the opals that night. 'Why did you bring that cruel man into my life?'

She might banish him as Adrianis had said, but she felt that she would never have courage to do it. Damer awed her. She felt something of what the poor women in the Salpétrière had felt, when he had hypnotised them, and made them believe that they clasped their hands on red-hot iron, or were being dragged by ropes to the scaffold. She strove to resist and conquer the impression, but she was subjugated by it against her will.

She buried her poor old servant that night, and followed the coffin in its gondola in her own, with her men in mourning and the torches burning at the prow.

From the casement of his high tower on the north of the city, which looked over the lagoon towards that island which is now the cemetery of Venice, with its tall mosque-like Campanile and its high sea-walls, Damer saw and recognised her on that errand of respect to the humble dead. He saw also the long-boat of the yacht of Adrianis, laden with flowers, following her gondola at a little distance, as though its owner were timid and uncertain of welcome. He recognised them both in the evening light, and through his binocular could discern their features, their hands, their garlands, as the torches flamed and the water, roughened by wind, broke against the black sides of her gondola and the white sides of the boat.

'Two children,' he thought, 'made for each other, with their flowers and fables and follies! I should do best to leave them together.'

Then he shut his window and turned from the sight of the silver water, the evening skies, the gliding vessels.

His work awaited him. Bound on a plank lay a young sheepdog, which he had bought from a peasant of Mazzorbo for a franc; he had cut its vocal chords; in his own jargon, had rendered it aphone; he had then cut open its body, and torn out its kidneys and pancreas. It was living; he reckoned it would live in its mute and unpitied agony for twelve hours more – long enough for the experiment which he was about to make.

These were the studies for which he had come to the tower on the Fondamenti.

The clang of hammers and the roar of furnaces drowned the cries of animals which it was not convenient to make aphone; and the people of the quarter were too engrossed in their labours to notice when he flung down into the water dead or half-dead mutilated creatures.

X

After the death of the serving-man, Biancon, the name of the English scientist and surgeon became known and revered amongst the persons of his own profession in Venice. The poor man had died certainly from the shock to the nerves, but that was of small moment. The operation had been eminently successful, as science counts success. It had been admirably performed, and had, as he had said to Veronica, cleared up a doubt which could not, without a human subject, have been satisfactorily dissipated. His skill, his manual dexterity, his courage, were themes of universal praise, and more than one rich person of the Veneto entreated his examination, and submitted to his treatment.

Adrianis saw but little of him in the daytime, but most evenings in *prima sera* they met in the Palazzo Zaranegra. There Damer spoke little, but he spoke with effect; and, when he was silent, it seemed to the young mistress of the house that his silence was odiously eloquent, for it appeared always to say to her, 'What a mindless creature you are! What a mindless creature you love!'

Sometimes it seemed to her to say more; to say across the length of the lighted, perfumed, flower-filled salon, 'And if I forbid your mutual passion? If I prevent its fruition?'

Out of his presence she ridiculed these ideas, but in his presence they were realities to her, and realities which alarmed and haunted her.

'How I wish you had never brought him here – oh, how I wish it!' she said once to Adrianis.

They were in the Piazza of S. Mark; it was late in the evening; the gay summer crowd was all around them; the band was playing; the full moon was above in all her glory; laughter and gay chatter mingled with the lapping of the water and the splash of oars. In the blaze of light under the colonnades people were supping and flirting and jesting, as though they were still in the days of Goldoni.

'Are you not a little unjust to me?' said Adrianis, gently. 'I could not do otherwise, in common honesty, than tell you that it was not I who had found your opals, and you wished to see and to thank the person who had done so.'

'Oh, I know! I know!' she said, with an impatient sigh. 'Such things are always one's own fault. But he killed Biancon, and his very presence now is painful to me.'

'Tell him so.'

'I dare not.'

'Shall I tell him for you?'

She looked at him with the wistful, alarmed gaze of a frightened child.

'Oh, no, no! He would be offended. He might quarrel with you. No! Pray do not do that.'

'His anger has no terrors for me,' he said, with a smile. 'But you know what you wish is my law for silence as for speech.'

'Limonate? Fragolone? Gelate? Confetti?' sang a boy, pushing against them with his tray of summer drinks, ices, fruits and sweetmeats.

'Let us go; it is late; and the crowd grows noisy,' said her duenna.

Adrianis accompanied them to their gondola, which was in waiting beyond the pillars. He did not venture to offer to accompany them, for the hour was late, and the elder lady, herself a Zaranegra, was rigid in her construction and observance of etiquette. He watched the gondola drift away amongst the many others waiting there, and then turned back to the piazza as the two Vulcans on the clock tower beat out on their anvil with their hammers the twelve strokes of midnight. He saw amongst the crowd the pale and thoughtful countenance of Damer. Had he heard what the young Countess had said of him? It was impossible to tell from his expression; he was looking up at the four bronze horses, as he sat, with an evening paper on his knee, at one of the little tables, an untouched lemonade standing at his elbow.

'I did not know you were here,' said Adrianis. 'It is too frivolous a scene for you. Are you longing to dissect the horses of S. Mark's?'

Damer smiled slightly.

'I fear I should find their anatomy faulty. I am no artist, or art critic either, or I should venture to say that I object to their attitude. Arrested motion is a thing too momentary to perpetuate in metal or in stone.'

Adrianis looked up at the rearing coursers.

'Surely we might as well object to the statue of Colleone because he sits erect and motionless through centuries?'

'No, that is quite another matter. Colleone is at rest. The horses yonder are leaping violently.'

'You are too subtle for me! I can only admire. I am an ignorant, you know. Have you been here long?'

'Half an hour.'

Had he heard? Adrianis wondered. It was impossible to tell.

'I seldom see you now,' he added. 'You have become very unsociable.'

'I was not aware that I was ever sociable. People much occupied cannot be so. You see, I have a newspaper and I do not read it; I have a *bevanda* and I do not drink it. I have seen the Contessa Zaranegra and I have not spoken to her.'

It seemed that the reply, which was longer and more jesting than was the wont of the speaker, was made with intention.

Adrianis was silent. He wished to tell Damer that his presence was unwelcome to the lady of whom he spoke, but he hesitated; he was afraid to compromise her, to seem to boast of some confidence from her.

'Did you know,' he asked in a low tone, 'that her poor serving-man would die under the knife?'

Damer gave him a cold, contemptuous glance.

'I do not speak on professional subjects to laymen,' he said curtly.

'I do not ask you,' replied Adrianis, 'from the professional point of view. I ask you from that of humanity.'

'Humanity does not enter into the question,' said Damer, slightingly. 'I hope you will not regard it as offensive if I ask you to limit yourself to speaking of what you understand.'

The blood rose into the cheek of Adrianis, and anger leapt to his lips. He restrained it with effort from utterance. The boundless scorn which Damer never scrupled to show for him was at times very chafing and provocative.

'You know, yourself, nothing of sculpture, you admit,' he

said, controlling his personal feeling, 'and yet you venture to criticise the horses of Lysippus.'

'My criticism is sound, and they are not the horses of Lysippus.'

'They may not be. But my criticism is sound too, I think, on your want of humanity towards poor Biancon.'

Damer cast an evil and disdainful glance at him.

'With regard,' he replied, 'to the man Biancon, there could be no question of either cruelty or kindness. These terms do not enter into surgical vocabularies. You are well aware that on the stage no actor could act who felt in any manner the real emotions of his part. In like degree no surgeon could operate who was unnerved by what you call "humanity" with regard to his patient. There is no more of feeling, or want of feeling, in the operator than in the actor. Is it impossible for you to comprehend that? As for yourself, you do not care the least for the dead facchino, you only care because a fair woman who is dear to you has wept.'

He spoke with insolence, but with apparently entire indifference. Adrianis coloured with displeasure and self-consciousness. It was the first time that the name of the Countess Zaranegra had been mentioned between them when out of her presence. It seemed to him an intolerable presumption in Damer to speak of her. But he scarcely knew how to reply. With a man of his own rank he would have quarrelled in such a manner that a sabre duel on the pastures by the Brenta river would have followed in the morning. But Damer was not socially his equal, and was a man to whom a year before he had owed, or had thought that he owed, his restoration to health and life.

'I should prefer that you left the name of that lady out of our discourse,' he said in a low tone, but with hauteur. 'In my world we do not venture to speak of women whom we respect.'

Damer understood the reproof and the lesson so conveyed.

'I am not of your world,' he said slightingly. 'I have no such pretensions. And women are to me but subjects of investigation, like cats – in their bodies, I mean; of their minds and hearts I have no knowledge. I leave such studies to Paul Bourget and you.'

Then he rose and walked away towards the end of the piazza, where the opening of the goldsmiths' street of the Merceria leads to the back of the clock tower and the network of narrow passages beyond it.

Adrianis did not detain him, but went himself to his gondola and was taken the few yards which parted S. Mark's from his hotel. Sometimes he slept on board his yacht, but sometimes at the hotel, because it was nearer to the Ca' Zaranegra, which he could not see from his windows, but which he knew were there on the bend of the canal towards Rialto.

However, he reflected with consolation, in a week or two more Veronica would go to her father's villa in the mountains of the Trentino, and she had given him to understand that she would tell the duke to invite him. Thither it would be impossible for Damer to go, even if he should desire to do so, which was improbable. For Adrianis never suspected the existence of any passion in Damer except the desire of command, the pleasure which the exercise of a strong will over weaker ones gave him from its sense of intellectual dominion.

The words of Damer seemed to him insolent; but he was used to his insolence, and he did not attribute them to any other feeling than that coldness of heart which was not new to him in the speaker.

To all interference in, or interrogation concerning, his scientific or surgical actions and purposes the Englishman had always replied with the same refusal to permit those whom he called laymen to judge either the deeds or the motives of his priesthood. It was precisely the same kind of arrogance and of inflexible secrecy to which Adrianis had been used in the ecclesiastics who had been set over him in his boyhood: the same refusal to be interrogated, the same mystic and unexplained claim of superiority and infallibility.

'If he would only go away!' thought Adrianis, as his gondola glided over the few hundred yards.

For the next few days he and Damer did not meet; he had arranged an excursion to Chioggia, and another to Grado, in which small cruises the Countess Zaranegra and other ladies were on board his schooner. It was beautiful weather; the sea was smooth and smiling; all that wealth could do to make the little voyages delightful was done, and he hoped in the course of them to have some opportunity to force from the lady of his thoughts some definite assurance of her acceptance of his love. In this hope he was disappointed.

Damer was not on board the yacht; but as she saw, over the distant water as they sailed away from Venice, the foundry flames and factory smoke of the Fondamenti, where his tower stood, she shuddered in the hot midsummer noon. It seemed as if even from that distance the eyes of the strange Englishman could see her and lay silence on her lips and terror on her heart. It was but a morbid fancy; she knew that; but she could not shake off the impression. Even when far out on the sunlit green waves of the Adriatic, when Venice had long dropped away out of sight, the chilliness and oppression of the hallucination remained with her.

Although she and everyone else knew that the water fêtes were solely in her honour and for her pleasure, she continued to accept the homage but to stop short of any actual and decisive words on her own part. Adrianis believed that her heart was his, and he could see nothing in the circumstances of either of them which need cause so much hesitation and doubt. Each was free, each young; each might run to meet happiness half-way, as children run to catch a ripe fruit before it has time to fall to earth, and pluck it, warm with sunlight, or pause, and let it drop ungathered. The position troubled and galled him, but his nature was sanguine and his temper optimistic.

Adrianis returned to the city, not wholly discouraged, but vexed and impatient of continual probation and uncertainty.

If he could not persuade her to promise herself to him in Venice he would follow her to the hills above Goritz, and there decide his fate. He had little doubt that he would succeed before the summer should have wholly fled.

'It is getting too warm here; let us go to the mountains,' said her companion.

'In a few days,' she answered. But the days passed, the weeks passed, the temperature grew higher, and she still did not move; and Adrianis stayed also, living chiefly on board his yacht, and Damer still delayed his departure, passing most of his time behind bolted doors in his two chambers on the Fondamenti.

What harm could he do? What harm should he do? He was going to the German university; he would pass out of her existence with the steamship which should bear him from the Giudecca to Trieste; he would vanish in the cold, grim, dark north, and she would remain in the sunshine and laughter and mirth of the south. They had nothing in common: could have nothing. He belonged to his ghastly pursuits, his sickening experiments, his merciless ambitions, and she belonged to herself – and another. So she told herself a hundred times, and out of his presence her reasoning served to reassure her. But whenever she saw him a vague, dull fear turned her heart cold. She felt as helpless as the blythe bird feels when suddenly in the flowering meadow, where it has made its nest, it sees a snake come gliding through the grass. The bird trembles, but does not fly away; dares not fly away. So she dared not dismiss this man from her house, and had not courage to go herself out of the city, out of reach from his magnetism. Her nerves felt the same cold terror as was felt by those of the Venetian brides who were borne away from the feasting on Castello by the brown arms of the Moorish sea-ravishers. She endeavoured to conceal what she felt, for she was ashamed of her own groundless and harmless fears, but they dulled for her the gaiety, the mirth, the beauty of the summer cruise on the emerald seas.

'You play with your happiness,' said her duenna, angrily, to her.

'I do not play, indeed,' she answered seriously. 'We will go to the hills the day after to-morrow.'

XI

Adrianis went out on the following day to make some purchases of glass and metal work for which one of his sisters had written to him. He thought that when they were completed it would be but courtesy to go and tell Damer that he himself was about to leave the city, and offer him his yacht to go in, if he desired it, to Trieste. Their last words had been chafing and cold. The indulgent kindliness of his nature made him wish to part friends with a man to whom he considered that he owed his life.

He bade his gondolier steer northwards to the Fondamenti. He had never been to the chambers occupied by Damer in the old watch-tower; the other had always discouraged all visits; but now he thought that he had better go there, or he might wholly miss seeing the Englishman again before his departure, for of late Damer had come but rarely to the Ca' Zaranegra. But before he could give the order to his gondolier, in passing the Ponte del Paradiso, a sandalo, in which there was one person alone, fouled his own in the narrow channel, and that solitary person was Damer.

'I was just going to your apartments,' cried Adrianis, whilst his gondolier swore loudly as his prow grazed the wall of Palazzo Narni.

'I am going to the hospital, and shall not be at home till dark,' replied Damer, ungraciously.

'I was coming to tell you,' said Adrianis, 'that I am about to leave Venice.'

'And are going to Goritz, no doubt,' said Damer, with a brief smile.

'I may be and I may not,' replied Adrianis, in a tone which implied that wherever he chose to go was no business of anyone's. 'Anyhow, I wished to say that the schooner is entirely at your disposition if you remain here or if you cross to Trieste.'

'Thanks. Yachts are rich men's toys for which I have no use,' answered Damer, without saying where he was going or what he intended to do. 'Send yours to her docks in Messina, if you do not require her yourself.'

'You might be a little more polite,' said Adrianis, half angrily, half jestingly. 'I should be glad to do you any services.'

'Poor men cannot accept such services.'

'Why do you constantly speak of your poverty? You have intellect; that is much rarer than riches.'

'And much less esteemed,' said Damer, with that brief, icy smile which always depressed and troubled Adrianis. 'I fear I cannot stay to gossip,' he added, 'I am already rather late for a conference at the hospital with my esteemed Venetian colleague.'

They were about to part, Damer to pass underneath the bridge, Adrianis to pursue his way to a copper-smith's workshop, when a weak infantine cry smote on their ears, echoed by other shriller childish voices.

There was a row of barges moored along the wall under the old grim Narni palace which stands just beyond the bridge, with its massive iron-studded doors, unaltered in appearance since the time when Tiziano walked a living presence over the Paradiso, and the sunshine shone on the golden hair of Palma Vecchio's daughter.

Some children were playing on the black barges which were laden with firewood and coal. They were small creatures, half naked in the warm air, and sportive as young rabbits; they ran, leaped, climbed the piles of fuel, caught each other in mimic wrestling, and screamed with glad laughter; there was only one who did not join in the games, a little boy, who lay languidly and motionless on some sacks, and watched the sports of others with heavy eyes.

There was no grown man or woman near; there were only the children, and the old palace, like a grey beard with closed eyes; it looked as if it had been shut when Dandolo was young, and had never been opened since; its white statues gazed down over the iron fencing of its garden wall; they, too, were very old.

As the gondola passed under that wall, the sporting children, growing wilder and more reckless, rushed in their
course past and over the little sick boy, and jostled him so
roughly that they pushed him over the edge of the barge, and
he fell, with a shrill cry, into the water. The others, frightened
at what had befallen them, gathered together, whimpering and
afraid, irresolute and incapable. The fallen child disappeared.
The water hereabouts is thick and dark, and sewage flows
unchecked into it. It was in that instant of his fall that his
cry, and the shrieks of his companions, rose shrilly on the
morning silence.

In a second Adrianis sprang from the gondola, dived for the
child, who had drifted underneath the barge, and brought him
up in his arms. He was a boy of some five years old, with a
pretty, pale face and naked limbs, his small, curly head fell in
exhaustion on the young man's shoulder, his ragged clothes
were dripping.

Damer looked at him with professional insight. 'That boy
is ill,' he said to Adrianis. 'You had better put him out of
your arms.'

'Poor little man!' said Adrianis, gently, holding the child
closer. 'What shall we do with him? We cannot leave him here
with only these children.'

'You are wet through yourself. You must go to your hotel,'
said Damer.

Adrianis was still standing in the water. At that moment
a woman rose up from the cabin of the farthest barge, and
came leaping wildly from one barge to another, screaming,
'The child! the child! my Carlino!'

She was his mother. Adrianis gave him to her outstretched
arms, and slipped some money into the little ragged shirt.

'I will come and see how he is in an hour,' he said to her,
amidst her prayers and blessings. 'He is not well. You must
take more care of him; you should not leave him alone.'

The child opened his eyes and smiled.

Adrianis stooped and kissed him.

'Go home by yourself. I will stay and see what is the matter

with him,' said Damer. Adrianis went. Damer, bidding the
woman go before him, walked over the barges until he reached
the one to which there was attached a rude deck-house or
cabin, in which she and five children lived. There he examined
the little boy.

'A sore throat,' he said simply. 'I will bring you remedies.'

He returned to his sandalo, and went on his way to the
hospital conference.

'What is amiss with him?' said Adrianis, later in the day.

'You would have done better to leave him in the canal
water,' replied Damer. 'He is a weak little thing; he has never
had any decent food; he will never recover.'

'But what is his illness?'

'A sore throat,' replied Damer, as he had replied to the
mother; and added, 'It is what the Faculty call Boulogne sore
throat.'

They went both to the Ca' Zaranegra that evening. There
were several people there; the night was very warm; the tall
lilies and palms on the balcony glistened in the light of a
full moon; there was music. Veronica held out the lute to
Adrianis.

'Will you not sing with me to-night?'

'Alas! You must forgive me. I am rather hoarse. I have no
voice,' he answered with regret.

'I heard of what you did this morning,' she murmured
in a low tone. 'Your gondolier told mine. Perhaps you
have taken a chill. I will go and see the little child to-
morrow.'

'We will go together,' he replied in the same soft whisper,
while his hand touched hers in seeming only to take the
lute. Damer saw the gesture where he sat, in the embrasure of a window, speaking of a frontier question of the
hour with a German Minister who was passing through
Venice.

When they left the house two or three other men accompanied them on to the water-steps. Warm though the night
was, Adrianis shivered a little as he wrapped his overcoat

round him. 'I could bear my sables,' he said as he descended the stairs. Damer looked at him in the moonlight, which was clear as the light of early morning.

'You should not plunge into sewage water and embrace little sick beggars,' he said coldly, as he accompanied one of the Venetian gentlemen whose palace was near the Fondamenti, and who had offered him a seat in his gondola.

Adrianis, refusing the entreaties of his companions to go and sup with them at Florian's, went to his rooms at the hotel. He had a flood of happiness at the well-springs of his heart, but in his body he felt feverish and cold.

'It is the sewage water. It got down my throat as I dived,' he thought, recalling the words of his friend. 'I shall sleep this chill off and be well again in the morning.'

But he did not sleep; he drank some iced drinks thirstily, and only fell into a troubled and heavy slumber as the morning dawned red over the roofs of Venice, and the little cannon on the Giudecca saluted a new day.

He felt ill when he rose, but he bathed and dressed, and, though he had no appetite for breakfast, went down to his gondola, which he had bidden to be before the hotel at nine o'clock.

At parting from her he had arranged with Veronica that they should go at that hour to see the little child of the Bridge of Paradise.

As he stood on the steps and was about to descend, Damer touched him on the arm.

'You are going to take the Countess Zaranegra to the sick boy?'

'Yes,' said Adrianis, with a haughty accent; he did not like the tone of authority in which he was addressed.

'I forbid you to do so, then,' said Damer. 'She would only see a dead body, and that body infectious with disease.'

Adrianis was painted.

'Is the little thing dead?' he said in a hushed voice. 'Dead already?'

'He died twenty minutes ago. He had been ill for three days.'

'Poor little pretty thing!' murmured Adrianis. 'I am sorry; I will go to the mother.'

'You had better go to your bed. You are unwell. You did a foolish act yesterday.'

'I am quite well. When I require your advice, I will ask it,' said Adrianis, impatiently; and he entered his gondola and went to the Ca' Zaranegra. Damer, standing on the steps of the hotel, looked after him with a gaze which would have killed him could a look have slain.

Her house was bright in the morning radiance, the green water lapping its marbles, the lilies and palms fresh from the night's dew, the doors standing open showing the blossoming acacias in the garden behind.

She came to him at once in one of the smaller salons.

'I am ready,' she said gaily. 'Look! I have got these fruits and toys for your little waif.'

Then something in his expression checked her gladness.

'What is it?' she asked.

'The child is dead,' said Adrianis.

'Oh, how sad!'

She put down the little gifts she had prepared on a table near her; she was tender-hearted and quickly moved; the tears came into her eyes for the little boy whom she had never seen.

Adrianis drew nearer to her.

'Mia cara,' he murmured. 'Do not play with me any longer. Death is so near us always. I have told you a hundred times that I love you. I will make you so happy if you will trust to me. Tell me – tell me –'

She was softened by emotion, conquered by the answering passion which was in her; she did not speak, but her breast heaved, her lips trembled; she let him take her hands.

'You will be mine – mine – mine!' he cried in delirious joy.

'I love you,' she answered, in a voice so low that it was like the summer breeze passing softly over the lilies.

'Hush! Leave me! Go now. Come back at three. I shall be alone.'

The doors were open and the windows; in a farther chamber two liveried servants stood; approaching through the ante-room was the figure of the major-domo of the palace.

Adrianis pressed her hands to his lips and left her. He was dizzy from ecstasy, or so he thought, as the busts and statues of the entrance hall reeled and swam before his sight, and his limbs felt so powerless and nerveless that, if one of his gondoliers had not caught and held him, he would have fallen headlong down the water-steps.

XII

When three of the clock chimed from the belfries of S. Mark's she awaited him, alone in her favourite room, clothed in white, with a knot of tea-roses at her breast; she was full of gladness; she looked at herself in the many mirrors and saw that she was as fair as the fair June day.

'How beautiful our lives will be!' she thought. 'Poor little dead child! It was his little hands joined ours. Perhaps he is an angel of God now, and will be always with us!'

She heard the swish of oars at the water-stairs below; she heard steps ascending those stairs; she heard the voice of her head servant speaking. It was he! She put her hand to her heart; it beat so wildly that the leaves of the roses fell; she crossed herself and murmured a prayer; such happiness seemed to merit gratitude.

Through the vista of the ante-chambers came the figure of a man. But it was not that of Adrianis.

Damer came up to her with his calm, expressionless face, his intent eyes, his air of authority and of indifference.

'You expected the Prince Adrianis,' he said to her. 'I regret to tell you, madame, that he is unable to keep his appointment with you. He has taken the disease of which that child on the barge died this morning. He has what the vulgar call diphtheria.'

XIII

Adrianis lay in the large salon where, two months earlier, they had dined together in the evening after finding the opal necklace. Damer had caused a bed to be taken into it and placed in the centre of the room, as affording more air from the four large windows than was to be obtained from the inner bed-chamber adjoining. He did not give the true name to the disease in speaking to the people of the hotel; he spoke merely of cold and fever from a plunge in the hot noonday into foul canal water; on the local doctor, whom he paid the compliment of calling in, he enjoined the same reserve.

'The prince is very rich,' he said, 'he will pay for any loss which may be incurred, any renewal of furniture and of draperies.'

From Adrianis he did not conceal the truth.

Indeed, Adrianis himself said, in a hoarse, faint voice, 'I have the disease which the child had. Cure me if you can, for –'

He did not add why life was more than ever beautiful to him, but the tears rose into his eyes; the other understood what remained unspoken.

When three in the afternoon sounded from the clock tower on the south side of the hotel he raised his head, and, with a despairing gesture, said to Damer, 'She expects me. Go, and explain to her; say I am ill. Tell her I would get up and keep my tryst if I died at her feet, but I fear – I fear – the contagion – for her.'

'Lie where you are and you will probably be well in a few days,' said Damer. 'I will leave Stefanio with you and take your message. I shall soon return. Meanwhile, your man knows what to do.'

Stefanio was the valet.

The eyes of Adrianis followed him from the room with longing and anguish. He was not yet so ill that the apathy of extreme illness dulled his desires and stilled his regrets. Both were intense as life still was intense in him. He would have risen and dragged himself to the Ca' Zaranegra; but, as he had said, he feared the infection for her which would be in his voice, in his touch, in his breath, in his mere presence.

He lay on his back, gazing wistfully at the great sunny windows, only veiled by the gauze of mosquito curtains. He could hear the churning of the water below as the canal steamers passed up and down; the softer ripple as oars parted it; he could see a corner of the marbles of the Salute, with two pigeons sitting side by side on it pruning their plumage in the sun.

He was not yet afraid, but he was very sorry; he longed to be up and out in the bright air, and he longed to be in the presence of his beloved, to ask again and again and again for the confession so dear to him; to hear it from her lips, to read it in her eyes.

'She loves me, she loves me,' he thought, and he, like a coward, like a knave, must be untrue to the first meeting she had promised him!

'Why is it,' he thought, as the tears welled up under his closed eyelids, 'that our better, kinder impulses always cost us so much more heavily than all our egotisms and all our vices?'

If he had left the little child underneath the barge to drown, would it not have been better even for the child? The little thing had only suffered some eighteen hours longer through his rescue.

'Let us do what we ought,' he murmured, in words his mother had often spoken to him. 'The gods will pay us.'

But the gods had been harsh in their payment to him.

He counted the minutes until Damer's return, holding his watch in his hot hand. He took docilely what his servant gave him, though to swallow was painful and difficult.

'What a while he stays!' he thought restlessly. He envied the other every moment passed at the Ca' Zaranegra.

'What did you tell her?' he asked breathlessly, when Damer at last returned.

'I told her the truth,' replied Damer, as he placed the thermometer under the sick man's armpit. 'You have worried and fretted; your fever has increased.'

'What did she say? She is not angry, or offended?'

'Who can be so at the misfortune of disease. Of course she knows that you have incurred this misfortune through your own folly.'

'Did she say so?'

'No; I am not aware that she said so. But she no doubt thought it. She bade me tell you not to agitate yourself.'

'Was that all?'

'She added – for her sake,' said Damer, with a cold, slight smile. He was truthful in what he repeated; he scorned vulgar methods of misrepresentation and betrayal. The heavy eyes of Adrianis gleamed and lightened with joy.

'Thanks,' he said softly, and his hot hand pressed that of his friend.

'I will write to her,' he added. 'You can disinfect a note?'

'Yes. But do not exert yourself. Try to sleep.'

He crossed the room and closed the green wooden blinds; he gave an order to Stefanio, and dipped his hands in a disinfecting fluid; then he sat down and took up a book. But he could not read. He saw before him that blanched and frightened face, which a little while before had been raised to his as the voice of Veronica had cried to him, 'Save him? You will save him! You have so much knowledge, so much power. You will save him for my sake?'

He had promised her nothing; he had only said briefly, in the language of people who were fools, that the issue of life and of death was in the hands of Deity. He had promised her nothing; in his own way he was sincere. Up to that time he had done everything which science and experience could suggest to combat the disease.

Adrianis wrote at intervals various pencilled notes to her; indistinct, feebly scrawled, but still coherent. He pointed to each when it was written and looked at his friend with supplicating eyes. He could not speak, for the false membrane filled his throat. Damer took each little note with apparent indifference.

'To the Countess Zaranegra?' he asked.

Adrianis signed a mute assent. Damer carried each scrap of paper to the next room, disinfected it, then sent it to its destination. He was of too proud a temper to use the usual small arts of the traitor.

This he did thrice.

Once she wrote in reply.

'I cannot see, my eyes are too weak,' Adrianis scrawled on its envelope as the letter was given to him. 'Read it to me.'

Damer opened it, and read it aloud. It was short, timid, simple, but a deep love and an intense anxiety spoke in it. Adrianis took it and laid his cheek on it with a smile of ineffable peace. It seemed to give him firmer hold on life.

Adrianis slept peacefully, his cheek on the little letter, as a child falls to sleep with a favourite toy on its pillow.

He called in a second medical man of the town, and two sisters of charity to replace Stefanio, who grew alarmed for his own safety and would no longer approach the bed.

'Send for my mother,' said Adrianis, in his choked voice.

'Certainly,' answered his friend. The disease which had fastened on Adrianis was not one which waits. But Damer telegraphed only to the Adrianis' palace in Palermo, and he knew that it was unlikely she would be in that city in the summer heats of the end of June.

The telegram might be forwarded or it might not; Italian households are careless in such matters.

But when he murmured once and again, 'Send for my mother!' Damer could, with a clear conscience, reply, 'I have telegraphed.'

He sat by the bedside and watched the sick man.

He believed that he would recover.

In the dusk he was told that a lady, who was below in her gondola, desired to see him. He descended the stairs, prepared to find Veronica Zaranegra. She was veiled; he could not see her features, but he knew her by the turn of her head, the shape of her hand, before she spoke.

'You come for news of the prince?' he said coldly and

harshly. 'I can give you none. The disease is always uncertain and deceptive.'

'Let me see him! oh, let me see him!' she murmured. 'I came for that. No matter what they say. No matter what danger there be. Only let me see him!'

'That is wholly impossible,' replied Damer, in an unchanged tone. 'Why do you come on such errands?'

'Who should see him if not I? Who are you that you should keep me from him?'

'I am a man of science, whose duty it is to protect you from yourself. Go home, madame, and pray for your betrothed. That is all that you can do.'

She burst into tears. He heard her sobs, he saw the heaving of her shoulders and her breast.

'Take your mistress home. She is unwell,' he said to the gondolier, who waited a moment for his lady's orders, then, receiving none, pushed his oar against the steps and slowly turned the gondola round to go back up the canal.

'Why does she love him?' thought Damer. 'Like to like. Fool to fool. Flower to flower!'

From his soul he despised her, poor, lovely, mindless, childlike creature! But her voice turned his blood to flame; the sound of her weeping deepened his scorn to hate; the touch of her ungloved hand was ecstasy and agony in one; he loved her with furious, brutal, unsparing passion, like lava under the ice of his self-restraint.

He stood in the twilight and looked after the black shape of the gondola.

'He shall never be yours,' he said in his heart. 'Never – never – never! unless I die instead of him to-night.'

He remained there some minutes, whilst the water traffic passed by him unnoticed and the crowds flocked out from a novena in the Salute.

The day became evening, the lovely roseate twilight of summer in Venice wore into night, and the night waned into dawn. All the animation of Venetian life began again to awake with the whirr of the wings of the pigeons taking their sunrise flight from dome, and cupola, and pinnacle, and gutter. To the sisters of charity their patient seemed better; to the surgeons of the city also; Damer said nothing.

'Is he not better?' asked the nun, anxiously.

'I see little amelioration,' replied Damer, and said in a louder tone to Adrianis, 'Your mother has telegraphed; she will soon be here.'

Adrianis smiled again a smile which lighted up his beautiful brown eyes and momentarily banished their languor. He felt disposed to sleep, but he drew his pencil and paper to him and wrote feebly, 'Mme Zaranegra?'

Damer read the name.

'She came to see you an hour or two ago,' he answered. 'But I could not allow it. Your illness is infectious.'

He spoke in his usual brief, calm, indifferent manner. Adrianis sighed, but it was a sigh of content; he was half asleep, he turned on his pillows and drew her little note, which he had hidden under them, once more against his cheek.

'He will sleep himself well,' said the nun.

'Let us hope so,' replied Damer; but she heard from his tone that he did not share her belief.

It was now eleven o'clock.

'Go and rest,' he said to her. 'You need it. I will watch to-night. If there be any necessity for aid I will summon you.'

'Will his mother soon be here?' asked the sister, whose heart was tender.

'I believe so,' replied Damer.

One of the medical men whom he had summoned came out on to the balcony to his side.

'The sisters say the prince is better; he seems so,' said his colleague.

'What do they know?' said Damer; and added less harshly, 'It is too early to be able to make sure of recovery; it is a disease which is very treacherous.'

'He has youth on his side.'

'Yes; but he is weakened by the effects of a wound he received last year, for which I treated him. His constitution is not prepared to make so soon again another struggle for existence.'

'You have more knowledge of him than I,' said the Venetian, who was a meek man, not very wise.

'Come to my laboratory in the Fondamenti, and I will show you something and tell you something,' said Damer.

His Italian colleague, flattered, complied with the request.

What he showed him were three animals, two rabbits and a cat, inoculated with and dying of diphtheria; what he explained to him were the theories of Lœffler and Klebs, and the discovery of the presumed antidote by Behring; he also displayed to him some serum which he had received from Roux, who was only then at the commencement of his applications of Behring's theory.

The Venetian doctor inspected and listened with deep respect.

'Why do you not try this treatment on the prince?' he said, which was what Damer desired and intended him to say.

'I will do so on my own responsibility if he be no better in the morning,' he replied. 'But you will admit that the responsibility will be great, the theory of the cure being at present unknown to the general public, and no one of his family being at present in Venice to authorise the experiment.'

'We are there as your colleagues, and we shall support you,' replies the more obscure man, touched and flattered by the deference of one who was in the confidence of French and German men of science.

'If there be no other way, I will take the risk; the risk is less than that of tracheotomy,' said Damer, as he put the small phial of serum back into a locked case.

XIV

When the Venetian doctor left him, he took the phial of serum, the inoculating syringe, and another smaller bottle containing a clear liquid, which was the toxin or virus of the malady, and which he had not shown to the Venetian. He put these together in the breast pocket of his coat. He had no belief in the efficacy of the serum, but he had prepared the venom of the toxin himself; and in that small glass tube there was poison enough to slay twelve men.

'If there be no other way,' he repeated to himself as he went back to the hotel through the moonlit canals and under the ancient houses.

The dual meaning which lay in the words was like a devil's laugh in his ears.

He looked up at the Ca' Zaranegra as he passed it; its windows were all dark, and the white lilies on the balconies had no light upon them save that from the rays of the moon.

As he entered the lighted hall of the hotel, they handed to him a telegram. It was from the Princess Adrianis. She had received his despatch twelve hours late, as she had been in her summer palace in the mountains; she had left Sicily immediately, and said that she would travel without pause at the utmost speed possible. She added, 'I commend my darling to God and to you.'

Damer crushed the paper up in his hand with a nervous gesture and flung it out, by the open doorway, into the water below.

Then he ascended the staircase and entered his patient's room.

The night was very warm; the windows stood wide open; there was a shaded porcelain lamp alight on the table. One nun watched whilst the other slept. Adrianis lay still on the great bed in the shadow; he was awake, his eyes were looking upward, his mouth was open but his breathing was easier and less hard.

The sister of charity whispered to Damer, 'I think he is better. The fungus growth seems loosening. We have given the wine and the meat essence. He could swallow.'

He lit a candle and approached the bed. Adrianis smiled faintly. He could not speak.

'Let me see your throat,' said Damer.

He saw that the nun had spoken truly; the fungus growth

was wasting, the false membrane was shrinking; there was a healthier look on the tongue. He set the lamp down and said nothing.

'Is he not better?' said the sister, anxiously.

'Perhaps,' he replied. 'If there be no re-formation of the false membrane he may be saved. Go, my good woman, and rest while you can.'

She went, nothing loth, to her supper and her bed. Damer was alone with the man who trusted him and whose mother trusted him.

He went away from the bedside and sat down by one of the windows. His heart had long years before been rendered dumb and dead; his mind alone remained alive and his passions.

He stayed in the open air, looking down on the green water.

'Man cannot control circumstances,' he thought, 'but the wise man can assist circumstance, the fool does not.'

He had in him that fell egotism of science which chokes the fountain of mercy at its well-springs in blood. He sat by the window, and looked out absently at the night.

He knew that the nun was right; he knew that the disease was passing away from the sick man; that, if left alone, sleep and youth would restore him to health, to love, and joy.

Should he leave him alone?

Should he let him live to become the lover and lord of Veronica Zaranegra? Should he let those two mindless, flowerlike lives lean together, and embrace, and multiply?

It would be what men called a crime, but his school despises the trivial laws of men, knowing that for the wise there is no such thing as crime and no such thing as virtue – only lesions of the brain, and absence of temptation and opportunity.

The mother of Adrianis could not be there before another day, travel as rapidly as she would. He knew the effect of affection on the nervous system, and that the sight and sense of a beloved person near them often gave to enfeebled frames the power of resistance and recovery. Those emotions were not in himself, but he recognised their existence, and he knew that in

Adrianis the emotions and the affections were very strong in proportion as the mental powers were slight.

He must not await the arrival of the princess. He had before been witness of her devotion, of her skill in illness, of her fortitude, and of the love existing between her and her son. They were powers he despised and never pitied, as he never pitied the love of the nursing bitch from whom he removed her litter that he might watch her die of the agony of her bursting teats. But he was conscious of the existence of such powers; and the physiologist ignores no facts which he has demonstrated, though they may belong to an order with which he has no sympathy.

He knew that he must not allow the mother of Adrianis to arrive in time to see her son alive.

'What thou doest, do quickly,' he murmured in words which he had heard in his childhood as he had sat in the old parish church of his native village.

He rose and walked to the bed.

Adrianis still seemed to sleep, the breathing was heavy and forced chiefly through the nasal passages; but there was a look of returning serenity on his features: a look which the man of science is well aware precedes recovery, not death.

As surely as anyone can gauge the unseen future, he was sure that if let alone the young man would recover, would in a week or two arise unharmed from his bed. He was equally sure that he had himself, in his breast, the means of changing that process of recovery into the agony of dissolution. He no longer hesitated; he no longer doubted. He went to the adjacent chamber, where the two nuns, still dressed, were sleeping. He awakened them.

'Come,' he said gently. 'He is worse. I am about to try the cure of Behring. It may succeed. There is no other chance. It will be necessary to hold him. I require you both.'

He was well aware that it would be unwise to essay that operation alone – it would rouse comment in the day to come.

'Hold him motionless,' he said to the two women. 'Do not awake him if you can avoid it.'

He filled the inoculating syringe from one of the little phials which he had brought from the Fondamenti. He stood in the full light of the lamp so that the two sisters could see all that he did.

'Loosen his shirt,' he said to them. Adrianis still slept; in his predisposition to sleep the few drops of chloral, which had been administered twenty minutes earlier, had sufficed to render him almost insensible.

Damer bent over him and inserted the injecting needle into one of the veins; the incision disturbed him without wholly loosening the bonds of the soporific; he struggled slightly, moaned a little, but the nuns succeeded in resisting his endeavour to rise; the inoculation was successfully made.

The face of Damer in the lamplight was not paler than usual, but his hand trembled as he withdrew the syringe.

'What is Behring's cure?' asked the nun who felt most interest in her patient.

'An antitoxin; the serum of an immune beast,' he answered calmly, as he turned slightly towards her. The nun did not understand, but she was afraid of troubling him with other questions.

He walked to the window and stood looking out at the moonlit water.

He had left on a table the syringe and the phial of serum which was half empty. But in the breast pocket of his coat he had the phial of toxin, and that phial was wholly empty. The nuns, engrossed in holding down Adrianis, had not seen that the glass tube on the table was not the one from which the syringe had been filled; and, when used, Damer had plunged the syringe immediately into a bowl of disinfecting acid. There was no trace anywhere that the toxin had been used instead of the serum; no trace whatever save in the tumefying vein of the sick man's throat.

'You had better stay near him, you may be wanted, and it is two o'clock,' said Damer to the nurses. 'I shall remain here. There will be, I hope, a great change soon.'

He went out on to the balcony and turned his back on the

watching women and leaned against the iron-work, looking down on the canal, where nothing moved except the slow, scarcely visible ripple or the water. He was human though he had killed his humanity, replacing it by intellect alone. He suffered in that moment; a vague sense of what ignorance calls crime was on him painfully; he had emancipated himself wholly from the superstitions and prejudices of men, but he was conscious that he had now done that which, if known, would put him outside the pale of their laws.

He did not repent or regret; he did not see any evil in his act. The right of the strong, the right of the sage was his; he had but exercised his reason to produce an issue he desired.

So he thought as he leaned against the iron scroll-work and watched the thick, dark water glide by past the marble steps of the Salute. There was a faint light in the sky on the east, but he could not see the east where he stood; it was still completely night between the walls of the Grand Canal. The voice of a man called up to him from the darkness below.

'Madame sends me to know how goes it with the prince?'

Damer looked down. 'Tell the Countess Zaranegra that things are as they were. A new remedy has been essayed.'

The man who had come by the calle retired by them, swinging a lantern in his hand.

The two Vulcans of the clock tower, hard by in S. Mark's square, struck four times upon their anvil. Damer looked up the darkness of the canal where nothing was to be seen but the lamps which burned on either side of it, with their reflections, and the lanthorns tied to poles before some of the palaces. He could not see the Ca' Zaranegra, which was not in sight even in the day, but he saw it in remembrance with its flowering balconies, its tapestried chambers, its red and white awnings, its great escutcheon over its portals. He saw her in his vision as she must be now – awake, listening for her messenger's return, in some white, loose gown no doubt, with her hair loose, too, upon her shoulders, her face white, her eyes strained in anxiety, as he had seen them that afternoon and evening.

If Adrianis had lived she would have been his wife: that was as certain as that the sea was beating on the bar of Malomocco underneath the moon.

'I have done well; I have exercised my supremacy,' he thought. 'We have right of life and death over all birds, and beasts, and things which swim and crawl, by virtue of our greater brain; in like manner has the greater brain the right to deal as it will with the weaker brain when their paths meet and one must yield and go under. The fool hath said that there is sanctity in life, but the man of science has never said it. To him one organism or another has the same measure in his scales.'

Strangely enough, at that moment, and incongruously, there came to him a remembrance of his own childish days: of sitting by his mother's side in the little, dark, damp church of their northern hamlet, and reading written on their tablets the Ten Commandments.

'Mother, what is it to do murder?' he had asked her; and she had answered, 'It is to take life; to destroy what we cannot recall.'

He remembered how, some weeks later, when he had killed from wantonness a mole which ran across a road, he had been frightened and had gone to his mother and said to her, 'Mother, mother, I have done murder. I have taken life and I cannot recall it.' And his mother had smiled and answered, 'That is not murder, my dear. A little mole is a dumb creature.'

But his mother had been wrong, as the world was wrong. Whether the organism were animal or human, what difference was there? Only a difference of brain.

The world and its lawgivers might and would still say that what destroyed the human organism was murder, that is, a crime; but to the trained, logical, strong reason of Damer the sophism was a premiss untenable. To slay a man was no more than to slay a mole. To do either was to arrest a mechanism, to dissolve tissues, to send elements back into the space they came from; it was nothing more. One organism or another, what matter?

Since that day in the dim long ago, he had taken life,

not once, not twice, but thousands of times, causing the greatest and most lingering agony in its inflictions. But, in his opinion, that had not been murder; it had been only torture and slaughter of dumb creatures according to human law. What difference could there be if, by accident, the creature to be removed were human?

He was consistent enough, and sincere enough to follow out the theories of the laboratory to their logical sequence without flinching. He honestly held himself without blame.

He was only a man, and therefore he felt some sickly sense of pain when he heard in the still and waning night the sound of his victim's convulsive struggles to gain breath; but he held himself without blame, for every thesis and every deduction of the priesthood of science justified and made permissible his action to bring about a catastrophe which was necessary to him.

Science bade him take all the other sentient races of earth and make them suffer as he chose and kill them as he chose. Those other races were organisms as susceptible as the human organisms. Why should the human organism enjoy immunity?

He had done no more than is done for sake of experiment or observation in the hospital or the laboratory every day all over the known world. The reluctance to face what he had done was merely that residue of early influences and impressions which remains in the soul of the strongest, haunting its remembrances and emasculating its resolution.

He called up to his command that volition, that power of will which had never failed him; he returned to the bedside as he would have returned to visit a dog dying under the pressure of eight atmospheres.

Adrianis still lay in the same position. About the almost invisible orifice where the needle had punctured there was a slight tumefied swelling.

'He seems worse,' whispered the nun.

'He cannot be either better or worse as yet,' replied Damer, truthfully. 'Give him a little wine, if he can take it.'

They might give him what they chose; they could not now

save him from death. He had received enough of the virus into his vein to slay a man in health. Passing as it did into an organ already diseased, he would die before the sun rose, or an hour after.

He had aided nature to destroy her own work. There was nothing new or criminal in that – nature was for ever creating and destroying. Once it had suited him to save that young man's life; now it suited him to end it.

One action was as wrong or as righteous as the other. It was an exercise of power, as when the monarch grants an amnesty or signs a death warrant. Who blames the monarch who does but use his power? The prerogative of superior reason is higher than the prerogative of a monarch. Moreover, who would ever know it? Who would ever be aware that the intenser virus of the toxin had mingled with the natural formation of the disease?

Even were there an autopsy, discovery would be impossible; the concentrated venom had mingled with and been absorbed in the common and usual growth of the false membrane. He had but aided death instead of hindering it.

His professional conscience would have shrunk from giving the disease, but it did not shrink from making death certain where it was merely possible. He did but add a stronger poison to that which nature had already poisoned.

Men slew their rivals in duels and no one blamed them; who should blame him because he used the finer weapon of science instead of the coarser weapon of steel? He did but carry out the doctrine of the laboratory to its just and logical sequence.

What he felt for Veronica was not love, but passion, and not passion alone, but the sense of dominion. He knew that the fair creature shrank from him, but submitted to him. All the intense instinctive tyranny of his nature longed to exercise itself on her, the beautiful and patrician thing, so far above him, so fragile and so fair. He knew that he would never possess her or command her except through fear; but this would suffice to him. The finer and more delicate elements of love were indifferent to him, were indeed unknown. They had existed in Adrianis, whom he had despised; but in his own temperament they could find no dwelling-place. His desires were brutal as had ever been those of Attila, whose throne lies low amongst the grass on Torcello.

Late at night and early at dawn messengers came from some noble families in the city, and the Ca' Zaranegra. Damer replied to all inquiries, 'It is impossible to say what turn the disease may take.'

Damer said nothing. He looked out at the marble church which had no message for him, and down the moonlit waters which had no beauty for him. He was absorbed in meditation. His will desired to do that from which his natural weakness shrank; for in his great strength he was still weak, being human. The infliction of death was nothing to him, could be nothing; he was used to kill as he was used to torture, with profound indifference, with no more hesitation than he ate or drank or fulfilled any natural function of his body. To obtain knowledge, even the approach of knowledge, he would have inflicted the most agonising and the most endless suffering without a moment's doubt or a moment's regret. From his boyhood upwards he had always lived in the hells created by modern science, wherein if the bodies of animals suffer the souls of men wither and perish. What was the man lying sleeping there to him? Only an organism like those which daily he broke up and destroyed and threw aside. Only an organism, filled by millions of other invisible organisms, by a myriad of parasite animalculæ, numerous as the star-dust in the skies.

The woman whom he desired was nothing more; he could not deem her more; he scorned himself for the empire over him of his own desire of her perishable form, of her foolish butterfly life. He himself was no more, but there was alight in him that light of the intellect which in his own esteem raised him above them into an empyrean unknown by them. His intellect made him as Cæsar, as Pharaoh; their foolishness made them as slaves.

The time is nigh at hand when there will be no priests and

no kings but those of science, and beneath their feet the nations will grovel in terror and writhe in death.

He went out again into the balcony, leaving the nuns to endeavour to administer the wine, which, however, their patient could not swallow, the fungus growth closed his larynx. His head was thrown back on the pillows; his eyes were staring but sightless; his face was pallid, and looked blue round the mouth and about the temples. He was now straining for breath; like a horse fallen on the road, blown and broken.

They called loudly to Damer, being frightened and horrified. He re-entered the chamber.

'He is worse,' he said gravely.

The nun, who had a tender heart, wept. Damer sat down by the bed. He had seen that struggle for air a thousand times in all the hospitals of Europe. It could now have but one end.

A little while after, they brought him a note and a telegram. The first was from the Countess Zaranegra. It said, 'You must let me see him. It is my right, my place.'

The second was from the mother of Adrianis; it said, 'I have reached Bologna; I shall soon be with you. God bless you for your goodness to my son.'

He read them, and tore the one in pieces and flung the pieces in the canal; the other he put in his breast pocket beside the empty phial of toxin.

The mother's letter would be useful if any called in question the too late usage of the Behring serum. It would show the complete confidence placed in him by the writer. At that moment his two Venetian colleagues arrived. The day had dawned. The women put out the light of the lamps.

'You have given the antitoxin?' said the elder of the Venetians, glancing at the syringe.

'I have,' replied Damer. 'But, I believe, too late.'

'I fear too late,' replied the Venetian. 'Not less admirable is your courage in accepting such responsibility.'

Damer bowed. He looked grave and worn, which was

natural in a man who had been in anxious vigil through thirty-six hours by the bedside of his friend.

'Have you any hope?' whispered the Venetian.

'I confess none, now,' he answered.

The pure light of earliest daybreak was in the whole of the vast chamber.

It shone on that ghastly sight, a man dying in his youth, struggling and straining for a breath of air, fighting against suffocation.

The fresh sea air was flowing through the room, sweet with the odours of fruits and flowers, free to the poorest wretch that lived. But in all that bounteous liberty and radiance of air he could not draw one breath, he could not reach one wave of it to slake his thirst of life.

The poisoned growth filled every chink of the air passages as though they were tubes mortared up and closed hermetically. His face grew purple and tumid, his eyes started from their sockets, his arms waved wildly, beckoning in space; he had no sense left except the mere instinctive mechanical effort to gasp for the air which he was never to breathe again. The five persons round him stood in silence, while the stifled sobs of the nun were heard; the splash of oars echoed from the water below; somewhere without a bird sang.

The Venetians spoke one with another, then turned to Damer.

'The end must be near. We ought to call in the assistance of the Church. We must not let him perish thus, unshrived, unannealed, like a pagan, like a dumb creature.'

'Do whatever you deem right,' replied Damer. 'With those matters I do not meddle.'

The minutes went on; the nuns sank on their knees; the one who wept hid her face on the coverlet of the bed. All which had so lately been the youth, the form, the vitality of Adrianis wrestled with death as a young lion tears at the walls of the den which imprisons him. The terrible choking sounds roared through the air to which his closed throat could not open. Blood foamed in froth from his lips, which were curled up over the white teeth, and were cracked and blue. His eyes, starting from their orbits, had not sight. Damer ceased to look; almost he regretted that which he had done.

Suddenly the convulsions ceased.

'He is out of pain,' said one of the Venetians, in a solemn and hushed voice.

'He is dead,' said Damer.

The women crossed themselves.

The little bird outside sang loudly.

The door opened, and the mother of Adrianis stood on the threshold.

Six months later the man who had killed him wedded Veronica Zaranegra. Her family opposed, and her friends warned her, in vain; she shrank from him, she feared him, she abhorred him, but the magnetism of his will governed hers till he shaped her conduct at his choice, as the hand of the sculptor moulds the clay.

He became master of her person, of her fortune, of her destiny; but her soul, frightened and dumb, forever escapes from him, and hides in the caverns of memory and regret.

The Courtship of Susan Bell

ANTHONY TROLLOPE

ANTHONY TROLLOPE (1815–1882) had a flourishing career in the Post Office as well as being a prolific novelist, best known for his Barchester and Palliser novels. He travelled widely and put much of his experience into short stories, such as this one about the days when building a railway was an exciting new pursuit. Poor Susan's happiness is nearly wrecked by the caution of her family, but in the end her railway engineer lover wins her.

JOHN Munroe Bell had been a lawyer in Albany, State of New York, and as such had thriven well. He had thriven well as long as thrift and thriving on this earth had been allowed to him. But the Almighty had seen fit to shorten his span.

Early in life he had married a timid, anxious, pretty, good little wife, whose whole heart and mind had been given up to do his bidding and deserve his love. She had not only deserved it but had possessed it, and as long as John Munroe Bell had lived, Henrietta Bell – Hetta as he called her – had been a woman rich in blessings. After twelve years of such blessings he had left her, and had left with her two daughters, a second Hetta, and the heroine of our little story, Susan Bell.

A lawyer in Albany may thrive passing well for eight or ten years, and yet not leave behind him any very large sum of money if he dies at the end of that time. Some small modicum, some few thousand dollars, John Bell had amassed, so that his widow and daughters were not absolutely driven to look for work or bread.

In those happy days when cash had begun to flow in plenteously to the young father of the family he had taken it into his head to build for himself, or rather for his young female brood, a small neat house in the outskirts of Saratoga Springs. In doing so he was instigated as much by the excellence of the investment for his pocket as by the salubrity of the place for his girls. He furnished the house well, and then during some summer weeks his wife lived there, and sometimes he let it.

How the widow grieved when the lord of her heart and master of her mind was laid in the grave, I need not tell. She had already counted ten years of widowhood, and her children had grown to be young women beside her at the time of which I am now about to speak. Since that sad day on which they had left Albany they had lived together at the cottage at the Springs. In winter their life had been lonely enough; but as soon as the hot weather began to drive the fainting citizens out from New York, they had always received two or three boarders – old ladies generally, and occasionally an old gentleman – persons of very steady habits, with whose pockets the widow's moderate demands agreed better than the hotel charges. And so the Bells lived for ten years.

That Saratoga is a gay place in July, August, and September the world knows well enough. To girls who go there with trunks full of muslin and crinoline, for whom a carriage and pair of horses is always waiting immediately after dinner, whose fathers' pockets are bursting with dollars, it is a very gay place. Dancing and flirtations come as a matter of course, and matrimony follows after with only too great rapidity. But the place was not very gay for Hetta or Susan Bell.

In the first place the widow was a timid woman, and among other fears feared greatly that she should be thought guilty of setting traps for husbands. Poor mothers! how often are they charged with this sin when their honest desires go no further than that their bairns may be 'respectit like the lave.' And then she feared flirtations; flirtations that should be that and nothing more, flirtations that are so destructive of the heart's sweetest essence. She feared love also, though she longed for that as well as feared it – for her girls, I mean; all such feelings for herself were long laid under ground; and then, like a timid creature as she was, she had other indefinite fears, and among them a great fear that those girls of hers would be left husbandless, a phase of life which after her twelve years of bliss she regarded as anything but desirable. But the upshot was – the upshot of so many fears and such small means, – that Hetta and Susan Bell had but a dull life of it.

Were it not that I am somewhat closely restricted in the number of my pages, I would describe at full the merits and beauties of Hetta and Susan Bell. As it is I can but say a few words. At our period of their lives Hetta was nearly one-and-twenty, and Susan was just nineteen. Hetta was a short, plump, demure, young woman, with the softest smoothed hair, and the brownest brightest eyes. She was very useful in the house, good at corn cakes, and thought much, particularly in these latter months, of her religious duties. Her sister in the privacy of their own little room would sometimes twit her with the admiring patience with which she would listen to the lengthened eloquence of Mr Phineas Beckard, the Baptist minister. Now Mr Phineas Beckard was a bachelor.

Susan was not so good a girl in the kitchen or about the house as was her sister; but she was bright in the parlour, and if that motherly heart could have been made to give out its inmost secret – which, however, it could not have been made to give out in any way painful to dear Hetta – perhaps it might have been found that Susan was loved with the closest love. She was taller than her sister, and lighter; her eyes were blue as were her mother's; her hair was brighter than Hetta's, but not always so singularly neat. She had a dimple on her chin, whereas Hetta had none; dimples on her cheeks too, when she smiled; and, oh, such a mouth! There; my allowance of pages permits no more.

One piercing cold winter's day there came knocking at the

widow's door – a young man. Winter days, when the ice of January is refrozen by the wind of February, are very cold at Saratoga Springs. In these days there was not often much to disturb the serenity of Mrs Bell's house; but on the day in question there came knocking at the door – a young man.

Mrs Bell kept an old domestic, who had lived with them in those happy Albany days. Her name was Kate O'Brien, but though picturesque in name she was hardly so in person. She was a thick-set, noisy, good-natured old Irishwoman, who had joined her lot to that of Mrs Bell when the latter first began housekeeping, and knowing when she was well off, had remained in the same place from that day forth. She had known Hetta as a baby, and, so to say, had seen Susan's birth.

'And what might you be wanting, sir?' said Kate O'Brien, apparently not quite pleased as she opened the door and let in all the cold air.

'I wish to see Mrs Bell. Is not this Mrs Bell's house?' said the young man, shaking the snow from out of the breast of his coat.

He did see Mrs Bell, and we will now tell who he was, and why he had come, and how it came to pass that his carpet-bag was brought down to the widow's house and one of the front bedrooms was prepared for him, and that he drank tea that night in the widow's parlour.

His name was Aaron Dunn, and by profession he was an engineer. What peculiar misfortune in those days of frost and snow had befallen the line of rails which runs from Schenectady to Lake Champlain, I never quite understood. Banks and bridges had in some way come to grief, and on Aaron Dunn's shoulders was thrown the burden of seeing that they were duly repaired. Saratoga Springs was the centre of these mishaps, and therefore at Saratoga Springs it was necessary that he should take up his temporary abode.

Now there was at that time in New York city a Mr Bell, great in railway matters – an uncle of the once thriving but now departed Albany lawyer. He was a rich man, but he liked his riches himself; or at any rate had not found himself called upon to share them with the widow and daughters of his nephew. But when it chanced to come to pass that he had a hand in despatching Aaron Dunn to Saratoga, he took the young man aside and recommended him to lodge with the widow. 'There,' said he, 'show her my card.' So much the rich uncle thought he might vouchsafe to do for the nephew's widow.

Mrs Bell and both her daughters were in the parlour when Aaron Dunn was shown in, snow and all. He told his story in a rough, shaky voice, for his teeth chattered; and he gave the card, almost wishing that he had gone to the empty big hotel, for the widow's welcome was not at first quite warm.

The widow listened to him as he gave his message, and then she took the card and looked at it. Hetta, who was sitting on the side of the fireplace facing the door, went on demurely with her work. Susan gave one glance round – her back was to the stranger – and then another; and then she moved her chair a little nearer to the wall, so as to give the young man room to come to the fire, if he would. He did not come, but his eyes glanced upon Susan Bell; and he thought that the old man in New York was right, and that the big hotel would be cold and dull. It was a pretty face to look on that cold evening as she turned it up from the stocking she was mending.

'Perhaps you don't wish to take winter boarders, ma'am?' said Aaron Dunn.

'We never have done so yet, sir,' said Mrs Bell timidly. Could she let this young wolf in among her lamb-fold? He might be a wolf – who could tell?

'Mr Bell seemed to think it would suit,' said Aaron.

Had he acquiesced in her timidity and not pressed the point, it would have been all up with him. But the widow did not like to go against the big uncle; and so she said, 'Perhaps it may, sir.'

'I guess it will, finely,' said Aaron. And then the widow seeing that the matter was so far settled, put down her work and came round into the passage. Hetta followed her, for there would be housework to do. Aaron gave himself another shake, settled the weekly number of dollars – with very little difficulty on his part, for he had caught another glance at Susan's face; and then went after his bag. 'Twas thus that Aaron Dunn obtained an entrance into Mrs Bell's house. 'But what if he be a wolf?' she said to herself over and over again that night, though not exactly in those words. Ay, but there is another side to that question. What if he be a stalwart man, honest-minded, with clever eye, cunning hand, ready brain, broad back, and warm heart; in want of a wife mayhap; a man that can earn his own bread and another's – half a dozen others, when the half-dozen come? Would not that be a good sort of lodger? Such a question as that too did flit, just flit, across the widow's sleepless mind. But then she thought so much more of the wolf! Wolves, she had taught herself to think, were more common than stalwart, honest-minded, wife-desirous men.

'I wonder mother consented to take him,' said Hetta when they were in the little room together.

'And why shouldn't she?' said Susan. 'It will be a help.'

'Yes, it will be a little help,' said Hetta. 'But we have done very well hitherto without winter lodgers.'

'But uncle Bell said she was to.'

'What is uncle Bell to us?' said Hetta, who had a spirit of her own. And she began to surmise within herself whether Aaron Dunn would join the Baptist congregation, and whether Phineas Beckard would approve of this new move.

He is a very well-behaved young man, at any rate,' said Susan, 'and he draws beautifully. Did you see those things he was doing?'

'He draws very well, I dare say,' said Hetta, who regarded this as but a poor warranty for good behaviour. Hetta also had some fear of wolves – not for herself, perhaps; but for her sister.

Aaron Dunn's work – the commencement of his work – lay at some distance from the Springs, and he left every morning with a lot of workmen by an early train – almost before daylight. And every morning, cold and wintry as the mornings were, the widow got him his breakfast with her own hands. She took his dollars and would not leave him altogether to the awkward mercies of Kate O'Brien; nor would she trust her girls to attend upon the young man. Hetta she might have trusted; but then Susan would have asked why she was spared her share of such hardship.

In the evening, leaving his work when it was dark, Aaron always returned, and then the evening was passed together. But they were passed with the most demure propriety. These women would make the tea, cut the bread and butter, and then sew; while Aaron Dunn, when the cups were removed, would always go to his plans and drawings.

On Sundays they were more together; but even on this day there was cause of separation, for Aaron went to the Episcopalian church, rather to the disgust of Hetta. In the afternoon however they were together; and then Phineas Beckard came in to tea on Sundays, and he and Aaron got to talking on religion; and though they disagreed pretty much, and would not give an inch either one or the other, nevertheless the minister told the widow, and Hetta too probably, that the lad had good stuff in him, though he was so stiff-necked.

'But he should be more modest in talking on such matters with a minister,' said Hetta.

The Rev. Phineas acknowledged that perhaps he should; but he was honest enough to repeat that the lad had stuff in him. 'Perhaps after all he is not a wolf,' said the widow to herself.

Things went on in this way for above a month. Aaron had declared to himself over and over again that that face was sweet to look upon, and had unconciously promised to himself certain delights in talking and perhaps walking with the owner of it. But the walkings had not been achieved – nor even the talkings as yet. The truth was that Dunn was bashful with young women, though he could be so stiff-necked with the minister.

And then he felt angry with himself, inasmuch as he had advanced no further; and as he lay in his bed – which perhaps those pretty hands had helped to make – he resolved that he would be a thought bolder in his bearing. He had no idea of making love to Susan Bell; of course not. But why should he not amuse himself by talking to a pretty girl when she sat so near him, evening after evening?

'What a very quiet young man he is,' said Susan to her sister.

'He has his bread to earn, and sticks to his work,' said Hetta. 'No doubt he has his amusement when he is in the city,' added the elder sister, not wishing to leave too strong an impression of the young man's virtue.

They had all now their settled places in the parlour. Hetta sat on one side of the fire, close to the table, having that side to herself. There she sat always busy. She must have made every dress and bit of linen worn in the house, and hemmed every sheet and towel, so busy was she always. Sometimes, once in a week or so, Phineas Beckard would come in, and then place was made for him between Hetta's usual seat and the table. For when there he would read out loud. On the other side, close also to the table, sat the widow, busy, but not savagely busy as her elder daughter. Between Mrs Bell and the wall, with her feet ever on the fender, Susan used to sit; not absolutely idle, but doing work of some slender pretty sort, and talking ever and anon to her mother. Opposite to them all, at the other side of the table, far away from the fire, would Aaron Dunn place himself with his plans and drawings before him.

'Are you a judge of bridges, ma'am?' said Aaron, the evening after he had made his resolution. 'Twas thus he began his courtship.

'Of bridges!' said Mrs Bell – 'oh dear, no, sir.' But she put out her hand to take the little drawing which Aaron handed to her.

'Because that's one I've planned for our bit of a new branch from Moreau up to Lake George. I guess Miss Susan knows something about bridges.'

'I guess I don't,' said Susan – 'only that they oughtn't to tumble down when the frost comes.'

'Ha, ha, ha; no more they ought. I'll tell McEvoy that.' McEvoy had been a former engineer on the line. 'Well, that won't burst with any frost, I guess.'

'Oh, my! how pretty!' said the widow, and then Susan of course jumped up to look over her mother's shoulder.

The artful dodger! He had drawn and coloured a beautiful little sketch of a bridge; not an engineer's plan with sections and measurements, vexatious to a woman's eye, but a graceful little bridge with a string of cars running under it. You could almost hear the bell going.

'Well; that is a pretty bridge,' said Susan. 'Isn't it, Hetta?'

'I don't know anything about bridges,' said Hetta, to whose clever eyes the dodge was quite apparent. But in spite of her cleverness Mrs Bell and Susan had soon moved their chairs round to the table, and were looking through the contents of Aaron's portfolio. 'But yet he may be a wolf,' thought the poor widow, just as she was kneeling down to say her prayers.

That evening certainly made a commencement. Though Hetta went on pertinaciously with the body of a new dress, the other two ladies did not put in another stitch that night. From his drawings Aaron got to his instruments, and before bedtime was teaching Susan how to draw parallel lines. Susan found that she had quite an aptitude for parallel lines, and altogether had a good time of it that evening. It is dull to go on week after week, and month after month talking only to one's mother and sister. It is dull though one does not oneself recognize it to be so. A little change in such matters is so very pleasant. Susan had not the slightest idea of regarding Aaron as even a possible lover. But young ladies do like the conversation of young gentlemen. Oh, my exceedingly proper, prim, old lady, you who are so shocked at this as a general doctrine, has it never occurred to you that the Creator has so intended it?

Susan, understanding little of the how and why, knew that she had had a good time, and was rather in spirits as she went to bed. But Hetta had been frightened by the dodge.

'Oh, Hetta, you should have looked at those drawings. He is so clever!' said Susan.

'I don't know that they would have done me much good,' replied Hetta.

'Good! Well, they'd do me more good than a long sermon, I know,' said Susan; 'except on a Sunday, of course,' she added apologetically. This was an ill-tempered attack both on Hetta and Hetta's admirer. But then why had Hetta been so snappish?

'I'm sure he's a wolf,' thought Hetta as she went to bed.

'What a very clever young man he is!' thought Susan to herself as she pulled the warm clothes round about her shoulders and ears.

'Well; that certainly was an improvement,' thought Aaron as he went through the same operation, with a stronger feeling of self-approbation than he had enjoyed for some time past.

In the course of the next fortnight the family arrangements all altered themselves. Unless when Beckard was there Aaron would sit in the widow's place, the widow would take Susan's chair, and the two girls would be opposite. And then Dunn would read to them; not sermons, but passages from Shakespeare, and Byron, and Longfellow. 'He reads much better than Mr Beckard,' Susan had said one night. 'Of course you're a competent judge!' had been Hetta's retort. 'I mean that I like it better,' said Susan. 'It's well that all people don't think alike,' replied Hetta.

And then there was a deal of talking. The widow herself, as unconscious in this respect as her youngest daughter, certainly did find that a little variety was agreeable on those long winter nights; and talked herself with unaccustomed freedom. And Beckard came there oftener and talked very much. When he was there the two young men did all the talking, and they pounded each other immensely. But still there grew up a sort of friendship between them.

'Mr Beckard seems quite to take to him,' said Mrs Bell to her eldest daughter.

'It is his great good nature, mother,' replied Hetta.

It was at the end of the second month when Aaron took another step in advance – a perilous step. Sometimes on evenings he still went on with his drawing for an hour or so; but during three or four evenings he never asked any one to look at what he was doing. On one Friday he sat over his work till late, without any reading or talking at all; so late that at last Mrs Bell said, 'If you're going to sit much longer, Mr Dunn, I'll get you to put out the candles.' Thereby showing, had he known it or had she, that the mother's confidence in the young man was growing fast. Hetta knew all about it, and dreaded that the growth was too quick.

'I've finished now,' said Aaron; and he looked carefully at the cardboard on which he had been washing in his water-colours. 'I've finished now.' He then hesitated a moment; but ultimately he put the card into his portfolio and carried it up to his bedroom. Who does not perceive that it was intended as a present to Susan Bell?

The question which Aaron asked himself that night, and which he hardly knew how to answer was this. Should he offer the drawing to Susan in the presence of her mother and sister, or on some occasion when they two might be alone together? No such occasion had ever yet occurred, but Aaron thought that it might probably be brought about. But then he wanted to make no fuss about it. His first intention had been to chuck the drawing lightly across the table when it was completed, and so make nothing of it. But he had finished it with more care than he had at first intended; and then he had hesitated when he had finished it. It was too late now for that plan of chucking it over the table.

On the Saturday evening when he came down from his room, Mr Beckard was there, and there was no opportunity that night. On the Sunday, in conformity with a previous engagement, he went to hear Mr Beckard preach, and walked to and from meeting with the family. This pleased Mrs Bell, and they were all very gracious that afternoon. But Sunday was no day for the picture.

On Monday the thing had become of importance to him. Things always do when they are kept over. Before tea that evening when he came down Mrs Bell and Susan only were in the room. He knew Hetta for his foe, and therefore determined to use this occasion.

'Miss Susan,' he said, stammering somewhat, and blushing too, poor fool! 'I have done a little drawing which I want you to accept,' and he put his portfolio down on the table.

'Oh! I don't know,' said Susan who had seen the blush.

Mrs Bell had seen the blush also, and pursed her mouth up, and looked grave. Had there been no stammering and no blush, she might have thought nothing of it.

Aaron saw at once that his little gift was not to go down smoothly. He was however in for it now, so he picked it out from among the other papers in the case and brought it over to Susan. He endeavoured to hand it to her with an air of indifference, but I cannot say that he succeeded.

It was a very pretty well-finished, water-coloured drawing, representing still the same bridge, but with more adjuncts. In Susan's eyes it was a work of high art. Of pictures probably she had seen but little, and her liking for the artist no doubt added to her admiration. But the more she admired it and wished for it, the stronger was her feeling that she ought not to take it.

Poor Susan! She stood for a minute looking at the drawing, but she said nothing; not even a word of praise. She felt that she was red in the face, and uncourteous to their lodger; but her mother was looking at her and she did not know how to behave herself.

Mrs Bell put out her hand for the sketch, trying to bethink herself as she did so in what least uncivil way she could refuse the present. She took a moment to look at it collecting her thoughts, and as she did so her woman's wit came to her aid.

'Oh dear, Mr Dunn, it is very pretty; quite a beautiful picture. I cannot let Susan rob you of that. You must keep that for some of your own particular friends.'

'But I did it for her,' said Aaron innocently.

Susan looked down at the ground, half pleased at the declaration. The drawing would look very pretty in a small gilt frame put over her dressing-table. But the matter now was altogether in her mother's hands.

'I am afraid it is too valuable, sir, for Susan to accept.'

'It is not valuable at all,' said Aaron, declining to take it back from the widow's hand.

'Oh, I am quite sure it is. It is worth ten dollars at least – or twenty,' said poor Mrs Bell, not in the very best taste. But she was perplexed and did not know how to get out of the scrape. The article in question now lay upon the tablecloth, appropriated by no one, and at this moment Hetta came into the room.

'It is not worth ten cents,' said Aaron, with something like a frown on his brow. 'But as we had been talking about the bridge, I thought Miss Susan would accept it.'

'Accept what?' said Hetta. And then her eye fell upon the drawing and she took it up.

'It is beautifully done,' said Mrs Bell, wishing much to soften the matter; perhaps the more so, that Hetta the demure was now present. 'I am telling Mr Dunn that we can't take a present of anything so valuable.'

'Oh dear, no,' said Hetta. 'It wouldn't be right.'

It was a cold frosty evening in March, and the fire was burning brightly on the hearth. Aaron Dunn took up the drawing quietly – very quietly – and rolling it up, as such drawings are rolled, put it between the blazing logs. It was the work of four evenings, and his chef-d'œuvre in the way of art.

Susan, when she saw what he had done, burst out into tears. The widow could very readily have done so also, but she was able to refrain herself, and merely exclaimed – 'Oh, Mr Dunn!'

'If Mr Dunn chooses to burn his own picture, he has certainly a right to do so,' said Hetta.

Aaron immediately felt ashamed of what he had done; and he also could have cried, but for his manliness. He walked away to one of the parlour-windows, and looked out upon the frosty night. It was dark, but the stars were bright, and he thought that he should like to be walking fast by himself along the line of rails towards Balston. There he stood, perhaps for three minutes. He thought it would be proper to give Susan time to recover from her tears.

'Will you please to come to your tea, sir?' said the soft voice of Mrs Bell.

He turned round to do so, and found that Susan was gone. It was not quite in her power to recover from her tears in three minutes. And then the drawing had been so beautiful! It had been done expressly for her too! And there had been something, she knew not what, in his eye as he had so declared. She had watched him intently over those four evenings' work, wondering why he did not show it, till her feminine curiosity had become rather strong. It was something very particular, she was sure, and she had learned that all that precious work had been for her. Now all that precious work was destroyed. How was it possible that she should not cry for more than three minutes?

The others took their meal in perfect silence, and when it was over the two women sat down to their work. Aaron had a book which he pretended to read, but instead of reading he was bethinking himself that he had behaved badly. What right had he to throw them all into such confusion by indulging in his passion? He was ashamed of what he had done, and fancied that Susan would hate him. Fancying that, he began to find at the same time that he by no means hated her.

At last Hetta got up and left the room. She knew that her sister was sitting alone in the cold, and Hetta was affectionate. Susan had not been in fault, and therefore Hetta went up to console her.

'Mrs Bell,' said Aaron, as soon as the door was closed, 'I beg your pardon for what I did just now.'

'Oh, sir, I'm so sorry that the picture is burnt,' said poor Mrs Bell.

'The picture does not matter a straw,' said Aaron. 'But I see that I have disturbed you all – and I am afraid I have made Miss Susan unhappy.'

'She was grieved because your picture was burnt,' said Mrs Bell, putting some emphasis on the 'your,' intending to show that her daughter had not regarded the drawing as her own. But the emphasis bore another meaning; and so the widow perceived as soon as she had spoken.

'Oh, I can do twenty more of the same if anybody wanted them,' said Aaron. 'If I do another like it, will you let her take it, Mrs Bell – just to show that you have forgiven me, and that we are friends as we were before?'

Was he, or was he not a wolf? That was the question which Mrs Bell scarcely knew how to answer. Hetta had given her voice, saying he was lupine. Mr Beckard's opinion she had not liked to ask directly. Mr Beckard she thought would probably propose to Hetta; but as yet he had not done so. And, as he was still a stranger in the family, she did not like in any way to compromise Susan's name. Indirectly she had asked the question, and, indirectly also, Mr Beckard's answer had been favourable.

'But it mustn't mean anything, sir,' was the widow's weak answer, when she had paused on the question for a moment.

'Oh no, of course not,' said Aaron, joyously, and his face became radiant and happy. 'And I do beg your pardon for burning it; and the young ladies' pardon too.' And then he rapidly got out his card-board, and set himself to work about another bridge. The widow meditating many things in her heart, commenced the hemming of a handkerchief.

In about an hour the two girls came back to the room and silently took their accustomed places. Aaron hardly looked up, but went on diligently with his drawing. This bridge should be a better bridge than that other. Its acceptance was now assured. Of course it was to mean nothing. That was a matter of course. So he worked away diligently, and said nothing to anybody.

When they went off to bed the two girls went into the mother's room. 'Oh, mother, I hope he is not very angry,' said Susan.

'Angry!' said Hetta, 'if anybody should be angry, it is mother. He ought to have known that Susan could not accept it. He should never have offered it.'

'But he's doing another,' said Mrs Bell.

'Not for her,' said Hetta.

'Yes he is,' said Mrs Bell, 'and I have promised that she shall take it.' Susan as she heard this sank gently into the chair behind her, and her eyes became full of tears. The intimation was almost too much for her.

'Oh mother!' said Hetta.

'But I particularly said that it was to mean nothing.'

'Oh mother, that makes it worse.'

Why should Hetta interfere in this way, thought Susan to herself. Had she interfered when Mr Beckard gave Hetta a testament bound in morocco? Had not she smiled, and looked gratified, and kissed her sister, and declared that Phineas Beckard was a nice dear man, and by far the most elegant preacher at the Springs? Why should Hetta be so cruel?

'I don't see that, my dear,' said the mother. Hetta would not explain before her sister, so they all went to bed.

On the Thursday evening the drawing was finished. Not a word had been said about it, at any rate in his presence, and he had gone on working in silence. 'There,' said he, late on the Thursday evening, 'I don't know that it will be any better if I go on daubing for another hour. There, Miss Susan; there's another bridge. I hope that will neither burst with the frost, nor yet be destroyed by fire,' and he gave it a light flip with his fingers and sent it skimming over the table.

Susan blushed and smiled, and took it up. 'Oh, it is beautiful,' she said. 'Isn't it beautifully done, mother?' and then all the three got up to look at it, and all confessed that it was excellently done.

'And I am sure we are very much obliged to you,' said Susan after a pause, remembering that she had not yet thanked him.

'Oh, it's nothing,' said he, not quite liking the word 'we'.

On the following day he returned from his work to Saratoga about noon. This he had never done before, and therefore no one expected that he would be seen in the house before the evening. On this occasion however he went straight thither, and as chance would have it, both the widow and her elder daughter were out. Susan was there alone in charge of the house.

He walked in and opened the parlour door. There she sat, with her feet on the fender, with her work unheeded on the table behind her, and the picture, Aaron's drawing, lying on her knees. She was gazing at it intently as he entered, thinking in her young heart that it possessed all the beauties which a picture could possess.

'Oh, Mr Dunn,' she said getting up and holding the tell-tale sketch behind the skirt of her dress.

'Miss Susan, I have come here to tell your mother that I must start for New York this afternoon and be there for six weeks, or perhaps longer.'

'Mother is out,' said she; 'I'm so sorry.'

'Is she?' said Aaron.

'And Hetta too. Dear me. And you'll be wanting dinner. I'll go and see about it.'

Aaron began to swear that he could not possibly eat any dinner. He had dined once, and was going to dine again – anything to keep her from going.

'But you must have something, Mr Dunn,' and she walked towards the door.

But he put his back to it. 'Miss Susan,' said he, 'I guess I've been here nearly two months.'

'Yes, sir, I believe you have,' she replied, shaking in her shoes and not knowing which way to look.

'And I hope we have been good friends.'

'Yes, sir,' said Susan, almost beside herself as to what she was saying.

'I'm going away now, and it seems to be such a time before I'll be back.'

'Will it, sir?'

'Six weeks, Miss Susan!' and then he paused, looking into her eyes, to see what he could read there. She leant against the table, pulling to pieces a morsel of half ravelled muslin which she held in her hand; but her eyes were turned to the ground, and he could hardly see them.

'Miss Susan,' he continued, 'I may as well speak out now as at another time.' He too was looking towards the ground, and clearly did not know what to do with his hands. 'The truth is just this. I – I love you dearly, with all my heart. I never saw any one I ever thought so beautiful, so nice, and so good – and what's more, I never shall. I'm not very good at this sort of thing, I know; but I couldn't go away from Saratoga for six weeks and not tell you.' And then he ceased. He did not ask for any love in return. His presumption had not got so far as that yet. He merely declared his passion, leaning against the door, and there he stood twiddling his thumbs.

Susan had not the slightest conception of the way in which she ought to receive such a declaration. She had never had a lover before; nor had she ever thought of Aaron absolutely as a lover, though something very like love for him had been crossing over her spirit. Now, at this moment, she felt that he was the *beau-idéal* of manhood, though his boots were covered with the railway mud, and though his pantaloons were tucked up in rolls round his ankles. He was a fine, well-grown, open-faced fellow, whose eye was bold and yet tender, whose brow was full and broad, and all his bearing manly. Love him! Of course she loved him. Why else had her heart melted with pleasure when her mother said that that second picture was to be accepted?

But what was she to say? Anything but the open truth; she well knew that. The open truth would not do at all. What

would her mother say and Hetta if she were rashly to say
that? Hetta, she knew, would be dead against such a lover,
and of her mother's approbation she had hardly more hope.
Why they should disapprove of Aaron as a lover she had
never asked herself. There are many nice things that seem
to be wrong only because they are so nice. Maybe that
Susan regarded a lover as one of them. 'Oh, Mr Dunn, you
shouldn't.' That in fact was all that she could say.

'Should not I?' said he. 'Well, perhaps not; but there's the
truth, and no harm ever comes of that. Perhaps I'd better not
ask you for an answer now, but I thought it better you should
know it all. And remember this – I only care for one thing
now in the world, and that is for your love.' And then he
paused, thinking possibly that in spite of what he had said
he might perhaps get some sort of an answer, some inkling
of the state of her heart's disposition towards him.

But Susan had at once resolved to take him at his word
when he suggested that an immediate reply was not necessary.
To say that she loved him was of course impossible, and to
say that she did not was equally so. She determined therefore
to close at once with the offer of silence.

When he ceased speaking there was a moment's pause,
during which he strove hard to read what might be written on
her down-turned face. But he was not good at such reading.
'Well, I guess I'll go and get my things ready now,' he said,
and then turned round to open the door.

'Mother will be in before you are gone, I suppose,'
said Susan.

'I have only got twenty minutes,' said he, looking at
his watch. 'But, Susan, tell her what I have said to you.
Good-bye.' And he put out his hand. He knew he should see
her again, but this had been his plan to get her hand in his.

'Good-bye, Mr Dunn,' and she gave him her hand.

He held it tight for a moment, so that she could not draw
it away, – could not if she would. 'Will you tell your mother?'
he asked.

'Yes,' she answered, quite in a whisper. 'I guess I'd better tell her.' And then she gave a long sigh. He pressed her hand again and got it up to his lips.

'Mr Dunn, don't,' she said. But he did kiss it. 'God bless you, my own dearest, dearest girl! I'll just open the door as I come down. Perhaps Mrs Bell will be here.' And then he rushed up stairs.

But Mrs Bell did not come in. She and Hetta were at a weekly service at Mr Beckard's meeting-house, and Mr Beckard it seemed had much to say. Susan, when left alone, sat down and tried to think. But she could not think; she could only love. She could use her mind only in recounting to herself the perfections of that demigod whose heavy steps were so audible overhead, as he walked to and fro collecting his things and putting them into his bag.

And then, just when he had finished, she bethought herself that he must be hungry. She flew to the kitchen, but she was too late. Before she could even reach at the loaf of bread he descended the stairs with a clattering noise, and heard her voice as she spoke quickly to Kate O'Brien.

'Miss Susan,' he said, 'don't get anything for me, for I'm off.'

'Oh, Mr Dunn, I am so sorry. You'll be so hungry on your journey,' and she came out to him in the passage.

'I shall want nothing on the journey, dearest, if you'll say one kind word to me.'

Again her eyes went to the ground. 'What do you want me to say, Mr Dunn?'

'Say, God bless you, Aaron.

'God bless you, Aaron,' said she; and yet she was sure that she had not declared her love. He however thought otherwise, and went up to New York with a happy heart.

Things happened in the next fortnight rather quickly. Susan at once resolved to tell her mother, but she resolved also not to tell Hetta. That afternoon she got her mother to herself in Mrs Bell's own room, and then she made a clean breast of it.

'And what did you say to him, Susan?'

'I said nothing, mother.'

'Nothing, dear!'

'No, mother; not a word. He told me he didn't want it.' She forgot how she had used his Christian name in bidding God bless him.

'Oh, dear!' said the widow.

'Was it very wrong?' asked Susan.

'But what do you think yourself, my child?' asked Mrs Bell after a while. 'What are your own feelings?'

Mrs Bell was sitting on a chair, and Susan was standing opposite to her against the post of the bed. She made no answer, but moving from her place, she threw herself into her mother's arms, and hid her face on her mother's shoulder. It was easy enough to guess what were her feelings.

'But, my darling,' said her mother, 'you must not think that it is an engagement.'

'No,' said Susan, sorrowfully.

'Young men say those things to amuse themselves.' Wolves, she would have said, had she spoken out her mind freely.

'Oh, mother, he is not like that.'

The daughter contrived to extract a promise from the mother that Hetta should not be told just at present. Mrs Bell calculated that she had six weeks before her; as yet Mr Beckard had not spoken out, but there was reason to suppose that he would do so before those six weeks would be over, and then she would be able to seek counsel from him.

Mr Beckard spoke out at the end of six days, and Hetta frankly accepted him. 'I hope you'll love your brother-in-law,' said she to Susan.

'Oh, I will indeed,' said Susan; and in the softness of her heart at the moment she almost made up her mind to tell; but Hetta was full of her own affairs, and thus it passed off.

It was then arranged that Hetta should go and spend a week with Mr Beckard's parents. Old Mr Beckard was a farmer living near Utica, and now that the match was declared and approved, it was thought well that Hetta should know her future husband's family. So she went for a week, and Mr

Beckard went with her. 'He will be back in plenty of time for me to speak to him before Aaron Dunn's six weeks are over,' said Mrs Bell to herself.

But things did not go exactly as she expected. On the very morning after the departure of the engaged couple, there came a letter from Aaron, saying that he would be at Saratoga that very evening. The railway people had ordered him down again for some days' special work; then he was to go elsewhere, and not to return to Saratoga till June. 'But he hoped,' so said the letter, 'that Mrs Bell would not turn him into the street even then, though the summer might have come, and her regular lodgers might be expected.'

'Oh dear, oh dear!' said Mrs Bell to herself, reflecting that she had no one of whom she could ask advice, and that she must decide that very day. Why had she let Mr Beckard go without telling him? Then she told Susan, and Susan spent the day trembling. Perhaps, thought Mrs Bell, he will say nothing about it. In such case, however, would it not be her duty to say something? Poor mother! She trembled nearly as much as Susan.

It was dark when the fatal knock came at the door. The tea-things were already laid, and the tea-cake was already baked; for it would at any rate be necessary to give Mr Dunn his tea. Susan, when she heard the knock, rushed from her chair and took refuge up stairs. The widow gave a long sigh, and settled her dress. Kate O'Brien with willing step opened the door, and bade her old friend welcome.

'How are the ladies?' asked Aaron, trying to gather something from the face and voice of the domestic.

'Miss Hetta and Mr Beckard be gone off to Utica, just man-and-wife like; and so they are, more power to them.'

'Oh indeed; I'm very glad,' said Aaron – and so he was; very glad to have Hetta the demure out of the way. And then he made his way into the parlour, doubting much, and hoping much.

Mrs Bell rose from her chair, and tried to look grave. Aaron glancing round the room saw that Susan was not there. He walked straight up to the widow, and offered her his hand, which she took. It might be that Susan had not thought fit to tell, and in such case it would not be right for him to compromise her; so he said never a word.

But the subject was too important to the mother to allow of her being silent when the young man stood before her. 'Oh, Mr Dunn,' said she, 'what is this you have been saying to Susan?'

'I have asked her to be my wife,' said he, drawing himself up and looking her full in the face. Mrs Bell's heart was almost as soft as her daughter's, and it was nearly gone; but at the moment she had nothing to say but, 'oh dear, oh dear!'

'May I not call you mother?' said he, taking both her hands in his.

'Oh dear – oh dear! But will you be good to her? Oh, Aaron Dunn, if you deceive my child!'

In another quarter of an hour, Susan was kneeling at her mother's knee, with her face on her mother's lap; the mother was wiping tears out of her eyes; and Aaron was standing by holding one of the widow's hands.

'You are my mother too, now,' said he. What would Hetta and Mr Beckard say, when they came back? But then he surely was not a wolf!

There were four or five days left for courtship before Hetta and Mr Beckard would return; four or five days during which Susan might be happy, Aaron triumphant, and Mrs Bell nervous. Days I have said, but after all it was only the evenings that were so left. Every morning Susan got up to give Aaron his breakfast, but Mrs Bell got up also. Susan boldly declared her right to do so, and Mrs Bell found no objection which she could urge. But after that Aaron was always absent till seven or eight in the evening, when he would return to his tea. Then came the hour or two of lovers' intercourse.

But they were very tame, those hours. The widow still felt an undefined fear that she was wrong, and though her heart yearned to know that her daughter was happy in the sweet happiness of accepted love, yet she dreaded to be too confident. Not a word had been said about money matters; not a word of Aaron Dunn's relatives. So she did not leave them by themselves, but waited with what patience she could for the return of her wise counsellors.

And then Susan hardly knew how to behave herself with her accepted suitor. She felt that she was very happy; but perhaps she was most happy when she was thinking about him through the long day, assisting in fixing little things for his comfort, and waiting for his evening return. And as he sat there in the parlour, she could be happy then too, if she were but allowed to sit still and look at him, – not stare at him but raise her eyes every now and again to his face for the shortest possible glance, as she had been used to do ever since he came there.

But he, unconsciable lover, wanted to hear her speak, was desirous of being talked to, and perhaps thought that he should by rights be allowed to sit by her, and hold her hand. No such privileges were accorded to him. If they had been alone together, walking side by side on the green turf, as lovers should walk, she would soon have found the use of her tongue – have talked fast enough no doubt. Under such circumstances, when a girl's shyness has given way to real intimacy, there is in general no end to her power of chatting. But though there was much love between Aaron and Susan, there was as yet but little intimacy. And then, let a mother be ever so motherly – and no mother could have more of a mother's tenderness than Mrs Bell – still her presence must be a restraint. Aaron was very fond of Mrs Bell; but nevertheless he did sometimes wish that some domestic duty would take her out of the parlour for a few happy minutes. Susan went out very often, but Mrs Bell seemed to be a fixture.

Once for a moment he did find his love alone, immediately as he came into the house. 'My own Susan, you do love me? do say so to me once.' And he contrived to slip his arm round her waist. 'Yes,' she whispered; but she slipped, like an eel, from his hands, and left him only preparing himself for a kiss. And then when she got to her room, half frightened, she clasped her hands together, and bethought herself that she did really love him with a strength and depth of love which filled her whole existence. Why could she not have told him something of all this?

And so the few days of his second sojourn at Saratoga passed away, not altogether satisfactorily. It was settled that he should return to New York on Saturday night, leaving Saratoga on that evening; and as the Beckards – Hetta was already regarded quite as a Beckard – were to be back to dinner on that day, Mrs Bell would have an opportunity of telling her wondrous tale. It might be well that Mr Beckard should see Aaron before his departure.

On that Saturday the Beckards did arrive just in time for dinner. It may be imagined that Susan's appetite was not very keen, nor her manner very collected. But all this passed by unobserved in the importance attached to the various Beckard arrangements which came under discussion. Ladies and gentlemen circumstanced as were Hetta and Mr Beckard are perhaps a little too apt to think that their own affairs are paramount. But after dinner Susan vanished at once, and when Hetta prepared to follow her, desirous of further talk about matrimonial arrangements, her mother stopped her, and the disclosure was made.

'Proposed to her!' said Hetta, who perhaps thought that one marriage in a family was enough at a time.

'Yes, my love – and he did it, I must say, in a very honourable way, telling her not to make any answer till she had spoken to me; now that was very nice, was it not, Phineas?' Mrs Bell had become very anxious that Aaron should not be voted a wolf.

'And what has been said to him since?' asked the discreet Phineas.

'Why – nothing absolutely decisive.' Oh, Mrs Bell! 'You see I know nothing as to his means.'

'Nothing at all,' said Hetta.

'He is a man that will always earn his bread,' said Mr Beckard; and Mrs Bell blessed him in her heart for saying it.

'But has he been encouraged?' asked Hetta.

'Well; yes, he has,' said the widow.

'Then Susan I suppose likes him?' asked Phineas.

'Well; yes, she does,' said the widow. And the conference ended in a resolution that Phineas Beckard should have a conversation with Aaron Dunn, as to his worldly means and position; and that he, Phineas, should decide whether Aaron might, or might not be at once accepted as a lover, according to the tenor of that conversation. Poor Susan was not told anything of all this. 'Better not,' said Hetta the demure. 'It will only flurry her the more.' How would she have liked it, if without consulting her, they had left it to Aaron to decide whether or no she might marry Phineas?

They knew where on the works Aaron was to be found, and thither Mr Beckard rode after dinner. We need not narrate at length the conference between the young men. Aaron at once declared that he had nothing but what he made as an engineer, and explained that he held no permanent situation on the line. He was well paid at that present moment, but at the end of summer he would have to look for employment.

'Then you can hardly marry quite at present,' said the discreet minister.

'Perhaps not quite immediately.'

'And long engagements are never wise,' said the other.

'Three or four months,' suggested Aaron. But Mr Beckard shook his head.

The afternoon at Mrs Bell's house was melancholy. The final decision of the three judges was as follows. There was to be no engagement; of course no correspondence. Aaron was to be told that it would be better that he should get lodgings elsewhere when he returned; but that he would be allowed to visit at Mrs Bell's house – and at Mrs Beckard's, which was very considerate. If he should succeed in getting a permanent appointment, and if he and Susan still held the same mind, why then – etc., etc. Such was Susan's fate, as communicated to her by Mrs Bell and Hetta. She sat still and wept when she heard it; but she did not complain. She had always felt that Hetta would be against her.

'Mayn't I see him, then?' she said through her tears.

Hetta thought she had better not. Mrs Bell thought she might. Phineas decided that they might shake hands, but only in full conclave. There was to be no lovers' farewell. Aaron was to leave the house at halfpast five; but before he went Susan should be called down. Poor Susan! She sat down and bemoaned herself; uncomplaining, but very sad.

Susan was soft, feminine, and manageable. But Aaron Dunn was not very soft, was especially masculine, and in some matters not easily manageable. When Mr Beckard in the widow's presence – Hetta had retired in obedience to her lover – informed him of the court's decision, there came over his face the look which he had worn when he burned the picture. 'Mrs Bell,' he said, 'had encouraged his engagement; and he did not understand why other people should now come and disturb it.'

'Not an engagement, Aaron,' said Mrs Bell piteously.

'He was able and willing to work,' he said, 'and knew his profession. What young man of his age had done better than he had?' and he glanced round at them with perhaps more pride than was quite becoming.

Then Mr Beckard spoke out, very wisely no doubt, but perhaps a little too much at length. Sons and daughters as well as fathers and mothers will know very well what he said; so I need not repeat his words. I cannot say that Aaron listened with much attention, but he understood perfectly what the upshot of it was. Many a man understands the purport of many a sermon without listening to one word in ten. Mr Beckard meant to be kind in his manner; indeed was so, only that Aaron could not accept as kindness any interference on his part.

'I'll tell you what, Mrs Bell,' said he. 'I look upon myself as engaged to her. And I look on her as engaged to me. I tell you so fairly; and I believe that's her mind as well as mine.'

'But, Aaron, you won't try to see her – or to write to her – not in secret, will you?

'When I try to see her, I'll come and knock at this door; and if I write to her, I'll write to her full address by the post. I never did and never will do anything in secret.'

'I know you're good and honest,' said the widow with her handkerchief to her eyes.

'Then why do you separate us?' asked he, almost roughly. 'I suppose I may see her at any rate before I go. My time's nearly up now, I guess.'

And then Susan was called for, and she and Hetta came down together. Susan crept in behind her sister. Her eyes were red with weeping, and her appearance was altogether disconsolate. She had had a lover for a week, and now she was to be robbed of him.

'Good-bye, Susan,' said Aaron, and he walked up to her without bashfulness or embarrassment. Had they all been compliant and gracious to him he would have been as bashful as his love; but now his temper was hot. 'Good-bye, Susan,' and she took his hand, and he held hers till he had finished. 'And remember this, I look upon you as my promised wife, and I don't fear that you'll deceive me. At any rate I sha'n't deceive you.'

'Good-bye, Aaron,' she sobbed.

'Good-bye, and God bless you, my own darling!' And then without saying a word to any one else, he turned his back upon them and went his way.

There had been something very consolatory, very sweet, to the poor girl in her lover's last words. And yet they had almost made her tremble. He had been so bold, and stern, and confident. He had seemed so utterly to defy the impregnable discretion of Mr Beckard, so to despise the demure propriety of Hetta. But of this she felt sure, when she came to question her heart, that she could never, never, never cease to love him better than all the world beside. She would wait – patiently if she could find patience – and then, if he deserted her, she would die.

In another month Hetta became Mrs Beckard. Susan brisked up a little for the occasion, and looked very pretty as bridesmaid. She was serviceable too in arranging household matters, hemming linen and sewing table-cloths; though of course in these matters she did not do a tenth of what Hetta did.

Then the summer came, the Saratoga summer of July, August, and September, during which the widow's house was full; and Susan's hands saved the pain of her heart, for she was forced into occupation. Now that Hetta was gone to her own duties, it was necessary that Susan's part in the household should be more prominent.

Aaron did not come back to his work at Saratoga. Why he did not, they could not then learn. During the whole long summer they heard not a word of him nor from him; and then when the cold winter months came and their boarders had left them, Mrs Beckard congratulated her sister in that she had given no further encouragement to a lover who cared so little for her. This was very hard to bear. But Susan did bear it.

That winter was very sad. They learned nothing of Aaron Dunn till about January; and then they heard that he was doing very well. He was engaged on the Erie trunk line, was paid highly, and was much esteemed. And yet he neither came nor sent! 'He has an excellent situation,' their informant told them. 'And a permanent one?' asked the widow. 'Oh, yes, no doubt,' said the gentleman, 'for I happen to know that they count greatly on him.' And yet he sent no word of love.

After that the winter became very sad indeed. Mrs Bell thought it to be her duty now to teach her daughter that in all probability she would see Aaron Dunn no more. It was open to him to leave her without being absolutely a wolf. He had been driven from the house when he was poor, and they had no right to expect that he would return, now that he had made some rise in the world. 'Men do amuse themselves in that way,' the widow tried to teach her.

'He is not like that, mother,' she said again.

'But they do not think so much of these things as we do,' urged the mother.

'Don't they?' said Susan, oh, so sorrowfully; and so through the whole long winter months she became paler and paler, and thinner and thinner.

And then Hetta tried to console her with religion, and that perhaps did not make things any better. Religious consolation is the best cure for all griefs; but it must not be looked for specially with regard to any individual sorrow. A religious man, should he become bankrupt through the misfortunes of the world, will find true consolation in his religion even for that sorrow. But a bankrupt, who has not thought much of such things, will hardly find solace by taking up religion for that special occasion.

And Hetta perhaps was hardly prudent in her attempts. She thought that it was wicked in Susan to grow thin and pale for love of Aaron Dunn, and she hardly hid her thoughts. Susan was not sure but that it might be wicked, but this doubt in no way tended to make her plump or rosy. So that in those days she found no comfort in her sister.

But her mother's pity and soft love did ease her sufferings, though it could not make them cease. Her mother did not tell her that she was wicked, or bid her read long sermons, or force her to go oftener to the meeting-house.

'He will never come again, I think,' she said one day, as with a shawl wrapped around her shoulders, she leant with her head upon her mother's bosom.

'My own darling,' said the mother, pressing her child closely to her side.

'You think he never will, eh, mother?' What could Mrs Bell say? In her heart of hearts she did not think he ever would come again.

'No, my child. I do not think he will.' And then the hot tears ran down, and the sobs came thick and frequent.

'My darling, my darling!' exclaimed the mother; and they wept together.

'Was I wicked to love him at the first?' she asked that night.

'No, my child; you were not wicked at all. At least I think not.'

'Then why —' Why was he sent away? It was on her tongue to ask that question; but she paused and spared her mother. This was as they were going to bed. The next morning Susan did not get up. She was not ill, she said; but weak and weary. Would her mother let her lie that day? And then Mrs Bell went down alone to her room, and sorrowed with all her heart for the sorrow of her child. Why, oh why, had she driven away from her door-sill the love of an honest man?

On the next morning Susan again did not get up; nor did she hear, or if she heard she did not recognize, the step of the postman who brought a letter to the door. Early, before the widow's breakfast the postman came, and the letter which he brought was as follows:

My dear Mrs Bell,

I have now got a permanent situation on the Erie line, and the salary is enough for myself and a wife. At least I think so, and I hope you will too. I shall be down at Saratoga to-morrow evening, and I hope neither Susan nor you will refuse to receive me.

Yours affectionately,

AARON DUNN.

That was all. It was very short, and did not contain one word of love; but it made the widow's heart leap for joy. She was rather afraid that Aaron was angry, he wrote so curtly and with such a brusque businesslike attention to mere facts; but surely he could have but one object in coming there. And then he alluded specially to a wife. So the widow's heart leapt with joy.

But how was she to tell Susan? She ran up stairs almost breathless with haste, to the bedroom door: but then she stopped: too much joy she had heard was as dangerous as too much sorrow; she must think it over for a while, and so she crept back again.

But after breakfast – that is, when she had sat for a while over her teacup – she returned to the room, and this time she entered it. The letter was in her hand, but held so as to be hidden – in her left hand as she sat down with her right arm towards the invalid.

'Susan dear,' she said, and smiled at her child, 'you'll be able to get up this morning? eh, dear?'

'Yes, mother,' said Susan, thinking that her mother objected to this idleness of her lying in bed. And so she began to bestir herself.

'I don't mean this very moment, love. Indeed, I want to sit with you for a little while,' and she put her right arm affectionately round her daughter's waist.

'Dearest mother,' said Susan.

'Ah! there's one dearer than me, I guess,' and Mrs Bell smiled sweetly, as she made the maternal charge against her daughter.

Susan raised herself quickly in the bed, and looked straight into her mother's face. 'Mother, mother,' she said, 'What is it? You've something to tell. Oh, mother!' And stretching herself over, she struck her hand against the corner of Aaron's letter. 'Mother, you've a letter. Is he coming, mother?' and with eager eyes and open lips, she sat up, holding tight to her mother's arm.

'Yes, love. I have got a letter.'

'Is he – is he coming?'

How the mother answered, I can hardly tell; but she did answer, and they were soon lying in each other's arms, warm with each other's tears. It was almost hard to say which was the happier.

Aaron was to be there that evening – that very evening. 'Oh, mother, let me get up,' said Susan.

But Mrs Bell said no, not yet; her darling was pale and thin, and she almost wished that Aaron was not coming for another week. What if he should come and look at her, and finding her beauty gone, vanish again and seek a wife elsewhere!

So Susan lay in bed, thinking of her happiness, dozing now

and again, and fearing as she waked that it was a dream, looking constantly at that drawing of his, which she kept outside upon the bed, nursing her love and thinking of it, and endeavouring, vainly endeavouring, to arrange what she would say to him.

'Mother,' she said, when Mrs Bell once went up to her, 'you won't tell Hetta and Phineas, will you? Not to-day, I mean?' Mrs Bell agreed that it would be better not to tell them. Perhaps she thought that she had already depended too much on Hetta and Phineas in the matter.

Susan's finery in the way of dress had never been extensive, and now lately, in these last sad winter days, she had thought but little of the fashion of her clothes. But when she began to dress herself for the evening, she did ask her mother with some anxiety what she had better wear. 'If he loves you he will hardly see what you have on,' said the mother. But not the less was she careful to smooth her daughter's hair, and make the most that might be made of those faded roses.

How Susan's heart beat – how both their hearts beat as the hands of the clock came round to seven! And then, sharp at seven, came the knock; that same short bold ringing knock which Susan had so soon learned to know as belonging to Aaron Dunn. 'Oh mother, I had better go up stairs,' she cried, starting from her chair.

'No dear; you would only be more nervous.'

'I will, mother.'

'No, no dear; you have not time;' and then Aaron Dunn was in the room.

She had thought much what she would say to him, but had not yet quite made up her mind. It mattered however but very little. On whatever she might have resolved, her resolution would have vanished to the wind. Aaron Dunn came into the room, and in one second she found herself in the centre of a whirlwind, and his arms were the storms that enveloped her on every side.

'My own, own darling girl,' he said over and over again,

as he pressed her to his heart, quite regardless of Mrs Bell, who stood by, sobbing with joy. 'My own Susan.'

'Aaron, dear Aaron,' she whispered. But she had already recognized the fact that for the present meeting a passive part would become her well, and save her a deal of trouble. She had her lover there quite safe, safe beyond anything that Mr or Mrs Beckard might have to say to the contrary. She was quite happy; only that there were symptoms now and again that the whirlwind was about to engulf her yet once more.

'Dear Aaron, I am so glad you are come,' said the innocent-minded widow, as she went up stairs with him, to show him his room; and then he embraced her also. 'Dear, dear mother,' he said.

On the next day there was, as a matter of course, a family conclave. Hetta and Phineas came down, and discussed the whole subject of the coming marriage with Mrs Bell. Hetta at first was not quite certain – ought they not to inquire whether the situation was permanent?

'I won't inquire at all,' said Mrs Bell, with an energy that startled both the daughter and son-in-law. 'I would not part them now; no, not if —' and the widow shuddered as she thought of her daughter's sunken eyes, and pale cheeks.

'He is a good lad,' said Phineas, 'and I trust she will make him a sober steady wife,' and so the matter was settled.

During this time, Susan and Aaron were walking along the Balston road; and they also had settled the matter – quite as satisfactorily.

Such was the courtship of Susan Dunn.

The Choice

EDITH WHARTON

EDITH WHARTON (1862–1937) was an American and a close friend of Henry James. As well as her novels she produced 11 collections of short stories. 'The Choice' is a dramatic story of illicit love, in which the wrong man survives.

I

STILLING, that night after dinner, had surpassed himself. He always did, Wrayford reflected, when the small fry from Highfield came to dine. He, Cobham Stilling, who had to find his bearings and keep to his level in the big heedless ironic world of New York, dilated and grew vast in the congenial medium of Highfield. The Red House was the biggest house of the Highfield summer colony, and Cobham Stilling was its biggest man. No one else within a radius of a hundred miles (on a conservative estimate) had as many horses, as many greenhouses, as many servants, and assuredly no one else had three motors and a motor-boat for the lake.

The motor-boat was Stilling's latest hobby, and he rode – or steered – it in and out of the conversation all the evening, to the obvious edification of every one present save his wife and his visitor, Austin Wrayford. The interest of the latter two who, from opposite ends of the drawing-room, exchanged a fleeting glance when Stilling again launched his craft on the thin current of the talk – the interest of Mrs Stilling and Wrayford had already lost its edge by protracted contact with the subject.

But the dinner-guests – the Rector, Mr Swordsley, his wife Mrs Swordsley, Lucy and Agnes Granger, their brother Addison, and young Jack Emmerton from Harvard – were all, for divers reasons, stirred to the proper pitch of feeling. Mr Swordsley, no doubt, was saying to himself: 'If my good parishioner here can afford to buy a motor-boat, in addition to all the other expenditures which an establishment like this must entail, I certainly need not scruple to appeal to him again for a contribution for our Galahad Club.' The Granger girls, meanwhile, were evoking visions of lakeside picnics, not unadorned with the presence of young Mr Emmerton; while that youth himself speculated as to whether his affable host would let him, when he came back on his next vacation, 'learn to run the thing himself'; and Mr Addison Granger, the elderly bachelor brother of the volatile Lucy and Agnes, mentally formulated the precise phrase in which, in his next letter to his cousin Professor Spildyke of the University of East Latmos, he should allude to 'our last delightful trip in my old friend Cobham Stilling's ten-thousand-dollar motor-launch' – for East Latmos was still in that primitive stage of culture on which five figures impinge.

Isabel Stilling, sitting beside Mrs Swordsley, her head slightly bent above the needlework with which on these occasions it was her old-fashioned habit to employ herself – Isabel also had doubtless her reflections to make. As Wrayford leaned back in his corner and looked at her across the wide flower-filled drawing-room he noted, first of all – for the how many hundredth time? – the play of her hands above the embroidery-frame, the shadow of the thick dark hair on her forehead, the listless droops of the lids over her somewhat full grey eyes. He noted all this with a conscious deliberateness of enjoyment, taking in unconsciously, at the same time, the particular quality in her attitude, in the fall of her dress and the turn of her head, which had set her for him, from the first day, in a separate world; then he said to himself: 'She is certainly thinking: "Where on earth will Cobham get the money to pay for it?" '

Stilling, cigar in mouth and thumbs in his waistcoat pockets, was impressively perorating from his usual dominant position on the hearth-rug.

'I said: "If I have the thing at all, I want the best that can be got." That's my way, you know, Swordsley; I suppose I'm what you'd call fastidious. Always was, about everything, from cigars to wom –' his eye met the apprehensive glance of Mrs Swordsley, who looked like her husband with his clerical coat cut slightly lower – 'so I said: "If I have the thing at all, I want the best that can be got." Nothing makeshift for me, no second-best. I never cared for the cheap and showy. I always say frankly to a man: "If you can't give me a first-rate cigar, for the Lord's sake let me smoke my own." ' He paused to do so. 'Well, if you have my standards, you can't buy a thing in a minute. You must look round, compare, select. I found there were lots of motor-boats on the market, just as there's lots of stuff called champagne. But I said to myself: "Ten to one there's only one fit to buy, just as there's only one champagne fit for a gentleman to drink." Argued like a lawyer, eh, Austin?' He tossed this to Wrayford. 'Take me for one of your own trade, wouldn't you? Well, I'm not such a fool as I look. I suppose you fellows who are tied to the treadmill – excuse me, Swordsley, but work's work, isn't it? – I suppose you think a man like me has nothing to do but take it easy: loll through life like a woman. By George, sir, I'd like either of you to see the time it takes – I won't say the *brains* – but just the time it takes to pick out a good motor-boat. Why, I went –'

Mrs Stilling set her embroidery-frame noiselessly on the table at her side, and turned her head toward Wrayford. 'Would you mind ringing for the tray?'

The interruption helped Mrs Swordsley to waver to her feet. 'I'm afraid we ought really to be going; my husband has an early service to-morrow.'

Her host intervened with a genial protest. 'Going already? Nothing of the sort! Why, the night's still young, as the poet says. Long way from here to the rectory? Nonsense! In our little twenty-horse car we do it in five minutes – don't we, Belle? Ah, you're walking, to be sure –' Stilling's indulgent gesture seemed to concede that, in such a case, allowances must be made, and that he was the last man not to make them. 'Well, then, Swordsley –' He held out a thick red hand that seemed to exude beneficence, and the clergyman, pressing it, ventured to murmur a suggestion.

'What, that Galahad Club again? Why, I thought my wife – Isabel, didn't we – No? Well, it must have been my mother, then. Of course, you know, anything my good mother gives is – well – virtually – You haven't asked her? Sure? I could have sworn; I get so many of these appeals. And in these times, you know, we have to go cautiously. I'm sure you recognize that yourself, Swordsley. With my obligations – here now, to show you don't bear malice, have a brandy and soda before you go. Nonsense, man! This brandy isn't liquor; it's liqueur. I picked it up last year in London – last of a famous lot from Lord St Oswyn's cellar. Laid down here, it stood me at – Eh?' he broke off as his wife moved toward him. 'Ah, yes, of course. Miss Lucy, Miss Agnes – a drop of soda-water? Look here, Addison, you won't refuse my tipple, I know. Well, take a cigar, at any rate, Swordsley. And, by the way, I'm afraid you'll have to go round the long way by the avenue to-night. Sorry, Mrs Swordsley, but I forgot to tell them to leave the gate into the lane unlocked. Well, it's a jolly night, and I daresay you won't mind the extra turn along the lake. And, by Jove! if the moon's out, you'll have a glimpse of the motor-boat. She's moored just out beyond our boat-house; and it's a privilege to look at her, I can tell you!'

The dispersal of his guests carried Stilling out into the hall, where his pleasantries reverberated under the oak rafters while the Granger girls were being muffled for the drive and the carriages summoned from the stables.

By a common impulse Mrs Stilling and Wrayford had moved together toward the fire-place, which was hidden by a tall screen from the door into the hall. Wrayford leaned his elbow against the mantel-piece, and Mrs Stilling stood beside him, her clasped hands hanging down before her.

'Have you anything more to talk over with him?' she asked.

'No. We wound it all up before dinner. He doesn't want to talk about it any more than he can help.'

'It's so bad?'

'No; but this time he's got to pull up.'

She stood silent, with lowered lids. He listened a moment, catching Stilling's farewell shout; then he moved a little nearer, and laid his hand on her arm.

'In an hour?'

She made an imperceptible motion of assent.

'I'll tell you about it then. The key's as usual?'

She signed another 'Yes' and walked away with her long drifting step as her husband came in from the hall. He went up to the tray and poured himself out a tall glass of brandy and soda.

'The weather is turning queer – black as pitch. I hope the Swordsleys won't walk into the lake – involuntary immersion, eh? He'd come out a Baptist, I suppose. What'd the Bishop do in such a case? There's a problem for a lawyer, my boy!'

He clapped his hand on Wrayford's thin shoulder and then walked over to his wife, who was gathering up her embroidery silks and dropping them into her work-bag. Stilling took her by the arms and swung her playfully about so that she faced the lamplight.

'What's the matter with you tonight?'

'The matter?' she echoed, colouring a little, and standing very straight in her desire not to appear to shrink from his touch.

'You never opened your lips. Left me the whole job of entertaining those blessed people. Didn't she, Austin?'

Wrayford laughed and lit a cigarette.

'There! You see even Austin noticed it. What's the matter, I say? Aren't they good enough for you? I don't say they're particularly exciting; but, hang it! I like to ask them here – I like to give people pleasure.'

'I didn't mean to be dull,' said Isabel.

'Well, you must learn to make an effort. Don't treat people as if they weren't in the room just because they don't happen to amuse you. Do you know what they'll think? They'll think it's because you've got a bigger house and more money than they have. Shall I tell you something? My mother said she'd noticed the same thing in you lately. She said she sometimes felt you looked down on her for living in a small house. Oh, she was half joking, of course; but you see you do give people that impression. I can't understand treating any one in that way. The more I have myself, the more I want to make other people happy.'

Isabel gently freed herself and laid the work-bag on her embroidery-frame. 'I have a headache; perhaps that made me stupid. I'm going to bed.' She turned toward Wrayford and held out her hand. 'Good night.'

'Good night,' he answered, opening the door for her.

When he turned back into the room, his host was pouring himself a third glass of brandy and soda.

'Here, have a nip, Austin? Gad, I need it badly, after the shaking up you gave me this afternoon.' Stilling laughed and carried his glass to the hearth, where he took up his usual commanding position. 'Why the deuce don't you drink something? You look as glum as Isabel. One would think you were the chap that had been hit by this business.'

Wrayford threw himself into the chair from which Mrs Stilling had lately risen. It was the one she usually sat in, and to his fancy a faint scent of her clung to it. He leaned back and looked up at Stilling.

'Want a cigar?' the latter continued. 'Shall we go into the den and smoke?'

Wrayford hesitated. 'If there's anything more you want to ask me about –'

'Gad, no! I had full measure and running over this afternoon. The deuce of it is, I don't see where the money's all gone to. Luckily I've got plenty of nerve; I'm not the kind of man to sit down and snivel because I've been touched in Wall Street.'

Wrayford got to his feet again. 'Then, if you don't want me, I think I'll go up to my room and put some finishing touches to a brief before I turn in. I must get back to town to-morrow afternoon.'

'All right, then.' Stilling set down his empty glass, and held out his hand with a tinge of alacrity. 'Good night, old man.'

They shook hands, and Wrayford moved toward the door.

'I say, Austin – stop a minute!' his host called after him. Wrayford turned, and the two men faced each other across the hearth-rug. Stilling's eyes shifted uneasily.

'There's one thing more you can do for me before you leave. Tell Isabel about that loan; explain to her that she's got to sign a note for it.'

Wrayford, in his turn, flushed slightly. 'You want me to tell her?'

'Hang it! I'm soft-hearted – that's the worst of me.' Stilling moved toward the tray, and lifted the brandy decanter. 'And she'll take it better from you; she'll *have* to take it from you. She's proud. You can take her out for a row to-morrow morning – look here, take her out in the motor-launch if you like. I meant to have a spin in it myself; but if you'll tell her –'

Wrayford hesitated. 'All right, I'll tell her.'

'Thanks a lot, my dear fellow. And you'll make her see it wasn't my fault, eh? Women are awfully vague about money, and she'll think it's all right if you back me up.'

Wrayford nodded. 'As you please.'

'And, Austin – there's just one more thing. You needn't say anything to Isabel about the other business – I mean about my mother's securities.'

'Ah?' said Wrayford, pausing.

Stilling shifted from one foot to the other. 'I'd rather put that to the old lady myself. I can make it clear to her. She idolizes me, you know – and, hang it! I've got a good record. Up to now, I mean. My mother's been in clover since I married; I may say she's been my first thought. And I don't want her to hear of this beastly business from Isabel. Isabel's a little harsh at times – and of course this isn't going to make her any easier to live with.'

'Very well,' said Wrayford.

Stilling, with a look of relief, walked toward the window which opened on the terrace. 'Gad! what a queer night! Hot as the kitchen-range. Shouldn't wonder if we had a squall before morning. I wonder if that infernal skipper took in the launch's awnings before he went home.'

Wrayford stopped with his hand on the door. 'Yes, I saw him do it. She's shipshape for the night.'

'Good! That saves me a run down to the shore.'

'Good night, then,' said Wrayford.

'Good night, old man. You'll tell her?'

'I'll tell her.'

'And mum about my mother!' his host called after him.

II

The darkness had thinned a little when Wrayford scrambled down the steep path to the shore. Though the air was heavy the threat of a storm seemed to have vanished, and now and then the moon's edge showed above a torn slope of cloud.

But in the thick shrubbery about the boat-house the darkness was still dense, and Wrayford had to strike a match before he could find the lock and insert his key. He left the door unlatched, and groped his way in. How often he had crept into this warm pine-scented obscurity, guiding himself by the edge of the bench along the wall, and hearing the soft lap of water through the gaps in the flooring! He knew just where one had to duck one's head to avoid the two canoes swung from the rafters, and just where to put his hand on the latch of the farther door that led to the broad balcony above the lake.

The boat-house represented one of Stilling's abandoned

whims. He had built it some seven years before, and for a time it had been the scene of incessant nautical exploits. Stilling had rowed, sailed, paddled indefatigably, and all Highfield had been impressed to bear him company, and to admire his versatility. Then motors had come in, and he had forsaken aquatic sports for the flying chariot. The canoes of birch-bark and canvas had been hoisted to the roof, the sail-boat had rotted at her moorings, and the movable floor of the boat-house, ingeniously contrived to slide back on noiseless runners, had lain undisturbed through several seasons. Even the key of the boat-house had been mislaid – by Isabel's fault, her husband said – and the locksmith had to be called in to make a new one when the purchase of the motor-boat made the lake once more the centre of Stilling's activity.

As Wrayford entered he noticed that a strange oily odor overpowered the usual scent of dry pine-wood; and at the next step his foot struck an object that rolled noisily across the boards. He lighted another match, and found he had overturned a can of grease which the boatman had no doubt been using to oil the runners of the sliding floor.

Wrayford felt his way down the length of the boat-house, and softly opening the balcony door looked out on the lake. A few yards away, he saw the launch lying at anchor in the veiled moonlight; and just below him, on the black water, was the dim outline of the skiff which the boatman kept to paddle out to her. The silence was so intense that Wrayford fancied he heard a faint rustling in the shrubbery on the high bank behind the boat-house, and the crackle of gravel on the path descending to it.

He closed the door again and turned back into the darkness; and as he did so the other door, on the land-side, swung inward, and he saw a figure in the dim opening. Just enough light entered through the round holes above the respective doors to reveal Mrs Stilling's cloaked outline, and to guide her to him as he advanced. But before they met she stumbled and gave a little cry.

'What is it?' he exclaimed.

'My foot caught; the floor seemed to give way under me. Ah, of course –' she bent down in the darkness – 'I saw the men oiling it this morning.'

Wrayford caught her by the arm. 'Do take care! It might be dangerous if it slid too easily. The water's deep under here.'

'Yes; the water's very deep. I sometimes wish –' She leaned against him without finishing her sentence, and he put both arms about her.

'Hush!' he said, his lips on hers.

Suddenly she threw her head back and seemed to listen.

'What's the matter? What do you hear?'

'I don't know.' He felt her trembling. 'I'm not sure this place is as safe as it used to be –'

Wrayford held her to him reassuringly. 'But the boatman sleeps down at the village; and who else should come here at this hour?'

'Cobham might. He thinks of nothing but the launch.'

'He won't to-night. I told him I'd seen the skipper put her shipshape, and that satisfied him.'

'Ah – he did think of coming, then?'

'Only for a minute, when the sky looked so black half an hour ago, and he was afraid of a squall. It's clearing now, and there's no danger.'

He drew her down on the bench, and they sat a moment or two in silence, her hands in his. Then she said: 'You'd better tell me.'

Wrayford gave a faint laugh. 'Yes, I suppose I had. In fact, he asked me to.'

'He asked you to?'

'Yes.'

She uttered an exclamation of contempt. 'He's afraid!'

Wrayford made no reply, and she went on: 'I'm not. Tell me everything, please.'

'Well, he's chucked away a pretty big sum again –'

'How?'

'He says he doesn't know. He's been speculating, I suppose. The madness of making him your trustee!'

She drew her hands away. 'You know why I did it. When we married I didn't want to put him in the false position of the man who contributes nothing and accepts everything; I wanted people to think the money was partly his.'

'I don't know what you've made people think; but you've been eminently successful in one respect. *He* thinks it's all his – and he loses it as if it were.'

'There are worse things. What was it that he wished you to tell me?'

'That you've got to sign another promissory note – for fifty thousand this time.'

'Is that all?'

Wrayford hesitated; then he said: 'Yes – for the present.'

She sat motionless, her head bent, her hand resting passively in his.

He leaned nearer. 'What did you mean just now, by worse things?'

She hesitated. 'Haven't you noticed that he's been drinking a great deal lately?'

'Yes; I've noticed.'

They were both silent; then Wrayford broke out, with sudden vehemence: 'And yet you won't –'

'Won't?'

'Put an end to it. Good God! Save what's left of your life.'

She made no answer, and in the stillness the throb of the water underneath them sounded like the beat of a tormented heart.

'Isabel –' Wrayford murmured. He bent over to kiss her. 'Isabel! I can't stand it! Listen –'

'No; no. I've thought of everything. There's the boy – the boy's fond of him. He's not a bad father.'

'Except in the trifling matter of ruining his son.'

'And there's his poor old mother. He's a good son, at any rate; he'd never hurt her. And I know her. If I left him, she'd never take a penny of my money. What she has of her own is not enough to live on; and how could he provide for her? If I put him out of doors, I should be putting his mother out too.'

'You could arrange that – there are always ways.'

'Not for her! She's proud. And then she believes in him. Lots of people believe in him, you know. It would kill her if she ever found out.'

Wrayford made an impatient movement. 'It will kill you if you stay with him to prevent her finding out.'

She laid her other hand on his. 'Not while I have you.'

'Have me? In this way?'

'In any way.'

'My poor girl – poor child!'

'Unless you grow tired – unless your patience gives out.'

He was silent, and she went on insistently: 'Don't you suppose I've thought of that too – foreseen it?'

'Well – and then?' he exclaimed.

'I've accepted that too.'

He dropped her hands with a despairing gesture. 'Then, indeed, I waste my breath!'

She made no answer, and for a time they sat silent again, a little between them. At length he asked: 'You're not crying?'

'No.'

'I can't see your face, it's grown so dark.'

'Yes. The storm must be coming.' She made a motion as if to rise.

He drew close and put his arm about her. 'Don't leave me yet. You know I must go to-morrow.' He broke off with a laugh. 'I'm to break the news to you to-morrow morning, by the way; I'm to take you out in the motor-launch and break it to you.' He dropped her hands and stood up. 'Good God! How can I go and leave you here with him?'

'You've done it often.'

'Yes; but each time it's more damnable. And then I've always had a hope –'

She rose also. 'Give it up! Give it up!'

'You've none, then, yourself?'

She was silent, drawing the folds of her cloak about her.

'None – none?' he insisted.

He had to bend his head to hear her answer. 'Only one!'

'What, my dearest? What?'

'Don't touch me! That he may die!'

They drew apart again, hearing each other's quick breathing through the darkness.

'You wish that too?' he said.

'I wish it always – every day, every hour, every moment!' She paused, and then let the words break from her. 'You'd better know it; you'd better know the worst of me. I'm not the saint you suppose; the duty I do is poisoned by the thoughts I think. Day by day, hour by hour, I wish him dead. When he goes out I pray for something to happen; when he comes back I say to myself: "Are you here again?" When I hear of people being killed in accidents, I think: "Why wasn't he there?" When I read the death-notices in the paper I say: "So-and-so was just his age." When I see him taking such care of his health and his diet – as he does, you know, except when he gets reckless and begins to drink too much – when I see him exercising and resting, and eating only certain things, and weighing himself, and feeling his muscles, and boasting that he hasn't gained a pound, I think of the men who die from overwork, or who throw their lives away for some great object, and I say to myself: "What can kill a man who thinks only of himself?" And night after night I keep myself from going to sleep for fear I may dream that he's dead. When I dream that, and wake and find him there it's worse than ever –'

She broke off with a sob, and the loud lapping of the water under the floor was like the beat of a rebellious heart.

'There, you know the truth!' she said.

He answered after a pause: 'People do die.'

'Do they?' She laughed. 'Yes – in happy marriages!'

They were silent again, and Isabel turned, feeling her way toward the door. As she did so, the profound stillness was broken by the sound of a man's voice trolling out unsteadily the refrain of a music-hall song.

The two in the boat-house darted toward each other with a simultaneous movement, clutching hands as they met.

'He's coming!' Isabel said.

Wrayford disengaged his hands.

'He may only be out for a turn before he goes to bed. Wait a minute. I'll see.' He felt his way to the bench, scrambled up on it, and stretching his body forward managed to bring his eyes in line with the opening above the door.

'It's as black as pitch. I can't see anything.'

The refrain rang out nearer.

'Wait! I saw something twinkle. There it is again. It's his cigar. It's coming this way – down the path.'

There was a long rattle of thunder through the stillness.

'It's the storm!' Isabel whispered. 'He's coming to see about the launch.'

Wrayford dropped noiselessly from the bench and she caught him by the arm.

'Isn't there time to get up the path and slip under the shrubbery?'

'No, he's in the path now. He'll be here in two minutes. He'll find us.'

He felt her hand tighten on his arm.

'You must go in the skiff, then. It's the only way.'

'And let him find you? And hear my oars? Listen – there's something I must say.'

She flung her arms about him and pressed her face to his.

'Isabel, just now I didn't tell you everything. He's ruined his mother – taken everything of hers too. And he's got to tell her; it can't be kept from her.'

She uttered an incredulous exclamation and drew back.

'Is this the truth? Why didn't you tell me before?'

'He forbade me. You were not to know.'

Close above them, in the shrubbery, Stilling warbled:

'*Nita, Juanita,*
Ask thy soul if we must part!'

Wrayford held her by both arms. 'Understand this – if he comes in, he'll find us. And if there's a row you'll lose your boy.'

She seemed not to hear him. 'You – you – you – he'll kill you!' she exclaimed.

Wrayford laughed impatiently and released her, and she stood shrinking against the wall, her hands pressed to her breast. Wrayford straightened himself and she felt that he was listening intently. Then he dropped to his knees and laid his hands against the boards of the sliding floor. It yielded at once, as if with a kind of evil alacrity; and at their feet they saw, under the motionless solid night, another darker night that moved and shimmered. Wrayford threw himself back against the opposite wall, behind the door.

A key rattled in the lock, and after a moment's fumbling the door swung open. Wrayford and Isabel saw a man's black bulk against the obscurity. It moved a step, lurched forward, and vanished out of sight. From the depths beneath them there came a splash and a long cry.

'Go! go!' Wrayford cried out, feeling blindly for Isabel in the blackness.

'Oh –' she cried, wrenching herself away from him.

He stood still a moment, as if dazed; then she saw him suddenly plunge from her side, and heard another splash far down, and a tumult in the beaten water.

In the darkness she cowered close to the opening, pressing her face over the edge, and crying out the name of each of the two men in turn. Suddenly she began to see: the obscurity was less opaque, as if a faint moon-pallor diluted it. Isabel vaguely discerned the two shapes struggling in the black pit below her; once she saw the gleam of a face. She glanced up desperately for some means of rescue, and caught sight of the oars ranged on brackets against the wall. She snatched down the nearest, bent over the opening, and pushed the oar down into the blackness, crying out her husband's name.

The clouds had swallowed the moon again, and she could see nothing below her; but she still heard the tumult in the beaten water.

'Cobham! Cobham!' she screamed.

As if in answer, she felt a mighty clutch on the oar, a clutch that strained her arms to the breaking-point as she tried to brace her knees against the runners of the sliding floor.

'Hold on! Hold on! Hold on!' a voice gasped out from below; and she held on, with racked muscles, with bleeding palms, with eyes straining from their sockets, and a heart that tugged at her as the weight was tugging at the oar.

Suddenly the weight relaxed, and the oar slipped up through her lacerated hands. She felt a wet body scrambling over the edge of the opening, and Stilling's voice, raucous and strange, groaned out, close to her: 'God! I thought I was done for.'

He staggered to his knees, coughing and sputtering, and the water dripped on her from his streaming clothes.

She flung herself down, again, straining over the pit. Not a sound came up from it.

'Austin! Austin! Quick! Another oar!' she shrieked.

Stilling gave a cry. 'My God! Was it Austin? What in hell – Another oar? No, no; untie the skiff, I tell you. But it's no use. Nothing's any use. I felt him lose hold as I came up.'

After that she was conscious of nothing till, hours later, as it appeared to her, she became dimly aware of her husband's voice, high, hysterical and important, haranguing a group of scared lantern-struck faces that had sprung up mysteriously about them in the night.

'Poor Austin! Poor Wrayford . . . terrible loss to me . . . mysterious dispensation. Yes, I do feel gratitude – miraculous escape – but I wish old Austin could have known that I was saved!'

The Conqueror

W. J. LOCKE

W. J. LOCKE (1863–1930) was a prolific and popular writer in the early years of this century. His story of 'The Conqueror' is unusual in that it tells of a life-long love that is never consummated.

MISS Winifred Goode sat in her garden in the shade of a clipped yew, an unopened novel on her lap, and looked at the gabled front of the Tudor house that was hers and had been her family's for many generations. In that house, Duns Hall, in that room beneath the southernmost gable, she had been born. From that house, save for casual absences rarely exceeding a month in duration, she had never stirred. All the drama, such as it was, of her life had been played in that house, in that garden. Up and down the parapeted stone terrace walked the ghosts of all those who had been dear to her – her father, a vague but cherished memory; a brother and a sister who had died during her childhood; her mother, dead three years since, to whose invalid and somewhat selfish needs she had devoted all her full young womanhood. Another ghost walked there, too; but that was the ghost of the living – a young man who had kissed and ridden away, twenty years ago. He had kissed her over there, under the old wistaria arbour at the end of the terrace. What particular meaning he had put into the kiss, loverly, brotherly, cousinly, friendly – for they had played together all their young lives, and were distantly connected – she had never been able to determine. In spite of his joy at leaving the lethargic country town of Dunsfield for America, their parting had been sad and sentimental. The kiss, at any rate, had been, on his side, one of sincere affection – an affection proven afterwards by a correspondence of twenty years. To her the kiss had been – well, the one and only kiss of her life, and she had treasured it in a neat little sacred casket in her heart. Since that far-off day no man had ever showed an inclination to kiss her, which, in one way, was strange, as she had been pretty and gentle and laughter-loving, qualities attractive to youths in search of a mate. But in another way it was not strange, as mate-seeking youths are rare as angels in Dunsfield, beyond whose limits Miss Goode had seldom strayed. Her romance had been one kiss, the girlish dreams of one man. At first, when he had gone fortune-hunting in America, she had fancied herself broken-hearted; but Time had soon touched her with healing fingers. Of late, freed from the slavery of a querulous bedside, she had grown in love with her unruffled and delicately ordered existence, in which the only irregular things were her herbaceous borders, between which she walked like a prim schoolmistress among a crowd of bright but unruly children. She had asked nothing more from life than what she had – her little duties in the parish, her little pleasures in the neighbourhood, her good health, her old house, her trim lawns, her old-fashioned garden, her black cocker spaniels. As it was at forty, she thought, so should it be till the day of her death.

But a month ago had come turmoil. Roger Orme announced his return. Fortune-making in America had tired him. He was coming home to settle down for good in Dunsfield, in the house of his fathers. This was Duns Lodge, whose forty acres marched with the two hundred acres of Duns Hall. The two places were known in the district as 'The Lodge' and 'The Hall.' About a century since, a younger son of The Hall had married a daughter of The Lodge, whence the remote tie of consanguinity between Winifred Goode and Roger Orme. The Lodge had been let on lease for many years, but now the lease had fallen in and the tenants gone. Roger had arrived in England yesterday. A telegram had bidden her expect him that afternoon. She sat in the garden expecting him, and stared wistfully at the old grey house, a curious fear in her eyes.

Perhaps, if freakish chance had not brought Mrs Donovan to Dunsfield on a visit to the Rector, a day or two after Roger's letter, fear – foolish, shameful, sickening fear – might not have had so dominant a place in her anticipation of his home-coming. Mrs Donovan was a contemporary, a Dunsfield girl, who had married at nineteen and gone out with her husband to India. Winifred Goode remembered a gipsy beauty riotous in the bloom of youth. In the Rector's drawing-room she met a grey-haired, yellow-skinned, shrivelled caricature, and she looked in the woman's face as in a mirror of awful truth in which she herself was reflected. From that moment she had known no peace. Gone was her placid acceptance of the footprints of the years, gone her old-maidish pride in dainty, old-maidish dress. She had mixed little with the modern world, and held to old-fashioned prejudices which prescribed the outward demeanour appropriate to each decade. One of her earliest memories was a homely saying of her father's – which had puzzled her childish mind considerably – as to the absurd-ity of sheep being dressed lamb fashion. Later she understood and cordially agreed with the dictum. The Countess of Ingles-wood, the personage of those latitudes, at the age of fifty showed the fluffy golden hair and peach-bloom cheeks and supple figure of twenty; she wore bright colours and dashing hats, and danced and flirted and kept a tame-cattery of adoring young men. Winifred visited with Lady Ingleswood because she believed that, in these democratic days, it was the duty of county families to outmarch the proletariat in solidarity; but, with every protest of her gentlewoman's soul, she disapproved of Lady Ingleswood. Yet now, to her appalling dismay, she saw that, with the aid of paint, powder, and peroxide, Lady Ingleswood had managed to keep young. For thirty years to Winifred's certain knowledge, she had not altered. The blasting hand that had swept over Madge Donovan's face had passed her by.

Winifred envied the woman's power of attraction. She read,

with a curious interest, hitherto disregarded advertisements. They were so alluring, they seemed so convincing. Such a cosmetic used by queens of song and beauty restored the roses of girlhood; under such a treatment, wrinkles disappeared within a week – there were the photographs to prove it. All over London bubbled fountains of youth, at a mere guinea or so a dip. She sent for a little battery of washes and powders, and, when it arrived, she locked herself in her bedroom. But the sight of the first unaccustomed – and unskilfully applied – dab of rouge on her cheek terrified her. She realised what she was doing. No! Ten thousand times no! Her old-maidishness, her puritanism revolted. She flew to her hand-basin and vigorously washed the offending bloom away with soap and water. She would appear before the man she loved just as she was – if need be, in the withered truth of a Madge Donovan . . . And, after all, had her beauty faded so utterly? Her glass said 'No.' But her glass mocked her, for how could she conjure up the young face of twenty which Roger Orme carried in his mind, and compare it with the present image?

She sat in the garden, this blazing July afternoon, waiting for him, her heart beating with the love of years ago, and the shrinking fear in her eyes. Presently she heard the sound of wheels, and she saw the open fly of 'The Red Lion' – Dunsfield's chief hotel – crawling up the drive, and in it was a man wearing a straw hat. She fluttered a timid handkerchief, but the man, not looking in her direction, did not respond. She crossed the lawn to the terrace, feeling hurt, and entered the drawing-room by the open French window and stood there, her back to the light. Soon he was announced. She went forward to meet him.

'My dear Roger, welcome home.'

He laughed and shook her hand in a hearty grip.

'It's you, Winifred? How good! Are you glad to see me back?'

'Very glad.'

'And I.'

'Do you find things changed?'

'Nothing,' he declared with a smile; 'the house is just the same.' He ran his fingers over the corner of a Louis XVI table near which he was standing. 'I remember this table, in this exact spot, twenty years ago.'

'And you have scarcely altered. I should have known you anywhere.'

'I should just hope so,' said he.

She realised, with a queer little pang, that time had improved the appearance of the man of forty-five. He was tall, strong, erect; few accusing lines marked his clean-shaven, florid, clear-cut face; in his curly brown hair she could not detect a touch of grey. He had a new air of mastery and success which expressed itself in the corners of his firm lips and steady, humorous gleam in his eyes.

'You must be tired after your hot train journey,' she said.

He laughed again. 'Tired? After a couple of hours? Now, if it had been a couple of days, as we are accustomed to on the other side — But go on talking, just to let me keep on hearing your voice. It's yours – I could have recognised it over a long-distance telephone – and it's English. You've no idea how delicious it is. And the smell of the room' – he drew in a deep breath – 'is you and the English country. I tell you, it's good to be back!'

She flushed, his pleasure was so sincere, and she smiled.

'But why should we stand? Let me take your hat and stick.'

'Why shouldn't we sit in the garden – after my hot and tiring journey?' They both laughed. 'Is the old wistaria still there, at the end of the terrace?'

She turned her face away. 'Yes, still there. Do you remember it?' she asked in a low voice.

'Do you think I could forget it? I remember every turn of the house.'

'Let us go outside, then.'

She led the way, and he followed, to the trellis arbour, a few steps from the drawing-room door. The long lilac blooms had gone with the spring, but the luxuriant summer leafage cast a grateful shade. Roger Orme sat in a wicker chair and fanned himself with his straw hat.

'Delightful!' he said. 'And I smell stocks! It does carry me back. I wonder if I have been away at all.'

'I'm afraid you have,' said Winifred – 'for twenty years.'

'Well, I'm not going away again. I've had my share of work. And what's the good of work just to make money? I've made enough. I sold out before I left.'

'But in your letters you always said you liked America.'

'So I did. It's the only country in the world for the young and eager. If I had been born there, I should have no use for Dunsfield. But a man born and bred among old, sleepy things has the nostalgia of old, sleepy things in his blood. Now tell me about the sleepy old things. I want to hear.'

'I think I have written to you about everything that ever happened in Dunsfield,' she said.

But still there were gaps to be bridged in the tale of births and marriages and deaths, the main chronicles of the neighbourhood. He had a surprising memory, and plucked obscure creatures from the past whom even Winifred had forgotten.

'It's almost miraculous how you remember.'

'It's a faculty I've had to cultivate,' said he.

They talked about his immediate plans. He was going to put The Lodge into thorough repair, bring everything up-to-date, lay in electric light and a central heating installation, fix bathrooms wherever bathrooms would go, and find a place somewhere for a billiard-room. His surveyor had already made his report, and was to meet him at the house the following morning. As for decorations, curtaining, carpeting, and such-like æsthetic aspects, he was counting on Winifred's assistance. He thought that blues and browns would harmonise with the oak-panelling in the dining-room. Until the house was ready, his headquarters would be 'The Red Lion.'

'You see, I'm going to begin right now,' said he.

She admired his vitality, his certainty of accomplishment.

The Hall was still lit by lamps and candles; and although, on her return from a visit, she had often deplored the absence of electric light, she had shrunk from the strain and worry of an innovation. And here was Roger turning the whole house inside out more cheerfully than she would turn out a drawer.

'You'll help me, won't you?' he asked. 'I want a home with a touch of the woman in it; I've lived so long in masculine stiffness.'

'You know that I should love to do anything I could, Roger,' she replied happily.

He remarked again that it was good to be back. No more letters – they were unsatisfactory, after all. He hoped she had not resented his business man's habit of typewriting. This was in the year of grace eighteen hundred and ninety-two, and, save for Roger's letters, typewritten documents came as seldom as judgment summonses to Duns Hall.

'We go ahead in America,' said he.

' "The old order changeth, yielding place to new." I accept it,' she said with a smile.

'What I've longed for in Dunsfield,' he said, 'is the old order that doesn't change. I don't believe anything has changed.'

She plucked up her courage. Now she would challenge him – get it over at once. She would watch his lips as he answered.

'I'm afraid I must have changed, Roger.'

'In what way?'

'I am no longer twenty.'

'Your voice is just the same.'

Shocked, she put up her delicate hands. 'Don't – it hurts!'

'What?'

'You needn't have put it that way – you might have told a polite lie.'

He rose, turned aside, holding the back of the wicker chair.

'I've got something to tell you,' he said abruptly. 'You would have to find out soon, so you may as well know now. But don't be alarmed or concerned. I can't see your face.'

'What do you mean?'

'I've been stone blind for fifteen years.'

'Blind?'

She sat for some moments paralysed. It was inconceivable. This man was so strong, so alive, so masterful, with the bright face and keen, humorous eyes – and blind! A trivial undercurrent of thought ran subconsciously beneath her horror. She had wondered why he had insisted on sounds and scents, why he had kept his stick in his hand, why he had touched things – tables, window jambs, chairs – now she knew. Roger went on talking, and she heard him in a dream. He had not informed her when he was stricken, because he had wished to spare her unnecessary anxiety. Also, he was proud, perhaps hard, and resented sympathy. He had made up his mind to win through in spite of his affliction. For some years it had been the absorbing passion of his life. He had won through like many another, and, as the irreparable detachment of the retina had not disfigured his eyes, it was his joy to go through the world like a seeing man, hiding his blindness from the casual observer. By dictated letter he could never have made her understand how trifling a matter it was.

'And I've deceived even you!' he laughed.

Tears had been rolling down her cheeks. At his laugh she gave way. An answering choke, hysterical, filled her throat, and she burst into a fit of sobbing. He laid his hand tenderly on her head.

'My dear, don't. I am the happiest man alive. And as for eyes, I'm rich enough to buy a hundred pairs. I'm a perfect Argus!'

But Winifred Goode wept uncontrollably. There was deep pity for him in her heart, but – never to be revealed to mortal – there was also horrible, terrifying joy. She gripped her hands and sobbed frantically to keep herself from laughter. A woman's sense of humour is often cruel, only to be awakened by tragic incongruities. She had passed through her month's agony and shame for a blind man.

At last she mastered herself. 'Forgive me, dear Roger. It was

a dreadful shock. Blindness has always been to me too awful
for thought – like being buried alive.'

'Not a bit of it,' he said cheerily. 'I've run a successful
business in the dark – real estate – buying and selling and
developing land, you know – a thing which requires a man
to keep a sharp look-out, and which he couldn't do if he were
buried alive. It's a confounded nuisance, I admit, but so is gout.
Not half as irritating as the position of a man I once knew who
had both hands cut off.'

She shivered. 'That's horrible.'

'It is,' said he, 'but blindness isn't.'

The maid appeared with the tea-tray, which she put on
a rustic table. It was then that Winifred noticed the little
proud awkwardnesses of the blind man. There was pathos
in his insistent disregard of his affliction. The imperfectly cut
lower half of a watercress sandwich fell on his coat and stayed
there. She longed to pick it off, but did not dare, for fear of
hurting him. He began to talk again of the house – the scheme
of decoration.

'Oh, it all seems so sad!' she cried.

'What?'

'You'll not be able to see the beautiful things.'

'Good Heavens,' he retorted, 'do you think I am quite
devoid of imagination? And do you suppose no one will enter
the house but myself?'

'I never thought of that,' she admitted.

'As for the interior, I've got the plan in my head, and
could walk about it now blindfold, only that's unnecessary;
and when it's all fixed up, I'll have a ground model made of
every room, showing every piece of furniture, so that, when I
get in, I'll know the size, shape, colour, quality of every blessed
thing in the house. You see if I don't.'

'These gifts are a merciful dispensation of Providence.'

'Maybe,' said he drily. 'Only they were about the size of
bacteria when I started, and it took me years of incessant toil
to develop them.'

He asked to be shown around the garden. She took him

up the gravelled walks beside her gay borders and her roses, telling him the names and varieties of the flowers. Once he stopped and frowned.

'I've lost my bearings. We ought to be passing under the shade of the old walnut tree.'

'You are quite right,' she said, marvelling at his accuracy. 'It stood a few steps back, but it was blown clean down three years ago. It had been dead for a long time.'

He chuckled as he strolled on. 'There's nothing makes me so mad as to be mistaken.'

Some time later, on their return to the terrace, he held out his hand.

'But you'll stay for dinner, Roger,' she exclaimed. 'I can't bear to think of you spending your first evening at home in that awful "Red Lion."'

'That's very dear of you, Winnie,' he said, evidently touched by the softness in her voice. 'I'll dine with pleasure, but I must get off some letters first. I'll come back. You've no objection to my bringing my man with me?'

'Why, of course not.' She laid her hand lightly on his arm. 'Oh, Roger, dear, I wish I could tell you how sorry I am, how my heart aches for you!'

'Don't worry,' he said – 'don't worry a little bit, and, if you really want to help me, never let me feel that you notice I'm blind. Forget it, as I do.'

'I'll try,' she said.

'That's right.' He held her hand for a second or two, kissed it, and dropped it, abruptly. 'God bless you!' said he. 'It's good to be with you again.'

When he was gone, Winifred Goode returned to her seat by the clipped yew and cried a little, after the manner of women. And, after the manner of women, she dreamed dreams oblivious of the flight of time till her maid came out and hurried her indoors.

She dressed with elaborate care, in her best and costliest, and wore more jewels than she would have done had her guest been of normal sight, feeling oddly shaken by the thought of his intense imaginative vision. In trying to fasten the diamond clasp of a velvet band round her neck, her fingers trembled so much that the maid came to her assistance. Her mind was in a whirl. Roger had left her a headstrong, dissatisfied boy. He had returned, the romantic figure of a conqueror, all the more romantic and conquering by reason of his triumph over the powers of darkness. In his deep affection she knew her place was secure. The few hours she had passed with him had shown her that he was a man trained in the significance not only of words, but also of his attitude towards individual men and women. He would not have said 'God bless you!' unless he meant it. She appreciated to the full his masculine strength; she took to her heart his masculine tenderness; she had a woman's pity for his affliction; she felt unregenerate exultancy at the undetected crime of lost beauty, and yet she feared him on account of the vanished sense. She loved him with a passionate recrudescence of girlish sentiment; but the very thing that might have, that ought to have, that she felt it indecent not to have, inflamed all her woman's soul and thrown her reckless into his arms, raised between them an impalpable barrier against which she dreaded lest she might be dashed and bruised.

At dinner this feeling was intensified. Roger made little or no allusion to his blindness; he talked with the ease of the cultivated man of the world. He had humour, gaiety, charm. As a mere companion, she had rarely met, during her long seclusion, a man so instinctive in sympathy, so quick in diverting talk into a channel of interest. In a few flashing yet subtle questions, he learned what she wore. The diamond clasp to the black velvet band he recognised as having been her mother's. He complimented her delicately on her appearance, as though he saw her clearly, in the adorable twilight beauty that was really hers. There were moments when it seemed impossible that he should be blind. But behind his chair, silent, impassive, arresting, freezing, hovered his Chinese body-servant, capped, pig-tailed, loosely clad in white, a creature as unreal in Dunsfield as gnome or merman, who, with the unobtrusiveness of a shadow from another world, served, in the mechanics of the meal, as an accepted, disregarded, and unnoticed pair of eyes for his master. The noble Tudor dining-room, with its great carved oak chimney-piece, its stately gilt-framed portraits, its Jacobean sideboards and presses, all in the gloom of the spent illumination of the candles on the daintily-set table, familiar to her from her earliest childhood, part of her conception of the cosmos, part of her very self, seemed metamorphosed into the unreal, the phantasmagoric, by the presence of this white-clad, exotic figure – not a man, but an eerie embodiment of the sense of sight.

Her reason told her that the Chinese servant was but an ordinary serving-man, performing minutely specified duties for a generous wage. But the duties were performed magically, like conjuror's tricks. It was practically impossible to say who cut up Roger's meat, who helped him to salt or to vegetables, who guided his hand unerringly to the wine glass. So abnormally exquisite was the co-ordination between the two, that Roger seemed to have the man under mesmeric control. The idea bordered on the monstrous. Winifred shivered through the dinner, in spite of Roger's bright talk, and gratefully welcomed the change of the drawing-room, whither the white-vestured automaton did not follow.

'Will you do me a favour, Winnie?' he asked during the evening. 'Meet me at The Lodge to-morrow at eleven, and help me interview these building people. Then you can have a finger in the pie from the very start.'

She said somewhat tremulously: 'Why do you want me to have a finger in the pie?'

'Good Heavens,' he cried, 'aren't you the only human creature in this country I care a straw about?'

'Is that true, Roger?'

'Sure,' said he. After a little span of silence he laughed. 'People on this side don't say "sure". That's sheer American.'

'I like it,' said Winifred.

When he parted from her, he again kissed her hand and

again said: 'God bless you!' She accompanied him to the hall, where the Chinaman, ghostly in the dimness, was awaiting him with hat and coat. Suddenly she felt that she abhorred the Chinaman.

That night she slept but little, striving to analyse her feelings. Of one fact only did the dawn bring certainty – that, for all her love of him, for all his charm, for all his tenderness towards her, during dinner she had feared him horribly.

She saw him the next morning in a new and yet oddly familiar phase. He was attended by his secretary, a pallid man with a pencil, note-book, and documents, for ever at his elbow, ghostly, automatic, during their wanderings with the surveyor through the bare and desolate old house.

She saw the master of men at work, accurate in every detail of a comprehensive scheme, abrupt, imperious, denying difficulties with harsh impatience. He leaned over his secretary and pointed to portions of the report just as though he could read them, and ordered their modification.

'Mr Withers,' he said once to the surveyor, who was raising objections, 'I always get what I want because I make dead sure that what I want is attainable. I'm not an idealist. If I say a thing is to be done, it has got to be done, and it's up to you or to someone else to do it.'

They went through the house from furnace to garret, the pallid secretary ever at Roger's elbow, ever rendering him imperceptible services, ever identifying himself with the sight-less man, mysteriously following his thoughts, co-ordinating his individuality with that of his master. He was less a man than a trained faculty, like the Chinese servant. And again Winifred shivered and felt afraid.

More and more during the weeks that followed, did she realise the iron will and irresistible force of the man she loved. He seemed to lay a relentless grip on all those with whom he came in contact and compel them to the expression of himself. Only towards her was he gentle and considerate. Many times she accompanied him to London to the great shops, the self-effacing secretary shadow-like at his elbow, and discussed with him colours and materials, and he listened to her with affectionate deference. She often noticed that the secretary translated into other terms her description of things. This irritated her, and once she suggested leaving the secretary behind. Surely, she urged, she could do all that was necessary. He shook his head.

'No, my dear,' he said very kindly. 'Jukes sees for me. I shouldn't like you to see for me in the way Jukes does.'

She was the only person from whom he would take advice or suggestion, and she rendered him great service in the tasteful equipment of the house and in the engagement of a staff of servants. So free a hand did he allow her in certain directions, so obviously and deliberately did he withdraw from her sphere of operations, that she was puzzled. It was not until later, when she knew him better, that the picture vaguely occurred to her of him caressing her tenderly with one hand, and holding the rest of the world by the throat with the other.

On the day when he took up his residence in the new home, they walked together through the rooms. In high spirits, boyishly elated, he gave her an exhibition of his marvellous gifts of memory, minutely describing each bit of furniture and its position in every room, the colour scheme, the texture of curtains, the pictures on the walls, the knick-knacks on mantelpieces and tables. And when he had done, he put his arm round her shoulders.

'But for you, Winnie,' said he, 'this would be the dreariest possible kind of place; but the spirit of you pervades it and makes it a fragrant paradise.'

The words and tone were lover-like, and so was his clasp. She felt very near him, very happy, and her heart throbbed quickly. She was ready to give her life to him.

'You are making me a proud woman,' she murmured.

He patted her shoulder and laughed as he released her.

'I only say what's true, my dear,' he replied, and then abruptly skipped from sentiment to practical talk.

Winifred had a touch of dismay and disappointment. Tears started, which she wiped away furtively. She had made up her mind to accept him, in spite of Wang Fu and Mr Jukes, if he should make her a proposal of marriage. She had been certain that the moment had come. But he made no proposal.

She waited. She waited a long time. In the meanwhile, she continued to be Roger's intimate friend and eagerly-sought companion. One day his highly-paid and efficient housekeeper came to consult her. The woman desired to give notice. Her place was too difficult. She could scarcely believe the master was blind. He saw too much, he demanded too much. She could say nothing explicit, save that she was frightened. She wept, after the nature of upset housekeepers. Winifred soothed her and advised her not to throw up so lucrative a post, and, as soon as she had an opportunity, she spoke to Roger. He laughed his usual careless laugh.

'They all begin that way with me, but after a while they're broken in. You did quite right to tell Mrs Strode to stay.'

And after a few months Winifred saw a change in Mrs Strode, and not only in Mrs Strode, but in all the servants whom she had engaged. They worked the household like parts of a flawless machine. They grew to be imperceptible, shadowy, automatic, like Wang Fu and Mr Jukes.

The months passed and melted into years. Roger Orme became a great personage in the neighbourhood. He interested himself in local affairs, served on the urban district council and on boards innumerable. They made him Mayor of Dunsfield. He subscribed largely to charities and entertained on a sumptuous scale. He ruled the little world, setting a ruthless heel on proud necks and making the humble his instruments. Mr Jukes died, and other secretaries came, and those who were not instantly dismissed grew to be like Mr Jukes. In the course of time Roger entered Parliament as member for the division. He became a force in politics, in public affairs. In the appointment of Royal Commissions, committees of inquiry, his name was the first to occur to ministers, and he was invariably respected, dreaded, and hated by his colleagues.

'Why do you work so hard, Roger?' Winifred would ask.

He would say, with one of his laughs: 'Because there's a dynamo in me that I can't stop.'

And all these years Miss Winifred Goode stayed at Duns Hall, leading her secluded, lavender-scented life when Roger was in London, and playing hostess for him, with diffident graciousness, when he entertained at The Lodge. His attitude towards her never varied, his need of her never lessened.

He never asked her to be his wife. At first she wondered, pined a little, and then, like a brave, proud woman, put the matter behind her. But she knew that she counted for much in his strange existence, and the knowledge comforted her. And as the years went on, and all the lingering shreds of youth left her, and she grew gracefully into the old lady, she came to regard her association with him as a spiritual marriage.

Then, after twenty years, the dynamo wore out the fragile tenement of flesh. Roger Orme, at sixty-five, broke down and lay on his death-bed. One day he sent for Miss Winifred Goode.

She entered the sick-room, a woman of sixty, white-haired, wrinkled, with only the beauty of a serene step across the threshold of old age. He bade the nurse leave them alone, and put out his hand and held hers as she sat beside the bed.

'What kind of a day is it, Winnie?'

'As if you didn't know! You've been told, I'm sure, twenty times.'

'What does it matter what other people say? I want to get at the day through you.'

'It's bright and sunny – a perfect day of early summer.'

'What things are out?'

'The may and the laburnum and the lilac –'

'And the wistaria?'

'Yes, the wistaria.'

'It's forty years ago, dear, and your voice is just the same. And to me you have always been the same. I can see you as you sit there, with your dear, sensitive face, the creamy cheek, in which the blood comes and goes – oh, Heavens, so different from the blowsy, hard-featured girls nowadays, who could not blush if – well – well – I know 'em, although I'm blind – I'm Argus, you know, dear. Yes, I can see you, with your soft, brown eyes and pale brown hair waved over your pure brow. There is a fascinating little kink on the left-hand side. Let me feel it.'

She drew her head away, frightened. Then suddenly she remembered, with a pang of thankfulness, that the queer little kink had defied the years, though the pale brown hair was white. She guided his hand and he felt the kink, and he laughed in his old, exultant way.

'Don't you think I'm a miracle, Winnie?'

'You're the most wonderful man living,' she said.

'I shan't be living long. No, my dear, don't talk platitudes. I know. I'm busted. And I'm glad I'm going before I begin to dodder. A seeing dodderer is bad enough, but a blind dodderer's only fit for the grave. I've lived my life. I've proved to this stupendous clot of ignorance that is humanity that a blind man can guide them wherever he likes. You know I refused a knighthood. Any tradesman can buy a knighthood – the only knighthoods that count are those that are given to artists and writers and men of science – and, if I could live, I'd raise hell over the matter, and make a differentiation in the titles of honour between the great man and the rascally cheesemonger –'

'My dear,' said Miss Winifred Goode, 'don't get so excited.'

'I'm only saying, Winnie, that I refused a knighthood. But – what I haven't told you, what I'm supposed to keep a dead secret – if I could live a few weeks longer, and I shan't, I should be a Privy Councillor – a thing worth being. I've had the official intimation – a thing that can't be bought. Heavens, if I were a younger man, and there were the life in me, I should be the Prime Minister of this country – the first great blind ruler that ever was in the world. Think of it! But I don't want anything now. I'm done. I'm glad. The whole caboodle is but leather and prunella. There is only one thing in the world that is of any importance.'

'What is that, dear?' she asked quite innocently, accustomed to, but never familiar with, his vehement paradox.

'Love,' said he.

He gripped her hand hard. There passed a few seconds of tense silence.

'Winnie, dear,' he said at last, 'will you kiss me?'

She bent forward, and he put his arm round her neck and drew her to him. They kissed each other on the lips.

'It's forty years since I kissed you, dear – that day under the wistaria. And, now I'm dying, I can tell you. I've loved you all the time, Winnie. I'm a tough nut, as you know, and whatever I do I do intensely. I've loved you intensely, furiously.'

She turned her head away, unable to bear the living look in the sightless eyes.

'Why did you never tell me?' she asked in a low voice.

'Would you have married me?'

'You know I would, Roger.'

'At first I vowed I would say nothing,' he said, after a pause, 'until I had a fit home to offer you. Then the blindness came, and I vowed I wouldn't speak until I had conquered the helplessness of my affliction. Do you understand?'

'Yes, but when you came home a conqueror –'

'I loved you too much to marry you. You were far too dear and precious to come into the intimacy of my life. Haven't you seen what happened to all those who did?' He raised his old knotted hands, clenched tightly. 'I squeezed them dry. I couldn't help it. My blindness made me a coward. It has been hell. The darkness never ceased to frighten me; I lied when I said it didn't matter. I stretched out my hands like tentacles and gripped everyone within reach in a kind of madness of self-preservation. I made them give up their souls and senses to me. It was some ghastly hypnotic power I seemed to have. When I had got them, they lost volition, individuality. They were about as much living creatures to me as my arm or my foot. Don't you see?'

The white-haired woman looked at the old face working passionately, and she felt once more the deadly fear of him.

'But with me it would have been different,' she faltered. 'You say you loved me.'

'That's the devil of it, my sweet, beautiful Winnie – it wouldn't have been different. I should have squeezed you, too, reduced you to the helpless thing that did my bidding, sucked your life's blood from you. I couldn't have resisted. So I kept you away. Have I ever asked you to use your eyes for me?'

Her memory travelled down the years, and she was amazed. She remembered Mr Jukes at the great shops and many similar incidents that had puzzled her.

'No,' she said.

There was a short silence. The muscles of his face relaxed, and the old, sweet smile came over it. He reached again for her hand and caressed it tenderly.

'By putting you out of my life, I kept you, dear. I kept you as the one beautiful human thing I had. Every hour of happiness I have had for the last twenty years has come through you.'

She said tearfully: 'You have been very good to me, Roger.'

'It's a queer mix-up, isn't it?' he said, after a pause. 'Most people would say that I've ruined your life. If it hadn't been for me, you might have married.'

'No, dear,' she replied. 'I've had a very full and happy life.'

The nurse came into the room to signify the end of the visit, and found them hand in hand like lovers. He laughed.

'Nurse,' said he, 'you see a dying but a jolly happy old man!'

Two days afterwards Roger Orme died. On the afternoon of the funeral, Miss Winifred Goode sat in the old garden in the shade of the clipped yew, and looked at the house in which she had been born, and in which she had passed her sixty years of life, and at the old wistaria beneath which he had kissed her forty years ago. She smiled and murmured aloud:

'No, I would not have had a single thing different.'

Full Moon

GEORGETTE HEYER

GEORGETTE HEYER (1902–1974) was born in Wimbledon. She wrote 12 crime novels, but she is best known for her Regency romances, a genre which she almost invented. Her 'Regencies' are still the best in their field, full of authentic detail and lively characters.

LORD Stavely prepared to descend from his chaise.

'We will stop here,' he announced.

It was certainly a charming inn. It stood at the end of the broad village street, with two great elms behind it and roses rambling over its old red brick frontage. It was not, of course, a posting house, which did not incline the two postilions in its favour. One of them said: 'If we was to drive on for another mile or two, we'd likely find a decent house for your honour to bait at.'

'My dear good fellow,' replied his lordship, 'you have no more notion of where we are than I have. Here we will stop. I like the place.'

The village seemed asleep in the moonlight, not a soul stirring. But the sound of carriage wheels brought the landlord out of the inn, all anxiety to oblige. Lord Stavely, alighting from the chaise, said: 'Arcadia, I presume. Tell me, what is the time?'

The landlord, slightly taken aback, said that it lacked but ten minutes to the hour.

'But what hour?' asked his lordship.

'Why, nine o'clock, sir!'

'How shocking! Am I anywhere in the neighbourhood of Melbury Place?'

'Melbury Place?' repeated the landlord. 'Yes, that you are, sir; it lies only a matter of ten miles from here, though the road's tricky, as you might say.'

'After the experiences of today, I should probably use a more forceful epithet. I imagine it will take me nearly an hour to reach the place. Obviously it behoves me to dine here. Or am I too late for dinner?'

The landlord was not one to turn away distinguished custom from his door. This gentleman, with his high crowned beaver hat, his driving coat of many capes, worn negligently open over a neat blue coat, a cut Venetian waistcoat, and the palest of fawn pantaloons, was plainly a member of the Quality. He assured Lord Stavely that, if he would step into the coffee-room, dinner should be served him in a very few minutes. A qualm then attacked him, and he faltered: 'I'm sorry I can't show your honour to a private parlour, but there's only Mr Tom in the coffee-room, after all.'

'Then if Mr Tom does not take exception to me, I shall do very well,' said his lordship. 'I wonder if I should remain here for the night? Shall I endear myself on my host by presenting myself at past eleven o'clock at night?'

'They do keep very early hours up at the Place, by what I hear, sir,' offered the landlord hopefully. 'Was the Squire expecting of you, sir?'

'He was, and I trust still is. Your manner leads me to fear that he will not be pleased by my tardy arrival?'

'Well, sir, begging your pardon, Squire is that pernickety in his ways, and – in a manner of speaking – a testy gentleman – not meaning any disrespect, I'm sure!'

'In fact, I shall *not* endear myself to him by arriving famished on his doorstep at dead of night. Very well. I'll put up here, then.'

The landlord, mentally resolving to have the best sheets instantly put on the bed in the larger of his two guest chambers, ushered his lordship into the coffee-room.

It had only one occupant, a young gentleman who sat in the window embrasure, with a bottle of brandy on the ledge beside him, and a glass in his hand. The landlord, casting a rather worried glance at the bottle, murmured that Mr Tom would not object to a gentleman's dining in the coffee-room. Mr Tom blinked at Lord Stavely, and inclined his head with dignity. He then resumed his scrutiny of the moon-washed street.

His lordship returned the civility by a slight bow, and a smile hovering about his mouth, but made no attempt to lure Mr Tom into conversation. It was apparent to him that care sat upon the young gentleman's brow. It would have been apparent to someone far less acute than Lord Stavely that Mr Tom was, very properly, drowning his troubles in brandy. He might have been any age between nineteen and twenty-five; he was certainly not older. Leanings towards dandyism were betrayed by the intricate but not entirely successful arrangement of his cravat, and by the inordinate height of his shirt collar, whose starched points reached almost to his cheek-bones. But there was little of the dandy in his sturdy figure and fresh-complexioned countenance. He looked like the son of a country gentleman, which, indeed, he was, and as though he would be very much at home in the hunting-field, or with a gun over his shoulder.

In a short time the landlord laid a simple but very tolerable meal before his new guest, and himself waited upon him. Lord Stavely pronounced the fare to be excellent, commended the burgundy, and tactfully declined the only port offered him on the score that he did not wish to encourage a tendency to the gout. He did not look as though he suffered from gout, or any other ailment; in fact, he looked as healthy as any other man of thirty-five; but the landlord did not question his words. He merely swept away the covers and set a bottle of old cognac before him.

For some minutes past Lord Stavely had been aware that the young gentleman in the window was subjecting him to an intent scrutiny. He knew well what was engaging this fixed attention, and when the landlord had withdrawn, he said gently: 'I call it the Nonchalant. It is not very difficult, once you acquire the knack of it.'

'Eh?' said the young gentleman, starting.

'My cravat,' explained Lord Stavely, smiling.

The young gentleman coloured and stammered that he begged pardon.

'Not at all,' said his lordship. 'I'll show you how to tie it, if you like.'

'Will you?' exclaimed the young gentleman eagerly. 'I tie mine in an Osbaldeston, but I don't like it above half.'

Lord Stavely waved one hand invitingly towards a chair at the table. 'Won't you join me?'

'Well – thank you!' The young gentleman got up and crossed the floor circumspectly. He brought his glass and the bottle with him, and set both down on the table. 'My name,' he announced carefully, 'is Hatherleigh.'

'Mine is Stavely,' returned his lordship.

They exchanged bows. Only a purist would have said that Mr Hatherleigh was drunk. He could, by taking only reasonable pains, walk and speak with dignity, and if his potations had had the effect of divorcing his brain a little from the normal, at least it was perfectly clear on all important matters. When Lord Stavely, for instance, touching lightly on the country through which he had driven, said that he should suppose it to be good hunting country, young Hatherleigh was able to expatiate on the subject with enthusiasm and really remarkable coherence. The cloud lifted from his brow, his eyes brightened, and he became quite animated. Then the cloud descended again abruptly, and he fetched a sigh, and said gloomily: 'But that is all at an end! I dare say I may think myself lucky if ever I get a leg across a good hunter again.'

'As bad as that?' said his lordship sympathetically.

Mr Hatherleigh nodded, and poured himself out some more brandy. 'I'm eloping with an heiress,' he announced dejectedly.

If Lord Stavely was startled by this intelligence, he managed to conceal his emotions most creditably. His lip did quiver a little, but he said in the politest way: 'Indeed?'

'Yes,' said Mr Hatherleigh, fortifying himself with a deep drink. 'Gretna Green,' he added.

'Forgive me,' said his lordship, 'but do you feel this to be a wise step to take?'

'No, of course I don't!' said Mr Hatherleigh. 'But what is a fellow to do? I can't draw back now! You must see that!'

'I expect it would be very difficult,' agreed Lord Stavely. 'When one has persuaded an heiress to elope with one –'

'No such thing!' interrupted Mr Hatherleigh. 'I dare say I may have said it would be rare sport to do it, if only to kick up a dust, but I never thought Annabella would think I really meant it! But that is Annabella all over. In fact, I think she's devilish like her father! Let her but once take a notion into her head, and there's no persuading her to listen to reason! Mind, though,' he added, bending a sudden, minatory scowl upon his auditor, 'you are not to be thinking that I wish to back out! I have loved Annabella for years. In fact, I swore a blood-oath to marry her when we were children. But that isn't to say that I want to drive off to the Border with her – and just now, too!'

'The moment is not quite convenient?'

Mr Hatherleigh shook his head. 'My uncle has invited me to Yorkshire for the grouse shooting!' he said bitterly. 'Only think what a splendid time I could have had! I have never tried my hand at grouse, you know, but I am accounted a pretty fair shot.'

'You could not, I suppose, postpone the elopement until after the shooting season?' suggested his lordship.

'No, because if we waited there would be no sense in eloping at all, because very likely Annabella will be tied up to the old fogy her father means her to marry. Besides, the moon's at the full now.'

'I see. And who is this old fogy? Is he *very* old?'

'I don't know, but I should think he must be, wouldn't you, if he's a friend of Sir Walter?'

His lordship paused in the act of raising his glass to his lips. 'Sir Walter?'

'Sir Walter Abingdon. He is Annabella's father.'

'Oh!' said his lordship, sipping his brandy. 'I collect that he does not look with favour on your suit?'

'No, and my father does not either. He says we are too young, and should not suit. So very likely I shall be cut off with a shilling, and be obliged to enter a counting-house, or some such thing, for Sir Walter will certainly cut Annabella off. But of course females never consider anything of that nature! They have not the least common sense, beside thinking that it is perfectly easy to hire a chaise for midnight without making anyone suspicious! And it is *not!*' said Mr Hatherleigh, a strong sense of grievance overcoming him. 'Let alone the expense of it – and that, let me tell you, has pretty well made my pockets to let! I have had to go twenty miles to do it, because a rare flutter I should have set up if I'd bespoke a chaise to go to Scotland at the George, or the Sun! Why, my father would have had wind of it within the hour!

'And then I had to rack my brains to think how best to meet it, because it would never do to have it driving up to my home to pick me up, you know. Luckily old Thetford here is very much attached to our interests, so I told the post-boys in the end to come to this inn at half-past ten tonight. Annabella thinks everyone will be asleep by half-past eleven, or twelve at latest, and she is to meet me in the shrubbery. Shrubbery at midnight!' he repeated scornfully. 'I can tell you, it makes me feel like a great cake! Such flummery!'

He picked up the bottle again as he spoke, and poured some more brandy into his glass. Some of the liquor spilled on to the table. Mr Hatherleigh glared at it, and set the bottle down with precision.

'Do you know,' said Lord Stavely conversationally, 'if I were going to elope at midnight I believe I would not drink too much brandy at ten o'clock?'

Mr Hatherleigh eyed him austerely. 'If you think I'm foxed,' he enunciated, 'you're wrong! I have a very hard head.'

'I'm sure you have,' said his lordship. 'But if Miss Annabella were to detect the fumes on your breath she might not be quite pleased.'

'Well, she shouldn't have insisted on eloping with me!' retorted Mr Hatherleigh.

'She must be very much attached to you?'

'Of course she is. Why, she's known me all her life! All the same, she never would have taken this silly notion into her head if that peppery old fool hadn't asked this fellow to stay, and told her she was to marry him. I must say, I was shocked when Annabella told me of it. I dare say he must be fifty at least, and a dead bore! Besides, she has never clapped eyes on him! I quite saw that as a gentleman I must rescue her, though I never though *then* that my uncle would invite me to stay with him in Yorkshire!'

'But surely even the most peppery of parents cannot in these days marry his daughter out of hand? Must you really elope?' said Lord Stavely.

'Annabella says so, and of course I am bound in honour to oblige her,' replied Mr Hatherleigh grandly. 'I dare say I shan't dislike being married so very much, once I get used to it.'

'I feel very strongly that you are making a mistake,' said his lordship, gently moving the bottle out of reach. 'Perhaps the dead bore will not wish to marry Annabella!'

'Then why is he coming to stay with the Abingdons?' demanded Mr Hatherleigh. 'I expect Sir Walter has it all arranged, in his famous style! My father says he is the most meddlesome, managing old fool in the country.' He drained his glass defiantly. ' 'T all events,' he pronounced, 'it'll be something to overset his precious plans!'

Half an hour later, the landlord, coming in to inform Mr Tom that his chaise was at the door, found that young gentleman stertorously asleep, with his head on the table.

'I don't think,' said Lord Stavely, 'that Mr Tom is in a fit case for travel.'

'There, now, I knew how it would be!' exclaimed Thetford,

looking down at Tom in some concern. 'Whatever can be the matter with him? When I see him this evening, I thought to myself: You're up to mischief, Mr Tom, or I don't know the signs! And here's a chaise and four come all the way from Whitworth to take him up! What's to be done?'

'You had better inform the postilions that Mr Tom is indisposed, and send them back to Whitworth,' said his lordship. 'And while you are about it, will you be so good as to inform my own postilions that I have changed my mind, and mean to go to Melbury Place tonight after all? Desire them to put the horses to at once, if you please.'

'Your lordship won't be staying here?' the landlord said, his face falling. 'And the bed made up, and a hot brick in it to air the sheets!'

'Carry Mr Tom up to it!' recommended Lord Stavely, with a smile. 'When he wakes –' He glanced down at Mr Tom's unconscious form. 'No, perhaps I had better leave a note for him.' He drew out his pocket-book, and after a moment's hesitation scribbled several lines in it in pencil, tore out the leaf, twisted it into a screw, and gave it to the landlord. 'When he wakes, give him that,' he said.

A quarter of an hour later, Thetford having furnished the post-boys with precise instructions. Lord Stavely was bowling along narrow country lanes to Melbury Place. When the gates came into sight, the post-boys would have turned in, but his lordship checked them, and said that he would get down.

They had long since decided that he was an eccentric, but this quite staggered them. 'It's Melbury Place right enough, my lord!' one assured him.

'I am aware. I have a fancy to stroll through the gardens in this exquisite moonlight. Wait here!'

He left them goggling after him. 'He must be as drunk as a wheelbarrow!' said one.

'Not him!' returned his fellow. 'Queer in his attic! I suspicioned it at the start.'

His lordship, meanwhile, was walking up the drive. He very soon left the gravel for the grass bordering it, so that no sound should betray his presence to anyone in the house. The air was heavy with the scent of roses, and the full moon, riding high overhead, cast ink-black shadows on the ground. It showed the house, outlined against a sky of deepest sapphire, and made it an easy matter for his lordship, traversing the flower gardens, to find the shrubbery. Here, neat walks meandered between high hedges, and several rustic seats were set at convenient spots. No one was present, and no light shone from the long, low house in the background. His lordship sat down to await events.

He had not long to wait. After perhaps twenty minutes, he heard the hush of skirts, and rose just as a cloaked figure came swiftly round a bend in the walk, carrying two band-boxes. He stepped forward, but before he could speak the newcomer exclaimed in a muted voice: 'I thought my aunt would never blow out her candle! But she is snoring now! Did you procure a chaise, Tom?'

Lord Stavely took off his hat, and the moonlight showed the lady the face of a complete stranger. She recoiled with a smothered shriek.

'Don't be afraid!' said his lordship reassuringly. 'I am Mr Hatherleigh's deputy. Let me take those boxes!'

'His *deputy*?' echoed Miss Abingdon, nervelessly relinquishing her baggage into his hands.

'Yes,' said Lord Stavely, setting the bandboxes down beside the seat. 'Shall we sit here while I explain it to you?'

'But who are you, and where is Tom?' demanded Miss Abingdon.

'Tom,' said his lordship diplomatically, 'is indisposed. He was good enough to confide his plans to me, and to – er – charge me with his deepest regrets.'

The lady's fright succumbed to a strong feeling of ill-usage. 'Well!' she said, her bosom swelling. 'If that is not the poorest spirited thing I ever heard! I suppose he was afraid?'

'Not at all!' said his lordship, gently propelling her towards the seat. 'He was overcome by a sudden illness.'

Miss Abingdon sat down, perforce, but peered suspiciously at him. 'It sounds to me like a fudge!' she said, not mincing matters. 'He was perfectly well yesterday!'

'His disorder attacked him unawares,' said Lord Stavely.

Miss Abingdon, who seemed to labour under few illusions, demanded forthrightly: 'Was he *foxed*?'

Lord Stavely did not answer for a moment. He looked at the lady, trying to see her face clearly in the moonlight. The hood had slipped back from her head. The uncertain light made it hard for him to decide whether her hair was dark or fair, but he was sure that it curled riotously, and that her eyes were both large and sparkling. He said: 'Foxed? Certainly not!'

'I don't believe you!' said Miss Abingdon. 'How could he be such a simpleton, on this of all nights?'

Lord Stavely returned no answer to this, and after pondering in silence for a few minutes, Miss Abingdon said: 'I did wonder if he quite liked the scheme. But why could he not have told me that he wanted to draw back from it?'

'That,' said Lord Stavely, 'is the last thing he meant to do. He informed me that you had plighted your troth many years ago.'

'Yes,' agreed Miss Abingdon. 'He cut my wrist with his knife, and we mixed our blood. He said I was chicken-hearted because I squeaked.'

'How very unfeeling of him!' said his lordship gravely. 'May I venture to ask if you love him very dearly?'

Miss Abingdon considered the matter. 'Well, I have always been prodigiously fond of him,' she answered at last. 'I dare say I might not have married him, in spite of the oath, had things not been so desperate, but what else could I do when my papa is behaving so abominably, and I am in such despair? I did hope that Papa would hire a house in London for the Season, for I am nearly twenty years old, and I have never been out of Shropshire, except to go to Bath, which I detest. And instead of that he means to marry me to a horrid old man I have never seen!'

'Yes, so Tom told me,' said his lordship. 'But – forgive me – it seems scarcely possible that he could do such a thing!'

'You don't know my papa!' said Miss Abingdon bitterly. 'He makes the most fantastic schemes, and forces everyone to fall in with them! And he says I must be civil to his odious friend, and if I am not he will pack me off to Bath to stay with my Aunt Charlotte! Sir, what could I do? Aunt Maria – who is Papa's other sister, and has lived with us since my mama died – will do nothing but say that I know what Papa is – and I *do*, and I dare say he would have not the least compunction in sending me to a stuffy house in Queen Square, with Aunt's pug wheezing at me, and Aunt scarcely stirring out of the house, but wishing me to play backgammon with her! *Backgammon!*' she reiterated, with loathing.

'That, certainly, is not to be thought of,' agreed his lordship. 'Yet I cannot help wondering if you are quite wise to elope to Gretna Green.'

'You don't think so?' Miss Abingdon said doubtfully.

'These Border marriages are not quite the thing, you know,' explained his lordship apologetically. 'Then, too, unless you are very much in love with Tom, you might not be perfectly happy with him.'

'No,' agreed Miss Abingdon, 'but how shocking it would be if I were to be an old maid!'

'If you will not think me very saucy for saying so,' said his lordship, a laugh in his voice, 'I cannot think that a very likely fate for you!'

'Yes, but it is!' she said earnestly. 'I have been kept cooped up here all my life, and Papa has not the least notion of taking me to London! He has made up his mind to it that his odious friend will be a very eligible match for me. He and this Lady Tenbury laid their heads together, I dare say –'

'So that was it!' interrupted his lordship. 'I should have guessed it, of course.'

Miss Abingdon was surprised. 'Are you acquainted with Lady Tenbury, sir?' she asked.

'My elder sister,' explained his lordship.

'Your – *w-what*?' gasped Miss Abingdon, recoiling.

'Don't be alarmed!' he begged. 'Though I shrink from owning to it, I think I must be your papa's odious friend. But I assure you, Miss Abingdon, his and my meddling sister's schemes come as a complete surprise to me!'

Miss Abingdon swallowed convulsively. 'D-do you m-mean to tell me, sir, that you are Lord Stavely?'

'Yes,' confessed his lordship. He added: 'But though I may be a dead bore, I am not really so very old!'

'You should have told me!' said Miss Abingdon, deeply mortified.

'I know I should, but I could not help nourishing the hope that I might not, after all, be the odious old man you and Tom have described in such daunting terms.'

She turned her face away, saying in a stifled tone: 'I would never . . . Oh, how could you let me run on so?'

'Don't mind it!' he said, taking one of her hands in a comforting clasp. 'Only pray don't elope to Gretna just to escape from my attentions!'

'No, no, but –' She lifted her head and looked at him under brows which he guessed rather than saw to be knit. 'But how *can* you be a friend of my papa?' she asked.

'To tell you the truth, I didn't know that I had the right to call myself so,' he replied. 'He and my family have been upon terms any time these twenty years, I suppose, and I know that he is a close friend of my sister and her husband.'

Miss Abingdon still appeared to be dissatisfied. 'Then how did you come to visit me?'

'If I must answer truthfully,' said his lordship, 'I found it impossible to refuse your parent's repeated invitations with the least degree of civility!'

She seemed to find this understandable. She nodded, and said: 'And you haven't come to – I mean, you didn't know –'

'Until this evening, ma'am,' said his lordship, 'I did not know that you existed! My sister, you see, though quite as meddlesome as your father, has by far more tact.'

'It is the most infamous thing!' declared Miss Abingdon. 'He made me think it had all been arranged, and I had nothing to do but encourage your advances! So naturally I made up my mind to marry Tom rather!' She gave a little spurt of involuntary laughter. 'Was ever anything so non sensical? I thought you had been fifty at least, and very likely fat!'

'I am thirty-five, and I do not *think* I am fat,' said his lordship meekly.

She was still more amused. 'No, I can see you are not! I am afraid I must seem the veriest goose to you! But Papa once thought for a whole month that he would like me to marry Sir Jasper Selkirk, and he is a widower, and has the gout besides! So there is never any telling what absurdity he may have taken into his head, you see.' A thought occurred to her; she turned more fully towards his lordship, and said: 'But how comes it that you are acquainted with Tom, and why are you so late? We were expecting you would arrive to dine, and Papa was in such a fume! And Aunt made them keep dinner back until the chickens were quite spoilt!'

'I cannot sufficiently apologize,' said Lord Stavely. 'A series of unfortunate accidents delayed me shockingly, and when I did at last reach Shropshire I found that your Papa's directions were not quite as helpful as I had supposed they would be. In fact, I lost my way.'

'It is a difficult country,' agreed Miss Abingdon. 'And of course Papa can never direct anyone properly. But how came you to meet Tom?'

'He was awaiting a chaise at the Green Dragon, where, being then so late, I stopped to dine. We fell into conversation, as one does, you know, and he was good enough to confide his intentions to me.'

'He *must* have been drunk!' interpolated Miss Abingdon.

'Let us say, rather, that he was a trifle worried over the propriety of eloping with you. I did what I could to persuade him against taking so ill-advised a step; he – er – succumbed to the disorder from which he was suffering, and I came here in his stead.'

'It was excessively kind of you, but I don't at all know why
you should have taken so much trouble for me!'

He smiled. 'But I could not let you kick your heels in this
shrubbery, could I? Besides, I had the liveliest curiosity to meet
you, Miss Abingdon!'

She tried to see his face. 'Are you quizzing me?' she
demanded.

'Not at all. You will allow that one's curiosity must be
aroused when one learns that a lady is prepared to elope to
escape from advances one had had not the least intention of
making!'

'It is quite dreadful!' she said, blushing. 'I wonder it did not
give you the most shocking disgust of me! But indeed I did
not think it would be improper to elope with Tom, because
he is almost like a brother, you know – and it would have been
such an adventure!'

She ended on a distinctly wistful note. Lord Stavely
responded promptly: 'If your heart is set on the adventure, my
chaise is waiting in the lane: you have only to command me!'

Another of her gurgling laughs escaped her. 'How can you
be so absurd? As though I would elope with a stranger!'

'Well, I do feel it might be better if you gave up the notion,'
he said. 'I fear I can hardly draw back now from Sir Walter's
invitation, but if I give you my word not to press an unwanted
suit upon you perhaps you may not find my visit insupportably
distasteful.'

'No, no!' she assured him. 'But I very much fear that Papa
may – may cause you a great deal of embarrassment, sir!'

'Quite impossible!' he said, smiling. 'Have no fear on
that head!'

'You are the most truly amiable man I ever met!' she
exclaimed warmly. 'Indeed, I am very much obliged to you,
and quite ashamed to think I should have misjudged you so!
You – you won't tell Papa?'

'Miss Abingdon, *that* is the unkindest thing you have yet
said to me!'

'No. I know you would not!' she said quickly. She rose

and held out her hand. 'I must go back to the house. But you?'

'In about twenty minutes' time,' said Lord Stavely, 'I shall drive up to the front door, with profuse apologies and excuses!'

'Oh, shall you indeed do that?' giggled Miss Abingdon. 'It must be close on midnight! Papa will be so cross!'

'Well, I must brave his wrath,' he said, raising her hand to his lips.

Her hand clung to his; Miss Abingdon jerked up her head and stood listening. In another instant Lord Stavely had also heard what had startled her: footsteps which tried to be stealthy, and a voice whose owner seemed to imagine himself to be speaking under his breath: 'Do you go that way, Mullins, and I'll go this, and mind, no noise!'

'Papa!' breathed Miss Abingdon, in a panic. 'He must have heard me: I tripped on the gravel! Depend upon it, he thinks we are thieves: Sir Jasper was robbed last month! What am I to do?'

'Can you reach the house without being observed if I draw them off?' asked his lordship softly.

'Yes, yes, but you? Papa will very likely have his fowling-piece!'

'Be sure I shall declare myself before he fires at me!' He picked up the bandboxes and gave them to her.

She clutched them and fled. Lord Stavely, having watched her disappear round a corner of the shrubbery, set his hat on his head and sauntered in the opposite direction, taking care to advertise his presence.

He emerged from the shrubbery into the rose garden, and was almost immediately challenged by an elderly gentleman who did indeed level a fowling-piece at him.

'Stand! I have you covered, rogue!' shouted Sir Walter. 'Mullins, you fool, here!'

Lord Stavely stood still, waiting for his host to approach him. This Sir Walter did not do until he had been reinforced by his butler, similarly armed, and sketchily attired in a nightshirt, a pair of breeches, and a greatcoat thrown over all. He then came forward, keeping his lordship covered, and said with gleeful satisfaction: 'Caught you, my lad!'

'How do you do, sir?' said Lord Stavely, holding out his hand. 'I must beg your pardon for presenting myself at this unconscionable hour, but I have been dogged by ill fortune all day. A broken lynch-pin and a lame horse must stand as my excuses.'

Sir Walter nearly dropped his piece. '*Stavely?*' he ejaculated, peering at his lordship in amazement.

Lord Stavely bowed.

'But what the devil are you doing in my garden?' Sir Walter demanded.

Lord Stavely waved an airy hand. 'Communing with Nature, sir, communing with Nature!'

'*Communing with Nature?*' echoed Sir Walter, his eyes fairly starting from his head.

'Roses bathed in moonlight!' said his lordship lyrically. 'Ah – must Mullins continue to point his piece at me?'

'Put it down, you fool!' commanded Sir Walter testily. 'Stavely, my dear fellow, are you feeling quite the thing?'

'Never better!' replied his lordship. 'Oh, you are thinking that I should have driven straight up to the house? Very true, sir, but I was lured out of my chaise by this exquisite scene. I am passionately fond of moonlight, and really, you know, your gardens present so charming a picture that I could not but yield to temptation, and explore them. I am sorry to have disturbed you!'

Sir Walter was staring at him with his jaw dropping almost as prodigiously as the butler's. 'Explore my gardens at midnight!' he uttered, in stupefied accents.

'Is it so late?' said his lordship. 'Yet I dare say one might see to read a book in this clear light!'

Sir Walter swallowed twice before venturing on a response. 'But where's your carriage?' he demanded.

'I told the post-boys to wait in the lane,' replied his lordship vaguely. 'I believe – yes, I believe I can detect the scent of jasmine!'

'Stavely,' said Sir Walter, laying an almost timid hand on his arm, 'do but come up to the house, and to bed! Everything is prepared, and this night air is most unwholesome!'

'On the contrary, I find that it awakens poetry in my soul,' said Lord Stavely. 'I am inspired to write a sonnet on roses drenched with moonshine.'

'Mullins, go and find his lordship's chaise, and direct the postilions to drive up to the house!' ordered Sir Walter, in an urgent under-voice. 'Sonnets, eh, Stavely? Yes, yes, I have been a rhymester in my time, too, but just come with me, my dear fellow, and you will soon feel better, I dare say! You have had a long and a tedious journey, that's what it is!'

He took his guest by the arm and firmly drew him towards the house. His lordship went with him unresisting, but maintained a slow pace, and frequently paused to admire some effect of trees against the night sky, or the sheen of moonlight on the lily-pond. Sir Walter, curbing his impatience, replied soothingly to these flights, and succeeded at last in coaxing him into the house, and upstairs to the chamber prepared for him. A suspicion that his noble guest had been imbibing too freely gave place to a far worse fear. Not until he was assured by the sound of my lord's deep breathing that he was sleeping soundly did Sir Walter retire from his post outside his guest's door and seek his own couch.

Lord Stavely and Miss Abingdon met officially at a late breakfast table. Sir Walter performed the introduction, eyeing his guest narrowly as he did so.

Lord Stavely, bowing first to Miss Maria Abingdon, apologized gracefully for having knocked the household up at such a late hour, and then turned to confront the heiress. For her part, she had been covertly studying him while he exchanged civilities with her aunt. She was very favourably impressed by what she saw. Lord Stavely was generally held to be a personable man. Miss Abingdon found no reason to quarrel with popular opinion. He had a pair of smiling grey eyes, a humorous mouth and an excellent figure. Both air and address were polished, and his raiment, without being dandified, was extremely elegant. He wore pantaloons and Hessians, which set off his legs to advantage; and Miss Abingdon noticed that his snow-white cravat was arranged in precise and intricate folds.

Miss Abingdon had surprised her aunt by choosing to wear quite her most becoming sprigged muslin gown. Miss Maria, who had despaired of detecting any such signs of docility in her niece, was further startled to observe that nothing could have been more demure than Annabella's behaviour. She seemed quite to have recovered from her sulks, curtsied shyly to the guest, and gave him her hand with the most enchanting and mischievous of smiles. Really, thought Miss Maria, watching her fondly, the child looked quite lovely!

Lord Stavely talked easily at the breakfast-table, ably assisted by both ladies. Sir Walter seemed a trifle preoccupied, and when they rose from the table, and his lordship begged leave to wander out into the sunlit garden, he acquiesced readily, and scarcely waited for his guest to step out through the long window before hurrying out of the room in his daughter's wake. He overtook her at the foot of the stairs, and peremptorily summoned her to his library. Shutting the door behind her, he said without preamble: 'Annabella, you need not be in a pet, for I have changed my plans for you! Yes, yes, I no longer think of Stavely for you, so let us have no more tantrums!'

Miss Abingdon's large blue eyes flew to his. 'Changed your plans for me, Papa?' she exclaimed.

He looked round cautiously, as though to be sure that his guest was not lurking in the room, and then said in an earnest tone: 'My dear, it is the most distressing circumstance! The poor fellow is deranged! You would never credit it, I dare say, but I found him wandering about the garden at midnight, talking of sonnets, and moonlight, and such stuff!'

Miss Abingdon lowered her gaze swiftly and faltered: 'Did you, Papa? How – how very strange, to be sure!'

'I was never more shocked in my life!' declared Sir Walter. 'I had not the least notion of such a thing, and I must say that I think Louisa Tenbury has not behaved as she should in concealing it from me!'

'It is very dreadful!' agreed Miss Abingdon. 'Yet he *seems* quite sane, Papa!'

'He seems sane *now*,' said her parent darkly, 'but we don't know what he may do when the moon is up! I believe some lunatics are only deranged at the full of the moon. And now I come to think of it, they used to say that his grandfather had some queer turns! Not that I believed it, but I see now that it may well have been so. I wish I had not pressed him to visit us! You had better take care, my child, not to be in his company unless I am at hand to protect you!'

Miss Abingdon, who, out of the tail of her eye, had seen Lord Stavely strolling in the direction of the rose garden, returned a dutiful answer, and proceeded without loss of time to follow his lordship.

She found him looking down at the sundial in the middle of a rose plot. He glanced up at her approach and smiled, moving to meet her. Her face was glowing with mischief, her eyes dancing. She said: 'Oh, my lord, Papa says you are mad, and he does not in the least wish me to marry you!'

He took her hands and held them. 'I know it. Now, what am I to do to convince him that I am in the fullest possession of my senses?'

'Why, what should it signify?' she asked. 'I am sure you do not care what he may think! I don't know how I kept my countenance! He says I must take care not to be in your company, unless he is at hand to protect me!'

'I see nothing to laugh at in that!' he protested.

She looked up innocently. 'I am so very sorry! But indeed I did not think that you would care!'

'On the contrary, it is of the first importance that your papa should think well of me.'

'Good gracious, why?'

'My dear Miss Abingdon, how can I persuade him to permit me to pay my addresses to you if he believes me to be mad?'

For a moment she stared at him; then her cheeks became suffused, and she pulled her hands away, saying faintly: '*Oh!* But you said you would not – you know you did!'

'I know nothing of the sort. I said I would not press an unwanted suit upon you. Do not take from me all hope of being able to make myself agreeable to you!'

Miss Abingdon, no longer meeting his eyes, murmured something not very intelligible, and began to nip off the faded blooms from a fine rose tree.

'I must study to please Sir Walter,' said his lordship. 'How is it to be done? I rely upon your superior knowledge of him!'

Miss Abingdon, bending down to pluck a half-blown rose, said haltingly: 'Well, if – if you don't wish him to believe you mad, perhaps – perhaps you had better remain with us for a little while, so that he may be brought to realize that you are quite sane!'

'An excellent plan!' approved his lordship. 'I shall be guided entirely by your advice, Miss Abingdon. May I have that rose?'

Sir Walter, informed by the gardener of the whereabouts of his guest and his daughter, came into the rose garden in time to see Miss Abingdon fix a pink rose-bud in the lapel of Lord Stavely's coat. His reflections on the perversity and undutifulness of females he was obliged to keep to himself, but he told Miss Abingdon, with some asperity, that her aunt was searching for her, and taking Lord Stavely by the arm, marched him off to inspect the stables.

Miss Abingdon found her aunt in a state of nervous flutter, having been informed by her brother of their guest's derangement. 'And I thought him such a sensible man! So handsome, too, and so truly amiable!'

'Oh, my dear aunt, is he not the most delightful creature?' confided Miss Abingdon, eyes and cheeks aglow. 'Only fancy his wishing to marry me!'

Miss Maria started. 'No, no, that is quite at an end! Your papa would never hear of it! And when I think that only yesterday you were vowing you would marry Tom Hatherleigh in spite of anything your papa could say, I declare I don't know what can have come over you!'

'Moon madness!' laughed Miss Abingdon. 'Just like Lord Stavely! *Poor* Papa!'

A Dunnet Shepherdess

from *The Country of the Pointed Firs*

SARAH ORNE JEWETT

SARAH ORNE JEWETT (1843–1909). This American novelist and short story writer was born and brought up in South Berwick, Maine, where her father was a doctor. In The Country of the Pointed Firs *she produced a minor classic of American literature.*

I

EARLY one morning at Dunnet Landing, as if it were still night, I waked, suddenly startled by a spirited conversation beneath my window. It was not one of Mrs Todd's morning soliloquies; she was not addressing her plants and flowers in words of either praise or blame. Her voice was declamatory though perfectly good-humoured, while the second voice, a man's, was of lower pitch and somewhat deprecating.

The sun was just above the sea, and struck straight across my room through a crack in the blind. It was a strange hour for the arrival of a guest, and still too soon for the general run of business, even in that tiny eastern haven where daybreak fisheries and early tides must often rule the day.

The man's voice suddenly declared itself to my sleepy ears. It was Mr William Blackett's.

'Why, sister Almiry,' he protested gently, 'I don't need none o' your nostrums!'

'Pick me a small han'ful,' she commanded. 'No, no, a *small* han'ful, I said, o' them large pennyr'yal sprigs! I go to all the trouble an' cossetin' of 'em just so as to have you ready to meet such occasions, an' last year, you may remember, you never stopped here at all the day you went up country. An' the frost come at last an' blacked it. I never saw any herb that so objected to gardin ground; might as well try to flourish mayflowers in a common front yard. There, you can come in now, an' set and eat what breakfast you've got patience for. I've found everything I want, an' I'll mash 'em up an' be all ready to put 'em on.'

I heard such a pleading note of appeal as the speakers went round the corner of the house, and my curiosity was so demanding, that I dressed in haste, and joined my friends a little later, with two unnoticed excuses of the beauty of the morning, and the early mail boat. William's breakfast had been slighted; he had taken his cup of tea and merely pushed back the rest on the kitchen table. He was now sitting in a helpless condition by the side window, with one of his sister's purple calico aprons pinned close about his neck. Poor William was meekly submitting to being smeared, as to his countenance, with a most pungent and unattractive lotion of pennyroyal and other green herbs which had been hastily pounded and mixed with cream in the little white stone mortar.

I had to cast two or three straightforward looks at William to reassure myself that he really looked happy and expectant in spite of his melancholy circumstances, and was not being overtaken by retribution. The brother and sister seemed to be on delightful terms with each other for once, and there was something of cheerful anticipation in their morning talk. I was reminded of Medea's anointing Jason before the great episode of the iron bulls, but to-day William really could not be going up country to see a railroad for the first time. I knew this to be one of his great schemes, but he was not fitted to appear in public, or to front an observing world of strangers. As I appeared he essayed to rise, but Mrs Todd pushed him back into the chair.

'Set where you be till it dries on,' she insisted. 'Land sakes, you'd think he'd get over bein' a boy some time or 'nother, gettin' along in years as he is. An' you'd think he'd seen full enough o' fish, but once a year he has to break loose like this, an' travel off way up back o' the Bowden place – far out o' my beat, 't is – an' go a trout fishin'!'

Her tone of amused scorn was so full of challenge that William changed colour even under the green streaks.

'I want some change,' he said, looking at me and not at her. ''T is the prettiest little shady brook you ever saw.'

'If he ever fetched home more'n a couple o' minnies, 't would seem worth while,' Mrs Todd concluded, putting a last dab of the mysterious compound so perilously near her brother's mouth that William flushed again and was silent.

A little later I witnessed his escape, when Mrs Todd had taken the foolish risk of going down cellar. There was a horse and waggon outside the garden fence, and presently we stood where we could see him driving up the hill with thoughtless speed. Mrs Todd said nothing, but watched him affectionately out of sight.

'It serves to keep the mosquitoes off,' she said, and a moment later it occurred to my slow mind that she spoke of the pennyroyal lotion. 'I don't know sometimes but William's kind of poetical,' she continued, in her gentlest voice. 'You'd think if anything could cure him of it, 't would be the fish business.'

It was only twenty minutes past six on a summer morning, but we both sat down to rest as if the activities of the day were over. Mrs Todd rocked gently for a time, and seemed to be lost, though not poorly, like Macbeth, in her thoughts. At last she resumed relations with her actual surroundings. 'I shall now put my lobsters on. They'll make us a good supper,' she announced. 'Then I can let the fire out for all day: give it a holiday, same's William. You can have a little one now, nice an' hot, if you ain't got all the breakfast you want. Yes, I'll put the lobsters on. William was very thoughtful to bring 'em over; William *is* thoughtful; if he only had a spark o' ambition, there be few could match him.'

This unusual concession was afforded a sympathetic listener from the depths of the kitchen closet. Mrs Todd was getting out her old iron lobster pot, and began to speak of prosaic affairs. I hoped that I should hear something more about her brother and their island life, and sat idly by the kitchen window looking at the morning glories that shaded it, believing that some flaw of wind might set Mrs Todd's mind on its former course. Then it occurred to me that she had spoken about our supper rather than our dinner, and I guessed that she might have some great scheme before her for the day.

When I had loitered for some time and there was no further word about William, and at last I was conscious of receiving no attention whatever, I went away. It was something of a disappointment to find that she put no hindrance in the way of my usual morning affairs, of going up to the empty little white schoolhouse on the hill where I did my task of writing. I had been almost sure of a holiday when I discovered that Mrs Todd was likely to take one herself; we had not been far afield to gather herbs and pleasures for many days now, but a little later she had silently vanished. I found my luncheon ready on the table in the little entry, wrapped in its shining old homespun napkin, and as if by way of special consolation, there was a stone bottle of Mrs Todd's best spruce beer, with a long piece of codline round it by which it could be lowered for coolness into the deep schoolhouse well.

I walked away with a dull supply of writing-paper and these provisions, feeling like a reluctant child who hopes to be called back at every step. There was no relenting voice to be heard, and when I reached the schoolhouse, I found that I had left an open window and a swinging shutter the day before, and the sea wind that blew at evening had fluttered my poor sheaf of papers all about the room.

So the day did not begin very well, and I began to recognise that it was one of the days when nothing could be done without company. The truth was that my heart had gone trouting with William, but it would have been too selfish to say a word even to one's self about spoiling his day. If there is one way above another of getting so close to nature that one simply is a piece of nature, following a primeval instinct with perfect self-forgetfulness and forgetting everything except the dreamy consciousness of pleasant freedom, it is to take the course of a shady trout brook. The dark pools and the sunny shallows beckon one on; the wedge of sky between the trees on either bank, the speaking, companioning noise of the water, the amazing importance of what one is doing, and the constant sense of life and beauty make a strange transformation of the quick hours. I had a sudden memory of all this, and another, and another. I could not get myself free from 'fishing and wishing.'

At that moment I heard the unusual sound of wheels, and I looked past the high-growing thicket of wild roses and straggling sumach to see the white nose and meagre shape of the Caplin horse; then I saw William sitting in the open waggon, with a small, expectant smile upon his face.

'I've got two lines,' he said. 'I was quite a piece up the road. I thought perhaps 'twas so you'd feel like going.'

There was enough excitement for most occasions in hearing William speak three sentences at once. Words seemed but vain to me at that bright moment. I stepped back from the schoolhouse window with a beating heart. The spruce-beer bottle was not yet in the well, and with that and my luncheon, and Pleasure at the helm, I went out into the happy world. The land breeze was blowing and, as we turned away, I saw a flutter of white go past the window as I left the schoolhouse and my morning's work to their neglected fate.

II

One seldom gave way to a cruel impulse to look at an ancient seafaring William, but one felt as if he were a growing boy; I only hope that he felt much the same about me. He did not wear the fishing clothes that belonged to his sea-going life, but a strangely shaped old suit of tea-coloured linen garments that might have been brought home years ago from Canton or Bombay. William had a peculiar way of giving silent assent when one spoke, but of answering your unspoken thoughts as if they reached him better than words. 'I find them very easy,' he said, frankly, referring to the clothes. 'Father had them in his old sea-chest.'

The antique fashion, a quaint touch of foreign grace and even imagination about the cut were very pleasing; if ever Mr William Blackett had faintly resembled an old beau, it was upon that day. He now appeared to feel as if everything had been explained between us, as if everything were quite understood; and we drove for some distance without finding it necessary to speak again about anything. At last, when it must have been a little past nine o'clock, he stopped the horse beside a small farmhouse, and nodded when I asked if I should get down from the waggon. 'You can steer about north-east right across the pasture,' he said, looking from under the eaves of his hat with an expectant smile. 'I always leave the team here.'

I helped to unfasten the harness, and William led the horse away to the barn. It was a poor-looking little place, and a forlorn woman looked at us through the window before she appeared at the door. I told her that Mr Blackett and I came up from the Landing to go fishing. 'He keeps a-comin', don't he?' she answered, with a funny little laugh, to which I was at a loss to find answer. When he joined us, I could not see that he took notice of her presence in any way, except to take an armful of dried salt fish from a corded stack in the back of the waggon which had been carefully covered with a piece of old sail. We had left a wake of their pungent flavour behind us all the way. I wondered what was going to become of the rest of them, and some fresh lobsters which were also disclosed to view, but he laid the present gift on the doorstep without a word, and a few minutes later, when I looked back as we crossed the pasture, the fish were being carried into the house.

I could not see any signs of a trout brook until I came close upon it in the bushy pasture, and presently we struck into the low woods of straggling spruce and fir mixed into a tangle of swamp maples and alders which stretched away on either hand up and down stream. We found an open place in the pasture where some taller trees seemed to have been overlooked rather than spared. The sun was bright and hot by this time, and I sat down in the shade while William produced his lines and cut and trimmed us each a slender rod. I wondered where Mrs Todd was spending the morning, and if later she would think that pirates had landed and captured me from the schoolhouse.

III

The brook was giving that live, persistent call to a listener that trout brooks always make; it ran with a free, swift current even here, where it crossed an apparently level piece of land. I saw two unpromising, quick barbel chase each other upstream from bank to bank as we solemnly arranged our hooks and sinkers. I felt that William's glances changed from anxiety to relief when he found that I was used to such gear; perhaps he felt that we must stay together if I could not bait my own hook, but we parted happily, full of a pleasing sense of companionship.

William had pointed me up the brook, but I chose to go down, which was only fair because it was his day, though one likes as well to follow and see where a brook goes as to find one's way to the places it comes from, and its tiny springs and headwaters, and in this case trout were not to be considered. William's only real anxiety was lest I might suffer from mosquitoes. His own complexion was still strangely impaired by its defences, but I kept forgetting it, and looking to see if we were treading fresh pennyroyal underfoot, so efficient was Mrs Todd's remedy. I was conscious, after we parted, and I turned to see if he were already fishing, and saw him wave his hand gallantly as he went away, that our friendship had made a great gain.

The moment that I began to fish the brook, I had a sense of

its emptiness; when my bait first touched the water and went lightly down the quick stream, I knew that there was nothing to lie in wait for it. It is the same certainty that comes when one knocks at the door of an empty house, a lack of answering consciousness and of possible response; it is quite different if there is any life within. But it was a lovely brook, and I went a long way through woods and breezy open pastures, and found a forsaken house and overgrown farm, and laid up many pleasures for future joy and remembrance. At the end of the morning I came back to our meeting-place hungry and without any fish. William was already waiting, and we did not mention the matter of trout. We ate our luncheons with good appetites, and William brought our two stone bottles of spruce beer from the deep place in the brook where he had left them cool. Then we sat awhile longer in peace and quietness on the green banks.

As for William, he looked more boyish than ever, and kept a more remote and juvenile sort of silence. Once I wondered how he had come to be so curiously wrinkled, forgetting, absent-mindedly, to recognise the effects of time. He did not expect anyone else to keep up a vain show of conversation, and so I was silent as well as he. I glanced at him now and then, but I watched the leaves tossing against the sky and the red cattle moving in the pasture. 'I don't know's we need head for home. It's early yet,' he said at last, and I was as startled as if one of the gray firs had spoken.

'I guess I'll go up-along and ask after Thankful Hight's folks,' he continued. 'Mother'd like to get word'; and I nodded a pleased assent.

IV

William led the way across the pasture, and I followed with a deep sense of pleased anticipation. I do not believe that my companion had expected me to make any objection, but I knew that he was gratified by the easy way that his plans for the day were being seconded. He gave a look at the sky to see if there were any portents, but the sky was frankly blue; even the doubtful morning haze had disappeared.

We went northward along a rough, clayey road, across a bare-looking, sunburnt country full of tiresome long slopes where the sun was hot and bright, and I could not help observing the forlorn look of the farms. There was a good deal of pasture, but it looked deserted, and I wondered afresh why the people did not raise more sheep when that seemed the only possible use to make of their land. I said so to Mr Blackett, who gave me a look of pleased surprise.

'That's what She always maintains,' he said eagerly. 'She's right about it too; well, you'll see!' I was glad to find myself approved, but I had not the least idea whom he meant, and waited until he felt like speaking again.

A few minutes later we drove down a steep hill and entered a large tract of dark spruce woods. It was delightful to be sheltered from the afternoon sun, and when we had gone some distance in the shade, to my great pleasure William turned the horse's head toward some bars, which he let down, and I drove through into one of those narrow, still, sweet-scented byways which seem to be paths rather than roads. Often we had to put aside the heavy drooping branches which barred the way, and once, when a sharp twig struck William in the face, he announced with such spirit that somebody ought to go through there with an axe, that I felt unexpectedly guilty. So far as I now remember, this was William's only remark all the way through the woods to Thankful Hight's folks, but from time to time he pointed or nodded at something which I might have missed: a sleepy little owl snuggled into the bend of a branch, or a tall stalk of cardinal flowers where the sunlight came down at the edge of a small, bright piece of marsh. Many times, being used to the company of Mrs Todd and other friends who were in the habit of talking, I came near making an idle remark to William, but I was for the most part happily preserved; to be with him only for a short time was to live on a different level, where thoughts served best because they were thoughts in common; the primary effect upon our

minds of the simple things and beauties that we saw. Once
when I caught sight of a lovely gay pigeon woodpecker eyeing
us curiously from a dead branch, and instinctively turned
toward William, he gave an indulgent, comprehending nod
which silenced me all the rest of the way. The wood-road
was not a place for common, noisy conversation; one would
interrupt the birds and all the still little beasts that belonged
there. But it was mortifying to find how strong the habit of
idle speech may become in one's self. One need not always be
saying something in this noisy world. I grew conscious of the
difference between William's usual fashion of life and mine;
for him there were long days of silence in a sea-going boat, and
I could believe that he and his mother usually spoke very little
because they so perfectly understood each other. There was
something peculiarly unresponding about their quiet island in
the sea, solidly fixed into the still foundations of the world,
against whose rocky shores the sea beats and calls and is
unanswered.

We were quite half an hour going through the woods; the
horse's feet made no sound on the brown, soft track under
the dark evergreens. I thought that we should come out at
last into more pastures, but there was no half-wooded strip
of land at the end; the high woods grew squarely against an
old stone wall and a sunshiny open field, and we came out
suddenly into broad daylight that startled us and even startled
the horse, who might have been napping as he walked, like an
old soldier. The field sloped up to a low unpainted house that
faced the east. Behind it were long, frost-whitened ledges that
made the hill, with strips of green turf and bushes between.
It was the wildest, most Titanic sort of pasture country up
there; there was a sort of daring in putting a frail wooden
house before it, though it might have the homely field and
honest woods to front against. You thought of the elements
and even of possible volcanoes as you looked up the stony
heights. Suddenly I saw that a region of what I had thought
gray stones was slowly moving, as if the sun was making my
eyesight unsteady.

'There's the sheep!' exclaimed William, pointing eagerly. 'You see the sheep?' and sure enough, it was a great company of woolly backs, which seemed to have taken a mysterious protective resemblance to the ledges themselves. I could discover but little chance for pasturage on that high sunburnt ridge, but the sheep were moving steadily in a satisfied way as they fed along the slopes and hollows.

'I never have seen half so many sheep as these, all summer long!' I cried with admiration.

'There ain't so many,' answered William soberly. 'It's a great sight. They do so well because they're shepherded, but you can't beat sense into some folks.'

'You mean that somebody stays and watches them?' I asked.

'She observed years ago in her readin' that they don't turn out their flocks without protection anywhere but in the State o' Maine,' returned William. 'First thing that put it into her mind was a little old book mother's got; she read it one time when she come out to the Island. They call it the *Shepherd o' Salisbury Plain*. 'T wasn't the purpose o' the book to most, but when she read it, 'There, Mis' Blackett!' she said, 'that's where we've all lacked sense; our Bibles ought to have taught us that what sheep need is a shepherd.' You see most folks about here gave up sheep-raisin' years ago 'count o' the dogs. So she gave up school-teachin' and went out to tend her flock, and has shepherded ever since, an' done well.'

For William, this approached an oration. He spoke with enthusiasm, and I shared the triumph of the moment. 'There she is now!' he exclaimed, in a different tone, as the tall figure of a woman came following the flock and stood still on the ridge, looking toward us as if her eyes had been quick to see a strange object in the familiar emptiness of the field. William stood up in the waggon, and I thought he was going to call or wave his hand to her, but he sat down again more clumsily than if the waggon had made the familiar motion of a boat, and we drove on toward the house.

It was a most solitary place to live – a place where one

might think that a life could hide itself. The thick woods were between the farm and the main road, and as one looked up and down the country, there was no other house in sight.

'Potatoes look well,' announced William. 'The old folks used to say that there wa'n't no better land outdoors than the Hight field.'

I found myself possessed of a surprising interest in the shepherdess, who stood far away in the hill pasture with her great flock, like a figure of Millet's high against the sky.

V

Everything about the old farmhouse was clean and orderly, as if the green dooryard were not only swept, but dusted. I saw a flock of turkeys stepping off carefully at a distance, but there was not the usual untidy flock of hens about the place to make everything look in disarray. William helped me out of the waggon as carefully as if I had been his mother, and nodded toward the open door with a reassuring look at me; but I waited until he had tied the horse and could lead the way, himself. He took off his hat just as we were going in, and stopped for a moment to smooth his thin gray hair with his hand, by which I saw that we had an affair of some ceremony. We entered an old-fashioned country kitchen, the floor scrubbed into unevenness and the doors well polished by the touch of hands. In a large chair facing the window there sat a masterful-looking old woman with the features of a warlike Roman emperor, emphasised by a bonnet-like black cap with a band of green ribbon. Her sceptre was a palm-leaf fan.

William crossed the room toward her, and bent his head close to her ear.

'Feelin' pretty well to-day, Mis' Hight?' he asked, with all the voice his narrow chest could muster.

'No, I ain't, William. Here I have to set,' she answered coldly, but she gave an inquiring glance over his shoulder at me.

'This is the young lady who is stopping with Almiry this

summer,' he explained, and I approached as if to give the countersign. She offered her left hand with considerable dignity, but her expression never seemed to change for the better. A moment later she said that she was pleased to meet me, and I felt as if the worst were over. William must have felt some apprehension, while I was only ignorant, as we had come across the field. Our hostess was more than disapproving, she was forbidding; but I was not long in suspecting that she felt the natural resentment of a strong energy that has been defeated by illness and made the spoil of captivity.

'Mother well as usual since you was up last year?' and William replied by a series of cheerful nods. The mention of dear Mrs Blackett was a help to any conversation.

'Been fishin', ashore,' he explained, in a somewhat conciliatory voice. 'Thought you'd like a few for winter,' which explained at once the generous freight we had brought in the back of the waggon. I could see that the offering was no surprise, and that Mrs Hight was interested.

'Well, I expect they're good as the last,' she said, but did not even approach a smile. She kept a straight, discerning eye upon me.

'Give the lady a cheer,' she admonished William, who hastened to place close by her side one of the straight-backed chairs that stood against the kitchen wall. Then he lingered for a moment like a timid boy. I could see that he wore a look of resolve, but he did not ask the permission for which he evidently waited.

'You can go search for Esther,' she said, at the end of a long pause that became anxious for both her guests. 'Esther'd like to see her'; and William in his pale nankeens disappeared with one light step and was off.

VI

'Don't speak too loud, it jars a person's head,' directed Mrs Hight plainly. 'Clear an' distinct is what reaches me best. Any news to the Landin'?'

I was happily furnished with the particulars of a sudden death, and an engagement of marriage between a Caplin, a seafaring widower home from his voyage, and one of the younger Harrises; and now Mrs Hight really smiled and settled herself in her chair. We exhausted one subject completely before we turned to the other. One of the returning turkeys took an unwarranted liberty, and, mounting the doorstep, came in and walked about the kitchen without being observed by its strict owner; and the tin dipper slipped off its nail behind us and made an astonishing noise, and jar enough to reach Mrs Hight's inner ear and make her turn her head to look at it; but we talked straight on. We came at last to understand each other upon such terms of friendship that she unbent her majestic port and complained to me as any poor old woman might of the hardships of her illness. She had already fixed various dates upon the sad certainty of the year when she had the shock, which had left her perfectly helpless except for a clumsy left hand which fanned and gestured, and settled and resettled the folds of her dress, but could do no comfortable time-shortening work.

'Yes'm, you can feel sure I use it what I can,' she said severely. "'T was a long spell before I could let Esther go forth in the mornin' till she'd got me up an' dressed me, but now she leaves things ready overnight, and I get 'em as I want 'em with my light pair o' tongs, and I feel very able about helpin' myself to what I once did. Then when Esther returns, all she has to do is to push me out here into the kitchen. Some parts o' the year Esther stays out all night, them moonlight nights when the dogs are apt to be after the sheep, but she don't use herself as hard as she once had to. She's well able to hire somebody, Esther is, but there, you can't find no hired man that wants to git up before five o'clock nowadays; 't aint as 't was in my time. They're liable to fall asleep too, and them moonlight nights she's so anxious she can't sleep, and out she goes. There's a kind of a fold, she calls it, up there in a sheltered spot, and she sleeps up in a little shed she's got – built it herself for lambin' time and when the poor foolish creatures gets hurt or anything. I've never seen it, but she says it's in a lovely spot and always pleasant in any weather. You see off, other side of the ridge, to the south'ard, where there's houses. I used to think some time I'd get up to see it again, and all them spots she lives in, but I shan't now. I'm beginnin' to go back; an' 't aint surprisin'. I've kind of got used to disappointments,' and the poor soul drew a deep sigh.

VII

It was long before we noticed the lapse of time; I not only told every circumstance known to me of recent events among the households of Mrs Todd's neighbourhood at the shore, but Mrs Hight became more and more communicative on her part, and went carefully into the genealogical descent and personal experience of many acquaintances, until between us we had pretty nearly circumnavigated the globe and reached Dunnet Landing from an opposite direction to that in which we had started. It was long before my own interest began to flag; there was a flavour of the best sort in her definite and descriptive fashion of speech. It may be only a fancy of my own that in the sound and value of many words, with their lengthened vowels and doubled cadences, there is some faint survival on the Maine coast of the sound of English speech of Chaucer's time.

At last Mrs Thankful Hight gave a suspicious look through the window.

'Where do you suppose they be?' she asked me. 'Esther must ha' been off to the far edge o' everything. I doubt William ain't been able to find her; can't he hear their bells? His hearin's all right?'

William had heard some herons that morning which were almost beyond the reach of my own ears, and almost beyond eyesight in the upper skies, and I told her so. I was luckily preserved by some unconscious instinct from saying that we had seen the shepherdess so near as we crossed the field. Unless she had fled faster than Atalanta, William must have been but a few minutes in reaching her immediate neighbourhood. I now discovered with a quick leap of amusement and delight in my heart that I had fallen upon a serious chapter of romance. The old woman looked suspiciously at me, and I made a dash to cover with a new piece of information; but she listened with lofty indifference, and soon interrupted my eager statements.

'Ain't William been gone some considerable time?' she demanded, and then in a milder tone: 'The time has re'lly flown; I do enjoy havin' company. I set here alone a sight o' long days. Sheep is dreadful fools; I expect they heerd a strange step, and set right off through bush and brier, spite of all she could do. But William might have the sense to return, 'stead o' searchin' about. I want to inquire of him about his mother. What was you goin' to say? I guess you'll have time to relate it.'

My powers of entertainment were on the ebb, but I doubled my diligence and we went on for another half hour at least with banners flying, but still William did not reappear. Mrs Hight frankly began to show fatigue.

'Somethin's happened, an' he's stopped to help her,' groaned the old lady, in the middle of what I had found to tell her about a rumour of disaffection with the minister of a town I merely knew by name in the weekly newspaper to which Mrs Todd subscribed. 'You step to the door, dear, an' look if you can't see 'em.' I promptly stepped, and once outside the house I looked anxiously in the direction which William had taken.

To my astonishment I saw all the sheep so near that I wonder we had not been aware in the house of every bleat and tinkle. And there, within a stone's throw, on the first long gray ridge that showed above the juniper, were William and the shepherdess engaged in pleasant conversation. At first I was provoked and then amused, and a thrill of sympathy warmed my whole heart. They had seen me and risen as if by magic; I had a sense of being the messenger of Fate. One could almost hear their sighs of regret as I appeared; they must have passed a lovely afternoon. I hurried into the house with the reassuring news that they were not only in sight but perfectly safe, with all the sheep.

VIII

Mrs Hight, like myself, was spent with conversation, and had ceased even the one activity of fanning herself. I brought a desired drink of water, and happily remembered some fruit that was left from my luncheon. She revived with splendid vigour, and told me the simple history of her later years since she had been smitten in the prime of her life by the stroke of paralysis, and her husband had died and left her alone with Esther and a mortgage on their farm. There was only one field of good land, but they owned a great region of sheep pasture and a little woodland. Esther had always been laughed at for her belief in sheep-raising when one by one their neighbours were giving up their flocks, and when everything had come to the point of despair she had raised all the money and bought all the sheep she could, insisting that Maine lambs were as good as any, and that there was a straight path by sea to Boston market. And by tending her flock herself she had managed to succeed; she had made money enough to pay off the mortgage five years ago, and now what they did not spend was safe in the bank. 'It has been stubborn work, day and night, summer and winter, an' now she's beginnin' to get along in years,' said the old mother sadly. 'She's tended me 'long o' the sheep, an' she's been a good girl right along, but she ought to have been a teacher'; and Mrs Hight sighed heavily and plied the fan again.

We heard voices and William and Esther entered; they did not know that it was so late in the afternoon. William looked almost bold, and oddly like a happy young man rather than an ancient boy. As for Esther, she might have been Jeanne d'Arc returned to her sheep, touched with age and gray with the ashes of a great remembrance. She wore the simple look of sainthood and unfeigned devotion. My heart was moved by the sight of her plain sweet face, weatherworn and gentle in its looks, her thin figure in its close dress, and the strong hand that clasped a shepherd's staff, and I could only hold William in new reverence; this silent farmer-fisherman who knew, and he alone, the noble and patient heart that beat within her breast. I am not sure that they acknowledged even to themselves that they had always been lovers; they could not consent to anything so definite or pronounced; but they were happy in being together in the world. Esther was untouched by the fret and fury of life; she had lived in sunshine and rain among her silly sheep, and been refined instead of coarsened, while her touching patience with a ramping old mother, stung by the sense of defeat and mourning her lost activities, had given back a lovely self-possession, and habit of sweet temper. I had seen enough of old Mrs Hight to know that nothing a sheep might do could vex a person who was used to the uncertainties and severities of her companionship.

IX

Mrs Hight told her daughter at once that she had enjoyed a beautiful call, and got a great many new things to think of. This was said so frankly in my hearing that it gave a consciousness of high reward, and I was indeed recompensed by the grateful look in Esther's eyes. We did not speak much together, but we understood each other. For the poor old woman did not read, and could not sew or knit with her helpless hand, and they were far from any neighbours, while her spirit was as eager in age as in youth, and expected even more from a disappointing world. She had lived to see the mortgage paid and money in the bank, and Esther's success acknowledged on every hand, and there were still a few pleasures left in life. William had his mother, and Esther had hers, and they had not seen each other for a year, though Mrs Hight had spoken of a year's making no change in William even at his age. She must have been in the far eighties herself, but of a noble courage and persistence in the world she ruled from her stiff-backed rocking-chair.

William unloaded his gift of dried fish, each one chosen with perfect care, and Esther stood by, watching him, and then she walked across the field with us beside the waggon. I believed that I was the only one who knew their happy secret, and she blushed a little as we said good-bye.

'I hope you ain't goin' to feel too tired, mother's so deaf; no, I hope you won't be tired,' she said kindly, speaking as if she well knew what tiredness was. We could hear the neglected sheep bleating on the hill in the next moment's silence. Then she smiled at me, a smile of noble patience, of uncomprehended sacrifice, which I can never forget. There was all the remembrance of disappointed hopes, the hardships of winter, the loneliness of single-handedness in her look, but I understood, and I love to remember her worn face and her young blue eyes.

'Good-bye, William,' she said gently, and William said good-bye, and gave her a quick glance, but he did not turn to look back, though I did, and waved my hand as she was putting up the bars behind us. Nor did he speak again until we had passed through the dark woods and were on our way homeward by the main road. The grave yearly visit had been changed from a hope into a happy memory.

'You can see the sea from the top of her pasture hill,' said William at last.

'Can you?' I asked with surprise.

'Yes, it's very high land; the ledges up there show very plain in clear weather from the top of our island, and there's a high upstandin' tree that makes a landmark for the fishin' grounds.' And William gave a happy sigh.

When we had nearly reached the Landing, my companion looked over into the back of the waggon and saw that the piece of sailcloth was safe, with which he had covered the dried fish. 'I wish we had got some trout,' he said wistfully. 'They always appease Almiry, and make her feel 't was worth while to go.'

I stole a glance at William Blackett. We had not seen a solitary mosquito, but there was a dark stripe across his mild face, which might have been an old scar won long ago in battle.

William's Wedding

from The Country of the Pointed Firs

SARAH ORNE JEWETT

I

THE hurry of life in a large town, the constant putting aside of preference to yield to a most unsatisfactory activity, began to vex me, and one day I took the train, and only left it for the eastward-bound boat. Carlyle says somewhere that the only happiness a man ought to ask for is happiness enough to get his work done; and against this the complexity and futile ingenuity of social life seems a conspiracy. But the first salt wind from the east, the first sight of a lighthouse set boldly on its outer rock, the flash of a gull, the waiting procession of seaward-bound firs on an island, made me feel solid and definite again, instead of a poor, incoherent being. Life was resumed, and anxious living blew away as if it had not been. I could not breathe deep enough or long enough. It was a return to happiness.

The coast had still a wintry look; it was far on in May, but all the shore looked cold and sterile. One was conscious of going north as well as east, and as the day went on the sea grew colder, and all the warmer air and bracing strength and stimulus of the autumn weather, and storage of the heat of summer, were quite gone. I was very cold and very tired when I came at evening up the lower bay, and saw the white houses of Dunnet Landing climbing the hill. They had a friendly look, these little houses, not as if they were climbing up the shore, but as if they were rather all coming down to meet a fond and weary traveller, and I could hardly wait with patience to step off the boat. It was not the usual eager company on the wharf. The coming-in of the mail-boat was the one large public event of a summer day, and I was disappointed at seeing none of my intimate friends but Johnny Bowden, who had evidently done nothing all winter but grow, so that his short sea-smitten clothes gave him a look of poverty.

Johnny's expression did not change as we greeted each other, but I suddenly felt that I had shown indifference and inconvenient delay by not coming sooner; before I could make an apology he took my small portmanteau, and walking before me in his old fashion he made straight up the hilly road toward Mrs Todd's. Yes, he was much grown – it had never occurred to me the summer before that Johnny was likely, with the help of time and other forces, to grow into a young man; he was such a well-framed and well-settled chunk of a boy that nature seemed to have set him aside as something finished, quite satisfactory, and entirely completed.

The wonderful little green garden had been enchanted away by winter. There were a few frostbitten twigs and some thin shrubbery against the fence, but it was a most unpromising small piece of ground. My heart was beating like a lover's as I passed it on the way to the door of Mrs Todd's house, which seemed to have become much smaller under the influence of winter weather.

'She hasn't gone away?' I asked Johnny Bowden with a sudden anxiety just as we reached the door-step.

'Gone away!' he faced me with blank astonishment – 'I see her settin' by Mis' Caplin's window, the one nighest the road, about four o'clock!' And eager with suppressed news of my coming, he made his entrance as if the house were a burrow.

Then on my homesick heart fell the voice of Mrs Todd. She stopped, through what I knew to be excess of feeling, to rebuke Johnny for bringing in so much mud, and I dallied for one moment during the ceremony; then we met again face to face.

II

'I daresay you can advise me what shapes they are goin' to wear. My meetin'-bunnit ain't goin' to do me again this year; no! I can't expect 't would do me forever,' said Mrs Todd, as soon as she could say anything. 'There! do set down and tell me how you have been! We've got a weddin' in the family, I s'pose you know?'

'A wedding!' said I, still full of excitement.

'Yes; I expect if the tide serves and the line storm don't overtake him they'll come in and appear out on Sunday. I shouldn't have concerned me about the bunnit for a month yet, nobody would notice, but havin' an occasion like this I shall show consider'ble. 'T will be an ordeal for William!'

'For *William!*' I exclaimed. 'What do you mean, Mrs Todd?'

She gave a comfortable little laugh. 'Well, the Lord's seen reason at last an' removed Mis' Cap'n Hight up to the farm, an' I don't know but the weddin's goin' to be this week. Esther's had a great deal of business disposin' of her flock, but she's done extra well – the folks that owns the next place goin' up country are well off. 'T is elegant land north side o' that bleak ridge, an' one o' the boys has been Esther's right-hand man of late. She instructed him in all matters, and after she markets the early lambs he's goin' to take the farm on halves, an' she's give the refusal to him to buy her out within two years. She's reserved the buryin'-lot, an' the right o' way in, an' –'

I couldn't stop for details. I demanded reassurance of the central fact.

'William going to be married?' I repeated; whereat Mrs Todd gave me a searching look that was not without scorn.

'Old Mis' Hight's funeral was a week ago Wednesday, and 't was very well attended,' she assured me after a moment's pause.

'Poor thing!' said I, with a sudden vision of her helplessness and angry battle against the fate of illness; 'it was very hard for her.'

'I thought it was hard for Esther!' said Mrs Todd without sentiment.

III

I had an odd feeling of strangeness: I missed the garden, and the little rooms, to which I had added a few things of my own the summer before, seemed oddly unfamiliar. It was like the hermit crab in a cold new shell, – and with the windows shut against the raw May air, and a strange silence and grayness of the sea all that first night and day of my visit, I felt as if I had after all lost my hold of that quiet life.

Mrs Todd made the apt suggestion that city persons were prone to run themselves to death, and advised me to stay and get properly rested now that I had taken the trouble to come. She did not know how long I had been homesick for the conditions of life at the Landing the autumn before – it was natural enough to feel a little unsupported by compelling incidents on my return.

Some one has said that one never leaves a place, or arrives at one, until the next day! But on the second morning I woke with the familiar feeling of interest and ease, and the bright May sun was streaming in, while I could hear Mrs Todd's heavy footsteps pounding about in the other part of the house as if something were going to happen. There was the first golden robin singing somewhere close to the house, and a lovely aspect of spring now, and I looked at the garden to see that in the warm night some of its treasures had grown a hand's breadth; the determined spikes of yellow daffies stood tall against the doorsteps, and the bloodroot was unfolding leaf and flower. The belated spring which I had left behind farther south had overtaken me on this northern coast. I even saw a presumptuous dandelion in the garden border.

It is difficult to report the great events of New England; expression is so slight, and those few words which escape us in moments of deep feeling look but meagre on the printed page. One has to assume too much of the dramatic fervour as one reads; but as I came out of my room at breakfast-time I met Mrs Todd face to face, and when she said to me, 'This weather'll bring William in after her; 't is their happy day!' I felt something take possession of me which ought to communicate itself to the least sympathetic reader of this cold page. It is written for those who have a Dunnet Landing of their own: who either kindly share this with the writer, or possess another.

'I ain't seen his comin' sail yet; he'll be likely to dodge round among the islands so he'll be the less observed,' continued Mrs Todd. 'You can get a dory up the bay, even a clean new painted one, if you know as how, keepin' it against the high land.' She stepped to the door and looked off to sea as she spoke. I could see her eye follow the grey shores to and fro, and then a bright light spread over her calm face. 'There he comes, and he's strikin' right in across the open bay like a man!' she said with splendid approval. 'See, there he comes! Yes, there's William, and he's bent his new sail.'

I looked too, and saw the fleck of white no larger than a gull's wing yet, but present to her eager vision.

I was going to France for the whole long summer that year, and the more I thought of such an absence from these simple scenes the more dear and delightful they became. Santa Teresa says that the true proficiency of the soul is not in much thinking, but in much loving, and sometimes I believed that I had never found love in its simplicity as I had found it at Dunnet Landing in the various hearts of Mrs Blackett and Mrs Todd and William. It is only because one came to know them, these three, loving and wise and true, in their own habitations. Their counterparts are in every village in the world, thank heaven, and the gift to one's life is only in its discernment. I had only lived in Dunnet until the usual distractions and artifices of the world were no longer in control, and I saw these simple natures clear. 'The happiness of life is in its recognitions. It seems that we are not ignorant of these truths, and even that we believe them;

but we are so little accustomed to think of them, they are so strange to us –'

'Well now, deary me!' said Mrs Todd, breaking into exclamation; 'I've got to fly round – I thought he'd have to beat; he can't sail far on that tack, and he won't be in for a good hour yet – I expect he's made every arrangement, but he said he shouldn't go up after Esther unless the weather was good, and I declare it did look doubtful this morning.'

I remembered Esther's weather-worn face. She was like a Frenchwoman who had spent her life in the fields. I remembered her pleasant look, her childlike eyes, and thought of the astonishment of joy she would feel now in being taken care of and tenderly sheltered from wind and weather after all these years. They were going to be young again now, she and William, to forget work and care in the spring weather. I could hardly wait for the boat to come to land, I was so eager to see his happy face.

'Cake an' wine I'm goin' to set 'em out!' said Mrs Todd. 'They won't stop to set down for an ordered meal, they'll want to get right out home quick's they can. Yes, I'll give 'em some cake an' wine – I've got a rare plum-cake from my best receipt, and a bottle o' wine that the old Cap'n Denton of all give me, one of two, the day I was married, one we had and one we saved, and I've never touched it till now. He said there wa'n't none like it in the State o' Maine.'

It was a day of waiting, that day of spring; the May weather was as expectant as our fond hearts, and one could see the grass grow green hour by hour. The warm air was full of birds, there was a glow of light on the sea instead of the cold shining of chilly weather which had lingered late. There was a look on Mrs Todd's face which I saw once and could not meet again. She was in her highest mood. Then I went out early for a walk, and when I came back we sat in different rooms for the most part. There was such a thrill in the air that our only conversation was in her most abrupt and incisive manner. She was knitting, I believe, and as for me I dallied with a book. I heard her walking to and fro, and, the door being wide open now, she went out and paced the front walk to the gate as if she walked a quarter-deck.

It is very solemn to sit waiting for the great events of life – most of us have done it again and again – to be expectant of life or expectant of death gives one the same feeling.

But at the last Mrs Todd came quickly back from the gate, and standing in the sunshine at the door, she beckoned me as if she were a sibyl.

'I thought you comprehended everything the day you was up there,' she added with a little more patience in her tone, but I felt that she thought I had lost instead of gained since we parted the autumn before.

'William's made this pretext o' goin' fishin' for the last time. 'T wouldn't done to take notice, 't would 'a scared him to death! but there never was nobody took less comfort out o' forty years courtin'. No, he won't have to make no further pretexts,' said Mrs Todd, with an air of triumph.

'Did you know where he was going that day?' I asked, with a sudden burst of admiration at such discernment.

'I did!' replied Mrs Todd grandly.

'Oh! but that pennyroyal lotion,' I indignantly protested, remembering that under pretext of mosquitoes she had besmeared the poor lover in an awful way – why, it was outrageous! Medea could not have been more conscious of high ultimate purposes.

'Darlin',' said Mrs Todd, in the excitement of my arrival and the great concerns of marriage, 'he's got a beautiful shaped face, and they pison him very unusual – you wouldn't have had him present himself to his lady all lop-sided with a mosquito-bite? Once when we was young I rode up with him, and they set upon him in concert the minute we entered the woods.' She stood before me reproachfully, and I was conscious of deserved rebuke. 'Yes, you've come just in the nick of time to advise me about a bunnit. They say large bows on top is liable to be worn.'

IV

The period of waiting was one of direct contrast to these high moments of recognition. The very slowness of the morning hours wasted that sense of excitement with which we had begun the day. Mrs Todd came down from the mount where her face had shone so bright, to the cares of common life, and some acquaintances from Black Island for whom she had little natural preference or liking came, bringing a poor, sickly child to get medical advice. They were noisy women, with harsh, clamorous voices, and they stayed a long time. I heard the clink of teacups, however, and could detect no impatience in the tones of Mrs Todd's voice; but when they were at last going away, she did not linger unduly over her leave-taking, and returned to me to explain that they were people she had never liked, and they had made an excuse of a friendly visit to save their doctor's bill; but she pitied the poor little child, and knew beside that the doctor was away.

'I had to give 'em the remedies right out,' she told me; 'they wouldn't have bought a cent's worth o' drugs down to the store for that dwindlin' thing. She needed feedin' up, and I don't expect she gets milk enough; they're great butter-makers down to Black Island, 't is excellent pasturage, but they use no milk themselves, and their butter is heavy laden with salt to make weight, so that you'd think all their ideas come down from Sodom.'

She was very indignant and very wistful about the pale little girl. 'I wish they'd let me kept her,' she said. 'I kind of advised it, and her eyes was so wishful in that pinched face when she heard me, so that I could see what was the matter with her, but they said she wa'n't prepared. Prepared!' And Mrs Todd sniffed like an offended war-horse, and departed; but I could hear her still grumbling and talking to herself in high dudgeon an hour afterward.

At the end of that time her arch enemy, Mari' Harris, appeared at the side-door with a gingham handkerchief over her head. She was always on hand for the news, and made some formal excuse for her presence – she wished to borrow the weekly paper. Captain Littlepage, whose housekeeper she was, had taken it from the post-office in the morning, but had forgotten, being of failing memory, what he had done with it.

'How is the poor old gentleman?' asked Mrs Todd with solicitude, ignoring the present errand of Maria and all her concerns.

I had spoken the evening before of intended visits to Captain Littlepage and Elijah Tilley, and I now heard Mrs Todd repeating my inquiries and intentions, and fending off with unusual volubility of her own the curious questions that were sure to come. But at last Maria Harris secured an opportunity and boldly inquired if she had not seen William ashore early that morning.

'I don't say he wasn't,' replied Mrs Todd; 'Thu'sday's a very usual day with him to come ashore.'

'He was all dressed up,' insisted Maria – she really had no sense of propriety. 'I didn't know but they was going to be married?'

Mrs Todd did not reply. I recognised from the sounds that reached me that she had retired to the fastnesses of the kitchen-closet and was clattering the tins.

'I expect they'll marry soon anyway,' continued the visitor.

'I expect they will if they want to,' answered Mrs Todd. 'I don't know nothin' 't all about it; that's what folks say.' And presently the gingham handkerchief retreated past my window.

'I routed her, horse and foot,' said Mrs Todd proudly, coming at once to stand at my door. 'Who's comin' now?' as two figures passed inward bound to the kitchen.

They were Mrs Begg and Johnny Bowden's mother, who were favourites, and were received with Mrs Todd's usual civilities. Then one of the Mrs Caplins came with a cup in hand to borrow yeast. On one pretext or another nearly all our acquaintances came to satisfy themselves of the facts, and see what Mrs Todd would impart about the wedding. But she firmly avoided the subject through the length of every call and errand, and answered the final leading question of each curious guest with her noncommittal phrase, 'I don't know nothin' 't all about it; that's what folks say!'

She had just repeated this for the fourth or fifth time and shut the door upon the last comers, when we met in the little front entry. Mrs Todd was not in a bad temper, but highly amused. 'I've been havin' all sorts o' social privileges, you may have observed. They didn't seem to consider that if they could only hold out till afternoon they'd know as much as I did. There wa'n't but one o' the whole sixteen that showed real interest, the rest demeaned themselves to ask out o' cheap curiosity; no, there wa'n't but one showed any real feelin'.'

'Miss Maria Harris, you mean?' and Mrs Todd laughed.

'Certain, dear,' she agreed, 'how you do understand poor human natur'!'

A short distance down the hilly street stood a narrow house that was newly painted white. It blinded one's eyes to catch the reflection of the sun. It was the house of the minister, and a waggon had just stopped before it; a man was helping a woman to alight, and they stood side by side for a moment, while Johnny Bowden appeared as if by magic, and climbed to the waggonseat. Then they went into the house and shut the door. Mrs Todd and I stood close together and watched; the tears were running down her cheeks. I watched Johnny Bowden, who made light of so great a moment by so handling the whip that the old white Caplin horse started up from time to time and was inexorably stopped as if he had some idea of running away. There was something in the back of the waggon which now and then claimed the boy's attention; he leaned over as if there were something very precious left in his charge; perhaps it was only Esther's little trunk going to its new home.

At last the door of the parsonage opened, and two figures came out. The minister followed them and stood in the doorway, delaying them with parting words; he could not have thought it was a time for admonition.

'He's all alone; his wife's up to Portland to her sister's,' said Mrs Todd aloud, in a matter-of-fact voice. 'She's a nice woman, but she might ha' talked too much. There! see, they're comin' here. I didn't know how 't would be. Yes, they're comin' up to see us before they go home. I declare, if William ain't lookin' just like a king!'

Mrs Todd took one step forward, and we stood and waited. The happy pair came walking up the street, Johnny Bowden driving ahead. I heard a plaintive little cry from time to time to which in the excitement of the moment I had not stopped to listen; but when William and Esther had come and shaken hands with Mrs Todd and then with me, all in silence, Esther stepped quickly to the back of the waggon, and unfastening some cords returned to us carrying a little white lamb. She gave a shy glance at William as she fondled it and held it to her heart, and then, still silent, we went into the house together. The lamb had stopped bleating. It was lovely to see Esther carry it in her arms.

When we got into the house, all the repression of Mrs Todd's usual manner was swept away by her flood of feeling. She took Esther's thin figure, lamb and all, to her heart and held her there, kissing her as she might have kissed a child, and then held out her hand to William and they gave each other the kiss of peace. This was so moving, so tender, so free from their usual fetter of self-consciousness, that Esther and I could not help giving each other a happy glance of comprehension. I never saw a young bride half so touching in her happiness as Esther was that day of her wedding. We took the cake and wine of the marriage feast together, always in silence, like a true sacrament, and then to my astonishment I found that sympathy and public interest in so great an occasion were going to have their way. I shrank from the thought of William's possible sufferings, but he welcomed both the first group of neighbours and the last with heartiness; and when at last they had gone, for there were thoughtless loiterers in Dunnet Landing, I made ready with eager zeal and walked with William and Esther to the water-side. It was only a little way, and kind faces nodded reassuringly from the windows, while kind voices spoke from the doors. Esther carried the lamb on one arm; she had found time to tell me that its mother had died that morning and she could not bring herself to the thought of leaving it behind. She kept the other hand on William's arm until we reached the landing. Then he shook hands with me, and looked me full in the face to be sure I understood how happy he was, and stepping into the boat held out his arms to Esther – at last she was his own.

I watched him make a nest for the lamb out of an old sea-cloak at Esther's feet, and then he wrapped her own shawl round her shoulders, and finding a pin in the lapel of his Sunday coat he pinned it for her. She looked at him fondly while he did this, and then glanced up at us, a pretty, girlish colour brightening her cheeks.

We stood there together and watched them go far out into the bay. The sunshine of the May day was low now, but there was a steady breeze, and the boat moved well.

'Mother'll be watching for them,' said Mrs Todd. 'Yes, mother'll be watching all day, and waiting. She'll be so happy to have Esther come.'

We went home together up the hill, and Mrs Todd said nothing more; but we held each other's hands all the way.

The Apple-tree

JOHN GALSWORTHY

JOHN GALSWORTHY (1807–1933) was both a novelist and a dramatist. He wrote more than 31 full length plays, as well as many one act dramas. As a novelist he is best known for The Forsyte Saga.

> The apple-tree, the singing, and the gold.
> GILBERT MURRAY *Hippolytus of Euripides*

ON their silver-wedding day Ashurst and his wife were motoring along the outskirts of the moor, intending to crown the festival by stopping the night at Torquay, where they had first met. This was the idea of Stella Ashurst, whose character contained a streak of sentiment. If she had long lost the blue-eyed, flower-like charm, the cool slim purity of face and form, the apple-blossom colouring, which had so swiftly and so oddly affected Ashurst twenty-six years ago, she was still at forty-three a comely and faithful companion, whose cheeks were faintly mottled, and whose grey-blue eyes had acquired a certain fullness.

It was she who had stopped the car where the common rose steeply to the left, and a narrow strip of larch and beech, with here and there a pine, stretched out towards the valley between the road and the first long high hill of the full moor. She was looking for a place where they might lunch, for Ashurst never looked for anything; and this, between the golden furze and the feathery green larches smelling of lemons in the last sun of April – this, with a view into the deep valley and up to the long moor heights, seemed fitting to the decisive nature of one who sketched in water-colours, and loved romantic spots. Grasping her paint box, she got out.

'Won't this do, Frank?'

Ashurst, rather like a bearded Schiller, grey in the wings, tall, long-legged, with large remote grey eyes which sometimes filled with meaning and became almost beautiful, with nose a little to one side, and bearded lips just open – Ashurst, forty-eight, and silent, grasped the luncheon basket, and got out too.

'Oh! Look, Frank! A grave!'

By the side of the road, where the track from the top of the common crossed it at right angles and ran through a gate past the narrow wood, was a thin mound of turf, six feet by one, with a moorstone to the west, and on it someone had thrown a blackthorn spray and a handful of bluebells. Ashurst looked, and the poet in him moved. At cross-roads – a suicide's grave! Poor mortals with their superstitions! Whoever lay there, though, had the best of it, no clammy sepulchre among other hideous graves carved with futilities – just a rough stone, the wide sky, and wayside blessings! And, without comment, for he had learned not to be a philosopher in the bosom of his family, he strode away up on to the common, dropped the luncheon basket under a wall, spread a rug for his wife to sit on – she would turn up from her sketching when she was hungry – and took from his pocket Murray's translation of the 'Hippolytus'. He had soon finished reading of 'The Cyprian' and her revenge, and looked at the sky instead. And watching the white clouds so bright against the intense blue, Ashurst, on his silver-wedding day, longed for – he knew not what. Mal-adjusted to life – man's organism! One's mode of life might be high and scrupulous, but there was always an undercurrent of greediness, a hankering, and sense of waste. Did women have it too? Who could tell? And yet, men who gave vent to their appetites for novelty, their riotous longings

for new adventures, new risks, new pleasures, these suffered,
no doubt, from the reverse side of starvation, from surfeit.
No getting out of it – a mal-adjusted animal, civilized man!
There could be no garden of his choosing, of 'the Apple-tree,
the singing, and the gold', in the words of that lovely Greek
chorus, no achievable elysium in life, or lasting haven of
happiness for any man with a sense of beauty – nothing which
could compare with the captured loveliness in a work of art,
set down for ever, so that to look on it or read was always
to have the same precious sense of exaltation and restful
inebriety. Life no doubt had moments with that quality of
beauty, of unbidden flying rapture, but the trouble was, they
lasted no longer than the span of a cloud's flight over the sun;
impossible to keep them with you, as Art caught beauty and
held it fast. They were fleeting as one of the glimmering or
golden visions one had of the soul in nature, glimpses of its
remote and brooding spirit. Here, with the sun hot on his face,
a cuckoo calling from a thorn tree, and in the air the honey
savour of gorse – here among the little fronds of the young
fern, the starry blackthorn, while the bright clouds drifted by
high above the hills and dreamy valleys – here and now was
such a glimpse. But in a moment it would pass – as the face of
Pan, which looks round the corner of a rock, vanishes at your
stare. And suddenly he sat up. Surely there was something
familiar about this view, this bit of common, that ribbon of
road, the old wall behind him. While they were driving he
had not been taking notice – never did; thinking of far things
or of nothing – but now he saw! Twenty-six years ago, just
at this time of year, from the farmhouse within half a mile of
this very spot he had started for that day in Torquay whence it
might be said he had never returned. And a sudden ache beset
his heart; he had stumbled on just one of those past moments
in his life, whose beauty and rapture he had failed to arrest,
whose wings had fluttered away into the unknown; he had
stumbled on a buried memory, a wild sweet time, swiftly
choked and ended. And, turning on his face, he rested his
chin on his hands, and stared at the short grass where the

little blue milkwort was growing . . .

And this is what he remembered.

I

On the first of May, after their last year together at college, Frank Ashurst and his friend Robert Garton were on a tramp. They had walked that day from Brent, intending to make Chagford, but Ashurst's football knee had given out, and according to their map they had still some seven miles to go. They were sitting on a bank beside the road, where a track crossed alongside a wood, resting the knee and talking of the universe, as young men will. Both were over six feet, and thin as rails; Ashurst pale, idealistic, full of absence; Garton queer, round-the-corner, knotted, curly, like some primeval beast. Both had a literary bent; neither wore a hat. Ashurst's hair was smooth, pale, wavy, and had a way of rising on either side of his brow, as if always being flung back; Garton's was a kind of dark unfathomed mop. They had not met a soul for miles.

'My dear fellow,' Garton was saying, 'pity's only an effect of self-consciousness; it's a disease of the last five thousand years. The world was happier without.'

Ashurst, following the clouds with his eyes, answered:

'It's the pearl in the oyster, anyway.'

'My dear chap, all our modern unhappiness comes from pity. Look at animals, and Red Indians, limited to feeling their own occasional misfortunes; then look at ourselves – never free from feeling the toothaches of others. Let's get back to feeling for nobody, and have a better time.'

'You'll never practise that.'

Garton pensively stirred the hotch-potch of his hair.

'To attain full growth, one mustn't be squeamish. To starve oneself emotionally's a mistake. All emotion is to the good – enriches life.'

'Yes, and when it runs up against chivalry?'

'Ah! That's so English! If you speak of emotion the English always think you want something physical, and are shocked.

They're afraid of passion, but not of lust – oh, no! – so long as they can keep it secret.'

Ashurst did not answer; he had plucked a blue floweret, and was twiddling it against the sky. A cuckoo began calling from a thorn tree. The sky, the flowers, the songs of birds! Robert was talking through his hat! And he said:

'Well, let's go on, and find some farm where we can put up.' In uttering these words, he was conscious of a girl coming down from the common just above them. She was outlined against the sky, carrying a basket, and you could see that sky through the crook of her arm. And Ashurst, who saw beauty without wondering how it could advantage him, thought: How pretty! The wind, blowing her dark frieze skirt against her legs, lifted her battered peacock tam-o'-shanter; her greyish blouse was worn and old, her shoes were split, her little hands rough and red, her neck browned. Her dark hair waved untidy across her broad forehead, her face was short, her upper lip short, showing a glint of teeth, her brows were straight and dark, her lashes long and dark, her nose straight; but her grey eyes were the wonder – dewy as if opened for the first time that day. She looked at Ashurst – perhaps he struck her as strange, limping along without a hat, with his large eyes on her, and his hair flung back. He could not take off what was not on his head, but put up his hand in a salute, and said:

'Can you tell us if there's a farm near here where we could stay the night? I've gone lame.'

'There's only our farm near, sir.' She spoke without shyness, in a pretty, soft, crisp voice.

'And where is that?'

'Down here, sir.'

'Would you put us up?'

'Oh! I think we would.'

'Will you show us the way?'

'Yes, sir.'

He limped on, silent, and Garton took up the catechism.

'Are you a Devonshire girl?'

'No, sir.'

'What then?'

'From Wales.'

'Ah! I *thought* you were a Celt; so it's not your farm?'

'My aunt's, sir.'

'And your uncle's?'

'He is dead.'

'Who farms it, then?'

'My aunt, and my three cousins.'

'But your uncle was a Devonshire man?'

'Yes, sir.'

'Have you lived here long?'

'Seven years.'

'And how d'you like it after Wales?'

'I don't know, sir.'

'I suppose you don't remember?'

'Oh, yes! But it is different.'

'I believe you!'

Ashurst broke in suddenly:

'How old are you?'

'Seventeen, sir.'

'And what's your name?'

'Megan David.'

'This is Robert Garton, and I am Frank Ashurst. We wanted to get on to Chagford.'

'It is a pity your leg is hurting you.'

Ashurst smiled, and when he smiled his face was rather beautiful.

Descending past the narrow wood, they came on the farm suddenly – a long, low, stone-built dwelling with casement windows, in a farmyard where pigs and fowls and an old mare were straying. A short steep-up grass hill behind was crowned with a few Scotch firs, and in front, an old orchard of apple-trees, just breaking into flower, stretched down to a stream and a long wild meadow. A little boy with oblique dark eyes was shepherding a pig, and by the house door stood a woman, who came towards them. The girl said:

'It is Mrs Narracombe, my aunt.'

'Mrs Narracombe, my aunt' had a quick, dark eye, like a mother wild-duck's, and something of the same snaky turn about her neck.

'We met your niece on the road,' said Ashurst. 'She thought you might perhaps put us up for the night.'

Mrs Narracombe, taking them in from head to heel, answered.

'Well, I can, if you don't mind one room. Megan, get the spare room ready, and a bowl of cream. You'll be wanting tea, I suppose.'

Passing through a sort of porch made by two yew-trees and some flowering-currant bushes, the girl disappeared into the house, her peacock tam-o'-shanter bright athwart that rosy-pink and the dark green of the yews.

'Will you come into the parlour and rest your leg? You'll be from college, perhaps?'

'We were, but we've gone down now.'

Mrs Narracombe nodded sagely.

The parlour, brick-floored, with bare table and shiny chairs and sofa stuffed with horsehair, seemed never to have been used, it was so terribly clean. Ashurst sat down at once on the sofa, holding his lame knee between his hands, and Mrs Narracombe gazed at him. He was the only son of a late professor of chemistry, but people found a certain lordliness in one who was often so sublimely unconscious of them.

'Is there a stream where we could bathe?'

'There's the strame at the bottom of the orchard, but sittin' down you'll not be covered!'

'How deep?'

'Well, 'tis about a foot and a half, maybe.'

'Oh! That'll do fine. Which way?'

'Down the lane, through the second gate on the right, an' the pool's by the big apple-tree that stands by itself. There's trout there, if you can tickle them.'

'They're more likely to tickle us!'

Mrs Narracombe smiled. 'There'll be the tea ready when you come back.'

The pool, formed by the damming of a rock, had a sandy bottom; and the big apple-tree, lowest in the orchard, grew so close that its boughs almost overhung the water; it was in leaf, and all but in flower – its crimson buds just bursting. There was not room for more than one at a time in that narrow bath, and Ashurst waited his turn, rubbing his knee and gazing at the wild meadow, all rocks and thorn trees and field flowers, with a grove of beeches beyond, raised up on a flat mound. Every bough was swinging in the wind, every spring bird calling, and a slanting sunlight dappled the grass. He thought of Theocritus, and the river Cherwell, of the moon, and the maiden with the dewy eyes; of so many things that he seemed to think of nothing; and he felt absurdly happy.

II

During a late and sumptuous tea with eggs to it, cream and jam, and thin, fresh cakes touched with saffron, Garton descanted on the Celts. It was about the period of the Celtic awakening, and the discovery that there was Celtic blood about this family had excited one who believed that he was a Celt himself. Sprawling on a horsehair chair, with a hand-made cigarette dribbling from the corner of his curly lips, he had been plunging his cold pin-points of eyes into Ashurst's and praising the refinement of the Welsh. To come out of Wales into England was like the change from china to earthenware! Frank, as a d – d Englishman, had not of course perceived the exquisite refinement and emotional capacity of that Welsh girl! And, delicately stirring in the dark mat of his still wet hair, he explained how exactly she illustrated the writings of the Welsh bard Morgan-ap-Something in the twelfth century.

Ashurst, full length on the horsehair sofa, and jutting far beyond its end, smoked a deeply-coloured pipe, and did not listen, thinking of the girl's face when she brought in a relay of cakes. It had been exactly like looking at a flower, or some other pretty sight in Nature – till, with a funny little shiver, she had lowered her glance and gone out, quiet as a mouse.

'Let's go to the kitchen,' said Garton, 'and see some more of her.'

The kitchen was a white-washed room with rafters, to which were attached smoked hams; there were flower-pots on the window-sill, and guns hanging on nails, queer mugs, china and pewter, and portraits of Queen Victoria. A long, narrow table of plain wood was set with bowls and spoons, under a string of high-hung onions; two sheep-dogs and three cats lay here and there. On one side of the recessed fireplace sat two small boys, idle, and good as gold; on the other sat a stout, light-eyed, red-faced youth with hair and lashes the colour of the tow he was running through the barrel of a gun; between them Mrs Narracombe dreamily stirred some savoury-scented stew in a large pot. Two other youths, oblique-eyed, dark-haired, rather sly-faced, like the two little boys, were talking together and lolling against the wall; and a short, elderly, clean-shaven man in corduroys, seated in the window, was conning a battered journal. The girl Megan seemed the only active creature – drawing cider and passing the jugs from cask to table. Seeing them thus about to eat, Garton said:

'Ah! If you'll let us, we'll come back when supper's over,' and without waiting for an answer they withdrew again to the parlour. But the colour in the kitchen, the warmth, the scents, and all those faces, heightened the bleakness of their shiny room, and they resumed their seats moodily.

'Regular gipsy type, those boys. There was only one Saxon – the fellow cleaning the gun. That girl is a very subtle study psychologically.'

Ashurst's lips twitched. Garton seemed to him an ass just then. Subtle study! She was a wild flower. A creature it did you good to look at. Study!

Garton went on:

'Emotionally she would be wonderful. She wants awakening.'

'Are you going to awaken her?'

Garton looked at him and smiled. 'How coarse and English you are!' that curly smile seemed saying.

And Ashurst puffed his pipe. Awaken her! This fool had the best opinion of himself! He threw up the window and leaned out. Dusk had gathered thick. The farm buildings and the wheel-house were all dim and bluish, the apple-trees but a blurred wilderness; the air smelled of wood-smoke from the kitchen fire. One bird going to bed later than the others was uttering a half-hearted twitter, as though surprised at the darkness. From the stable came the snuffle and stamp of a feeding horse. And away over there was the loom of the moor, and away and away the shy stars which had not as yet full light, pricking white through the deep blue heavens. A quavering owl hooted. Ashurst drew a deep breath. What a night to wander out in! A padding of unshod hoofs came up the lane, and three dim, dark shapes passed – ponies on an evening march. Their heads, black and fuzzy, showed above the gate. At the tap of his pipe, and a shower of little sparks, they shied round and scampered. A bat went fluttering past, uttering its almost inaudible 'chip, chip'. Ashurst held out his hand; on the upturned palm he could feel the dew. Suddenly from overhead he heard little burring boys' voices, little thumps of boots thrown down, and another voice, crisp and soft – the girl's putting them to bed, no doubt; and nine clear words: 'No, Rick, you can't have the cat in bed'; then came a skirmish of giggles and gurgles, a soft slap, a laugh so low and pretty that it made him shiver a little. A blowing sound, and the glim of the candle which was fingering the dusk above, went out; silence reigned. Ashurst withdrew into the room and sat down; his knee pained him, and his soul felt gloomy.

'You go to the kitchen,' he said; 'I'm going to bed.'

III

For Ashurst the wheel of slumber was wont to turn noiseless and slick and swift, but though he seemed sunk in sleep when his companion came up, he was really wide awake; and long after Garton, smothered in the other bed of that low-roofed room, was worshipping darkness with his upturned nose, he heard the owls. Barring the discomfort of his knee, it was not unpleasant – the cares of life did not loom large in night watches for this young man. In fact he had none; just enrolled a barrister, with literary aspirations, the world before him, no father or mother, and four hundred a year of his own. Did it matter where he went, what he did, or when he did it? His bed, too, was hard, and this preserved him from fever. He lay, sniffing the scent of the night which drifted into the low room through the open casement close to his head. Except for a definite irritation with his friend, natural when you have tramped with a man for three days, Ashurst's memories and visions that sleepless night were kindly and wistful and exciting. One vision, specially clear and unreasonable, for he had not even been conscious of noting it, was the face of the youth cleaning the gun; its intent, stolid, yet startled uplook at the kitchen doorway, quickly shifted to the girl carrying the cider jug. This red, blue-eyed, light-lashed, tow-haired face stuck as firmly in his memory as the girl's own face, so dewy and simple. But at last, in the square of darkness through the uncurtained casement, he saw day coming, and heard one hoarse and sleepy caw. Then followed silence, dead as ever, till the song of blackbird, not properly awake, adventured into the hush. And, from staring at the framed brightening light, Ashurst fell asleep.

Next day his knee was badly swollen; the walking tour was obviously over. Garton, due back in London on the morrow, departed at midday with an ironical smile which left a scar of irritation – healed the moment his loping figure vanished round the corner of the steep lane. All day Ashurst rested his knee, in a green-painted wooden chair on the patch of grass by the yew-tree porch, where the sunlight distilled the scent of stocks and gillyflowers, and a ghost of scent from the flowering-currant bushes. Beatifically he smoked, dreamed, watched.

A farm in spring is all birth – young things coming out of bud and shell, and human beings watching over the process with faint excitement feeding and tending what has been born. So still the young man sat, that a mother-goose, with stately cross-footed waddle, brought her six yellow-necked grey-backed goslings to strop their little beaks against the grass blades at his feet. Now and again Mrs Narracombe or the girl Megan would come and ask if he wanted anything, and he would smile and say: 'Nothing, thanks. It's splendid here.' Towards tea-time they came out together, bearing a long poultice of some dark stuff in a bowl, and after a long and solemn scrutiny of his swollen knee, bound it on. When they were gone, he thought of the girl's soft 'Oh!' – of her pitying eyes, and the little wrinkle in her brow. And again he felt that unreasoning irritation against his departed friend, who had talked such rot about her. When she brought out his tea, he said:

'How did you like my friend, Megan?'

She forced down her upper lip, as if afraid that to smile was not polite. 'He was a funny gentleman; he made us laugh. I think he is very clever.'

'What did he say to make you laugh?'

'He said I was a daughter of the bards. What are they?'

'Welsh poets, who lived hundreds of years ago.'

'Why am I their daughter, please?'

'He meant that you were the sort of girl they sang about.'

She wrinkled her brows. 'I think he likes to joke. Am I?'

'Would you believe me, if I told you?'

'Oh, yes.'

'Well, I think he was right.'

She smiled.

And Ashurst thought: You *are* a pretty thing!

'He said, too, that Joe was a Saxon type. What would that be?'

'Which is Joe? With the blue eyes and red face?'

'Yes. My uncle's nephew.'

'Not your cousin, then?'

'No.'

'Well, he meant that Joe was like the men who came over to England about fourteen hundred years ago, and conquered it.'

'Oh! I know about them; but is he?'

'Garton's crazy about that sort of thing; but I must say Joe does look a bit Early Saxon.'

'Yes.'

That 'Yes' tickled Ashurst. It was so crisp and graceful, so conclusive, and politely acquiescent in what was evidently Greek to her.

'He said that all the other boys were regular gipsies. He should not have said that. My aunt laughed, but she didn't like it, of course, and my cousins were angry. Uncle was a farmer – farmers are not gipsies. It is wrong to hurt people.'

Ashurst wanted to take her hand and give it a squeeze, but he only answered:

'Quite right, Megan. By the way, I heard you putting the little ones to bed last night.'

She flushed a little. 'Please to drink your tea – it is getting cold. Shall I get you some fresh?'

'Do you ever have time to do anything for yourself?'

'Oh, yes.'

'I've been watching, but I haven't seen it yet.'

She wrinkled her brows in a puzzled frown, and her colour deepened.

When she was gone, Ashurst thought: Did she think I was chaffing her? I wouldn't for the world! He was at that age when to some men 'Beauty's a flower', as the poet says, and inspires in them the thoughts of chivalry. Never very conscious of his surroundings, it was some time before he was aware that the youth whom Garton had called 'a Saxon type' was standing outside the stable door; and a fine bit of colour he made in his soiled brown velvet-cords, muddy gaiters, and blue shirt; red-armed, red-faced, the sun turning his hair from tow to flax; immovably stolid, persistent, unsmiling he stood. Then, seeing Ashurst looking at him, he crossed the yard at that gait of the young countryman always ashamed not to be slow and heavy-dwelling on each leg, and disappeared round the end of the house towards the kitchen entrance. A chill came over Ashurst's mood. Clods! With all the good will in the world, how impossible to get on terms with them! And yet – see that girl! Her shoes were split, her hands rough; but – what was it? Was it really her Celtic blood, as Garton had said? – she was a lady born, a jewel, though probably she could do no more than just read and write!

The elderly, clean-shaven man he had seen last night in the kitchen had come into the yard with a dog, driving the cows to their milking. Ashurst saw that he was lame.

'You've got some good ones there!'

The lame man's face brightened. He had the upward look in his eyes which prolonged suffering often brings.

'Yeas; they'm praaper buties; gude milkers tu.'

'I bet they are.'

''Ope as yure leg's better, zurr.'

'Thank you, it's getting on.'

The lame man touched his own: 'I know what 'tes, meself; 'tes a main worritin' thing, the knee. I've a 'ad mine bad this ten year.'

Ashurst made the sound of sympathy which comes so readily from those who have an independent income, and the lame man smiled again.

'Mustn't complain, though – they mighty near 'ad it off.'

'Ho!'

'Yeas; an' compared with what 'twas, 'tes almost so gude as nu.'

'They've put a bandage of splendid stuff on mine.'

'The maid she picks et. She'm a gude maid wi' the flowers. There's folks zeem to know the healin' in things. My mother was a rare one for that. 'Ope as yu'll zune be better, zurr. Goo ahn, therr!'

Ashurst smiled. 'Wi' the flowers!' A flower herself.

That evening, after his supper of cold duck, junket, and cider, the girl came in.

'Please, auntie says – will you try a piece of our Mayday cake?'

'If I may come to the kitchen for it.'

'Oh, yes! You'll be missing your friend.'

'Not I. But are you sure no one minds?'

'Who would mind? We shall be very pleased.'

Ashurst rose too suddenly for his stiff knee, staggered, and subsided. The girl gave a little gasp, and held out her hands. Ashurst took them, small, rough, brown; checked his impulse to put them to his lips, and let her pull him up. She came close beside him, offering her shoulder. And leaning on her he walked across the room. That shoulder seemed quite the pleasantest thing he had ever touched. But he had presence of mind enough to catch his stick out of the rack, and withdraw his hand before arriving at the kitchen.

That night he slept like a top, and woke with his knee of almost normal size. He again spent the morning in his chair on the grass patch, scribbling down verses; but in the afternoon he wandered about with the two little boys Nick and Rick. It was Saturday, so they were early home from school; quick, shy, dark little rascals of seven and six, soon talkative, for Ashurst had a way with children. By four o'clock they had shown him all their methods of destroying life, except the tickling of trout; and with breeches tucked up, lay on their stomachs over the trout stream, pretending they had this accomplishment also. They tickled nothing, of course, for their giggling and shouting scared every spotted thing away. Ashurst, on a rock at the edge of the beech clump, watched them, and listened to the cuckoos, till Nick, the elder and less persevering, came up and stood beside him.

'The gipsy bogle zets on that stone,' he said.

'What gipsy bogle?'

'Dunno; never zeen 'e. Megan zays 'e zets there; an' old Jim zeed 'e once. 'E was zettin' there naight afore our pony kicked-in father's 'ead. 'E plays the viddle.'

'What tune does he play?'

'Dunno.'

'What's he like?'

''E's black. Old Jim zays 'e's all over 'air. 'E's a praaper bogle. 'E don' come only at naight.' The little boy's oblique dark eyes slid round. 'D'yu think 'e might want to take me away? Megan's feared of 'e.'

'Has she seen him?'

'No. She's not afeared o' yu.'

'I should think not. Why should she be?'

'She zays a prayer for yu.'

'How do you know that, you little rascal?'

'When I was asleep, she said: "God bless us all, an' Mr Ashes." I yeard 'er whisperin'.'

'You're a little ruffian to tell what you hear when you're not meant to hear it!'

The little boy was silent. Then he said aggressively:

'I can skin rabbets. Megan, she can't bear skinnin' 'em. I like blood.'

'Oh! you do; you little monster!'

'What's that?'

'A creature that likes hurting others.'

The little boy scowled. 'They'm only dead rabbets, what us eats.'

'Quite right, Nick. I beg your pardon.'

'I can skin frogs, tu.'

But Ashurst had become absent. 'God bless us all, and Mr Ashes!' and puzzled by that sudden inaccessibility, Nick ran back to the stream where the giggling and shouts again uprose at once.

When Megan brought his tea, he said:

'What's the gipsy bogle, Megan?'

She looked up, startled.

'He brings bad things.'

'Surely you don't believe in ghosts?'

'I hope I will never see him.'

'Of course you won't. There aren't such things. What old Jim saw was a pony.'

'No! There are bogles in the rocks; they are the men who lived long ago.'

'They aren't gipsies, anyway; those old men were dead long before gipsies came.'

She said simply: 'They are all bad.'

'Why? If there are any, they're only wild, like the rabbits. The flowers aren't bad for being wild; the thorn trees were never planted – and you don't mind them. I shall go down at night and look for your bogle, and have a talk with him.'

'Oh, no! Oh, no!'

'Oh, yes! I shall go and sit on his rock.'

She clasped her hands together: 'Oh, please!'

'Why! What does it matter if anything happens to me?'

She did not answer; and in a sort of pet he added:

'Well, I daresay I shan't see him, because I suppose I must be off soon.'

'Soon?'

'Your aunt won't want to keep me here.'

'Oh, yes! We always let lodgings in summer.'

Fixing his eyes on her face, he asked:

'Would you like me to stay?'

'Yes.'

'I'm going to say a prayer for *you* tonight!'

She flushed crimson, frowned, and went out of the room. He sat cursing himself, till his tea was stewed. It was as if he had hacked with his thick boots at a clump of bluebells. Why had he said such a silly thing? Was he just a towny college ass like Robert Garton, as far from understanding this girl?

IV

Ashurst spent the next week confirming the restoration of his leg, by exploration of the country within easy reach. Spring was a revelation to him this year. In a kind of intoxication he would watch the pink-white buds of some backward beech-tree sprayed up in the sunlight against the deep blue sky, or the trunks and limbs of the few Scotch firs, tawny in violent light, or again on the moor, the gale-bent larches which had such a look of life when the wind streamed in their young green, above the rusty black underboughs. Or he would lie on the banks, gazing at the clusters of dog-violets, or up in the dead bracken, fingering the pink, transparent buds of the dewberry, while the cuckoos called and yaffles laughed, or a lark, from very high, dripped its beads of song. It was certainly different from any spring he had ever known, for spring was within him, not without. In the daytime he hardly saw the family; and when Megan brought in his meals she always seemed too busy in the house or among the young things in the yard to stay talking long. But in the evenings he installed himself in the window seat in the kitchen, smoking and chatting with the lame man Jim, or Mrs Narracombe, while the girl sewed, or moved about, clearing the supper things away. And sometimes with the sensation a cat must feel when it purrs, he would become conscious that Megan's eyes – those dew-grey eyes – were fixed on him with a sort of lingering soft look which was strangely flattering.

It was on Sunday week in the evening, when he was lying in the orchard listening to a blackbird and composing a love poem, that he heard the gate swing to, and saw the girl come running among the trees, with the red-cheeked, stolid Joe in swift pursuit. About twenty yards away the chase ended, and the two stood fronting each other, not noticing the stranger in the grass – the boy pressing on, the girl fending him off. Ashurst could see her face, angry, disturbed; and the youth's – who would have thought that red-faced yokel could look so distraught! And painfully affected by that sight, he jumped up. They saw him then. Megan dropped her hands, and shrank behind a tree-trunk; the boy gave an angry grunt, rushed at the bank, scrambled over and vanished. Ashurst went slowly up to her. She was standing quite still, biting her lip – very pretty, with her fine, dark hair blown loose about her face, and her eyes cast down.

'I beg your pardon,' he said.

She gave him one upward look, from eyes much dilated; then, catching her breath, turned away. Ashurst followed.

'Megan!'

But she went on; and taking hold of her arm, he turned her gently round to him.

'Stop and speak to me.'

'Why do you beg my pardon? It is not to me you should do that.'

'Well, then, to Joe.'

'How dare he come after me?'

'In love with you, I suppose.'

She stamped her foot.

Ashurst uttered a short laugh. 'Would you like me to punch his head?'

She cried with sudden passion:

'You laugh at me – you laugh at us!'

He caught hold of her hands, but she shrank back, till her passionate little face and loose dark hair were caught among the pink clusters of the apple blossom. Ashurst raised one of her imprisoned hands and put his lips to it. He felt how chivalrous he was, and superior to that clod Joe – just brushing that small, rough hand with his mouth! Her shrinking ceased suddenly; she seemed to tremble towards him. A sweet warmth overtook Ashurst from top to toe. This slim maiden, so simple and fine and pretty, was pleased, then, at the touch of his lips! And, yielding to a swift impulse, he put his arms round her, pressed her to him, and kissed her forehead. Then he was frightened – she went so pale, closing her eyes, so that the long, dark lashes lay on her pale cheeks; her hands, too, lay inert at her sides. The touch of her breast sent a shiver through him. 'Megan!' he sighed out, and let her go. In the utter silence a blackbird shouted. Then the girl seized his hand, put it to her cheek, her heart, her lips, kissed it passionately, and fled away among the mossy trunks of the apple-trees, till they hid her from him.

Ashurst sat down on a twisted old tree growing almost along the ground, and, all throbbing and bewildered, gazed vacantly at the blossom which had crowned her hair – those pink buds with one white open apple star. What had he done? How had he let himself be thus stampeded by beauty – or – just the spring! He felt curiously happy, all the same; happy and triumphant, with shivers running through his limbs, and a vague alarm. This was the beginning of – what? The midges bit him, the dancing gnats tried to fly into his mouth, and all the spring around him seemed to grow more lovely and alive; the songs of the cuckoos and the blackbirds, the laughter of the yaffles, the level-slanting sunlight, the apple blossom which had crowned her head –! He got up from the old trunk and strode out of the orchard, wanting space, an open sky, to get on terms with these new sensations. He made for the moor, and from an ash-tree in the hedge a magpie flew out to herald him.

Of man – at any age from five years on – who can say he has never been in love? Ashurst had loved his partners at his dancing class; loved his nursery governess; girls in school-holidays; perhaps never been quite out of love, cherishing always some more or less remote admiration. But this was different, not remote at all. Quite a new sensation; terribly delightful, bringing a sense of completed manhood. To be holding in his fingers such a wild flower, to be able to put it to his lips, and feel it tremble with delight against them! What intoxication, and – embarrassment! What to do with it – how meet her next time? His first caress had been cool, pitiful; but the next could not be, now that, by her burning little kiss on his hand, by her pressure of it to her heart, he knew that she loved him. Some natures are coarsened by love bestowed on them; others, like Ashurst's, are swayed and drawn, warmed and softened, almost exalted, by what they feel to be a sort of miracle.

And up there among the tors he was racked between the passionate desire to revel in this new sensation of spring fulfilled within him, and a vague but very real uneasiness. At one moment he gave himself up completely to his pride at having captured this pretty, trustful, dewy-eyed thing! At the next he thought with factitious solemnity: Yes, my boy! But look out what you're doing! You know what comes of it!

Dusk dropped down without his noticing – dusk on the carved, Assyrian-looking masses of the rocks. And the voice of Nature said: 'This is a new world for you!' As when a man gets up at four o'clock and goes out into a summer morning, and beasts, birds, trees stare at him and he feels as if all had been made new.

He stayed up there for hours, till it grew cold, then groped his way down the stones and heather roots to the road, back into the lane, and came again past the wild meadow to the orchard. There he struck a match and looked at his watch. Nearly twelve! It was black and unstirring in there now, very different from the lingering, bird-befriended brightness of six hours ago! And suddenly he saw this idyll of his with the eyes of the outer world – had mental vision of Mrs Narracombe's snake-like neck turned, her quick dark glance taking it all in, her shrewd face hardening; saw the gipsy-like cousins coarsely mocking and distrustful; Joe stolid and furious; only the lame man, Jim, with the suffering eyes, seemed tolerable to his mind. And the village pub! – the gossiping matrons he passed on his walks; and then – his own friends – Robert Garton's smile when he went off that morning ten days ago; so ironical and knowing! Disgusting! For a minute he literally hated this earthly, cynical world to which one belonged, willy-nilly. The gate where he was leaning grew grey, a sort of shimmer passed before him and spread into the bluish darkness. The moon! He could just see it over the bank behind; red, nearly round – a strange moon! And turning away, he went up the lane which smelled of the night and cow-dung and young leaves. In the straw-yard he could see the dark shapes of cattle, broken by the pale sickles of their horns, like so many thin moons, fallen ends-up. He unlatched the farm gate stealthily. All was dark in the house. Muffling his footsteps, he gained the porch, and, blotted against one of the yew-trees, looked up at Megan's window. It was open. Was she sleeping, or lying awake perhaps, disturbed – unhappy at his absence? An owl hooted while he stood there peering up, and the sound seemed to fill the whole night, so quiet was all else, save for the never-ending murmur of the stream running below the orchard. The cuckoos by day, and now the owls – how wonderfully they voiced this troubled ecstasy within him! And suddenly he saw her at her window, looking out. He moved a little from the yew-tree, and whispered: 'Megan!' She drew back, vanished, reappeared, leaning far down. He stole forward on the grass patch, hit his shin against the green-painted chair, and held his breath at the sound. The pale blur of her stretched-down arm and face did not stir; he moved the chair, and noiselessly mounted it. By stretching up his arm he could just reach. Her hand held the huge key of the front door, and he clasped that burning hand with the cold key in it. He could just see her face, the glint of teeth between her lips, her tumbled hair. She was still dressed – poor child, sitting up for him, no doubt! 'Pretty Megan!' Her hot, roughened fingers clung to his; her face had a strange, lost look. To have been able to reach it – even with his hand! The owl hooted, a scent of sweetbriar crept into his nostrils. Then one of the farm dogs barked; her grasp relaxed, she shrank back.

'Good-night, Megan!'

'Good-night, sir!' She was gone! With a sigh he dropped back to earth, and sitting on that chair, took off his boots. Nothing for it but to creep in and go to bed; yet for a long while he sat unmoving, his feet chilly in the dew, drunk on the memory of her lost, half-smiling face, and the clinging grip of her burning fingers, pressing the cold key into his hand.

V

He awoke feeling as if he had eaten heavily overnight, instead of having eaten nothing. And far off, unreal, seemed yesterday's romance! Yet it was a golden morning. Full spring had burst at last – in one night the 'goldie-cups', as the little boys called them, seemed to have made the field their own, and from his window he could see apple blossoms covering the orchard as with a rose and white quilt. He went down almost dreading to see Megan; and yet, when not she but Mrs Narracombe brought in his breakfast, he felt vexed and disappointed. The woman's quick eye and snaky neck seemed to have a new alacrity this morning. Had she noticed?

'So you an' the moon went walkin' last night, Mr Ashurst! Did ye have your supper anywheres?'

Ashurst shook his head.

'We kept it for you, but I suppose you was too busy in your brain to think o' such a thing as that?'

Was she mocking him, in that voice of hers, which still kept some Welsh crispness against the invading burr of the West Country? If she knew! And at that moment he thought: No, no; I'll clear out. I won't put myself in such a beastly false position.

But, after breakfast, the longing to see Megan began and increased with every minute, together with fear lest something should have been said to her which had spoiled everything. Sinister that she had not appeared, not given him even a glimpse of her! And the love poem, whose manufacture had been so important and absorbing yesterday afternoon under the apple-trees, now seemed so paltry that he tore it up and rolled it into pipe spills. What had he known of love, till she seized his hand and kissed it! And now – what did he not know? But to write of it seemed mere insipidity! He went up to his bedroom to get a book, and his heart began to beat violently, for she was in there making the bed. He stood in the doorway watching; and suddenly with turbulent joy, he saw her stoop and kiss his pillow, just at the hollow made by his head last night. How let her know he had seen that pretty act of devotion? And yet, if she heard him stealing away, it would be even worse. She took the pillow up, holding it as if reluctant to shake out the impress of his cheek, dropped it, and turned round.

'Megan!'

She put her hands up to her cheeks, but her eyes seemed to look right into him. He had never before realized the depth and purity and touching faithfulness in those dew-bright eyes, and he stammered:

'It was sweet of you to wait up for me last night.'

She still said nothing, and he stammered on:

'I was wandering about on the moor; it was such a jolly night. I – I've just come up for a book.'

Then, the kiss he had seen her give the pillow afflicted him with sudden headiness, and he went up to her. Touching her eyes with his lips, he thought with queer excitement: I've done it! Yesterday all was sudden – anyhow; but now – I've done it! The girl let her forehead rest against his lips, which moved downwards till they reached hers. That first real lover's kiss – strange, wonderful, still almost innocent – in which heart did it make the most disturbance?

'Come to the big apple-tree tonight, after they've gone to bed. Megan – promise!'

She whispered back: 'I promise!'

Then, scared at her white face, scared at everything, he let her go, and went downstairs again. Yes! he had done it now! Accepted her love, declared his own! He went out to the green chair as devoid of a book as ever; and there he sat staring vacantly before him, triumphant and remorseful, while under his nose and behind his back the work of the farm went on. How long he had been sitting in that curious state of vacancy he had no notion when he saw Joe standing a little behind him to the right. The youth had evidently come from hard work in the fields, and stood shifting his feet, breathing loudly, his face coloured like a setting sun, and his arms, below the rolled-up sleeves of his blue shirt, showing the hue and furry sheen of ripe peaches. His red lips were open, his blue eyes with their flaxen lashes stared fixedly at Ashurst, who said ironically:

'Well, Joe, anything I can do for you?'

'Yeas.'

'What, then?'

'Yu can goo away from yere. Us don' want yu.'

Ashurst's face, never too humble, assumed its most lordly look.

'Very good of you, but, do you know, I prefer the others should speak for themselves.'

The youth moved a pace or two nearer, and the scent of his honest heat afflicted Ashurst's nostrils.

'What d'yu stay yere for?'

'Because it pleases me.'

'Twon't please yu when I've bashed yure head in!'

'Indeed! When would you like to begin that?'

Joe answered only with the loudness of his breathing, but his eyes looked like those of a young and angry bull. Then a sort of spasm seemed to convulse his face.

'Megan don' want yu.'

A rush of jealousy, of contempt, and anger with this thick, loud-breathing rustic got the better of Ashurst's self-possession; he jumped up and pushed back his chair.

'You can go to the devil!'

And as he said those simple words, he saw Megan in the doorway with a tiny brown spaniel puppy in her arms. She came up to him quickly:

'Its eyes are blue!' she said.

Joe turned away; the back of his neck was literally crimson.

Ashurst put his finger to the mouth of the little brown bullfrog of a creature in her arms. How cosy it looked against her!

'It's fond of you already. Ah! Megan, everything is fond of *you*.'

'What was Joe saying to you, please?'

'Telling me to go away, because you didn't want me here.'

She stamped her foot; then looked up at Ashurst. At that adoring look he felt his nerves quiver, just as if he had seen a moth scorching its wings.

'Tonight!' he said. 'Don't forget!'

'No.' And smothering her face against the puppy's little fat, brown body, she slipped back into the house.

Ashurst wandered down the lane. At the gate of the wild meadow he came on the lame man and his cows.

'Beautiful day, Jim!'

'Ah! 'Tes brave weather for the grass. The ashes be later than th' oaks this year. "When th' oak before th' ash –" '

Ashurst said idly: 'Where were you standing when you saw the gipsy bogle, Jim?'

'It might be under that big apple-tree, as you might say.'

'And you really do think it was there?'

The lame man answered cautiously:

'I shouldn't like to say rightly that 't *was* there. 'Twas in my mind as 'twas there.'

'What do you make of it?'

The lame man lowered his voice.

'They do zay old master, Mist' Narracombe, come o' gipsy stock. But that's tellin'. They'm a wonderful people, yu know, for claimin' their own. Maybe they knu 'e was goin', and sent this feller along for company. That's what I've a-thought about it.'

'What was he like?'

"E 'ad 'air all over 'is face, an' goin' like this, he was, zame as if 'e 'ad a viddle. They zay there's no such thing as bogles, but I've a-zeen the 'air on this dog standin' up of a dark naight, when I couldn' zee nothin', meself.'

'Was there a moon?'

'Yeas, very near full, but 'twas on'y just risen, gold-like be'ind them trees.'

'And you think a ghost means trouble, do you?'

The lame man pushed his hat up; his aspiring eyes looked at Ashurst more earnestly than ever.

"Tes not for me to zay that – but 'tes they bein' so unrestin'-like. There's things us don' understand, that's zartin, for zure. There's people that zee things, tu, an' others that don't never zee nothin'. Now, our Joe – yu might putt anything under 'is eyes an' 'e'd never see it; and them other boys, tu, they'm rattlin' fellers. But yu take an' putt our Megan where there's suthin', she'll zee it, an' more tu, or I'm mistaken.'

'She's sensitive, that's why.'

'What's that?'

'I mean, she feels everything.'

'Ah! She'm very lovin'-'earted.'

Ashurst, who felt colour coming into his cheeks, held out his tobacco pouch.

'Have a fill, Jim?'

'Thank 'ee, sir. She'm one in an 'underd, I think.'

'I expect so,' said Ashurst shortly, and folding up his pouch, walked on.

'Lovin'-'earted!' Yes! And what was he doing? What were his intentions – as they say – towards this loving-hearted girl? The thought dogged him, wandering through fields bright with buttercups, where the little red calves were feeding, and the swallows flying high. Yes, the oaks were before the ashes, brown-gold already; every tree in different stage and hue. The cuckoos and a thousand birds were singing; the little streams were very bright. The ancients believed in a golden age, in the garden of the Hesperides! A queen wasp settled on his sleeve. Each queen wasp killed meant two thousand fewer wasps to thieve the apples which would grow from that blossom in the orchard; but who, with love in his heart, could kill anything on a day like this? He entered a field where a young red bull was feeding. It seemed to Ashurst that he looked like Joe. But the young bull took no notice of this visitor, a little drunk himself, perhaps, on the singing and the glamour of the golden pasture, under his short legs. Ashurst crossed out unchallenged to the hillside above the stream. From that slope a tor mounted to its crown of rocks. The ground there was covered with a mist of bluebells, and nearly a score of crab-apple trees were in full bloom. He threw himself down on the grass. The change from the buttercup glory and oak-goldened glamour of the fields to this ethereal beauty under the grey tor filled him with a sort of wonder; nothing the same, save the sound of running water and the songs of the cuckoos. He lay there a long time, watching the sunlight wheel till the crab-trees threw shadows over the bluebells, his only companions a few wild bees. He was not quite sane, thinking of that morning's kiss, and of tonight under the apple-tree. In such a spot as this, fauns and dryads surely lived; nymphs, white as the crab-apple blossom, retired within those trees; fauns, brown as the dead bracken with pointed ears, lay in wait for them. The cuckoos were still calling when he woke, there was the sound of running water; but the sun had couched behind the tor, the hillside was cool, and some rabbits had come out. Tonight! he thought. Just as from the earth everything was pushing up, unfolding under the soft insistent fingers of an unseen hand, so were his heart and senses being pushed, unfolded. He got up and broke off a spray from a crab-apple tree. The buds were like Megan – shell-like, rose-pink, wild, and fresh; and so, too, the opening flowers, white, and wild, and touching. He put the spray into his coat. And all the rush of the spring within him escaped in a triumphant sigh. But the rabbits scurried away.

VI

It was nearly eleven that night when Ashurst put down the pocket *Odyssey* which for half an hour he had held in his hands without reading, and slipped through the yard down to the orchard. The moon had just risen, very golden, over the hill, and like a bright, powerful, watching spirit peered through the bars of an ash-tree's half-naked boughs. In among the apple-trees it was still dark, and he stood making sure of his direction, feeling the rough grass with his feet. A black mass close behind him stirred with a heavy grunting sound, and three large pigs settled down again close to each other, under the wall. He listened. There was no wind, but the stream's burbling whispering chuckle had gained twice its daytime strength. One bird, he could not tell what, cried, 'Pip – pip, pip – pip,' with perfect monotony; he could hear a night-jar spinning very far off; an owl hooting. Ashurst moved a step or two, and again halted, aware of a dim living whiteness all round his head. On the dark unstirring trees innumerable flowers and buds all soft and blurred were being bewitched to life by the creeping moonlight. He had the oddest feeling of actual companionship, as if a million

white moths or spirits had floated in and settled between
dark sky and darker ground, and were opening and shutting
their wings on a level with his eyes. In the bewildering, still,
scentless beauty of that moment he almost lost memory of
why he had come to the orchard. The flying glamour which
had clothed the earth all day had not gone now that night had
fallen, but only changed into this new form. He moved on
through the thicket of stems and boughs covered with that
live powdering whiteness, till he reached the big apple-tree.
No mistaking that, even in the dark, nearly twice the height
and size of any other, and leaning out towards the open
meadows and the stream. Under the thick branches he stood
still again, to listen. The same sounds exactly, and a faint
grunting from the sleepy pigs. He put his hands on the dry,
almost warm tree trunk whose rough mossy surface gave
forth a peaty scent at his touch. Would she come – would she?
And among these quivering, haunted, moon-witched trees
he was seized with doubts of everything! All was unearthly
here, fit for no earthly lovers; fit only for god and goddess,
faun and nymph – not for him and this little country girl.
Would it not be almost a relief if she did not come? But all
the time he was listening. And still that unknown bird went
'Pip – pip, pip – pip,' and there rose the busy chatter of the
little trout stream, whereon the moon was flinging glances
through the bars of her tree-prison. The blossom on a level
with his eyes seemed to grow more living every moment,
seemed with its mysterious white beauty more and more
a part of his suspense. He plucked a fragment and held it
close – three blossoms. Sacrilege to pluck fruit-tree blossom
– soft, sacred, young blossom – and throw it away! Then
suddenly he heard the gate close, the pigs stirring again
and grunting; and leaning against the trunk, he pressed his
hands to its mossy sides behind him, and held his breath.
She might have been a spirit threading the trees, for all the
noise she made! Then he saw her quite close – her dark form
part of a little tree, her white face part of its blossom; so
still, and peering towards him. He whispered: 'Megan!' and

held out his hands. She ran forward, straight to his breast.
When he felt her heart beating against him, Ashurst knew
to the full the sensations of chivalry and passion. Because
she was not of his world, because she was so simple and
young and headlong, adoring and defenceless, how could
he be other than her protector, in the dark! Because she
was all simple Nature and beauty, as much a part of this
spring night as was the living blossom, how should he not
take all that she would give him – how not fulfil the spring
in her heart and his! And torn between these two emotions
he clasped her close, and kissed her hair. How long they
stood there without speaking he knew not. The stream went
on chattering, the owls hooting, the moon kept stealing up
and growing whiter; the blossom all round them and above
brightened in suspense of living beauty. Their lips had sought
each other's, and they did not speak. The moment speech
began all would be unreal! Spring has no speech, nothing
but rustling and whispering. Spring has so much more than
speech in its unfolding flowers and leaves, and the coursing of
its streams, and in its sweet restless seeking! And sometimes
spring will come alive, and, like a mysterious Presence, stand,
encircling lovers with its arms, laying on them the fingers
of enchantment, so that, standing lips to lips, they forget
everything but just a kiss. While her heart beat against him,
and her lips quivered on his, Ashurst felt nothing but simple
rapture – Destiny meant her for his arms, Love could not be
flouted! But when their lips parted for breath, division began
again at once. Only, passion now was so much the stronger,
and he sighed:

'Oh! Megan! Why did you come?'

She looked up, hurt, amazed.

'Sir, you asked me to.'

'Don't call me "sir", my pretty sweet.'

'What should I be callin' you?'

'Frank.'

'I could not. Oh, no!'

'But you love me – don't you?'

'I could not help lovin' you. I want to be with you – that's all.'

'All!'

So faint that he hardly heard, she whispered:

'I shall die if I can't be with you.'

Ashurst took a mighty breath.

'Come and be with me, then!'

'Oh!'

Intoxicated by the awe and rapture in that 'Oh!' he went on, whispering:

'We'll go to London. I'll show you the world. And I *will* take care of you, I promise, Megan. I'll never be a brute to you!'

'If I can be with you – that is all.'

He stroked her hair, and whispered on:

'To-morrow I'll go to Torquay and get some money, and get you some clothes that won't be noticed, and then we'll steal away. And when we get to London, soon perhaps, if you love me well enough, we'll be married.'

He could feel her hair shiver with the shake of her head.

'Oh, no! I could not. I only want to be with you!'

Drunk on his own chivalry, Ashurst went on murmuring:

'It's I who am not good enough for you. Oh! Megan, when did you begin to love me?'

'When I saw you in the road, and you looked at me. The first night I loved you; but I never thought you would want me.'

She slipped down suddenly to her knees, trying to kiss his feet.

A shiver of horror went through Ashurst; he lifted her up bodily and held her fast – too upset to speak.

She whispered: 'Why won't you let me?'

'It's I who will kiss your feet!'

Her smile brought tears into his eyes. The whiteness of her moonlit face so close to his, the faint pink of her opened lips, had the living unearthly beauty of the apple blossom.

And then, suddenly, her eyes widened and stared past

him painfully; she writhed out of his arms, and whispered: 'Look!'

Ashurst saw nothing but the brightened stream, the furze faintly gilded, the beech-trees glistening, and behind them all the wide loom of the moonlit hill. Behind him came the frozen whisper: 'The gipsy bogle!'

'Where?'

'There – by the stone – under the trees!'

Exasperated, he leapt the stream, and strode towards the beech clump. Prank of the moonlight! Nothing! In and out of the boulders and thorn trees, muttering and cursing, yet with a kind of terror, he rushed and stumbled. Absurd! Silly! Then he went back to the apple-tree. But she was gone; he could hear a rustle, the grunting of the pigs, the sound of a gate closing. Instead of her, only this old apple-tree! He flung his arms around the trunk. What a substitute for her soft body; the rough moss against his face – what a substitute for her soft cheek; only the scent, as of the woods, a little the same! And above him, and around, the blossoms, more living, more moonlit than ever, seemed to glow and breathe.

VII

Descending from the train at Torquay station, Ashurst wandered uncertainly along the front, for he did not know this particular queen of English watering places. Having little sense of what he had on, he was quite unconscious of being remarkable among its inhabitants, and strode along in his rough. Norfolk jacket, dusty boots, and battered hat, without observing that people gazed at him rather blankly. He was seeking a branch of his London bank, and having found one, found also the first obstacle to his mood. Did he know anyone in Torquay? No. In that case, if he would wire to his bank in London, they would be happy to oblige him on receipt of the reply. That suspicious breath from the matter-of-fact world somewhat tarnished the brightness of his visions. But he sent the telegram.

Nearly opposite to the post office he saw a shop full of ladies' garments, and examined the window with strange sensations. To have to undertake the clothing of his rustic love was more than a little disturbing. He went in. A young woman came forward; she had blue eyes and a faintly puzzled forehead. Ashurst stared at her in silence.

'Yes, sir?'

'I want a dress for a young lady.'

The young woman smiled. Ashurst frowned – the peculiarity of his request struck him with sudden force.

The young woman added hastily:

'What style would you like – something modish?'

'No. Simple.'

'What figure would the young lady be?'

'I don't know; about two inches shorter than you, I should say.'

'Could you give me her waist measurement?'

Megan's waist!

'Oh! anything usual!'

'Quite!'

While she was gone he stood disconsolately eyeing the models in the window, and suddenly it seemed to him incredible that Megan – his Megan – could ever be dressed save in the rough tweed skirt, coarse blouse, and tam-o'-shanter cap he was wont to see her in. The young woman had come back with several dresses in her arms, and Ashurst eyed her laying them against her own modish figure. There was one whose colour he liked, a dove-grey, but to imagine Megan clothed in it was beyond him. The young woman went away, and brought some more. But on Ashurst there had now come a feeling of paralysis. How choose? She would want a hat too, and shoes, and gloves; and, suppose, when he had got them all, they commonized her, as Sunday clothes always commonized village folk! Why should she not travel as she was? Ah! But conspicuousness would matter; this was a serious elopement. And, staring at the young woman, he thought: I wonder if she guesses, and thinks me a blackguard?'

'Do you mind putting aside that grey one for me?' he said desperately at last. 'I can't decide now; I'll come in again this afternoon.'

The young woman sighed.

'Oh! certainly. It's a very tasteful costume. I don't think you'll get anything that will suit your purpose better.'

'I expect not,' Ashurst murmured, and went out.

Freed again from the suspicious matter-of-factness of the world, he took a long breath, and went back to visions. In fancy he saw the trustful, pretty creature who was going to join her life to his; saw himself and her stealing forth at night, walking over the moor under the moon, he with his arm round her, and carrying her new garments, till, in some far-off wood, when dawn was coming, she would slip off her old things and put on these, and an early train at a distant station would bear them away on their honeymoon journey, till London swallowed them up, and the dreams of love came true.

'Frank Ashurst! Haven't seen you since Rugby, old chap!'

Ashurst's frown dissolved; the face, close to his own, was blue-eyed, suffused with sun – one of those faces where sun from within and without join in a sort of lustre. And he answered:

'Phil Halliday, by Jove!'

'What are you doing here?'

'Oh! nothing. Just looking round, and getting some money. I'm staying on the moor.'

'Are you lunching anywhere? Come and lunch with us; I'm here with my young sisters. They've had measles.'

Hooked in by that friendly arm Ashurst went along, up a hill, down a hill, away out of the town, while the voice of Halliday, redolent of optimism as his face was of sun, explained how 'in this mouldy place the only decent things were the bathing and boating', and so on, till presently they came to a crescent of houses a little above and back from the sea, and into the centre one – an hotel – made their way.

'Come up to my room and have a wash. Lunch'll be ready in a jiffy.'

Ashurst contemplated his visage in a looking-glass. After his farm-house bedroom, the comb and one spare shirt régime of the last fortnight, this room littered with clothes and brushes was a sort of Capua; and he thought: Queer – one doesn't realize – But what – he did not quite know.

When he followed Halliday into the sitting-room for lunch, three faces, very fair and blue-eyed, were turned suddenly at the words: 'This is Frank Ashurst – my young sisters.'

Two were indeed young, about eleven and ten. The third was perhaps seventeen, tall and fair-haired too, with pink-and-white cheeks just touched by the sun, and eyebrows, rather darker than the hair, running a little upwards from her nose to their outer points. The voices of all three were like Halliday's, high and cheerful; they stood up straight, shook hands with a quick movement, looked at Ashurst critically, away again at once, and began to talk of what they were going to do in the afternoon. A regular Diana and attendant nymphs! After the farm this crisp, slangy, eager talk, this cool, clean, off-hand refinement, was queer at first, and then so natural that what he had come from became suddenly remote. The names of the two little ones seemed to be Sabina and Freda; of the eldest, Stella.

Presently the one called Sabina turned to him and said:

'I say, will you come shrimping with us? It's awful fun!'

Surprised by this unexpected friendliness, Ashurst murmured:

'I'm afraid I've got to get back this afternoon.'

'Oh!'

'Can't you put it off?'

Ashurst turned to the new speaker, Stella, shook his head, and smiled. She was very pretty! Sabina said regretfully: 'You might!' Then the talk switched off to caves and swimming.

'Can you swim far?'

'About two miles.'

'Oh!'

'I say!'

'How jolly!'

The three pairs of blue eyes, fixed on him, made him conscious of his new importance. The sensation was agreeable. Halliday said:

'I say, you simply must stop and have a bathe. You'd better stay the night.'

'Yes, do!'

But again Ashurst smiled and shook his head. Then suddenly he found himself being catechized about his physical achievements. He had rowed – it seemed – in his college boat, played in his college football team, won his college mile; and he rose from table a sort of hero. The two little girls insisted that he must see 'their' cave, and they set forth chattering like magpies, Ashurst between them, Stella and her brother a little behind. In the cave, damp and darkish like any other cave, the great feature was a pool with possibility of creatures which might be caught and put into bottles. Sabina and Freda, who wore no stockings on their shapely brown legs, exhorted Ashurst to join them in the middle of it, and help sieve the water. He too was soon bootless and sockless. Time goes fast for one who has a sense of beauty, when there are pretty children in a pool and a young Diana on the edge, to receive with wonder anything you can catch! Ashurst never had much sense of time. It was a shock when, pulling out his watch, he saw it was well past three. No cashing his cheque today – the bank would be closed before he could get there. Watching his expression, the little girls cried out at once:

'Hurrah! Now you'll have to stay!'

Ashurst did not answer. He was seeing again Megan's face, when at breakfast he had whispered: 'I'm going to Torquay, darling, to get everything; I shall be back this evening. If it's fine we can go tonight. Be ready.' He was seeing again how she quivered and hung on his words. What would she think? Then he pulled himself together, conscious suddenly of the calm scrutiny of this other young girl, so tall and fair and Diana-like, at the edge of the pool, of her wondering blue eyes under those brows which slanted up a little. If they knew what was in his mind – if they knew that this very night he had meant –! Well, there would be a little sound of disgust, and he would be alone in the cave. And with a curious mixture of anger, chagrin, and shame, he put his watch back into his pocket and said abruptly:

'Yes; I'm dished for today.'

'Hurrah! Now you can bathe with us.'

It was impossible not to succumb a little to the contentment of these pretty children, to the smile on Stella's lips, to Halliday's 'Ripping, old chap! I can lend you things for the night!' But again a spasm of longing and remorse throbbed through Ashurst, and he said moodily:

'I must send a wire!'

The attractions of the pool palling, they went back to the hotel. Ashurst sent his wire, addressing it to Mrs Narracombe: 'Sorry, detained for the night back tomorrow.' Surely Megan would understand that he had too much to do; and his heart grew lighter. It was a lovely afternoon, warm, the sea calm and blue, and swimming his great passion; the favour of these pretty children flattered him, the pleasure of looking at them, at Stella, at Halliday's sunny face; the slight unreality, yet extreme naturalness of it all – as of a last peep at normality before he took this plunge with Megan! He got his borrowed bathing dress, and they all set forth. Halliday and he undressed behind one rock, the three girls behind another. He was first into the sea, and at once swam out with the bravado of justifying his self-given reputation. When he turned he could see Halliday swimming along shore, and the girls flopping and dipping, and riding the little waves, in the way he was accustomed to despise, but now thought pretty and sensible, since it gave him the distinction of the only deep-water fish. But drawing near, he wondered if they would like him, a stranger, to come into their splashing group; he felt shy, approaching that slim nymph. Then Sabina summoned him to teach her to float, and between them the little girls kept him so busy that he had no time even to notice whether Stella was accustomed to his presence, till suddenly he heard a startled sound from her. She was standing submerged to the waist, leaning a little forward, her slim white arms stretched out and pointing, her wet face puckered by the sun and an expression of fear.

'Look at Phil! Is he all right? Oh, look!'

Ashurst saw at once that Phil was not all right. He was splashing and struggling out of his depth, perhaps a hundred yards away; suddenly he gave a cry, threw up his arms, and went down. Ashurst saw the girl launch herself towards him, and crying out: 'Go back, Stella! Go back!' he dashed out. He had never swum so fast, and reached Halliday just as he was coming up a second time. It was a case of cramp, but to get him in was not difficult, for he did not struggle. The girl, who had stopped where Ashurst told her to, helped as soon as he was in his depth, and once on the beach they sat down one on each side of him to rub his limbs, while the little ones stood by with scared faces. Halliday was soon smiling. It was – he said – rotten of him, absolutely rotten! If Frank would give him an arm, he could get to his clothes all right now. Ashurst gave him the arm, and as he did so caught sight of Stella's face, wet and flushed and tearful, all broken up out of its calm; and he thought: I called her Stella! Wonder if she minded?

While they were dressing, Halliday said quietly:

'You saved my life, old chap!'

'Rot!'

Clothed, but not quite in their right minds, they went up all together to the hotel and sat down to tea, except Halliday, who was lying down in his room. After some slices of bread and jam, Sabina said:

'I say, you know, you *are* a brick!' And Freda chimed in: 'Rather!'

Ashurst saw Stella looking down; he got up in confusion, and went to the window. From there he heard Sabina mutter:

'I say, let's swear blood bond. Where's your knife, Freda?' and out of the corner of his eye could see each of them solemnly prick herself, squeeze out a drop of blood and dabble on a bit of paper. He turned and made for the door.

'Don't be a stoat! Come back!' His arms were seized; imprisoned between the little girls he was brought back to the table. On it lay a piece of paper with an effigy drawn in blood, and the three names Stella Halliday, Sabina Halliday, Freda Halliday – also in blood, running towards it like the rays of a star. Sabina said:

'That's you. We shall have to kiss you, you know.'

And Freda echoed:

'Oh! Blow – yes!'

Before Ashurst could escape, some wettish hair dangled against his face, something like a bite descended on his nose, he felt his left arm pinched, and other teeth softly searching his cheek. Then he was released, and Freda said:

'Now – Stella.'

Ashurst, red and rigid, looked across the table at a red and rigid Stella. Sabina giggled; Freda cried:

'Buck up – it spoils everything!'

A queer, ashamed eagerness shot through Ashurst: then he said quietly:

'Shut up, you little demons!'

Again Sabina giggled.

'Well, then, she can kiss her hand, and you can put it against your nose. It *is* on one side!'

To his amazement the girl did kiss her hand and stretch it out. Solemnly he took that cool, slim hand and laid it to his cheek. The two little girls broke into clapping, and Freda said:

'Now, then, we shall have to save your life at any time; that's settled. Can I have another cup, Stella, not so beastly weak?'

Tea was resumed, and Ashurst, folding up the paper, put it in his pocket. The talk turned on the advantages of measles, tangerine oranges, honey in a spoon, no lessons, and so forth. Ashurst listened, silent, exchanging friendly looks with Stella,

whose face was again of its normal sun-touched pink and
white. It was soothing to be so taken to the heart of this jolly
family, fascinating to watch their faces. And after tea, while
the two little girls pressed seaweed, he talked to Stella in the
window seat and looked at her water-colour sketches. The
whole thing was like a pleasurable dream; time and incident
hung up, importance and reality suspended. To-morrow he
would go back to Megan, with nothing of all this left save
the paper with the blood of these children, in his pocket.
Children! Stella was not quite that – as old as Megan! Her
talk – quick, rather hard and shy, yet friendly – seemed to
flourish on his silences, and about her there was something
cool and virginal – a maiden in a bower. At dinner, to which
Halliday, who had swallowed too much sea-water, did not
come, Sabina said:

'I'm going to call you Frank.'

Freda echoed:

'Frank, Frank, Franky.'

Ashurst grinned and bowed.

'Every time Stella calls you Mr Ashurst, she's got to pay a
forfeit. It's ridiculous.'

Ashurst looked at Stella, who grew slowly red. Sabina
giggled; Freda cried:

'She's "smoking" – "smoking!" – Yah!'

Ashurst reached out to right and left, and grasped some
fair hair in each hand.

'Look here,' he said, 'you two! Leave Stella alone, or I'll
tie you together!'

Freda gurgled:

'Ouch! You *are* a beast!'

Sabina murmured cautiously:

'*You* call *her* Stella, you see!'

'Why shouldn't I? It's a jolly name!'

'All right; we give you leave to!'

Ashurst released the hair. Stella! What would she call him
– after this? But she called him nothing; till at bedtime he
said, deliberately:

'Good-night, Stella!'

'Good-night, Mr – Good-night, Frank! It *was* jolly of you, you know!'

'Oh – that! Bosh!'

Her quick, straight handshake tightened suddenly, and as suddenly became slack.

Ashurst stood motionless in the empty sitting-room. Only last night, under the apple-tree and the living blossom, he had held Megan to him, kissing her eyes and lips. And he gasped, swept by that rush of remembrance. Tonight it should have begun – his life with her who only wanted to be with him! And now, twenty-four hours and more must pass, because – of not looking at his watch! Why had he made friends with this family of innocents just when he was saying good-bye to innocence, and all the rest of it? But I mean to marry her, he thought. I told her so!

He took a candle, lighted it, and went to his bedroom, which was next to Halliday's. His friend's voice called as he was passing:

'Is that you, old chap? I say, come in.'

He was sitting up in bed, smoking a pipe and reading.

'Sit down a bit.'

Ashurst sat down by the open window.

'I've been thinking about this afternoon, you know,' said Halliday rather suddenly. 'They say you go through all your past. I didn't. I suppose I wasn't far enough gone.'

'What did you think of?'

Halliday was silent for a little, then said quietly:

'Well, I did think of one thing – rather odd – of a girl at Cambridge that I might have – you know; I was glad I hadn't got her on my mind. Anyhow, old chap, I owe it to you that I'm here; I should have been in the big dark by now. No more bed, or baccy; no more anything. I say, what d'you suppose happens to us?'

Ashurst murmured:

'Go out like flames, I expect.'

'Phew!'

'We may flicker, and cling about a bit, perhaps.'

'H'm! I think that's rather gloomy. I say, I hope my young sisters have been decent to you?'

'Awfully decent.'

Halliday put his pipe down, crossed his hands behind his neck, and turned his face towards the window.

'They're not bad kids!' he said.

Watching his friend, lying there, with that smile, and the candle-light on his face, Ashurst shuddered. Quite true! He might have been lying there with no smile, with all that sunny look gone out for ever! He might not have been lying there at all, but 'sanded' at the bottom of the sea, waiting for resurrection on the – ninth day, was it? And that smile of Halliday's seemed to him suddenly something wonderful, as if in it were all the difference between life and death – the little flame – the all! He got up, and said softly:

'Well, you ought to sleep, I expect. Shall I blow out?'

Halliday caught his hand.

'I can't say it, you know; but it must be rotten to be dead. Goodnight, old boy!'

Stirred and moved, Ashurst squeezed the hand, and went downstairs. The hall door was still open, and he passed out on to the lawn before the Crescent. The stars were bright in a very dark blue sky, and by their light some lilacs had that mysterious colour of flowers by night which no one can describe. Ashurst pressed his face against a spray; and before his closed eyes Megan started up, with the tiny brown spaniel pup against her breast. 'I thought of a girl that I might have – you know. I was glad I hadn't got her on my mind!' He jerked his head away from the lilac, and began pacing up and down over the grass, a grey phantom coming to substance for a moment in the light from the lamp at either end. He was with her again under the living, breathing whiteness of the blossom, the stream chattering by, the moon glinting steel-blue on the bathing-pool; back in the rapture of his kisses on her upturned face of innocence and humble passion, back in the suspense and beauty of that pagan night. He stood still once more in the shadow of the lilacs. Here the sea, not the stream, was Night's voice; the sea with its sigh and rustle; no little bird, no owl, no nightjar called or spun; but a piano tinkled, and the white houses cut the sky with solid curve, and the scent from the lilacs filled the air. A window of the hotel, high up, was lighted; he saw a shadow move across the blind. And most queer sensations stirred within him, a sort of churning, and twining, and turning of a single emotion on itself, as though spring and love, bewildered and confused, seeking the way, were baffled. This girl, who had called him Frank, whose hand had given his that sudden little clutch, this girl so cool and pure – what would *she* think of such wild, unlawful loving? He sank down on the grass, sitting there cross-legged, with his back to the house, motionless as some carved Buddha. Was he really going to break through innocence, and steal? Sniff the scent out of a wild flower, and – perhaps – throw it away? '. . . of a girl at Cambridge that I might have – you know!' He put his hands to the grass, one on each side, palms downwards, and pressed; it was just warm still – the grass, barely moist, soft and firm and friendly. What am I going to do? he thought. Perhaps Megan was at her window, looking out at the blossom, thinking of him! Poor little Megan! Why not? he thought. I love her! But do I – really love her? or do I only want her because she is so pretty, and loves me? What am I going to do? The piano tinkled on, the stars winked; and Ashurst gazed out before him at the dark sea, as if spell-bound. He got up at last, cramped and rather chilly. There was no longer light in any window. And he went to bed.

VIII

Out of a deep and dreamless sleep he was awakened by the sound of thumping on the door. A shrill voice called:

'Hi! Breakfast's ready.'

He jumped up. Where was he –? Ah!

He found them already eating marmalade, and sat down

in the empty place between Stella and Sabina, who, after
watching him a little, said:

'I say, do buck up; we're going to start at half-past nine.'

'We're going to Berry Head, old chap; you *must* come!'

Ashurst thought: 'Come! Impossible. I shall be getting
things and going back.' He looked at Stella. She said quickly:

'Do come!'

Sabina chimed in:

'It'll be no fun without you.'

Freda got up and stood behind his chair.

'You've got to come, or else I'll pull your hair!'

Ashurst thought: 'Well – one day more – to think it over!
One day more!' And he said:

'All right! You needn't tweak my mane!'

'Hurrah!'

At the station he wrote a second telegram to the farm,
and then – tore it up; he could not have explained why.
From Brixham they drove in a very little wagonette. There,
squeezed between Sabina and Freda, with his knees touching
Stella's, they played 'Up Jenkins'; and the gloom he was
feeling gave way to frolic. In this one day more to think
it over, he did not want to think! They ran races, wrestled,
paddled – for today nobody wanted to bathe – they sang
catches, played games, and ate all they had brought. The
little girls fell asleep against him on the way back, and
his knees still touched Stella's in the wagonette. It seemed
incredible that thirty hours ago he had never set eyes on any
of those three flaxen heads. In the train he talked to Stella of
poetry, discovering her favourites, and telling her his own
with a pleasing sense of superiority; till suddenly she said,
rather low:

'Phil says you don't believe in a future life, Frank. I think
that's dreadful.'

Disconcerted, Ashurst muttered:

'I don't either believe or not believe – I simply don't
know.'

She said quickly:

'I couldn't bear that. What would be the use of living?'

Watching the frown of those pretty oblique brows, Ashurst answered:

'I don't believe in believing things because one wants to.'

'But why should one *wish* to live again, if one isn't going to?'

And she looked full at him.

He did not want to hurt her, but an itch to dominate pushed him on to say:

'While one's alive one naturally wants to go on living for ever; that's part of being alive. But it probably isn't anything more.'

'Don't you believe in the Bible at all, then?'

Ashurst thought: Now I shall really hurt her!

'I believe in the Sermon on the Mount, because it's beautiful and good for all time.'

'But don't you believe Christ was divine?'

He shook his head.

She turned her face quickly to the window, and there sprang into his mind Megan's prayer, repeated by little Nick: 'God bless us all, and Mr Ashes!' Who else would ever say a prayer for him, like her who at this moment must be waiting – waiting to see him come down the lane? And he thought suddenly: What a scoundrel I am!

All that evening this thought kept coming back; but, as is not unusual, each time with less poignancy, till it seemed almost a matter of course to be a scoundrel. And – strange! – he did not know whether he was a scoundrel if he meant to go back to Megan, or if he did not mean to go back to her.

They played cards till the children were sent off to bed; then Stella went to the piano. From over on the window seat, where it was nearly dark, Ashurst watched her between the candles – that fair head on the long, white neck bending to the movement of her hands. She played fluently, without much expression; but what a picture she made, the faint golden radiance, a sort of angelic atmosphere – hovering about her! Who could have passionate thoughts or wild desires in the presence of that swaying, white-clothed girl with the seraphic head? She played a thing of Schumann's called '*Warum?*' Then Halliday brought out a flute, and the spell was broken. After this they made Ashurst sing, Stella playing him accompaniments from a book of Schumann songs, till, in the middle of '*Ich grolle nicht*', two small figures clad in blue dressing-gowns crept in and tried to conceal themselves beneath the piano. The evening broke up in confusion, and what Sabina called 'a splendid rag'.

That night Ashurst hardly slept at all. He was thinking, tossing and turning. The intense domestic intimacy of these last two days, the strength of this Halliday atmosphere, seemed to ring him round, and make the farm and Megan – even Megan – seem unreal. Had he really made love to her – really promised to take her away to live with him? He must have been bewitched by the spring, the night, the apple blossom! This May madness could but destroy them both! The notion that he was going to make her his mistress – that simple child not yet eighteen – now filled him with a sort of horror, even while it still stung and whipped his blood. He muttered to himself: 'It's awful, what I've done – awful!' And the sound of Schumann's music throbbed and mingled with his fevered thoughts, and he saw again Stella's cool, white, fair-haired figure and bending neck, the queer, angelic radiance about her. I must have been – I must be – mad! he thought. What came into me? Poor little Megan! 'God bless us all, and Mr Ashes!' 'I want to be with you – only to be with you!' And burying his face in his pillow, he smothered down a fit of sobbing. Not to go back was awful! To go back – more awful still!

Emotion, when you are young, and give real vent to it, loses its power of torture. And he fell asleep, thinking: What was it – a few kisses – all forgotten in a month!

Next morning he got his cheque cashed, but avoided the shop of the dove-grey dress like the plague; and, instead, bought himself some necessaries. He spent the whole day in a queer mood, cherishing a kind of sullenness against himself. Instead of the hankering of the last two days, he felt nothing but a blank – all passionate longing gone, as if quenched in that outburst of tears. After tea Stella put a book down beside him, and said shyly:

'Have you read that, Frank?'

It was Farrar's *Life of Christ*. Ashurst smiled. Her anxiety about his beliefs seemed to him comic, but touching. Infectious, too, perhaps, for he began to have an itch to justify himself, if not to convert her. And in the evening, when the children and Halliday were mending their shrimping nets, he said:

'At the back of orthodox religion, so far as I can see, there's always the idea of reward – what you can get for being good; a kind of begging for favours. I think it all starts in fear.'

She was sitting on the sofa making reefer knots with a bit of string. She looked up quickly:

'I think it's much deeper than that.'

Ashurst felt again that wish to dominate.

'You think so,' he said; 'but wanting the *quid pro quo* is about the deepest thing in all of us! It's jolly hard to get to the bottom of it!'

She wrinkled her brows in a puzzled frown.

'I don't think I understand.'

He went on obstinately:

'Well, think, and see if the most religious people aren't those who feel that this life doesn't give them all they want. I believe in being good because to be good is good in itself.'

'Then you do believe in being good?'

How pretty she looked now – it was easy to be good with her! And he nodded and said:

'I say, show me how to make that knot!'

With her fingers touching his, in manoeuvring the bit of string he felt soothed and happy. And when he went to bed he wilfully kept his thoughts on her, wrapping himself in her fair, cool sisterly radiance, as in some garment of protection.

Next day he found they had arranged to go by train to Totnes, and picnic at Berry Pomeroy Castle. Still in that resolute oblivion of the past, he took his place with them in the landau beside Halliday, back to the horses. And, then, along the sea front, nearly to the turning to the railway station, his heart almost leaped into his mouth. Megan – Megan herself! – was walking on the far pathway, in her old skirt and jacket and her tam-o'-shanter, looking up into the faces of the passers-by. Instinctively he threw his hand up for cover, then made a feint of clearing dust out of his eyes; but between his fingers he could see her still, moving, not with her free country step, but wavering, lost-looking, pitiful – like some little dog which has missed its master and does not know whether to run on, to run back – where to run. How had she come like this? What excuse had she found to get away? What did she hope for? But with every turn of the wheels bearing him away from her, his heart revolted and cried to him to stop them, to get out, and go to her! When the landau turned the corner to the station he could stand it no more, and opening the carriage door, muttered: 'I've forgotten something! Go on – don't wait for me! I'll join you at the castle by the next train!' He jumped, stumbled, spun round, recovered his balance, and walked forward, while the carriage with the astonished Hallidays rolled on.

From the corner he could only just see Megan, a long way ahead now. He ran a few steps, checked himself, and dropped into a walk. With each step nearer to her, further from the Hallidays, he walked more and more slowly. How did it alter anything – this sight of her? How make the going to her, and that which must come of it, less ugly? For there was no hiding it – since he had met the Hallidays he had become gradually sure that he would not marry Megan. It would only be a wild love-time, a troubled, remorseful, difficult time – and then – well, then he would get tired, just because she gave him everything, was so simple, and so trustful, so dewy. And dew – wears off! The little spot of faded colour, her tam-o'-shanter cap, wavered on far in front of him; she was

looking up into every face, and at the house windows. Had
any man ever such a cruel moment to go through? Whatever
he did, he felt he would be a beast. And he uttered a groan
which made a nursemaid turn and stare. He saw Megan stop
and lean against the sea-wall, looking at the sea; and he too
stopped. Quite likely she had never seen the sea before, and
even in her distress could not resist that sight. Yes – she's
seen nothing, he thought; everything's before her. And just
for a few weeks' passion, I shall be cutting her life to ribbons.
I'd better go and hang myself rather than do it! And suddenly
seemed to see Stella's calm eyes looking into his, the wave of
fluffy hair on her forehead stirred by the wind. Ah! it would
be madness, would mean giving up all that he respected, and
his own self-respect. He turned and walked quickly back
towards the station. But memory of that poor, bewildered little figure, those anxious eyes searching the passers-by, smote
him too hard again, and once more he turned towards the
sea. The cap was no longer visible; that little spot of colour
had vanished in the stream of the noon promenaders. And
impelled by the passion of longing, the dearth which comes
on one when life seems to be whiling something out of reach,
he hurried forward. She was nowhere to be seen; for half an
hour he looked for her; then on the beach flung himself face
downward in the sand. To find her again he knew he had
only to go to the station and wait till she returned from her
fruitless quest, to take her train home; or to take train himself
and go back to the farm, so that she found him there when she
returned. But he lay inert in the sand, among the indifferent
groups of children with their spades and buckets. Pity at her
little figure wandering, seeking, was well-nigh merged in
the spring-running of his blood; for it was all wild feeling
now – the chivalrous part, what there had been of it, was
gone. He wanted her again, wanted her kisses, her soft, little
body, her abandonment, all her quick, warm, pagan emotion;
wanted the wonderful feeling of that night under the moonlit
apple boughs; wanted it all with a horrible intensity, as the
faun wants the nymph. The quick chatter of the little bright

trout-stream, the dazzle of the buttercups, the rocks of the old
'wild men'; the calling of the cuckoos and yaffles, the hooting
of the owls; and the red moon peeping out of the velvet dark
at the living whiteness of the blossom; and her face just out
of reach at the window, lost in its love-look; and her heart
against his, her lips answering his, under the apple tree –
all this besieged him. Yet he lay inert. What was it which
struggled against pity and this feverish longing, and kept
him there paralysed in the warm sand? Three flaxen heads –
a fair face with friendly blue-grey eyes, a slim hand pressing
his, a quick voice speaking his name – 'So you do believe
in being good?' Yes, and a sort of atmosphere as of some
old walled-in English garden, with pinks, and corn-flowers,
and roses, and scents of lavender and lilac – cool and fair,
untouched, almost holy – all that he had been brought up
to feel was clean and good. And suddenly he thought: She
might come along the front again and see me! and he got up
and made his way to the rock at the far end of the beach.
There, with the spray biting into his face, he could think more
coolly. To go back to the farm and love Megan out in the
woods, among the rocks, with everything around wild and
fitting – that, he knew, was impossible, utterly. To transplant
her to a great town, to keep, in some little flat or rooms,
one who belonged so wholly to Nature – the poet in him
shrank from it. His passion would be a mere sensuous revel,
soon gone; in London, her very simplicity, her lack of all
intellectual quality, would make her his secret plaything –
nothing else. The longer he sat on the rock, with his feet
dangling over a greenish pool from which the sea was ebbing,
the more clearly he saw this; but it was as if her arms and all
of her were slipping slowly, slowly down from him, into the
pool, to be carried away out to sea; and her face looking
up, her lost face with beseeching eyes, and dark, wet hair –
possessed, haunted, tortured him! He got up at last, scaled the
low rock-cliff, and made his way down into a sheltered cove.
Perhaps in the sea he could get back his control – lose this
fever! And stripping off his clothes, he swam out. He wanted

to tire himself so that nothing mattered, and swam recklessly, fast and far; then suddenly, for no reason, felt afraid. Suppose he could not reach shore again – suppose the current set him out – or he got cramp, like Halliday! He turned to swim in. The red cliffs looked a long way off. If he were drowned they would find his clothes. The Hallidays would know; but Megan perhaps never – they took no newspaper at the farm. And Phil Halliday's words came back to him again: 'A girl at Cambridge I might have – Glad I haven't got her on my mind!' And in that moment of unreasoning fear he vowed he would not have her on his mind. Then his fear left him; he swam in easily enough, dried himself in the sun, and put on his clothes. His heart felt sore, but no longer ached; his body cool and refreshed.

When one is as young as Ashurst, pity is not a violent emotion. And, back in the Hallidays' sitting-room, eating a ravenous tea, he felt much like a man recovered from fever. Everything seemed new and clear; the tea, the buttered toast and jam tasted absurdly good; tobacco had never smelt so nice. And walking up and down the empty room, he stopped here and there to touch or look. He took up Stella's work-basket, fingered the cotton reels and a gaily-coloured plait of sewing silks, smelt at the little bag filled with woodroffe she kept among them. He sat down at the piano, playing tunes with one finger, thinking: 'Tonight she'll play; I shall watch her while she's playing; it does me good to watch her.' He took up the book, which still lay where she had placed it beside him, and tried to read. But Megan's little, sad figure began to come back at once, and he got up and leaned in the window, listening to the thrushes in the Crescent gardens, gazing at the sea, dreamy and blue below the trees. A servant came in and cleared the tea away, and he still stood, inhaling the evening air, trying not to think. Then he saw the Hallidays coming through the gate of the Crescent, Stella a little in front of Phil and the children, with their baskets, and instinctively he drew back. His heart, too sore and dis-comfited, shrank from this encounter, yet wanted its friendly solace – bore a grudge against this influence, yet craved its cool innocence, and the pleasure of watching Stella's face. From against the wall behind the piano he saw her come in and stand looking a little blank as though disappointed; then she saw him and smiled, a swift, brilliant smile which warmed yet irritated Ashurst.

'You never came after us, Frank.'

'No; I found I couldn't.'

'Look! We picked such lovely late violets!' She held out a bunch. Ashurst put his nose to them, and there stirred within him vague longings, chilled instantly by a vision of Megan's anxious face lifted to the faces of the passers-by.

He said shortly: 'How jolly!' and turned away. He went up to his room, and, avoiding the children, who were coming up the stairs, threw himself on his bed, and lay there with his arms crossed over his face. Now that he felt the die really cast, and Megan given up, he hated himself, and almost hated the Hallidays and their atmosphere of healthy, happy English homes. Why should they have chanced here, to drive away first love – to show him that he was going to be no better than a common seducer? What right had Stella, with her fair, shy beauty, to make him know for certain that he would never marry Megan; and, tarnishing it all, bring him such bitterness of regretful longing and such pity? Megan would be back by now, worn out by her miserable seeking – poor little thing! – expecting, perhaps, to find him there when she reached home. Ashurst bit at his sleeve, to stifle a groan of remorseful longing. He went to dinner glum and silent, and his mood threw a dinge even over the children. It was a melancholy, rather ill-tempered evening, for they were all tired; several times he caught Stella looking at him with a hurt, puzzled expression, and this pleased his evil mood. He slept miserably; got up quite early, and wandered out. He went down to the beach. Alone there with the serene, the blue, the sunlit sea, his heart relaxed a little. Conceited fool – to think that Megan would take it so hard! In a week or two she would almost have forgotten! And he – well, he would have the reward of virtue! A good young man! If Stella knew, she would give him her blessing for resisting that devil she believed in; and he uttered a hard laugh. But slowly the peace and beauty of sea and sky, the flight of the lonely seagulls, made him feel ashamed. He bathed, and turned homewards.

In the Crescent gardens Stella herself was sitting on a camp stool, sketching. He stole up close behind. How fair and pretty she was, bent diligently, holding up her brush, measuring, wrinkling her brows.

He said gently:

'Sorry I was such a beast last night, Stella.'

She turned round, startled, flushed very pink, and said in her quick way:

'It's all right. I knew there was something. Between friends it doesn't matter, does it?'

Ashurst answered:

'Between friends – and we are, aren't we?'

She looked up at him, nodded vehemently, and her upper teeth gleamed again in that swift, brilliant smile.

Three days later he went back to London, travelling with the Hallidays. He had not written to the farm. What was there he could say?

On the last day of April in the following year he and Stella were married . . .

Such were Ashurst's memories, sitting against the wall among the gorse, on his silver-wedding day. At this very spot, where he had laid out the lunch, Megan must have stood outlined against the sky when he had first caught sight of her. Of all queer coincidences! And there moved in him a longing to go down and see again the farm and the orchard, and the meadow of the gipsy bogle. It would not take long; Stella would be an hour yet, perhaps.

How well he remembered it all – the little crowning group of pine trees, the steep-up grass hill behind! He paused at the farm gate. The low stone house, the yew-tree porch, the flowering currants – not changed a bit; even the old green chair was out there on the grass under the window, where he had reached up to her that night to take the key. Then he turned down the lane, and stood leaning on the orchard gate – grey skeleton of a gate, as then. A black pig even was wandering in there among the trees. Was it true that twenty-six years had passed, or had he dreamed and awakened to find Megan waiting for him by the big apple-tree? Unconsciously he put up his hand to his grizzled beard and brought himself back to reality. Opening the gate, he made his way down through the docks and nettles till he came to the edge, and the old apple-tree itself. Unchanged! A little more of the grey-green lichen, a dead branch or two, and for the rest it might have been only last night that he had embraced that mossy trunk after Megan's flight and inhaled its woody savour, while above his head the moonlit blossom had seemed to breathe and live. In that early spring a few buds were showing already; the blackbirds shouting their songs, a cuckoo calling, the sunlight bright and warm. Incredibly the same – the chattering trout-stream, the narrow pool he had lain in every morning, splashing the water over his flanks and chest; and out there in the wild meadow the beech clump and the stone where the gipsy bogle was supposed to sit. And an ache for lost youth, a hankering, a sense of wasted love and sweetness, gripped Ashurst by the throat. Surely, on this earth of such wild beauty, one was meant to hold rapture to one's heart, as this earth and sky held it! And yet, one could not!

He went to the edge of the stream, and looking down at the little pool, thought: Youth and spring! What has become of them all, I wonder? And then, in sudden fear of having this memory jarred by human encounter, he went back to the lane, and pensively retraced his steps to the cross-roads.

Beside the car an old, grey-bearded labourer was leaning on a stick, talking to the chauffeur. He broke off at once, as though guilty of disrespect, and touching his hat, prepared to limp on down the lane.

Ashurst pointed to the narrow green mound. 'Can you tell me what this is?'

The old fellow stopped; on his face came a look as though he were thinking: You've come to the right shop, mister!

''Tes a grave,' he said.

'But why out here?'

The old man smiled. 'That's a tale, as yu may say. An' not the first time as I've a-told et – there's plenty folks asks 'bout that bit o' turf. "Maid's Grave" us calls et, 'ereabouts.'

Ashurst held out his pouch. 'Have a fill?'

The old man touched his hat again, and slowly filled an old clay pipe. His eyes, looking upward out of a mass of wrinkles and hair, were still quite bright.

'If yu don' mind, zurr, I'll zet down – my leg's 'urtin' a bit today.' And he sat down on the mound of turf.

'There's always a vlower on this grave. An' 'taint' so very lonesome, neither; brave lot o'folks goes by now, in they new motor cars an' things – not as 'twas in th' old days. She've a-got company up 'ere. 'Twas a poor soul killed 'erself.'

'I see!' said Ashurst. 'Cross-roads burial. I didn't know that custom was kept up.'

'Ah! but 'twas a main long time ago. Us 'ad a parson as was very God-fearin' then. Let me see, I've a 'ad my pension six year come Michaelmas, an' I were just on fifty when t'appened. There's none livin' knows more about et than what I du. She belonged close 'ere; same farm as where I used to work along o' Mrs Narracombe – 'tes Nick Narracombe's now; I dus a bit for 'im still, odd times.'

Ashurst, who was leaning against the gate, lighting his pipe, left his curved hands before his face for long after the flame of the match had gone out.

'Yes?' he said, and to himself his voice sounded hoarse and queer.

'She was one in an 'underd, poor maid! I putts a vlower 'ere every time I passes. Pretty maid an' gude maid she was, though they wouldn't burry 'er up tu th' church, nor where she wanted to be burried neither.' The old labourer paused, and put his hairy, twisted hand flat down on the turf beside the bluebells.

'Yes?' said Ashurst.

'In a manner of speakin',' the old man went on, 'I think as 'twas a love-story – though there's no one never knu for zartin. Yu can't tell what's in a maid's 'ead – but that's wot I think about it.' He drew his hand along the turf. 'I was fond o' that maid – don' know as there was anyone as wasn' fond of 'er. But she was tu lovin'-'earted – that's where 'twas, I think.' He looked up. And Ashurst, whose lips were trembling in the cover of his beard, murmured again: 'Yes?'

''Twas in the spring, 'bout now as 't might be, or a little later – blossom time – an' we 'ad one o' they young college gentlemen stayin' at the farm – nice feller tu, with 'is 'ead in the air. I liked 'e very well, an' I never see nothin' between 'em, but to my thinkin' 'e turned the maid's fancy.' The old man took the pipe out of his mouth, spat, and went on:

'Yu see, 'e went away sudden one day, an' never come back. They got 'is knapsack and bits o' things down there still. That's what stuck in my mind – 'is never sendin' for 'em. 'Is name was Ashes, or somethen' like that.'

'Yes?' said Ashurst once more.

The old man licked his lips.

''Er never said nothin', but from that day 'er went kind of dazed lukin'; didn' seem rightly therr at all. I never knu a 'uman creature so changed in me life – never. There was another young feller at the farm – Joe Biddaford 'is name wer', that was praaperly sweet on 'er, tu; I guess 'e used to plague 'er wi' 'is attentions. She got to luke quite wild. I'd zee her sometimes of an avenin' when I was bringin' up the calves; ther' she'd stand in th' orchard, under the big appletree, lukin' straight before 'er. Well, I used t'think, I dunno what 'tes that's the matter wi' yu, but yu'm lukin' pittiful, that yu be!'

The old man relit his pipe, and sucked at it reflectively.

'Yes?' said Ashurst.

'I remembers one day I said to 'er: "What's the matter,

Megan?" – 'er name was Megan David, she come from Wales same as 'er aunt, ol' Missis Narracombe. "Yu'm frettin' about somethin," I says. "No, Jim," she says, "I'm not frettin'." 'Yes, yu be!' I says. 'No,' she says, and tu tears cam' rollin' out. 'Yu'm cryin' – what's that, then?' I says. She putts 'er 'and over 'er 'eart: 'It 'urts me,' she says; 'but 'twill sune be better,' she says. 'But if anything shude 'appen to me, Jim, I wants to be burried under this 'ere apple-tree.' I laughed. 'What's goin' to 'appen to yu?' I says. 'Don't 'ee be fulish.' 'No,' she says, 'I won't be fulish.' Well, I know what maids are, an' I never thought no more about et, till tu days arter that, 'bout six in the avenin' I was comin' up wi' the calves, when I see somethin' dark lyin' in the strame, close to that big apple-tree. I says to meself: 'Is that a pig – funny place for a pig to get to!' an' I goes up to et, an' I see what 'twas.'

The old man stopped: his eyes, turned upward, had a bright, suffering look.

''Twas the maid, in a little narrer pool ther' that's made by the stoppin' of a rock – where I see the young gentleman bathin' once or twice. 'Er was lyin' on 'er face in the watter. There was a plant o' goldie-cups growin' out o' the stone just above 'er 'ead. An' when I come to luke at 'er face, 'twas luvly, butiful, so calm's a baby's – wonderful butiful et was. When the doctor saw 'er, 'e said: "'Er culdn' never a-done it in that little bit o' watter ef'er 'adn't a-been in an extarsy." Ah! an' judgin' from 'er face, that was just 'ow she was. Et made me cry praaper – butiful et was! 'Twas June then, but she'd a-found a little bit of apple-blossom left over somewheres, and stuck et in 'er 'air. That's why I thinks 'er must a-been in an extarsy, to go to et gay, like that. Why! there wasn't more than a fute and 'arf o' watter. But I tell 'ee one thing – that meadder's 'arnted; I knu et, an' she knu et; an' no one'll persuade me as 'tesn't. I told 'em what she said to me 'bout bein' burried under th' apple-tree. But I think that turned 'em – made et luke tu much 's ef she'd 'ad it in 'er mind deliberate; an' so they buried 'er up 'ere. Parson we 'ad then was very particular, 'e was.'

Again the old man drew his hand over the turf.

'Tes wonderful, et seems,' he added slowly, 'what maids 'll du for love. She 'ad a lovin' 'eart; I guess 'twas broken. But us never *knu* nothin'!'

He looked up as if for approval of his story, but Ashurst had walked past him as if he were not there.

Up on top of the hill, beyond where he had spread the lunch, over, out of sight, he lay down on his face. So had his virtue been rewarded, and 'the Cyprian', goddess of love, taken her revenge! And before his eyes, dim with tears, came Megan's face with the sprig of apple blossom in her dark, wet hair. What did I do that was wrong? he thought. What *did* I do? But he could not answer. Spring, with its rush of passion, its flowers and song – the spring in his heart and Megan's! Was it just Love seeking a victim! The Greek was right, then – the words of the 'Hippolytus' as true today!

> For mad is the heart of Love,
> And gold the gleam of his wing;
> And all to the spell thereof
> Bend when he makes his spring.
> All life that is wild and young
> In mountain and wave and stream,
> All that of earth is sprung,
> Or breathes in the red sunbeam;
> Yea, and Mankind. O'er all a royal throne,
> Cyprian, Cyprian, is thine alone!

The Greek was right! Megan! Poor little Megan – coming over the hill! Megan under the old apple-tree waiting and looking! Megan dead, with beauty printed on her . . .

A voice said:

'Oh, there you are! Look!'

Ashurst rose, took his wife's sketch, and stared at it in silence.

'Is the foreground right, Frank?'

'Yes.'

'But there's something wanting, isn't there?'

Ashurst nodded. Wanting? The apple-tree, the singing, and the gold!